MIRROR
of
the
MARVELOUS

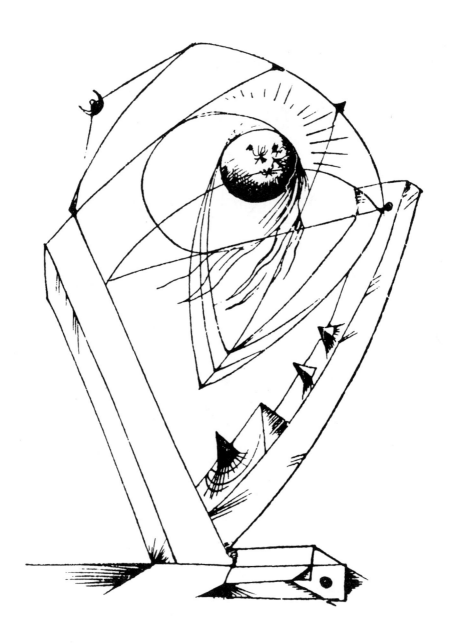

MIRROR
of
the
MARVELOUS

THE CLASSIC SURREALIST WORK ON MYTH

PIERRE MABILLE

Illustrations by André Masson

Translated from the French
by Jody Gladding

Inner Traditions
Rochester, Vermont

To Jeanne Mégnen, whose inestimable collaboration
made this book possible.

Inner Traditions wishes to express its appreciation for assistance given
by the government of France through the ministère de la Culture
in the preparation of this translation.

᪣

We thank Madame Elisa Breton and Jérôme Lindon of Les Éditions
de Minuit for their help in preparing this work, especially for their
kind permission to publish the preface written for the
1962 French edition by André Breton.

Inner Traditions International
One Park Street
Rochester, Vermont 05767
www.innertraditions.com

Copyright © 1998 by Jean-Pierre Mabille and Claudie Mabille

Translation copyright © 1998 by Inner Traditions International

Library of Congress Cataloging-in-Publication Data

Mabille, Pierre.
    [Miroir du merveilleux. English]
    Mirror of the marvelous : the classic surrealist work on myth / Pierre Mabille ; translated from
the French by Jody Gladding.
       p. cm.
    Includes bibliographical references.
    ISBN 0-89281-650-3 (hardcover : alk. paper)
    1. Marvelous, The, in literature. 2. Supernatural in literature.
I. Gladding, Jody, 1955– . II. Title.
PN56.M3M313   1998
809'.91163—dc21   98-14998
                                                  CIP

Printed and bound in the United States

10 9 8 7 6 5 4 3 2 1

Text design and layout by Kristin Camp
This book was typeset in New Baskerville with Trajan as the display typeface

CONTENTS

Foreword:

DRAWBRIDGES

A man of great counsel, the only one I've known to grasp the whole nexus of communication lines best tracked along the most ancient trails, commonly leading to dead ends these days, but which, for him, retained their attraction and their promise, such a presence was Pierre Mabille, and still is now, judging by the light emanating from him. A scout in the full sense of the word, among the most active of medical practitioners, and, as such, a participant in the most advanced scientific research, his speculative field, far from being reduced only to what science revealed to him, never ceased to embrace at the same time the whole of esoteric thought, about which, above and beyond his very brilliant medical and surgical studies, he educated himself. These ideas, their traditional nature, would attest to him alone that they harbored a "soul of truth," and, as passionate about truth as he was, one would find him totally immersed in them at the most profound depths. Thus, it was within him that the quarrel between the ancients and the moderns worked toward its resolution, not without clashes and occasional uncertainties, which had great human resonance and resulted in his own distinct ways of moving, leading, in large part, to his peculiar charm. For all the incidental details of his life, for all the quick decisions—such as medical operations require— no one knew better how to replicate daydream's great soaring flights, in the evening, while he spoke, rallying together more and more remote points of hermetic philosophy and with each one, regaining vigor. There are few looks that have pleased me as much as his, and for me, his physical disappearance has not diminished this in the least.

I see us again, he and I, in 1934, as if it were yesterday, working out the meaning of our respective roles in *Minotaure*, and again now as then, I feel the fire he brought to bear there, beginning with his own, a "Preface to the Praise of Popular Prejudices,"[1] which constituted a profession of faith (a bit clumsy, but all the more moving for it: he still signed it "Doctor Pierre Mabille"). This paper centered around his research into physical and psychological morphology, which would remain his primary focus, and which he had every reason to think of as supporting surrealism.[2] At that time and place, one of the most important encounters I have ever had took place, a determining encounter, I think I am able to say, for both of us, and one in which our mutual confidence was sealed without the least possibility of retraction.

Two years would pass before he would unveil publicly, in *Minotaure* number 8,[3] any of his sources, and that was in his "Notes on Symbolism," which, with the magazine's perspective in mind, he illustrated with reproductions of Théodore de Bry's superb engravings that originally illustrated Michel Maier's *Atalanta Fugiens* (1618). Rigorously adapted to their alchemical context, these plates, in and of themselves— that is to say, considered independently—offer the most decisive touchstone to the evaluation, as much in the timeless figurative art as in what today boasts of promoting new "signs," of all that is supposed to leap into the unknown and seize upon the mystery. From Pierre Mabille's text, which these images support, his two main preoccupations become clear: first, his desire to establish that, contrary to current opinion, the symbol belongs to *external* reality, and is linked *organically* with the object, the functioning of the human mind being entirely dependent on symbolic representation thus conceived, and second, his suggestion that certain human groups, with a shared allegiance, can constitute a dynamic whole capable of subduing external forces.[4]

Allow me a moment of subjectivity here: I couldn't forgive myself if it appears that I have forgotten that completely cheerful being whom he knew how to portray, the expressive ease of his gestures under all circumstances, his incredibly warm presence, the comfort that I drew

1. *Minotaure*, no. 6 (Winter 1935).
2. He would treat this fully in his work *La Construction de l'homme* (Jean Flory, 1936).
3. June 15, 1936.
4. He began working this idea out in *Egrégores* (J. Flory, 1938).

from him so many times. With the same beautiful hands that brought her into the world, I see him the very next day, tracing out for me on paper my daughter's birth chart "to the nearest minute," and I again hear his discourse on this subtle method—multidialectic and artless—of prediction. Totally agreeing that in our day, astrology hardly survives against traditional memory, which is rarely sufficient for legitimizing it, his intention was to retain the symbolic sense of the ancient language. He also deemed the astrological method itself fertile, the principle on which it was based worth retaining for its simple hypothesis. On those darker days when I had to take recourse to his office for matters of health, the care he provided, far from being limited to physical needs, extended to the moral, because of that rare gift he had for restoring serenity. This power he drew from his conviction that "spirituality is stronger than material forces," should they be opposed, and that "consequently, the transformation of these latter into moral possibilities" was the final human end.[5] This art "of rising instead of descending"—which conforms not even to the slightest demand in poetry—he indicated several times he owed to alchemy, throughout which this schema is inscribed like a watermark. Considering this in the light of his resilient good humor, the wonder was that the debt I contracted, always growing larger as the days passed, weighed him down no more than an armful of wildflowers.

The long, sensitive exchanges, which our then frequent discussions permitted, perhaps do not give the complete measure of his personality. That would require the whole network of circumstances that the armistice, signed in June 1940, decided. Demobilized in the "French zone" and then stripped of all means of existence, I thought first of seeking asylum wherever he was. That was in Salon-de-Provence, and I rejoined him there. He welcomed me with opened arms and we did not leave each other's side for several months. In these extremely troubled times when no one could know for sure how the dice would fall, when deception and impudence were the official currency, when the future could tolerate only the shortest intervals of sunlight, Pierre Mabille was still the best conspirator and the most adept at safeguarding, at shelving away, whatever would keep of what was most sacred to the rights of the spirit. Few people possessed, and even fewer at that time, a mind such as his which drew upon the work of the medieval

---

5. *La Construction de l'homme.*

seekers for its life force. Few could be as articulate as he was when he knew he had someone's ear, nor as naturally receptive and mobile, which, in the face of current events, he opposed to oppression and spinelessness.

Always faithful to his anthropological vocation, he remained one for whom the terms *solve* and *coagule* ceased to be dead language, absorption and expenditure, to act and to suffer. In both the specific and the general, he recognized and rejuvenated once and for all the six constraints or primal tendencies ascribable to existence. In this way, he assured himself that no *external* constraints could prevail against them. But one of his most endearing traits was that he was also a man of great conjecture. How many times, under the trees at a café in Salon—in Salon, where Nostradamus lies buried—did I see him grappling with the enigma of the *Centuries*, which he continued to debate with Pierre Piobb, his late teacher, as if the latter were still in this world. It's impossible to exaggerate the role of Pierre Piobb—who was the first translator of the general astrology and geomancy tracts of Robert Fludd—in Pierre Mabille's spiritual development. In this regard, it is of great importance to refer to his works, among others, *The Secret of Nostradamus*, and the admirable *Venus*,[6] which, in his collection of the Mysteries, is followed by only one *Hecate*,[7] awakened from a half-century sleep. All I can do here is offer a glimpse of Pierre Mabille's part in that discursive kind of thinking based upon the most solid knowledge and a taste for examining things with one's antennae.

It is especially to this last tendency that I wanted to pay homage when I dedicated to him my poem, "Pleine marge," which I began at the end of our stay in Salon and finished in Martigues, always in his light. We were camped then in a sort of hazy territory, which he brightened with his very ingenious solutions to shortages and his witticisms. And yet it was there that the news reached us—for me, like a horrible, fateful blow—of Leon Trotsky's assassination. Having experienced deeply the hopes that October's revolution had given birth to and having followed its demise step by step, certainly he took full measure of what had suddenly exploded, how desperately unjust it was, offering no hope of recourse on the human scale. But he did so without collapsing, as I did, into sobs. There again, at the end of that day, I discovered

6. *Venus* (Paris: H. Daragon, 1909).
7. *Hecate* (Omnium lettéraire, 1961).

how, as if by the soaring of his mind, he alone knew how to look toward *the large*, although always with absolute regard for my pain.

As we both spent time away from France, some years would separate us before we met up again in Haiti, where he had sent for me. I'll skip over the incidents that marked the beginning of my trip because, to my great unhappiness, they were to have unfortunate repercussions on his activities as the cultural attaché in Port-au-Prince, jeopardizing a mission that was close to his heart, that of founding and organizing the Institut Français in this city. Even though he was justified in attributing the chance responsibility for his disgrace to me, he was, once more, generous enough to bear me no grudge and to see to it that our relationship was not affected by it in the least. It was still very early and, as was true every morning, his schedule for operations at the hospital was full. As if guided by radar, his car charged through the suburbs, barely dispersing the continually moving, solid human masses, which immediately reformed behind him like mercury. The incredible deftness of his driving made itself evident to me once again, testifying to his perfect self-control on the level of practical action. Which again I saw during an hour of relaxation at the beach, when he reemerged dripping wet, laden with red and pink coral which he had brought up from the water's depths. Because I know no other person who would give himself over so avidly, with so much fervor, to the spectacle of nature. That this fell within his share of total knowledge was because he made it his own and his one ambition to justify according to his own methods a resolutely *monistic* view of the world. According to this view, not only, in fact, must the separation between mind and matter be rejected, but also the human being can only conceive of itself as a microcosm called upon to advance its knowledge by interrogating the laws that regulate— itself included—the entire universe.

For whoever holds such a conviction and constantly maintains himself at that level—and that was the case with Pierre Mabille—great spaces open, which Hölder in and Nerval had discovered in their time, and where each, for himself, can advance no further except silently. Mabille has alluded to this "word of light" which must somewhere be preserved.[8] At the end of the present work, where he tackles the mystery of love, it is as if he puts his finger to his lips: "Beyond this threshold, not a word..." because it is absolutely incontestable that he was also a man of great

---

8. *Le Merveilleux* (Quatre Vents, 1946).

secrecy. This aspect coincides with the image that, perhaps more precisely than all the others, I retain of him. As slowly as possible he paddles, facing me, among the reeds in a lake, as if there could be nothing more mysterious or more beautiful (it seems to me that, without knowing it, Max Ernst expressed this in a canvas accurately entitled *Eye of Silence*). We had gone there between three and four in the morning, the crescent moon still very bright and, at this latitude, in the position of a horizontal boat, which always surprised me. The trick was to enter cautiously enough not to arouse their suspicions, to be able to witness a great variety of large birds as they awakened. A bit later I saw there again, rising from every side, white egrets. I could not deny that only one vision of the world, Pierre Mabille's vision, had been able to reveal to me this burst of flight.

Not a page has been turned, and nevertheless, the scenery has changed. The sky is furiously swept aside, drained of its blue. It pulls in opposite directions toward shades of acid and smoky black as in the "heavy" paintings of Hector Hyppolite. In the low light, the further we advance, the more the gray *bayahonde* bushes loom up, closing in on us in their disquieting way, which Jacques Roumain could not avoid being haunted by in his beautiful book *Governor of the Dew*. These bushes are all the more impenetrable because, the closer we approach to our destination, the more intensely the bewitching reverberations of tomtoms seem to condense in them. Pierre Mabille leads me toward one of those *houmforts,* or voodoo temples, where in a little while, more or less clandestinely, a ceremony is going to take place—and this will be repeated about eight times during my stay on the island. The complexity of the voodoo ritual is so great that, without recourse to specialized works,[9] one can only formulate a poor idea of it; and to try to shed some light on it here would be, in my eyes, to profane it. Besides, I have a completely different purpose: to show what I valued most in witnessing these authentic ceremonies (from which, in general, Whites were excluded). And that remains the extent to which Pierre Mabille's friendship was all that was required to spontaneously grant me all the privileges he had earned. He was always received with great consideration by the *houngan* or the *mambo* who would preside over the ritual and who conducted him first toward the *pé,* that is, the alter stone, where, using his hands, he would mime the sacred acts. The pathos of the voodoo cer-

9. See Milo Rigaud, *La Tradition voudoo et le Vaudou haïtien* (Niclaus, 1953).

emony has left such a lasting impression that I cannot claim to be able to extricate its generative spirit from the persistent vapors of rum and blood, or to assess its real significance. What the ceremonies offered me was the chance to immerse myself in their atmosphere, to open myself to the flood of primal forces that they awakened. If I often discussed them with Pierre Mabille, whose knowledge in this regard ran much deeper than mine, I'm sure, it was nearly always indirectly, in this case from the angle of "being possessed," something about which we both knew (from the Salpêtrière hospital) through clinical antecedents. In view of the syncretism culminating in the voodoo cult, we spent much time wondering out loud together about the "style" of these possessions, doubting that they were entirely African imports. We were both inclined to find traces of mesmerism there, which was rendered plausible—and perfectly fascinating—by the fact that in 1772, accompanied by a Black with "psychic powers," Martinez de Pasqually, in my opinion one of the most enigmatic and captivating of figures, debarked at Santa Domingo. He was to endow the island with a "Sovereign Tribunal," found a lodge in Port-au-Prince, another one in Léogane, and bring his *Statut de l'Ordre des Elus Cohens* into its final, definitive form before dying there in 1774. We would never give up following up those tidbits of information we heard that might lead us to the exact spot where he was buried, still a mystery, and who knows, perhaps even let us lift the phosphorescent veil that kept it hidden.[10]

However I benefited from these exchanges, which most often took place in the evening, under the shade trees of a terrace in the residential quarter of Pétionville, where two intrepid lizards encircled the foot of the lamp as soon as it went on, what I found most satisfying about Pierre Mabille's company then was exactly what I valued when he slid open the door of the *houmfort:* his ability, beyond all barriers of rank, origin, and culture, to be on equal footing with ethnic groups so fundamentally different from his own, to empathize immediately with their aspirations, and to know how to profit from letting them contribute to his own inner growth and perfection. And therein lies perhaps his most distinctive trait: he was a man of great human kinships, par excellence. And what is more, his final message was, unconditionally, to extol them.

If, as some see it, Pierre Mabille's objective was "to achieve a

---

10. See Gérard Van Rijnberk, *Un thaumaturge du XVIIIe siècle: Martinez de Pasqually* (Librairie Félix Alcan, 1935).

synthetic comprehension of the world and to bring humans back into this knowledge," it goes without saying that, on the other hand, he never sacrificed to it the contributions of the most advanced psychological analysis. Not only did Freud and Piaget always very precisely inform his thinking, but again, no one went further than he did in emphasizing the weaknesses of the "projective techniques" as used in psychological exploration, to which he believed it was nonetheless necessary to devote himself. As he proved himself to be concerned above all with balance, one would expect him to require that experimental psychology be founded on solid biological knowledge and rigorous practices of observation. Here again, this is not an abstraction for me but what I saw with my own eyes as he drew the pieces of some sort of child's construction game from a box and placed them all upon the table from which our dinner had just been cleared away (the game, I learned afterward, he had meticulously perfected himself). "Make your village," he said to me. Because of the succinctness of the phrase and his irrefutable expression, my departure was now out of the question. The scarcity of pieces that would make that task easy only emphasized the overabundance of those one could gladly do without, which lent themselves more or less badly to serving as substitutes. I left, sufficiently humbled by this test. To compensate, Pierre Mabille, with his usual simplicity and vivaciousness, revealed to me its rationale.[11] Far from concerning himself with exploiting the fundamental corrections that he had made to his data by subjecting it to long personal experimentation, or with the discoveries that this experiment had already revealed, he showed himself to be lying in wait for whatever else awaited him, to the point of wanting to make me a partner in his subsequent research in this direction. Here again, what I hope to make understood is how exemplary and exceptional his attitude was for our time. He himself said that he had reembraced one of the most thoroughly abandoned ideas, that of the "realists" of the Middle Ages, for whom "no fundamental difference exists between the elements of thought and the phenomena of the world." He denounced the growing conflict between human needs on the one side, and, on the other, the state of the sciences, which had ceased to nurture human inner transformation. It was exactly through the rehabilitation and exaltation of values of the *heart* that he expected

---

11. See Pierre Mabille, "La technique du test du village," in *The Review of Human Morpho-Physiology* (Paris, 1950).

human understanding to be set right again.

It was ten years ago that, without warning for either his friends or himself, Pierre Mabille left us. Ten years—about the time it takes for a mind as expansive as his to pit itself against the darkness and reemerge from it—for his message to settle out and gain both clarity and the power to reach those who have not yet heard it. While waiting for critical studies covering the whole of his work—and no studies could be more fruitful—there is no greater imperative than the reissue of *Mirror of the Marvelous*. Indeed, there the reader finds himself at the very source of Pierre Mabille's radiance, and, I will permit myself to add, facing one of those monumental works that to leave unread would be to renounce, once and for all, any hope of comprehending the *surrealist* spirit. Completed in close collaboration with those who claim that spirit, it brings to bear considerable resources which were Mabille's alone. Who else, to the extent that he dared, and risking such asymmetry, could merge the accents of certain modern poetry with those of the texts we classify as "sacred"? That task required precisely the freedom and capacity for flight conferred only upon a master of so many diverse disciplines.

Mirror of the Marvelous... let there be no doubt that Pierre Mabille weighed—in gold dust—the two terms in this title. The marvelous, nothing defines this better than setting it in opposition to "the fantastic," which, unfortunately, our contemporaries tend more and more to use as its replacement. The problem is that the fantastic nearly always falls under the order of inconsequential fiction, while the marvelous illuminates the furthest extremity of vital movement and engages the entire emotional realm. As to mirror, he lets us know that, if it is possible to find a comparison for our minds there, we must admit that "its silvering consists of the red flow of desire."[12]

André Breton
Paris, May 1962

---

12. Pierre Mabille, "Miroirs," *Minotaure*, no. 11 (Spring 1938).

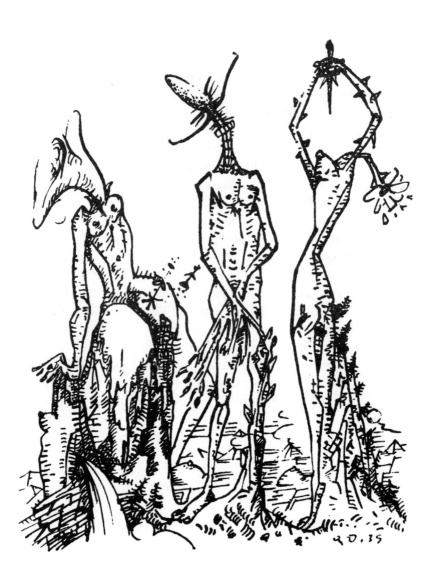

INTRODUCTION

Perhaps what the reader is looking for here is a nice collection of stories with all the charm of those pressed flower arrangements young girls used to love to make. Between the pages of gray blotting paper, the colored petals of some long ago spring slowly faded, while their scent remained, despite the passing years. They were chosen for their rarity, of course; however, the memory of a day of intoxicating freedom, of rambling and dreaming, was not an uncommon reason for preserving them. Such books, tenderhearted confessions, in which natural treasures testify to the movements of the heart, possess great value. And a collection of ancient stories could have the same evocative power. It could feel like a wood fire in a big, cold house in autumn on the moors. It could suggest the deeply moving forms that trees design on the night of the first quarter moon, the mirages that appear on ponds in full sunlight. Shivers of exquisite terror could be mixed with the sensual desire for some undefined happiness.

Although I love to abandon myself to the charm of such accounts and to feel them echoing through me, I have decided to take this work in an entirely different direction. I want it to be a collection of maps, going from the map of passionate feelings to the celestial planisphere, by way of the diagrams left by pirates to show the location of their buried treasure.

These admittedly enigmatic plans lie like a grid over the routes used by tourists and officials. They permit the discovery of a mysterious castle, not far from the well-traveled paths, hidden by undergrowth and thickets. If, for practical reasons, most people declare that they want to follow the official route, guided by the reassuring sight of milestone markers, we will acknowledge with regret that, for the majority, this seems to be their inescapable fate.

No one lives in the castle now. Nevertheless, the crowd gathered there indicates that this is the center of life. I gain access toward the middle of the summer, at noon, when the cicadas' shrill breathing filters through everything. The garden, grown wild, cultivates nothing but scents. It's the domain of insects and birds. Giant butterflies, which seem like transitory forms of enchanted genies, frolic about, guarded by praying mantises.

I hope that the reader doesn't expect me to show him around like a museum guide or a rental agent, clutching a chain of carefully labeled keys. But neither should he imagine attempting some dangerous break-in. Those eager to plunder report scanty spoils. Sacking the place, they seize the costume jewelry and don't see the diamonds lying in plain view on the tables.

Access to the marvelous remains hidden by too many misinterpretations. And why, after defending itself against indifferent wanderers or unwanted thieves, should it welcome roaming ghosts, mounting the thick walls as they please? Far from abandoning the body and condemning it as so much annoying weight, we will demand true testimony from our heightened senses. Since we have decided never to separate the dream from the conscious act, it won't be possible to hear our words as simple, allegorical tales.

At the determined hour, the door, up till then hopelessly sealed, opens, welcoming us because we haven't given up hope. This hour marks the consent of things to the will of humans. It indicates an extraordinary harmony between the beating of the heart and the rhythm of the stars. Each makes her way toward the place where she is led by her predisposition and the diligent course of her past thoughts. May every step be so fruitful! May the noble passion with which the conquest begins not abandon a single one of the visitors!

Stepping over the threshold, we find everything in place. A good many instructions await us which can bring the sleeping building back to life. Some papers have been burned despite the haste. Our instructions tell us to sort through the others, which have collected in the library. The library contains many ancient books, and a few more recent ones; all languages are represented. Some of them aren't even written in words, but in signs representing monuments that people have constructed over the course of centuries. Through various means of expression and appearing in many versions, a limited number of essential themes becomes obvious.

Most of the works describe in detail ways into the castle, which is paradoxical since it's only possible to read them after having already gone through ordeals and succeeded in penetrating the castle walls. Still, it's true that one can only really benefit by hearing what one already knows and has totally recreated through personal experience. After having given it much thought, I understand how the variety of these accounts is far from useless. People need to know that others before them, using different means, have reached the same end. The diverse paths leading to knowledge are no less interesting. Knowledge cannot be "abstracted" from the means used to acquire it. Doesn't a theory of mechanics have a different value for the one who makes the difficult discovery oneself and for the student who learns it from a book, for the one who considers it on paper, and for the one who sees its enactment in a moving body?

I understand that with changing circumstances, with historical developments, the same truths, the same fundamental assertions must find specific expression. Guests only for a moment ourselves in the mysterious castle, we will come around to giving our own account of our journey and our stay. Then we, too, will have provided new evidence regarding the marvelous.

Before this great work can be completed, before a new systemization of the myths, with appropriate revelations, and formulations adapted to the present needs, is possible, it is useful to assemble on some fragile arch the most significant texts from the past and the present. When one is pressed to choose between the thousands of documents from all epochs and every country, that decision always includes something of the arbitrary.

But, what does it matter? Even if it were a hundred volumes, this book would be no less incomplete. Another selection would have been open to the same criticism. I've aimed less at establishing impartiality than at making a clear and concerted effort here. Some great names are intentionally omitted. Others are left out only for the single reason that these authors are found within the familiar realms of my universe.

Giving up all concern to be encyclopedic, my attempt is to provide some hypothetical traveler with a suggestion of the great adventure's perilous itinerary.[1]

The maps I've mentioned are diagrams that represent geographic reality just as words represent beings and things in the work of thought. Knowing the sign leads to knowing the thing. That's why examining the word "marvelous" will help me to explore the marvelous itself. In recent years, some revolutionaries, wanting to break with the past, have called for understanding terms according to their present meaning only and no longer as a function of etymology. This advice would be very useful if our understanding of the present were not so inadequate and if furthering that understanding were not exactly our goal.

Because it is used indiscriminately and interchangeably with other superlatives, the adjective "marvelous" has lost all meaning. In contrast, the noun has retained more of its power. It evokes all the extraordinary and unbelievable phenomena that together constitute the essential domain of fantasy. The usual audience for these accounts—children, enthusiasts, or melancholics—want to escape the sordid conditions of daily life and be transported to a world custom-built according to their desires. However, after the initial shock, their attention turns quickly toward exploring powers unknown to humans and aspects unknown to nature. They hardly stop to look at the devices and mechanisms these stories use. Their desire is to rip away the veil that hides from them the total reality of an incomprehensible universe.

As it sets out upon this endless search, the mind worries about the elements in play; it questions their power. It wants to distinguish with certainty the truly marvelous from the fantastic, the strange, the illusory. Once intoxicated by discovery, the real disorientation that expanded horizons create can easily be confused with the lesser emotions that literary artifices or reprehensible parodies elicit. I know that a true sensibility rarely makes mistakes. Instinctively, it can distinguish between the true and the false; that is its essential characteristic. It knows which closed door leads to the treasure and which is only stage set. But how many pitfalls it must overcome! The force of feelings, the weight of set mental habits can undermine its vigilance at any moment.

Yet, finding no good definition of the marvelous in current collec-

---

1. I regret not being able to include enough romantic texts. The question of the marvelous in German romanticism deserves a study all to itself which cannot be undertaken here.

tive thought on the one hand, and worried about overextending the search on the other, I cannot simply accept a definition dictated by my own personal taste either.

What's necessary is to let one's own sensibility verify the testimony of the centuries, weighing it a piece at a time, and then comparing the conclusions to the age-old evidence.

The name is a condensation of all past experience. So let us subject the marvelous to an official inquiry, but let us conduct it without the hostility of a judge or the indifference of a scholar, as this is the first stage of the journey.

The science of language summarizes all the other sciences. How many feelings I owe to it, despite the deplorable atmosphere of dry abstraction in which grammarians and specialized scholars have embalmed the study of words. The science of the Word, a science linked to the development of life, has become the preoccupation of librarians. Faced with the expanse of ancient languages, I feel how much my present effort costs. Sometimes, I feel like a powerful being on the shores of an ocean that has swallowed into its depths thousands of cities of Ys. The water and sand, which seized them when they were fully operating, keep them guarded. They are mine under the condition that I can discover the elements of this lost empire. At other moments, the layers of words, grammars, and syntaxes look to me like the geological strata visible in a mine shaft. Etymological exploration is then a veritable descent in search of the primitive ground that borders the central fire, the ground where the first emotions were translated, the first moment was fixed, or the first incandescent desire found its form.

In the end, the familiar symbol of "root" is no less satisfactory since it calls up the way dormant minerals are transformed into ever-regenerating vegetable life. I hope that my insistence on linguistics here won't be seen as merely a wish to envelop my etymological research on the word "marvelous" in an easy lyricism. The problem is more general. This is where we come upon one of the keys we need most for our endeavor.

Faced with the messages left in the castle, on the walls as well as in the library, faced with other vital messages that our poets never stop transmitting, what would become of someone incapable of fully understanding the meanings of the terms? In ancient initiations, the first and the longest ordeal consisted of learning to read.

The dictionary says that "marvel" comes from *mirabilia* which itself comes from *miror,* "Things worth looking at." You could go back through the Latin to find the origin of the root *mir* in Sanskrit, but we trace it so far. The official etymology shows clearly enough how astonishing it is that "admirable" comes down to us relatively intact, while "marvelous" has been subjected to such great changes. No doubt the course taken in these two cases has been different, with different peoples and social strata coming into play.

Whatever the case, around the root *miror* a very strange family has proliferated: "to mirror, to be mirrored, to admire, admirable, marvelous, and its derivatives miracle, mirage, and finally mirror." Searching for the definition of the marvelous leads us here, to the mirror, the most banal and most extraordinary magical instrument of all.

The reflecting surface of calm water, the first natural mirror, divides the universe. On the one side, where our voluntary actions take place, are all tangible objects together; on the other, the images, the reversed, fugitive world that a breath of wind or a falling leaf distorts and obliterates. The mirror engenders our first metaphysical questions. It makes us doubt our senses. It poses the problem of illusions.

By their very nature, reflections resemble the images from which thought is constructed. They share the elusive fragility of mental representations, vanishing as quickly as they appear.

As soon as we approach the polished surface, we see ourselves. Up until that moment, we felt as if we lived enclosed in the deep warmth of our flesh, the world we knew as the obstacle limiting our movements. Now we see ourselves as if we were looking at strangers. We must learn to recognize ourselves as people like others and yet different from them in a thousand small ways that we gradually discover in our appearances. An effort of judgment and long habit are needed to link this confused mass of internal sensations with that objective representation of being, to join the I with the self.

Confronting the experience of the mirror, thought enters into an endless series of unsettling questions. Between objects and their reflections, the play of dialectical interchange never stops. One supposes, one hopes, one infers. Between the material and the immaterial, innumerable scholastic arguments are assembled. Logic, that obliging servant, proposes false certainties and false solutions. Since the images are reversed, the mind deduces that they must possess qualities and attributes opposite to those of the tangible universe.

Thanks to the mirror, we have been able to escape the confines enclosing us. We have been able to transform our feelings of existence into a representation—we have discovered ourselves. The hope is that the reverse phenomenon will occur with regard to objects. Normally perceived as the shapes their exterior surfaces take, couldn't they, through the play of reflection, let us penetrate the mystery of their contents to arrive at their essence?

The domain of images where our immediate actions have no impact, in which our beings become objects, seems outside of the real world to us, superimposed upon it, subject to other laws. But, at the same time, the analogy between reflections and the tools of our mental life allows us to assimilate this abstract domain at the very depths of our being. Reflections and echoes lead to the center of the unconscious, to the origins of dream, to the place where desire manages to express itself in some confused way.

Thus, in front of the mirror, we are led to ask ourselves about the exact nature of reality, about the links connecting mental representations with the objects prompting them. The problem arises of reconciling human necessity, which stems from our desires, with a natural necessity that obeys implacable laws. These are the questions that allow us to reach an exact definition of the marvelous. Apart from all its charm and curiosity, all the feelings that stories, tales, and legends hold for us, outside of the need for distraction and forgetting, for pleasant or terrifying sensations, the real purpose of the marvelous voyage, as we may already understand, is to explore universal reality more thoroughly.

Lewis Carroll is one of those authors who best understands this mechanism of the imagination. He transmits it directly, without recourse to dry philosophical language. He was qualified for this task, combining a mathematician's lucid precision with the greatest poetic sensibility. The titles of his works illustrate this best: *Alice in Wonderland, Through the Looking Glass.* Through the play of suppositions and by a maneuver that deconstructs logic, Alice manages to break down the limits of common sense and build herself a marvelous world.

Through the Looking Glass
Lewis Carroll

And Alice got the Red Queen off the table, and set it up before the kitten as a model for it to imitate; however the thing didn't succeed, principally, Alice said, because the kitten wouldn't fold its arms properly. So to punish it, she held it up to the Looking-glass, that it might see how sulky it was, "—and if you're not good directly," she added, "I'll put you through into Looking-glass House. How would you like *that*?

"Now, if you'll only attend, Kitty, and not talk so much, I'll tell you all my ideas about Looking-glass House. First, there's the room you can see through the glass—that's just the same as our drawing room, only the things go the other way. I can see all of it when I get upon a chair—all but the bit behind the fire-place. Oh! I do wish I could see *that* bit! I want so much to know whether they've a fire in the winter: you never *can* tell, you know, unless our fire smokes, and then smoke comes up in that room too—but that may be only pretense, just to make it look as if they had a fire. Well then, the books are something like our books, only the words go the wrong way: I know *that*, because I've held up one of our books to the glass, and then they hold up one in the other room.

"How would you like to live in Looking-glass House, Kitty? I wonder if they'd give you milk in there? Perhaps Looking-glass milk isn't good to drink—but oh, Kitty! now we come to the passage. You can just see a little *peep* of the passage in Looking-glass House! I'm sure it's got, oh! such beautiful things in it. Let's pretend there's a way of getting through into it, somehow, Kitty. Let's pretend the glass has got all soft like gauze, so that we can get through. Why, it's turning into a sort of mist now, I declare! It'll be easy enough to get through—." She was up on the chimney-piece while she said this, though she hardly knew how she got there. And certainly the glass *was* beginning to melt away, just like a bright silvery mist.

In another moment Alice was through the glass, and had jumped lightly down into the Looking-glass room. The very first thing she did was to look whether there was a fire in the fireplace, and she was quite pleased to find that there was a real one, blazing away as brightly as the one she had left behind. "So I shall be as warm here as I was in the old room," thought Alice: "warmer, in fact, because there'll be no one here to scold me away from the fire. Oh, what fun it'll be, when they see me through the glass in here, and can't get at me!"

Then she began looking about, and noticed that what could be seen from the old room was quite common and uninteresting, but that all the rest was as different as possible. For instance, the pictures on the wall next to the fire seemed to be all alive, and the very clock on the chimney-piece (you know you can only see the back of it in the Looking-glass) had got the face of a little old man and grinned at her.

"They don't keep this room so tidy," Alice thought to herself, as she noticed several of the chessmen down in the hearth among the cinders; but in another moment with a little "Oh!" of surprise, she was down on her hands and knees watching them. The chessmen were walking about, two and two!

"Here are the Red King and the Red Queen," Alice said (in a whisper, for fear of frightening them), "and there are the White King and the White Queen sitting on the edge of the shovel—and here are the two castles walking arm in arm—I don't think they can hear me," she went on as she put her head closer down, "and I'm nearly sure they can't see me. I feel somehow as if I was getting invisible—."[2]

Alice's adventures in the rabbit burrow or through the mantelpiece mirror encourage us to search for other gaps where we can penetrate the marvelous. There are a great many of them. In certain places, where the mystery is less carefully guarded, it seems accessible, either because nature lets us detect the elements' unrest there or because humankind has succeeded in taking control of the barrier: the inside of craters, volcanoes with flames shooting out of them; mist-covered countries where the horizon is lost as sky and water become one; deep tropical forests where life takes on a monstrous exuberance; modern laboratories in which machines, the products of dreams, transform a world of invisible forces into tangible forms. At first sight, the Palace of Illusions at the Musée Grévin doesn't seem to be one of these exceptional places, but rather an outdated fairground attraction. That's how I remembered it until this afternoon when, out walking with my lover in Paris, and

2. Lewis Carroll (Charles Lutwidge Dodgson). Born January 27, 1832. Professor of mathematics 1855 to 1881. Lived in Oxford almost all his life. Publications: *Pieces of Verse* (1856), *A Syllabus of Plane Algebraical Geometry* (1860), *Formulas of Trigonometry* (1861), *Alice in Wonderland, Russian Travels with Dr. Liddon, A Basic Tract on Determinants* (1867), *New Steeple* (1872), *The Hunting of the Snark, Phantasmagoria* (1876), *Euclid and His Modern Rivals* (1879), *Rhyme? and Reason?* (1883), *The Principles of Parlimentary Representation* (1884), *A Mixed Up Story* (1885), *The Play of Logic* (1887), *Curiosa Mathematica*, 3 parts (1888 to 1893), *Sylvie and Bruno* (1889), *The Nursery Alice* (1990), and *Symbolic Logic* (1896). Died in 1898. To my great surprise, I found recently that Carroll's poetic work forms an integral part of his mathematical contributions. It contains conscious symbolic significance. The fantastic, the comic, and the humorous are used deliberately to conceal an almost hermetic message. Carroll employs the burlesque just as Rabelais does the trivial to mislead the inattentive reader. The marriage of the chess queen in *Alice* is very similar to *The Chemical Wedding* of Valentin Andreae, from which I will give an extract later.

trying to escape from the bustle of the working city, we went in there together. Lovers are infallible diviners. Renewed by emotion, their eyes wash clean habit's dust from things and so perceive their total reality.

We moved through the dark galleries where wax figures were poised in comic attitudes. I imagined we were visiting the underground site of a magician, an occult master, using his power to enchant these mannequins. A great social tragedy seemed to be underway there in which the actors would go line up their skeletons when their roles were over, like useless cast-offs. (I've seen the dead arranged like dolls in dusty convent catacombs from Capuccini to Palermo.)

Still troubled by these impressions, we arrived at the Palace of Illusions. The hermetically sealed room seemed to be located at the center of the earth. The mirror walls were erected in the shape of a regular polygon, a column with horrid artificial greenery supporting each of its peaks. In the middle of this polygon hung a lighting fixture and there were lamps at each corner. We waited in the dark like people awaiting their fate or prisoners in the cellars of the "castle." I thought about initiation ceremonies during which the initiate hopes to gain access to the luminous temple to contemplate truth. Our attendant, a semiconscious automaton, served as the great lighting director. Suddenly, thanks to a magical device, we were transported to an immense temple. In the distance, our images multiplied. The hundreds of columns recalled the central room of the "Great Mosque" of Kairouan; they receded with an architectural rhythm even more perfect than the most beautiful oriental monuments. Our excited gestures repeated themselves to infinity in smaller and smaller, less and less precise images.

The proportion between them was not simple, but was regulated by the laws of a well-known geometric progression, which would certainly not have been impossible to calculate, but which, for the moment, held us in the spell of its mysterious charm and vital harmony. It was as mysterious as the appearance of happiness in a life, as the repetition of similar epics throughout history, as the unwinding of the spring in the great celestial clock. When we held each other close, our images organized themselves between the rows of columns like musical notes written on a huge stave, at set intervals, composing the haunting symphony of desire. We reached the height of emotion. Cut off from the activity of society, we escaped duration; except for the blood we felt coursing through us, everything took part in the eternity of the moment. Enclosed in the magic circle, the polygon of mirrors recreated the infinity of space for us, a space entirely inhabited by our presence and submitting absolutely to our pleasure.

That is the magic circle where Lewis Carroll would have loved to hold class for Alice. There he could have shown her the play of equations through which she could have entered the enchanted kingdom more easily than she did by going down a rabbit's hole.

Alas! The high school teachers who teach us optics hardly resemble Lewis Carroll. They conscientiously present this branch of physics as one particular science with its own subject matter and practical applications. The idea that science is a language, a way of exploring, much like poetry and the arts, and that all these different paths lead to one unique mystery doesn't seem to occur to them. In contrast, when I was a student, I had the clearest sense of this. Already I understood that you could make substitutions for scientific notations so that the same diagrams could represent the most diverse thought processes. Geometry's universal value and significance, interior for the mind and exterior for reality simultaneously, made a great impression on me. All the possibilities for metaphysical constructs are in these simple figures; and that's where both the danger and temptation lie. Those very outlines which are so useful for solving practical problems become traps. The real object and the virtual image can be reversed at will. This freedom is not peculiar to optics; it's the rule throughout the abstract world of mathematics and it results in the play of intelligence, Alice's play.

But outside of the mind's self-imposed conditions, nothing corresponds to the circle, the triangle, this sense of a movement. To the contrary, in our experience of the world, all abstraction disappears. Nothing is reversible. Things have one situation, one function, and one direction which belongs to them. If we begin to believe that it's not the man who approaches the table, but the table that approaches the man, that it's the objects that light up the lamp and not the lamp that illuminates the objects, our minds are seized with vertigo. Are these examples, crude and cartoonish as they may seem, really so far from the questions that metaphysics asks? In optics, it's exactly a matter of metaphysics when we consider that the same lines represent both the trajectory of light bringing outside energy from the world to the eye and the distance that we can see going from our eyes out into space. Ordinary circumstances in life tend not to raise these discussions, but they become essential as soon as an unusual phenomenon arises.

Sometimes, images appear in the mirror with no exterior object to explain them. Their perception may be spontaneous, or coincide with a heightened emotional state, or follow some ceremony of invocation.

What are you? Strange forms in which human traits become tragic or comic and merge with animal shapes? Visions of those absent who, at that very moment, are moving around somewhere else, very far away? Touching silhouettes of lost beings? The power of the imagination? The particular powers of a certain mirror? Or yet again, reflections of the real existence of angels, demons, ghosts, or doubles peopling space with your invisible presence?

Where does the marvelous reside? Is it simply the human mind's creative capacity that becomes conscious of it, expresses it, gives it a form, first poetic, then plastic, and finally makes it into concrete objects? Does it belong to the outside world? And are we incapable of apprehending it ordinarily, our senses dulled by the habits of daily life? Isn't it internal and external at the same time, like a higher plane belonging to a greater reality that shares only narrow flood zones with ordinary planes of existence, those rare points of intersection or tangency corresponding to particular states of the soul or singular circumstances? I will retain this last image, the most generous of them; it invites us to investigate the gaping holes left in the wall of our insensitivity by these bursts of contact.

The Magic Mirror in *The Monk*
Matthew Lewis

"Though you shunned my presence, all your proceedings were known to me; nay, I was constantly with you in some degree, thanks to this most precious gift!"

With these words she drew from beneath her habit a mirror of polished steel, the borders of which were marked with various strange and unknown characters.

"Amidst all my sorrows, amidst all my regrets for your coldness, I was sustained from despair by the virtues of this talisman. On pronouncing certain words, the person appears in it on whom the observer's thoughts are bent: thus, though *I* was exiled from *your* sight, you, Ambrosio, were ever present to mine."

The friar's curiosity was strongly excited.

"What you relate is incredible! Matilda, are you not amusing yourself with my credulity?"

"Be your own eyes the judge."

She put the mirror into his hand. Curiosity induced him to take it, and love, to wish that Antonia might appear. Matilda pronounced the magic words. Immediately a thick smoke rose from the characters traced upon the borders, and spread itself over the surface. It dispersed again gradually; a confused mixture of colors and images presented themselves to the friar's eyes, which at length arranging themselves in their proper places, he beheld in miniature Antonia's lovely form.

The scene was a small closet belonging to her apartment. She was undressing to bathe herself. The long tresses of her hair were already bound up. The amorous monk had full opportunity to observe the voluptuous contours and admirable symmetry of her person. She threw off her last garment, and advancing to the bath prepared for her, put her foot into the water. It struck cold, and she drew it back again. Though unconscious of being observed, an in-bred sense of modesty induced her to veil her charms; and she stood hesitating upon the brink, in the attitude of the Venus de Médicis. At this moment a tame linnet flew toward her, nestled its head between her breasts, and nibbled them in wanton play. The smiling Antonia strove in vain to shake off the bird, and at length raised her hands to drive it from its delightful harbour. Ambrosio could bear no more. His desires were worked up to frenzy.

"I yield!" he cried, dashing the mirror upon the ground.[3]

Ambrosio abandons himself to passion, and to satisfy his desires, he gives his soul to the diabolical powers. Enclosed within a mystical metaphysical system, he attributes moral value to all thought, thus forcing himself to choose between the divine order, whereby desire is annihilated, and a so-called satanic rule, the domain of life and passion. His spirit is lost in the vertiginous dialectic, which makes up the reality of his universe.

A no less grave danger would be to arbitrarily separate the domain of tangible reality from that of images and thought, all in an effort to escape this preoccupation with morality. The marvelous, thus reduced to the play of the imagination, would lose all objective solidity.

For me, as for the realists of the Middle Ages, there is no fundamental difference between the elements of thought and the phenomena of the world, between the visible and the comprehensible, between the perceptible and the imaginable.

---

3. Matthew Lewis, *The Monk* (reprint, Grove Press), 268–69. Lewis was an English writer (1775–1818).

Consequently, *the marvelous is everywhere.* In things, it appears as soon as one succeeds in penetrating any object whatever. The most humble of them, just by itself, raises every issue. Its form, which reveals its individual structure, is the result of transformations which have been going on since the world began. And it contains the germs of countless possibilities that will be realized in the future.

The marvelous is also between all things and all beings, interpenetrating space, where our senses perceive nothing directly; but the space is filled with energy, waves, and forces in continual motion, where equilibrium is achieved for a moment, where all the transformations are in preparation. Far from being independent, isolated units, objects are part of compositions, huge fragile assemblies or solid constructs, realities that the eyes perceive only as fragments but that the mind conceives as whole.

Knowing the structure of the external world, discovering the play of forces, tracing the movements of energy—this is science's agenda. Thus it would seem that the sciences ought to provide the true keys to the marvelous. If they no longer do, it's because they aren't interested in the complete human being. Their strict disciplines exclude perceptible feeling. In seeking knowledge, they reject subjective factors in favor of mechanical and impersonal investigations.

Paradoxically, the more humanity extends its knowledge and mastery over the world, the more estranged it feels from the life of this world, and the more it separates the needs of the whole being from the information intelligence provides. A definite antinomy seems to exist today between the ways of the marvelous and those of science.

For the scientist, perceptible feeling survives at the moment of discovery when he perceives the obstacle overcome, the door opening onto unexplored territory. As for the uneducated, they feel it when they go ecstatic over the wonders of modern technology without understanding them in the least.

Others, students and teachers, are not so engaged by a mechanism. Nor is their memory and intelligence such a clean slate. Knowledge is like a suitcase they carry around. For them, no internal transformation seems necessary for understanding a theorem or following a curve in space. They acquire, one after the other, the particular techniques and specialized vocabularies of each limited science. Becoming more and more precise and abstract, these languages avoid poetic and concrete images, any words with more general meanings that engender emotion.

The biologist would be embarrassed to describe the evolution of the blood cell in terms of the phoenix story, the functions of the spleen as parallel to the myth of Saturn who produces children in order to eventually eat them.

Such compartmentalization, such analytical willfulness will come to an end. Soon, thanks to a vast synthesis, humanity will establish its authority over the systems of knowledge that it has acquired. Science will become a key into the world as soon as it becomes capable of expressing universal mechanisms in a language accessible to the collective emotion. This language will constitute a new and communal poetry, a poetry that finally doesn't waver, play illusive games, and rely on quaint images.

Then the conscience will stop binding life's passionate impulses in an iron corset. It will be as the service of desire. Rising above the squalid plane of common sense and logic where now it drags itself along, reason will rejoin the great possibilities of imagination and dream at their transcendent level.

If I allow for the external reality of the marvelous, if I hope that the sciences will allow for its exploration, it's because I'm certain that soon the interior life of the individual will no longer be separated from the knowledge and development of the external world.

Because it is only too apparent that the mystery is within us as well as in things, that the country of the marvelous is first and foremost within our very beings.

The adventure follows the paths of the world and those leading to the hidden center of the self at the same time. Along the first, courage, patience, attentiveness, and reason's good leadership are indispensable. Along the second, other things are necessary to gain access to the sources of emotion.

Those who wish to attain the marvelous deep within must let go of their conventional ties, ties always dominated by utilitarian decisions. They must learn to see the person behind the social function, destroy the table of so-called moral values and replace it with one of real values, rise above taboos, the weight of ancient prohibitions, and stop associating the object with whatever profit can be made from it, whatever price society will pay for it, or whatever purpose it serves. This liberation begins as soon as, one way or another, the guilty conscience's voluntary censorship is lifted, as soon as there is no longer anything to hinder the mechanisms of dream. Then a new world appears where the blue-eyed passerby becomes king, where red coral is more precious than diamonds, and the toucan less dispensable than the workhorse.

The fork has left its enemy, the knife, on the restaurant table. Now it is between Aristotle's categories and the piano. Giving in to an irresistible urge, the sewing machine has taken to the fields to plant beets. The world is on holiday, subject only to the absolute rule of pleasure. It all seems so free; nevertheless, a truer order, based on profound reason and strict hierarchy, is soon established.

In this mysterious domain, which opens as soon as the intelligence, social in origin and purpose, has been relinquished, the traveler feels disturbingly disoriented. After the first moments of amusement or fear pass, she must explore the unconscious, limitless as the ocean, and just as alive with opposing movements. It quickly becomes apparent that this unconscious is not of one piece. There is one layer on top of another, just as in the material world, each with its own values and laws, its sequences and rhythms.

Paraphrasing Hermes who said, "all is above as it is below to make up the miracle of a single thing," we could say that all is within us as it is outside of us to make up a single reality. Within us, scattered fantasies, distorted reflections of reality, and repressed expressions of unfulfilled desires mingle with shared and familiar symbols. From the confused to the simple, from the glare of personal emotion to the vague perception of cosmic drama, the dreamer's imagination makes its journey. Endlessly, it dives and resurfaces, bringing back great, blind fish from the depths of consciousness's threshold. Nevertheless, the pearl fisherman arrives to guide it through all the dangers and currents. He succeeds in finding his way among the passages hidden in the semidark where points of light only glimmer faintly. Little by little he becomes a master of the dark waters.

Achieving this inner lucidity within a more expansive sensibility is no less necessary to a person than mastering scientific disciplines and technology. Because of the tension they produce, magical ceremonies, psychic exercises leading to concentration and ecstatic states, the freedom of mental automatism, and simulating morbid attitudes are some of the means by which the normal faculties can be increased, resulting in clairvoyance. There lie the ways into the realm of the marvelous.

But the mind is not content to simply enjoy contemplating the magnificent images seen in dreams. It wants to translate these visions, to give expression to the new world into which it has penetrated, to have others share it, to produce the inventions suggested there. The dream takes on material form in writing, in the plastic arts, in the building of monuments, and finally, in the construction of machines. Nonetheless, all the work accomplished and the knowledge acquired do little to alleviate, indeed, may even increase, that human uneasiness which is always searching for an individual and collective finality, which is always haunted by the fear of disrupting our solitude and the hope of acting directly upon the minds of others to change the way they feel or direct their actions, and finally and above all, which is always driven by the desire to realize absolute love.

Having admitted that the marvelous is both external to humankind and contained within us, requiring an outward conquest of nature and a constant inward searching, having come to understand this dialect between dream and action, between the interior life and continuous revolutionary social action, the history of humanity no longer seems like a succession of accidental events, but more like a long voyage directed toward conquering a marvelous realm, a land we have promised to ourselves. Discoveries of universal laws as well as political and economic changes and works of art testify to the species' constant drive toward raising its level of knowledge and happiness, its perpetual struggle against the forces of ignorance and death. Humanity's driving passion ought to be examined as the epic of a single human's development in vast space, ignorant of personal demise. Whether we accept this idea as true or see it as a poetic comparison hardly matters. The essential thing is to recognize the single set of mechanisms at work governing our behavior, both as a group and as individuals.

The architecture of the individual, which begins at the ground level of the unconscious and ascends to the lit heights of voluntary, logical, intelligent consciousness, is found in the social structure. People, collectively, aren't aware of the present realities. They are pawns in a gigantic game and they don't comprehend its stakes. They are driven by inexorable social determinism, and their thinking reflects the necessity to which they submit.

When they are equal to the task, the ruling classes embody the intelligence, concentrated on well-defined and altruistic goals. Beyond this plane, which corresponds to simple rationalism, groups that seem to possess more complete knowledge and more extensive powers exist. They appear as far back into the past as you can look, under different names. The castle I've alluded to is the traditional dwelling for these exclusive brotherhoods.

What was this high science hidden in well-guarded books and transmitted by word of mouth only under an oath of secrecy? It was certainly not of the same order as today's scholarly science, aimed only at practical results. It seems to have been more general and, by its very nature, capable of quieting fundamental human fears. Men succeeded each other, understanding the meaning of the myths and the ceremonies that they performed. Directly or indirectly, their words were passed along to the popular masses to bring them to some previously conceived evolutionary stage. There is no doubt that the true keys to the marvelous were held by these gentlemen, so removed from the world and exerting so great a power over it at the same time.

The lay masses, made up of rich and poor, masters and slaves, the crowd that sticks to the main road, is not aware of, or denies, the castle's existence. Those with some intuitive sense of it are often able only to dream of the mysterious life going on there. Indeed, those led by their destiny to abandon the ordinary way and overcome the obstacles have been so profoundly changed by the time they enter the marvelous building that they haven't been able to return to the crowd afterward to give them their impressions and tell them what they've seen. With an altered mental state comes an altered language that makes communication impossible, whether or not it's desired.

A book on the marvelous ought to be an initiation tract; in fact, age-old experience shows that such a book can't be written, at least not in clear terms. The most that's possible is to suggest some well-defined direction.

Peoples have always lived, and still live, concerned mainly with their immediate needs, working constantly to satisfy them, however well or badly. They are driven by simple passions, which control the collective unconscious and which we find in every one of us. People subjected to life's necessities have never had the time nor the necessary mental freedom to develop their consciousness. The rare moments free from work have been taken up by play, religious ceremonies, or rites connected to the accepted myths; the leisure hours have allowed for singing and storytelling. These more or less mythical accounts represent in poetic language some basic explanations of the world; they express real history and social life as it has existed, but beyond that, they reflect the permanent passionate needs of the human species.

The unconscious of peoples, like that of individuals, has a double nature. Memories of the past are mingled with desires stemming from the needs of the living flesh and extending toward the future. This duality explains why, in local customs as well as in the stories and songs that make up the domain of folklore, we find humanity's hopes linked to bits of knowledge established and accumulated little by little over the course of centuries. These are very fortunate circumstances. Since we can't delineate the science of the initiated here, we will look to how such knowledge is reflected in the collective soul for reference. The high science concealed, it is to folklore, "the science of the people," that we will turn to ask the way to the realm of the marvelous.[4]

The word "folklore" evokes regional traditions: headdresses, costumes and dances, songs and rural dialects, local customs and stories. One thinks either of whatever it is that characterizes some savage tribe or what distinguishes a country amidst these great political and economic structures we call modern nations.

Historical development tends toward unification. Successive revolutions, wars, and the blending of different peoples have eroded local characteristics. Some efforts have been made, both deliberately and unconsciously, to resist this evolution. Reactionary politicians and priests have devoted themselves to conserving and even reviving traditions, even if it has meant giving them an artificial life. They have been aided in their efforts by the old timers' sentimentalism, by the taste of certain artists for the picturesque, and by the tourist business.

Thanks to the dialectical movement that directs social phenomena, these reactionary intentions can lead to progressive results. In proclaiming their ancestral heritage, certain minorities struggle for their freedom. They resist being absorbed by an overpowering imperialism. They help to keep alive the unrest associated with the revolutionary efforts of the economically oppressed classes.

The problem of primitive folklore is of even greater importance, because knowledge of it, by its very nature, can transform the basis of thought. The deadly weight of inertia creates conformity and custom in societies, and art becomes fixed in an official, classical, academic style. People believe their representation of the universe to be the only one possible; beyond it, they see only barbarism and fanciful illusion. The individual bases his definition of all human nature upon himself. To prove that these stagnant ideas are mistaken, innovators are forced to look to other traditions for examples, other representations of the world, and other systems of feeling and thought.

This necessity is a law of history. The Christian subversion of Rome

---

4. Folk: people. Lore: science.

exploited the snobbery that had developed in favor of Greece, Egypt, and Asia Minor.

Romanticism revitalized its emotional sources by drawing from the exotic and from the gothic and medieval past. At the beginning of this century, African and Oceanic folklore, as well as that of pre-Columbian America, served as a springboard for the artistic revolution of cubism and surrealism.

But whatever motivates those undertaking folkloric research, the important thing is that their numbers have multiplied. Travelers, anthropologists, and linguists, out to discover local traditions, are recording customs and rites, and writing down songs and stories. At present, the transcribed and translated stories comprise an immense literature. Unless we suppose that this phase has come to its end, all we can see before us are sensational discoveries. But after the era of inventory must follow one of examination. We have arrived at the same critical point the natural sciences reached at the end of the eighteenth century, when it was necessary to go beyond an enthusiasm for collections to the difficult work of classification, of establishing the laws.

Preliminary attempts at interpretation have already taken place in the domain of folklore. The difficulty is distinguishing that which characterizes one cultural group from that which belongs to the enduring universal tradition. While the dress, the customs, and the dances are particular to a certain society, the stories often contain universal elements. Thus, it is to an examination of the stories that our inquiry into the marvelous leads. Having absorbed current popular opinion, I thought I would begin this work by classifying the various texts according to their age and where they were collected, and then conclude by noting their common characteristics. The original plan included systematic borrowings from the folklore of Egypt, Scandinavia, Ireland, etc. Geographic identification would take the place of the name of the author. I've been obliged to abandon this method that, by insisting on insignificant differences in expression, gives too little value to the profound similarities. The Egyptian stories, which date back to the second millennium B.C., are indistinguishable from modern stories. The story of the two brothers, in Gustave Lefebvre's remarkable translation from which I will later give an excerpt, is nearly identical to a popular German story collected in Hesse by Wolff, to a Hungarian story transmitted by J. Mailath, and to a Russian heroic legend cited by Rimbaud. It is found in modern Greece, in eighteenth-century France, in Italy, India (Deccan), Bengal, Vietnam, and some twenty other places. When I say that it is found there, I mean that not only is the general sense of the narrative similar, but even the internal mechanisms of the story and the poetic images are repeated. And I could give countless more examples.

So it is that in her important work, Miss Marian Roalf Cox has been able to draw together more than one hundred and thirty versions of the story of Cinderella, collected in the widest variety of regions and coming from ancient and modern eras. These findings lead me to follow the example of folklorists and abandon chronological and geographical classification in favor of concentrating on the general sense of the accounts to isolate a few essential themes. Having established how uniform popular accounts of the marvelous are by looking at them all together, it is still interesting to understand how and why these stories take on their regional characteristics. It seems as though the different human races, all theoretically equal, have each developed their own faculties with regard to the marvelous as a function of the particular qualities displayed in their everyday lives. We would no doubt come to this conclusion if we gathered together a modern-day European enamored with material comfort, a Chinese, an imaginative and talkative Arab, a fetishistic African. These ethnic gifts are much less pronounced if we look for them not in specific individuals, but in the whole collection of folklore. Following Grimm, Müller, and M. de Hahn, German scholars try their best to attribute the authorship of the great legends to the Aryans. E. Cosquin locates their origin in India. Knowing the traditions of Oceania, Africa, and pre-Columbian America invalidates these theses. We would have to suppose that the Aryans were the most primitive race and that their culture extended over the entire globe, or that, originally sown in India, the seeds for these stories could have been dispersed to every corner of the planet, hypotheses that have no justification and that give rise only to a wretched sort of racial pride.

Furthermore, it seems that the human unconscious has always been extraordinarily uniform with regard to the fundamental directions it takes and even the symbols it employs.

I think the present moment, with its outbreaks of racism, nationalism, and wars, is a good time to repeat the words of William Blake: "According to the poetic spirit, men are all alike," and Lautréamont's assertion: "Poetry must be made by all." Whatever holds for a nation holds for all of humanity.

Since the last century, the attempt has been to explain works according to the background out of which they derive. Materialist notions of history have made this way of seeing even more precise by giving an overriding importance to the social economy and to the means of production and exchange. According to this philosophy, stories would, above all, reflect society at one moment in its evolution. Indeed, they do reflect it, transforming historic events into epics, letting the traces of social structures appear in narratives. Stories from the Middle Ages have knights for heroes, whereas later on, the middle class adopts the same themes and they are adapted to a new economic hierarchy. Here the dreaded figure of the master is a king, there a caliph, elsewhere an overlord or a patron. But these changes in costume and scenery do nothing to alter the deep sense of the stories.

In contrast, the natural environment plays a much greater role. Proximity to the sea or forest, landscapes of granite ledge or fertile plains have an influence on the composition of folklore. If no class has a special claim on the marvelous, there is a link between the marvelous and the natural elements, the marvelous and place: legends of the sea, the steppes, the mountains. But even here the differences reside more in presentation than in any deep transformation of the principal themes.

We need not be charmed by this remarkable continuity. The idea that humanity submits to such great monotony, even when it comes to exercising the imagination, is not very comforting. We can understand the boredom of oriental sovereigns who, exhausted by never-ending stories, wanted to perceive other dream vistas beyond the ordinary marvelous. After having been induced to read many hundreds of legends in order to prepare this work, each more extraordinary than the last, I must say that I have had my fill of them. One quickly loses interest in the society of fairies and princes. The mind grows weary of too many riches, miracles, and parallel adventures.

That thematic consistency in folklore: Is it a function of human nature that, animated by the same passions, lives one single dream among the unchanging cosmic rhythms? Does it come solely from a kind of passive repetition, a poverty of the imagination which, one day, we will be able to break out of?

To clarify this issue, insofar as that's possible, it may be helpful to examine how we acquire the traditional elements of the marvelous.

From the moment of birth, the infant begins his slow education. His movements become coordinated, his consciousness is formed and oriented toward the accomplishment of necessary gestures. Some disciplines are developed. This training occurs without difficulties, except in those exceptional cases where a serious emotional conflict develops early and hinders its progress.

At first glance, playing seems opposed to practical work because the actions and objects seem so splendidly unmotivated. Although it seems entirely subject to fantasy and pleasure, playing, in fact, serves as an apprenticeship to life in society, since the most highly valued play imitates the life of "big people." Children anticipate the activities they will later feel enslaved by. The little boy imagines himself a soldier, sailor, police officer, thief, merchant. The little girl dreams of being a wife, mother, actress. Children create theatrical spectacles in which people and things are replaced by stand-ins, for lack of access to the real things. The adult eye perceives only the illusory character of such play in which arbitrary convention doesn't trouble the players in the least. From a simple piece of wood, they create a doll that they dress and cradle in their arms as tenderly as they would a "flesh and blood" baby. Thanks to these surrogates, a dream is lived out here, but it is a dream that copies and leads to life as it is observed and cannot properly be called a search for the marvelous. This continues as long as the child retains the goodwill of a conformist, as long as he is afraid of calling attention to himself, as long as he wants to blend into the shared reality. The situation changes as soon as the family or social atmosphere makes him suffer, as soon as he encounters obstacles in the way of his desire for knowledge or the satisfaction of his emotional impulses. Then he feels all the poverty of the imperfect world. He feels nostalgic for other countries and better people. He stops deifying his parents and their world. He begins to revolt and assert his need for evasion. The marvelous is born. At about seven years old, the child creates his mystery, which is a personal treasure.

Rimbaud retains a lucid memory of this time, and expresses it with bitterness and violence:

The Seven-Year-Old Poets
Arthur Rimbaud

And the mother, shutting the book of exercises,
Went off satisfied and very proud, not seeing
In the blue eyes under a bump-covered brow
The soul of her child given over to aversion.

Throughout the day he sweated obedience; very
Intelligent; however, dark nervous tics, several traits

Seemed to affirm bitter hypocrisy within him!
In the shadow of the corridors with their moldy drapes,
When passing through he stuck out his tongue, his two fists
At his crotch, and saw spots in his closed eyes.
A door opened onto evening: by the lamp
He could be seen, on high, grousing on the stairway,
Under a gulf of daylight suspended from the roof. In summer
Especially, overcome and stupid, he stubbornly sought
To shut himself up in the cool air of the outhouses;
There he would think, in tranquillity, nostrils gaping wide.

When washed clean of the day's odors, the small garden
Behind the house, in winter, moonlit,
Lying at the foot of a wall, buried in the marl
And rubbing his dizzy eyes to force visions,
He listened to the teeming movement of the mangy espaliers,
For pity's sake! These children alone were his friends
Who, wretched, bare-headed, with eyes running onto their cheeks,
Hiding scrawny fingers black and yellow with mud
Under old-fashioned clothes reeking of diarrhea and age
Conversed with the sweetness of idiots!
And if, having caught him in these deeds of rank mercy
His mother was shocked; the profound tenderness
Of her child seized on that astonishment
That was as it should be. She had a blue gaze—that lies!

At seven, he wrote novels about life
In the great desert, where enraptured Freedom shines,
Forests, suns, riverbanks, savannahs!—He was aided
By illustrated newspapers where, blushing, he looked
At the laughing girls of Spain and Italy.
When the daughter of the workers next door came by,
Eight years old, brown-eyed, crazed and wearing a calico dress,
The little brute had jumped him in the corner,

Pushing him on his back and shaking her long hair,
As he was under her, he bit her buttocks,
Because she never wore panties;
—And battered by her fists and heels,
Took the taste of her skin back to his room.

He feared the wan Sundays in December,

When, with hair pomaded, on a small mahogany table,
He read a Bible with cabbage-green edges;
Dreams oppressed him every night in his alcove.
He did not love God, but the men whom in the tawny evening,
Black, in smocks, he saw going home to the suburbs,
Where town criers, with three drum rolls,
Make the crowd laugh and rumble over edicts.
—He dreamed of the amorous prairie, where luminous
Swells, fresh perfumes, golden puberties,
Move tranquilly and take flight!

And as he especially savored things of darkness,
When, in his bare room with the blinds drawn,
High and blue, in the grip of a bitter humidity,
He read his endlessly pondered upon novel,
Full of heavy ocherous skies and drowned forests,
Of flesh flowers that unfurl in sidereal woods—
Vertigo, collapse, disorder, and mercy!
—While the noise of the neighborhood went on,
Below, alone, and lying on pieces of unbleached
Canvas that are violently foreshadowing a sail! [5]

The world the child dreamed of had all the vivid color of illustrated magazines. From the stories he heard, he remembered the marvelous forms. It was the legendary country that old sailors described so precisely, sitting along the quays among their nets and barrels.

If you think about it, nothing is more complex than the ancient human need to tell children stories, the narrator's penchant for showing off, for capturing the attention of an audience easily mystified and incapable of gauging the story's plausibility. A desire both to charm and to terrorize accounts for the images of wealth and happiness coming after the worst misfortunes and horrible crimes. But there's more to it. People feel vaguely ashamed at seeing the eyes of the child opening up to such an imperfect world. They experience the same feelings as the

---

5. Arthur Rimbaud, "The Seven-Year-Old Poets" (May 26, 1871), trans. Jon Graham.

lover who, when the woman he desires arrives, suddenly discovers how poor he is and hides this behind flowers and garlands. In the same way, stories serve to mask life's mediocrity. Moreover, they constitute the most complete confession human beings can make: a confession of their hope. In returning to children the message of the marvelous, we give them the best of the tradition. By providing the child's imagination with the fundamental elements of dream, the first stories leave an indelible imprint on it. The woman desired will always be that far-off princess whose conquest requires a thousand trials. The idea of a just prince arriving at the climactic moment to save the innocent will endure, like that of grateful beasts and friendly fairies helping to vanquish evil demons. Whatever more there is to be learned and reflected upon, to transform consciousness, desire's spontaneous expression will remain associated with these first impressions of the marvelous.

It's remarkable that in the strictest families where every detail is carefully considered (the choice of teachers, the child's relationships, the precise etiquette of his habits), the responsibility for storytelling is left to domestics, to old women, or even ancient, slightly senile relatives. The importance of hired help and old people in the development of the imagination is well worth noting. It establishes a sort of sympathy between the classes and the generations that goes against social custom. Thus, it's particularly strange how little White American children, raised in an atmosphere of scorn for the Black race, go to sleep to the songs of their Black mammies. Even in its transmission, then, folklore retains its character as a "science of the people." The images, which carry human hope and clothe our passions, pass from one subconscious to another undeterred by boundaries of race, state, or class. The continuity we've noted deep within the structure of humanity derives partly from this method of propagating the marvelous. If a radical change in the stories intended for the young doesn't bring it about, no valid human transformation can be hoped for. I won't risk claiming that such a change is possible, since most that have taken place up till now have occurred only on the surface.

The way in which these stories reach children and shape their imaginations illustrates how the core of our inner emotional life is, at the same time, that part of our being we all have in common. This idea, which we have already encountered with regard to the experience of mirrors, becomes clearest here. Even as conscious volition, knowledge, intelligence, and social ambition are so many barriers isolating us, the domain of the unconscious makes us partake of the riches of community, riches represented by poetic symbols, which allow for exchange between all.

The inquiry into the marvelous, leading to the study of the collective unconscious and the folklore that expresses it, raises the problem of religious myths. The feelings of respect, faith, or disdain that surround these questions continue to make their examination difficult. Thus, a well-informed scholar like E. Cosquin, devoted to Christian dogma, refrains from establishing connections between stories and sacred accounts. At the very most, he takes a timid glance at ancient religions because they seem to him imaginary, on the order of fantastic legends. Such a position is untenable. Myths and stories are so interwoven and interconnected, sometimes to the point of being indistinguishable, that it's impossible to see a separation between them.

Among the different opinions that have been expressed on this subject, I keep coming back to the interesting theory of Saint-Yves. According to this author, most stories and popular traditions are echoes of ancient religious rites that have gradually lost their sacred character.

This explanation is valid for most local customs and regional dances, in which reminders of organized religious ceremonies are easily found. This is also true of seasonal holidays, and customs surrounding birth, engagement, and death.

Because we are familiar with Roman, Greek, and Egyptian antiquity, it is not difficult to uncover the origins of folklore traditions in the Mediterranean. Ancient affiliations are less easy to trace in Nordic countries whose primitive religions are less well known to us. In Sicily, Italy, and Provence, crosses made of earth and sprouting seeds are displayed in the streets for the Easter holidays. Despite its Christian form, this custom imitates those practiced in Egypt for celebrating the resurrection of Osiris. And it's likely that those derived from an even more ancient cult devoted to the vegetation god. Even though religions change, customs remain linked to the same ritual preoccupations.

The same is true of play. In his very remarkable work, Yrjö Hirn studies its origin.[6] He shows, for example, how the rattle, which is now used to entertain babies, is a very ancient ritual object. Its noise served to banish evil powers. Among certain Indian tribes, it was used to heal diseases and cast spells. Its music, however rudimentary, prepared Siberian shamans for their ecstatic trances.

---

6. Yrjö Hirn, *Les jeux d'enfants* (Stock).

By reading a text drawn from the Popol-Vuh, we can understand the importance of tennis from a sacred point of view. Tracing a game of snakes and ladders reminds us of labyrinths: arriving at certain points, the adept was obliged to turn around, go back, and undergo tests. Like a bad player, he fell down a shaft, stayed in prison, waited to get over a bridge, or encountered death. Everyone knows that our playing cards represent a simplified version of the tarot. The tarot, like dice, like knucklebones, aided the hierophant in predicting fate. In Asia, the games of chess and mah-jongg were sacred.

Not all play derives from religion. On the other hand, we can say that all aspects of ancient religion have become playthings. All rites have been transformed into customs that are generally pleasant. This "profanation" in the literal sense of the word—passage from the sacred to the profane—is a fundamental law of history. It's impossible to see how humans could have overcome the terrors of religion without acting in this way.

Turning from games to stories, we can see the same mechanism at work. Stories come from myths, from initiation narratives that have lost their original seriousness. This observation explains why we feel a kind of hermetic significance underlying popular stories. But interpreters are wrong in claiming that legendary figures are symbols of natural and cosmic forces. Their error lies in their desire to reduce all the explanations to only one—according to one school, the cycle of the day, according to another, the seasons of the year—as if initiatory instructions had only one chapter, and as if layers of reasoning could not be found superimposed there.

This ambivalence, or should we say multivalence, which is the very law of initiatory symbolism, has not been understood any better than the dialectic that translates personal fears into cosmic realities. When humans read the sky, they connect the points of the stars into figures: lion, bull, eagle, serpent..., just as the seer "reads" an ink blot, a coffee stain, molten lead, just as Leonardo da Vinci examined the forms of mold on an old wall. Thus humans project thought into space. They see the images that obsess them. But the moment the dream becomes external or is linked to objects in the universe, it gives up the rhythm of dream and takes on the rhythm of the cosmos. The lion no longer pounces with brusque and angry authority. Now, with stately grace, he follows behind the virgin. He no longer elicits fear but becomes the symbol of the sun's power at the height of summer.

Before our scholars pointed it out, popular storytellers were well aware of the initiatory content in traditional stories. They gave their accounts a hieratic form on purpose to keep the audience's attention and to create a more mysterious atmosphere. Folklore often makes use of a kind of hermeticism, which is nothing more than a matter of style: the seven brothers of the kings, the seven sons, the ten princes, the three princesses, etc. Often too, the use of sacred numbers is a simple *trompe l'oeil* meant to divert inquiries.

Explaining stories in terms of the ancient myths they contain is one facet of the truth. To understand the entire picture, we must invert the proposition and show how myths and rites are born and grow out of the fertile ground of folklore. Stories constitute a common wealth, a spontaneous expression of the collective unconscious. Religions take possession of them, building them into a stable construction equipped with a moral purpose. Religious systemization captures the marvelous and strips it of its novelty, its freedom. It exploits it for metaphysical and social ends. Dream images are organized according to an iconography precisely calculated to promote a certain dogma.

I've noticed that there's often been confusion between those bursts of mysticism associated with the highest levels of spirituality and the development of imaginative and dream faculties. Despite the miracles it surrounds itself with, despite the fantastic elements it employs, a religion always begins as a reaction against an earlier paganism that it exposes as fantasmagorical and childish. It triumphs because of its rational usefulness. It tends to limit the field of the marvelous by providing answers to fears, security based on dogmatic assertions, and a more complete explanation of the universe. The marvelous, on the other hand, proposes fewer solutions in favor of exploring unknown territory. The true believer ignores the unknown as soon as he possesses faith. Thus there's an equilibrium at work between the domains of the religious and the marvelous. The latter never disappears entirely. Even during periods when orthodox mysticism is the most strict, popular stories survive. They adapt to a new vocabulary and become permeated with new precepts. These changes are rarely for the better. When Buddhism appeared, Hindu folklore suffered for a long time. A deliberate desire to moralize changed stories into apologues. The change takes the same form we see in poems that exalt one individual or develop one particular thesis. The marvelous cannot be made into examples or demonstrations. European legends have suffered much by being incorporated into the Christian edifice. They have been safeguarded only where the popular imagination has escaped the stranglehold of dogma, in regions where only the superficial pomp of Christianity has mingled with earlier religions still existing above ground. I'm thinking of Ireland, Brittany, the Black Forest, and certain areas of Spain.

The fantastic legends that center on places or natural phenomena (caves, for example) derive less from ancient rites than from that spontaneous emotion these places and sights elicit, emotions that psychoanalysis seems able to explain. For the unconscious, the cave evokes feminine sexuality and its great mystery. It simultaneously suggests all the ardor of desire and the torpid hope of returning to prenatal calm. It's a good place to dream. It makes you want to hide away there, to make love or to die. In such an atmosphere, remarkable things happen. A traveler hears strange noises, he notices voices, he witnesses apparitions. Dozing, he has unusual dreams. These incidences are then exploited, a cult is organized, the place becomes sacred. In Lourdes, the theme of the enchanted cave recurs all the way back to the beginning of time.

A recent myth about Thérèse of Lisieux doesn't depend upon the power of place, but on another unconscious dream. The success of the saint is largely due to her promise to make it rain roses. The theme of the virgin whose mouth spills roses is a classic one in folklore. This power is usually given to a poor and virtuous girl by a fairy as a reward for her merits. The complete tradition includes female tears being changed into pearls and drops of blood becoming rubies. It is from that universal legend that this particular myth derives its energy. The power of the traditional folkloric image is such that, despite her Christian training, the heroine herself imagines an angelic existence more in keeping with traditional stories than with orthodox Catholicism.

The themes of the marvelous are not only systematized in doctrinal and mythic structures. Often they are also transformed into living realities. One hopes for the liberating prince, and he comes. One fears the wolf, the monster, the destructive spirit, and they appear. One prays for the Messiah, and someone arrives to play the part.

A constant dialectic operates between dream and reality. If legends are created around heroes, heroes, in turn, are incarnated out of legends.

Religious groups are not the only exploiters of the marvelous. It has been made the tool of writers, poets, and artists as well.

Taking an overview, the evolution is simple. At the beginning of each civilization, art is a collective phenomenon. The people, priests, architects, and painters are all connected by close bonds. Songs and incantations, out of which poems will grow, have an impersonal character. Troubadours and storytellers travel about with their various talents, performing pieces from their repertoire for their audiences. Their primary role is to remember the stories, to assemble them, and most important, to circulate them. No one takes pride in being original. On the contrary, the aim is to faithfully reproduce the tradition. The idea of a creative artist, submissive to some personal genius, surfaces later in a civilization's evolution. It appears at the time when conscious technical exploration predominates in the work of art, when concern for form and style, a taste for technique for its own sake, becomes the essential preoccupation. The exploitation of the collective treasure by a few individuals seeking self-glorification is equivalent to what the propertied classes do when they appropriate the work of the community and the resources of the past.

Removed from the people, the marvelous became the opportunity for individual works and was weakened. Its emotional value and authentic mystery are diminished by the author's desire for perfection according to conventional rules of expression. The classic search for a noble style, concern for a majestic or pleasing order, often results in the use of "beautiful," "lyric," or "elegant" images. The popular image, which possesses a magical, emotional charge, is rejected. That is how the marvelous gets extinguished, by being disassociated from certain key images: a pin going through a woman's head to change her into a bird, a ring swallowed by a fish, a lost shoe, a flying horse, a spot of red blood on the snow, an apple with a woman inside, etc.

Let us now take a look at this idea of key images.

Man produces a sort of small, limited universe, a closed microcosm, a "monad" as Leibniz called it. His most vital problem is communicating with other beings. Contact is established directly by a physical mechanism that calls the elements and cosmic energies into play. Erotic desire, fear, calm, anguish pass from one skin to another as heat or electricity. I am convinced that all thought can be transmitted in this way, without words or gestures. This type of contact troubles those with impure hearts. Subject to unknown laws, it doesn't provide that efficient consistency societies demand. And it assures the supremacy of feeling beings, something that mediocre and practical minds could never accept.

Thus, humans have resorted to words. Words have the advantage of being something like things (at least I believe this), of containing in their very structure the heavy inheritance of centuries' long collective efforts toward gaining knowledge, of being a convenient code. They have the disadvantage of being meaningless to anyone who isn't familiar with their subject. Without personal memory, words evoke nothing. Very often, the ideas that the same word suggests to different minds have nothing in common. Each of us possesses a code of symbols that is ours alone, that is the result of our individual past.

Those words that move me most deeply may mean nothing to you.

But the key images open the doors of our collective sensibility. Moreover, they resonate in the unconscious with a singular depth. The proof of their vital worth lies in the fact that, despite all the different forms stories take on over the ages, the key words remain intact. Studying these images, we arrive at the science of the Word, that truly magical science, which is not in any way related to formal examinations of the classics.

Surrealism has had the virtue of clarifying the problem of inspiration, which, until now, has been seen as a divine gift, mysterious and personal. The systematic use of dreams and automatic writing, the rejection of deliberate control, and the abolition of artistic rankings have all reopened the sources of the marvelous. Timid forays into the unconscious for personal ends have been replaced by methodical exploration. Free access must be extended to the collective unconscious and to the consciousness of the individual. The first examinations of this sort will make it necessary to revamp our literary and artistic halls of fame.

Prompted by my work on this book to reread the most celebrated texts of Western civilization, I've been struck by their poverty compared to the riches of universal folklore. I've given up citing them for the most part, preferring anonymous sources. That is why Dante, the Christian prince of the marvelous, doesn't appear in this collection. In his place, I offer Ishtar's descent into hell, a Mesopotamian account from the third millennium B.C., which itself is a transcription of an even more ancient theme.

Examining the tradition of stories and legend, one finds that the marvelous grows out of uneasiness, from the revolutionary desire to lift the veil of mystery. This palpable tension has no connection to preoccupations with style. Those who can reclaim this tradition and maintain a real connection with it are not the museum curators or guardians of the academy. They are the innovators who continue the great adventure. By listening most attentively to their unconscious, they can better hear the voice of the universe and so hope to extend the domain of the collective marvelous.

Having shown how religious systems and individual works grow from folklore, having seen how folklore enacts the movement toward the unknown and reveals human unconscious desires, our next task is to uncover the nature of these desires, that is, to begin psychoanalysis of the collective soul. That idea I'm so fond of, viewing the whole of humanity as one entity similar to an individual and subject to the same laws, leads me to believe we can extend psychoanalysis's range by simply transposing its already classical teachings. I share this opinion with contemporary writers who try to link recent findings concerning personal psychology to sociological observations. But in changing dimension, in moving from one plane to another, we can't forget that even if they operate according to the same mechanism, phenomena change in meaning. If not used with the greatest care, analogies and generalizations lead only to error.

The problems that present themselves to the whole aren't the same as those that disturb the individual. These center on his struggle within the family. His psychology is constructed around the oedipal complex, around the conflict between father and son. The man of traditional folklore has supposedly resolved his internal difficulties. At the time of his heroic adventures, at the hour when the curtain rises on the stage of the marvelous, the father, that symbol of the last generation, is dead. He is no longer the master possessing all the oppressive powers of guardianship. He appears vanquished, the victim of treachery, ignorance, or age. He has succumbed, not, as Freud says, to his murderous son's attacks, but rather to the damaging forces of nature. He has been beaten by the perversity of the evil spirits he has fought against. Besides corresponding to reality, this defeat is necessary, we can see. Why should these stories inspire our courage, our curiosity, our hope, if our parents have been successful and if all we need to do is maintain and imitate their conquests? The marvelous requires a revolutionary will to escape mediocrity, to assert the power of desire over the laws of the universe. But, and this is what characterizes the collective unconscious, paternal defeat doesn't lead to filial remorse but to solidarity. The son considers himself obliged to follow through with the effort already underway. He must increase his knowledge and his abilities so as not to fall into the traps set by hostile gods and that enemy, nature.

He must discover the secret paths and magic formulas that will win him the aid of benevolent powers. Then the vanquished father can be avenged. The remarkable thing is that folklore, which assumes the father's disappearance to be necessary, retains the presence of the grandfather. However, he is removed from the action. He makes his voice heard to the audience. He informs the hero about human destiny, the difficulties awaiting him, and the role assigned to him. In real life, elders have the privilege of effectively shaping the unconscious of the child with their stories before action begins. The characters of the grandparents can be disguised. Often a wise old man or an old woman somewhat like a sorceress appears at the right moment to put an end to the hero's hesitations. At other times, the allusion is less direct and the familial chain is represented by an inheritance with draconian conditions attached, or a stolen good that must be recovered at the risk of very great danger.

As for the mother, she is found to have all the feminine charm she possesses in the personal unconscious. Very often, the widow is depicted as a sensitive, nervous, timid being who may provide emotional comfort but is prevented from actually intervening. She rarely plays an important role.

On the other hand, the person who sparks amorous feelings is described with a great wealth of poetic comparisons meant to evoke the listener's desire. The beloved combines all those attributes that can inspire a man to persevere on his difficult journey through the world and surmount the most perilous obstacles. She possesses beauty, virtue, power. Like the individual unconscious, the collective unconscious makes love the essential motivating force behind human actions. Generally in the stories, taking possession of the woman desired corresponds to attaining knowledge.

Modern scholars see an allegory in this traditional assimilation. For them, giving truth the features of a woman derives from poetic license. I do not accept this explanation. This is not a matter of allegory, but of reality. There is good reason for the tradition not to separate knowledge from love. Because of the feeling it provokes, love alone opens the doors to the unknown. Love alone allows real contact between a man and another being, and thus, with the rest of the cosmos. What the intelligence learns can remain separate from love, but true understanding, true knowledge, cannot.

There are some deep hidden caverns with walls of rock crystal. When someone enters there by way of a secret gorge, leaving the light of day behind, when she penetrates deeper, equipped with her lantern, the marvelous seizes her. The fantastic architecture doesn't obey practical necessity as human constructions do, but a subtle necessity of mineral pressures. The single flame of a candle is enough to set huge fires ablaze. Thousands of images are reflected, and, merging with one another, create the strangest forms. With its rigorous geometry and regular harmony, the Palace of Illusions pales in comparison. The effect is all the more powerful because the way the crevices are arranged creates a complex play of echoes. One word, or a simple sound like a drop of water falling, fills the place with voices, murmurs that repeat themselves as if innumerable presences were greeting the visitor. For me, nothing better evokes the inner life of humans. When, thanks to sleep, we descend toward the depths of our beings, the unconscious seems just like an enchanted cave. The images from our waking hours are multiplied, distorted, and call up monsters and phantoms. Conversations are carried on, and the words spoken by the inner voice change in timbre and seem to be those of other, stranger voices.

Given our emotional reactions and beliefs, the whole of humanity could not operate differently. Each individual constitutes one facet, large or small, upright or oblique, brilliant or dull, by which the images of the universe are reflected and transformed. The stories repeated from person to person, from generation to generation, follow a trajectory comparable to that of a gigantic echo extending into infinity.

But where does that resonating voice originate? From a god who spoke when time began and whose speech continues to make the walls of the world shake? Do we interpret in spoken words the sound of the storm, the crash of thunder, the murmur of the forest? Do we give human meaning to the symphony of the spheres? Perhaps also the spirit, lost in the immensity of the palace, no longer recognizes its own beating heart among the sounds there, the look of its wondering eye in that light. The mystery surrounding the origin of folklore is no different from that which hides from us the origin of the species.

And to try to trace the line of descent back to one single source: that is no less futile than the attempts to prove a single disseminated and continuous creation.

What we have learned from our methods of discovery tends to show creation taking place everywhere at once. It is a collective phenomenon, its form and time imposed by the rhythms of the cosmos.

The Transmission of Knowledge
W. Blake

*I was in a Printing house in Hell, & saw the method in which
knowledge is transmitted from generation to generation.*

*In the first chamber was a Dragon-Man, clearing away the rubbish
from a cave's mouth; within, a number of Dragons were hollowing
the cave.*

*In the second chamber was a Viper folding round the rock & the cave
and others adorning it with gold, silver and precious stones.*

*In the third chamber was an Eagle with wings and feathers of air: he
caused the inside of the cave to be infinite; around were numbers of
Eagle-like men who built palaces in the immense cliffs.*

*In the fourth chamber were Lions of flaming fire, raging around &
melting the metals into living fluids.*

*In the fifth chamber were Unnam'd forms, which cast the metals into
the expanse.*

*There they were received by Men who occupied the sixth chamber, and
took the forms of books & were arranged in libraries.* [7]

Let us quickly leave this problem of general ontogeny behind and
see if we can shed some light on the matter by analyzing a story originating in the present. The circumstances of life today (much more rapid

---

7. "A Memorable Vision," in *The Marriage of Heaven and Hell* (1790). Blake
(1757–1827) is, for me, one of the most important prophets of modern times.
He never stopped living totally connected to the reality of the world. When
the French Revolution changed the human condition, Blake set forth what is,
and for centuries will be, our truth. As a prophet, we don't ask him for predictions of events or philosophical understanding (this is weak in his work). It is
enough that he sets forth the indispensable. The words engraved by him will
remain engraved on the tables of those who love the new law. When the rock
of doctrine crystallizes from our work, it will begin:

> *Man's body is not distinct from his soul, because what is called body is part
> of the soul.*
> *Energy is the only life and it comes from the body and Reason is the limit or
> exterior circumference of Energy.*
> *Energy is the eternal law.*

To my thinking, there is a direct line connecting Blake's message and
Nietzsche's, that other great inspirer of future change.

communication, wider dissemination of news) do not noticeably alter human reactions.

Toward the end of September 1938, the following story circulated among the intellectuals who gather in the Saint-Germain-des-Prés quarter: A driver happened to meet an old woman on the road where his car had broken down. She looked like a witch, said a few unimportant things, and then announced that Hitler would die in January 1939. She added, "And if you don't believe me, you will soon have proof of my clairvoyance. Tomorrow, in fact, you will transport a cadaver in your car." The traveler went away troubled. The next day, he gave a friend of his a ride, and, during the trip, his friend slumped over dead.... Here the story ends. The first part of the prophecy having come true, the audience remains troubled about the imminent future. This story was told to me more than ten times by different people. In December, I heard it from a merchant who was clearly not part of the intelligentsia.

Each of the accounts was different. Sometimes the traveler was a close relative of the speaker, sometimes he was a famous person, the names of André Gide and Paul Valéry came up. The circumstances of the meeting with the old woman varied also. Sometimes she approached the automobile. More often she was waiting in a passage or under the porch of a house. According to some, she was from Brittany, according to others, she was a Gypsy. The death of the companion was, generally, natural and sudden. The way André Gide heard the story, it took place within André Breton's inner circle. He consulted with Breton. None of the details provided stood up to examination.

So what had happened? At the end of September, international tensions were high. France wanted Hitler's death, and that wish, more than war, which for the moment had been avoided, seemed to many to have unfortunately prolonged the German dictator's rule. The assassination of the chief by terrorist methods thus presented itself as a solution to the general imagination at a time when the hope for a satisfactory collective settlement was vanishing. This mechanism is well known in sociology. Moreover, the story was first told to me by a Jew who would, of course, have a particularly strong desire to see the master of Germany disappear.

There is no doubt that originally a clairvoyant did predict to someone that Hitler would be assassinated in January 1939. If the story had been told that way, it wouldn't have had much credibility. So many of these kinds of predictions have been made in the last few years, and they've all proven false. So it then becomes useful to hide the identity of the Parisian clairvoyant, to locate her in the country, to edit out the consultation and invent a chance meeting. Last of all, to build trust, the example of a prophecy that comes true becomes necessary. No doubt the clairvoyant in question had already predicted a mishap like the one that later occurred. And because this first prophecy had come true, she was consulted again and her words were taken into consideration. The story reverses the order of the propositions. It responds to the listener's growing doubts with the words of the old woman: "If you don't believe me, I predict that you...." This is a mechanism of the dreaming mind. Freud analyzes it brilliantly. The progression of thought, of conflicting feelings, are represented in dreams by so many different characters engaged in conversation or struggle. Internal debate is transformed into theatrical drama. That explains the theatrical nature of stories. Each character symbolizes an idea or feeling in its pure state. None has the complexity of a real being.

But let us return to the analysis of our story. The secondary prophecy cannot be insignificant. The prediction of the assassination of a dictator must be guaranteed by some unusual and serious event involving the death of a man, and that death must be unforeseeable. That's why it's an embolism, the sudden collapse of a young and healthy individual. The assassination of the chancellor would be the same kind of event, escaping all probability, given the precautions taken to safeguard his life and the failure of all attempts made against him. The unexpected death of a friend or parent corresponds to an inverted reduplication of the motif.

Here the unconscious lets us witness its functional law in operation: to divide mythic heroes into their various aspects, like figures in dreams. (This process takes place throughout ancient mythology, especially in Greece.) On the other hand, we also have here an example of magic thought. The enchantment requires the character's duality (and all prophecy constitutes a kind of enchantment). The friend's death serves as an enactment of the dictator's assassination. The story takes on a moral aspect. Since a sympathetic character has been sacrificed, the same thing could happen to the despised figure. This idea of atonement is among the most ancient. Here we find it underlying modern aims.

This story, which spread throughout Paris, expressed nothing but a collective desire. The prediction did not come true. To my knowledge, no serious danger threatened Hitler in January. The prophecy was shown to be false too quickly to serve as a basis for an enduring story. If it had come partially or wholly true, the account would have been transformed. The circumstances serving only to substantiate the prophecy would have been eliminated and replaced with an attempt to explain it.

The identity of the clairvoyant would still be kept secret. Our Western mentality doesn't hold these types in high regard. Instead, a supernatural being, a messenger from God, would be made to intervene, one whom the church had no doubt persecuted. This celestial messenger would be shown announcing the prophecy to a privileged, virtuous few in a moralizing speech expressing the Lord's grievances against the German master.

Prophecies that don't come true are not necessarily forgotten. If what happens isn't in keeping with what we want to happen, we consider the apparent reality false. This is the reasoning behind deranged interpretations. The most typical example is provided by those women who fall prey to a pathological kind of love. The men they pester with their devoted attentions have clearly declared that they don't love them, but the women don't believe it. They know that their love is shared, and that their lovers' denials, be it from fear or spitefulness, only serve to make them suffer. We find a similar interpretational mechanism at work on the story that concerns us here. Apparently, Hitler is not dead, but perhaps we are being fooled and his assassination has been kept a secret. In New York, in January 1939, with the help of the Macauley and Cy firm, a book entitled *The Strange Death of Adolf Hitler* appeared. Under this title, recalling the names of certain popular films of this era, an author (who remains anonymous) recounts in the smallest and most precise detail how the chancellor was made a victim of poisoning and how he was replaced by a double. The idea that famous people can disappear without the public's knowing it, and that dummies or doubles can take their places without anyone's noticing is, again, a classic theme of folklore. Complex feelings are expressed by it. This belief allows the popular unconscious to seek vengeance for the excessive dominance certain individuals gain on the international scene. It is very comforting for common mortals to think that a great man's death may not change anything and that anyone could replace him in his high position. The obsession with the superman is thus overcome. Furthermore, these legends free the collective unconscious from its desire to kill the chiefs. By persuading themselves that such a death would have no beneficial effects upon events, the common people render assassination attempts useless.

That was how the story heard around the cafés developed. And we would have been less taken by it if we had seen how the mechanisms of collective storytelling were being employed.

Tibetan Legend
Alexandra David-Neel

Once upon a time, a trader was traveling with his caravan on a stormy day, and his hat was carried away by the wind.

Tibetans believe that to pick up a hat which has fallen down in such circumstances in the course of a journey will bring bad luck. So yielding to that superstition, the merchant abandoned his hat.

It was a soft felt hat, with fur laps that can be worn turned up or covering the ears, as the weather requires. Buried between the thorny shrubs where it had been violently tossed by the wind, its shape was hardly recognizable.

A few weeks later a man passing by that place at dusk noticed an indistinguishable form which seemed to be crouched among the thickets. He was not too brave and hurriedly passed his way. On the morrow he told some villagers that he had seen "something strange" at a short distance from the path. Other travelers also remarked at that very spot, a peculiar object whose nature they could not ascertain, and spoke of it to the villagers. Then, others again and again had a look at the innocent hat and called the attention of the country people to it.

Now sun, rain and dust helped to make the hat a still more mysterious-looking object. The felt had taken on a dirty yellowish-brown color and the fur laps looked vaguely like an animal's ears.

Traders and pilgrims stopping in the village were warned that, at the skirt of the forest, a "thing," neither man nor beast, remained in ambush and it was necessary to be on the watch. Someone suggested that the "thing" must be a demon and soon the object, anonymous till then, was promoted to the rank of a devil.

As months went by, more people cast a fearful glance at the old hat, more people spoke about it and the whole country came to talk of the "demon" hidden at the border of the wood.

Then one day it happened that some passers-by saw the rag moving. Another day it tried to extricate itself from the thorns that had grown around it, and finally it followed a party of wayfarers who ran, panic-stricken, for their lives.

The hat had been animated by the many thoughts concentrated on it.[8]

⤳

The study of personal psychology has recently begun. More precise knowledge of biological phenomena, psycho-physiological experimentation, and finally, psychoanalysis and the methods growing out of it have all allowed for this. Psychoses (normal tendencies exaggerated), dreams, Freudian slips, abortive gestures, and lies are the pathways leading to the normal mechanisms of the mind. (Let me note that the various forms of lies, described by novelists in particular, have not been examined as carefully as one would wish.) By contrast, collective psychology remains obscure. For a long time it was the domain reserved for priests, a few directors of the conscience, and a small group of "handlers." Their sacred science was, above all, a science of the social. The development of today's press and radio has changed all that. Now there is open access to the popular soul. Experiences are multiplied. Practical experience has more to teach us than abstract observations made by yesterday's philosophers. Whatever disgust we feel when we note how public opinion is at the mercy of mercenary publicists without ideals, who know nothing but the details of their trade, it is unfortunately true that they can provide us with a window on the laws of the collective unconscious, the large waves of popular feeling, and, thus, certain aspirations to the marvelous. And, no matter what the price, we need to learn to know how false reports are created, how they are spread and come to impose themselves upon the masses, how they arouse or divert the passions.

"False" reports are generally not inventions, pure and simple. They grow from inexact or terribly overblown accounts. A piece of information is exaggerated and changed as it is passed by word of mouth. The complex trajectory it follows is like that of the echoes created in the cave of the marvelous. The transmission itself is an absolute necessity, known and exploited by the specialists. Here is an example: A newspaper sends a dispatch, but only incidentally and with qualifications. The dispatch is telegraphed and reproduced in a foreign country. There it is changed, interpretations are added. It is reprinted in its new form two days later by the original newspaper. It now depends upon references that are all the better for being so far removed. Thus

---

8. *Magic and Mystery in Tibet* (Claude Kendall, 1932; reprint, Dover, 1971).

created, the false report can only evolve in such a way if it is plausible. It is because it falls into the category of likely events that, very often, it constitutes a simple anticipation of them. But, verified or not, it has played its part, made its contribution as an element of social determinism, provoked certain manifestations, wars, financial upheavals, etc. Even if immediate reactions to it have been prevented, it remains in the collective memory as an obscure component of public opinion.

To understand how receptive minds become when they are given over to the violence of public passions, it is necessary to have been part of a seething crowd during some revolutionary or dramatic event. A crowd grows by multiplication, not addition. As soon as critical reason is abandoned and social constraints are thrown aside, reactions far exceed in intensity, power, and duration the excitement that caused them. The same is true for the intense reactions of artists, poets, and sleepers. During sleep, a light touch felt at the neck elicits a dramatic dream of execution. Dream activity combines the burlesque with the dramatic. The life of the crowd has that same quality. For a nervous crowd afraid of being attacked, the slightest sharp noise is heard as a gunshot. It leads to what is thought to be a defensive assault. This passionate intensity, the fundamental fact of crowd dynamics, is what keeps scientific historians from understanding how revolutions and religions originate. It all appears absurd if you limit yourself to official documents and administrative reports. Yet none of it is absurd when seen through the lightning flash of passion, which illuminates more brightly than all reasonable advice.

In the heightened atmosphere of the crowd, nothing is humanly impossible. An individual no longer perceives social and material barriers; these effectively disappear, and the power of the human being is then truly increased tenfold. I'm thinking of Barcelona in 1936 when the unarmed masses threw themselves into battle against troops equipped with cannons and machine guns and managed, against all odds, to defeat them. A kind of supernatural protection seems to be given to those who go beyond the limits of their ordinary timidity. Yet if you think about it, what is really supernatural is the way millions of beings accept lives that fall so short of their potential, ignorant of the power contained within them.

A very curious example of what mass excitement at its height can do appears in Louis Figuier's history of the marvelous.[9] During the

---

9. L. Figuier, *Histoire du Merveilleux dans les temps modernes* (Hachette, 1881).

reign of Louis XIV, the Protestants of Midi were subjected to both the most brutal and subtle kinds of persecution. Directed by a Machiavellian Jesuit, the royal administration had resolved to suppress the Protestant movement in France. Using faith as an excuse, people were stripped of their possessions, imprisoned, subjected to cruel moral and physical tortures, and deprived of their children. The fugitive Protestants gathered in the woods or on the mountain at night to prepare themselves for resistance or emigration, which was forbidden. Protestantism, that rational, philosophical, and moral reformation of Catholicism, which suppressed all the magical apparatus of Christianity, wouldn't seem to be fruitful ground for the development of the marvelous. Nevertheless, for more than twenty years it witnessed a series of very extraordinary phenomena. A school of prophets was established in Dauphiné in 1689, under the aegis of a master of Serre, a gentleman glassworker of Dieu-le-fit. There, children would fall into ecstatic states of sleep. They remained in the strangest postures and, without waking, they preached against the Roman Church, repeating their inspired prophecies to whomever approached them. Similar occurrences took place simultaneously in the country of Castres and in Haut-Languedoc. Angels appeared to assemblies made up of many hundreds of the faithful. A young shepherdess of Crest, a holy prophetess, remained in a permanent state of frenzy. She wandered the mountain villages evangelizing, remembering not a word of what she said. Everywhere she went, her audiences were touched by the Holy Spirit. One of the preachers, Gabriel Astier, who was badly beaten on April 2, 1690, like so many others, saw the heavens open during his ecstatic fits, and there sat the Protestant martyrs on the brilliant clouds. He also had visions of paradise and the angels, Satan, and hell.

In Vivarais, melodious concerts were heard in the air and luminous fires rose in the sky. Today such phenomena have scientific names that medicine has given to them. For all that, they are no more explicable. However questionable the quality of the marvelous here, it is nevertheless certain that this was the mysterious climate in which large numbers of people lived for a long time.

These examples, which could be multiplied, are testimony to the way the marvelous is linked to a palpable tension, a growing emotion and passion. This observation is no less relevant today. People currently live in a state of permanent anguish. They have lost confidence in the solutions conformists advocate. Where military dictatorships rule, or that other dictatorship, hunger, it is not a question of choosing between remedies, but only of obeying, of submitting. Escape into the marvelous is the only possible freedom. The nervous world will ask for its safety. The danger is that, once more, the dream will simply be a flight, a forgetting, a renouncement of the struggle and of life, since it must necessarily be linked to everyday needs and tangible realities, since it must serve to effectively surmount that miserable state that is our own. We are currently paying for the inadequacies of outdated mysticism and academic rationalism. An explosion of the passions is inescapable, but knowledge of the laws of the individual and collective unconscious can keep it from fostering a kind of mysticism that is sterile because it is reactionary. I believe it is possible to direct the need for the marvelous so that it can lead to human victory and not become a means of mutilation.

The marvelous stays perfectly in tune with the inner necessity of our desires and the ultimate necessity of the universe. Sometimes a breakthrough results from a series of conscious steps (a calculated equation, an experiment confirming some findings). Sometimes, spontaneously and to our great surprise, someone we have been thinking about, or speaking of, or wishing to see, suddenly appears, and his arrival can't be logically explained. Communication between the self and things occurs again when the object found by chance turns out to be the indispensable instrument we wanted, the miraculous response to a question that was haunting us.

Living thus depends, on the one hand, upon a certain conception of the world, on the other, upon a particular state of sensitivity. This conception of the world is what children have by nature, no matter what peoples or what civilization they are part of. Piaget has shown (and his works are of primary importance) that the child is first and foremost a realist and animist.

At the beginning of his development, he doesn't distinguish the psychic world from the physical world. He doesn't observe the precise limits between himself and the external world. He considers as alive and conscious a great number of bodies that, for us, are inert.[10]

The social intelligence adapts this representation of the universe. In becoming reasonable, the adult becomes an agnostic, skeptic, specialist, and nominalist. He has then ruptured the sacred bonds. Only

---

10. Jean Piaget, *The Child's Conception of the World, Birth of the Intelligence in the Child* (Littlefield, 1975).

the poet, the seer, the magus, bound by a desire for general understanding, for synthesis in the hermetic sense of the term, escapes this
evolution.

Attaining the marvelous requires that the power and knowledge
gradually acquired with age help to extend and nourish the child's spontaneous thought process, rather than to destroy it. In short, a person
remains faithful to his own nature rather than fighting it in order to
benefit the artificial social personality he has made himself into.

If the exploration of the marvelous requires emotion, that's because
an emotional shock temporarily reestablishes our communication with
the world, which the intelligence has cut off. Preoccupied, aroused by
a violent internal passion, we give up being voluntary spectators viewing objects as separate from us. We project onto them our anxiety. Thus
we integrate them into the necessity of our desire.

The external world can play a variety of roles in producing that
emotion. It can be of primary importance when it's a matter of unusual
spectacles. In such cases, the world seems to take the first step and
initiate a meeting with us. It is no longer we who are appealing to indifferent or hostile nature, but nature that speaks and provokes our unease. Even though the marvelous should not be confused with the exceptional, with natural wonders or supernatural phenomena, these are
doors into the mystery.

What is strange and bizarre manages to disorient us in such a way
that the ordinary boundaries separating us from the world are destroyed.
Observations of natural curiosities and freakish scenes, because of their
violence, their feverish pitch, thus acquire immense importance, as the
romantics clearly understood.

Aware of their natural inertia and the pressing need to live in a state
of palpable tension, people are inclined to artificially provoke or pro-
long these experiences. The arts serve to rekindle in us a spark that
society tries to extinguish, to maintain a fire whose place is not on the
temple altars, but within the depths of our flesh. The overwhelming
images we create multiply those occasions of emotional shock. It is in
this sense that art is truly the sum of "artifices," that it distances itself
from ordinary reality and familiar representations. It tends toward the
exceptional, toward unique testimony.

Having brought the marvelous to bear on the exploration of mystery, I must emphasize the need for achieving some *limited psychological
states* that can be located within or on this side of consciousness, in
dream, or beyond, in a superrational, hyperconscious lucidity, if the

geography of the interior can be so schematized. It is interesting to note in this regard that the mind corresponds in its functions to a circle along the periphery of which each point possesses a diametrical or dialectical double. The descent toward dream and the ascent toward the highest levels of consciousness are as similar as two symmetrical triangles, as two sides of a hyperbola. That's why it's equally accurate to say "to ascend toward dream" or "to descend toward consciousness." In practice, the dream ceases as soon as the sleeper's mind becomes fixed on a precise image that is too disturbing. Conversely, consciousness is lost when attention remains centered for too long on the same object (this process produces hypnosis). Something like intoxication comes over us, whether we abandon our ordinary mental representations to arrive at a feeling of pure physical contact, or whether we go beyond familiar images to extend our minds toward a mathematical formulation becoming ever more abstract, ever more vast.

Over the course of these processes, we encounter certain critical zones, like those mysterious moments the material world knows when water cools down below zero degrees but doesn't turn to ice, or when a supersaturated solution does not crystallize, or when an impending storm doesn't break. In these brief moments, all sorts of exacerbations precede the changed states. Our mental faculties, which are usually distinct, become exceptionally synthesized. Even though its threshold has been passed, consciousness remains. We are in the dream state and still we enjoy the most rational sanity. We act, while, at the same time, being absent from our action. We are within ourselves and also like strangers observing ourselves from the outside. There is not just one side of the mirror. Both sides exist at the same time.

The marvelous does not lie within that rational equilibrium extolled by the classics, which can seem as static as death. It is at the most extreme point of movement, at the height of vital effort, where nothing more could be added without everything collapsing at once.

To the Limits of the Self
Julien Gracq

She raised her arms and without an effort, like a living caryatid, supported the skies on her hands. It seemed that the flow of the captivating and mysterious grace could not continue another instant without the vessels bursting in their perilously pounding hearts. Then she threw back her head, and in a frail sweet gesture raised her shoulders, and the foam that blew against her belly sent such an intolerably voluptuous sensation coursing through her that her lips drew back over her teeth in a passionate grimace—and to the surprise of the two spectators, at that instant there burst from this exultant figure the disordered and fragile movements of a woman.

Herminien, lingering on the shore, was fixing a tumultuous image. He was living over again that moment when the sun, breaking through the mists suddenly with its fiery darts, imprinted Heide in the depth of his heart—and those tragic moments when, with head thrown back between her shoulders as from too violent a shock, there escaped like an involuntary admission the gestures of possession. Then her long and liquid eyes rolled back, her hands opened, each finger slowly unfolding as in the free surrender of a last resistance, her teeth glittered in the sunlight one by one in all their insolence, her lips parted like a wound henceforth impossible to conceal, her whole body trembled all through its solid thickness, and the toes rose as though all the nerves of the body were stretched to the breaking point, like the rigging of a ship ravaged by an unknown wind.

They swam, the three of them, toward the high sea. Lying almost on the surface of the water, they watched the heavy waves come rolling toward them from the horizon in regular succession, and in the vertiginous tumult of their senses it seemed to them that the entire weight of the waters fell on their shoulders and must surely crush them—before forming beneath them a swell of softness and of silence which would lift them lazily on its weary back with a sensation of exquisite lightness. Sometimes the crest of a wave would brusquely throw its shadow over Heide's face, sometimes the salty gleam of her wet cheek would reappear. It seemed to them that, little by little, their muscles began to partake of the dissolving power of the element that bore them along: their flesh seemed to lose some of its density and to become identified, by an obscure osmosis, with the liquid meshes that entangled them. They felt a matchless parity, an incomparable freedom being born in them— they smiled, all three of them, a smile unknown to men, as they braved the incalculable horizon. They were headed *out to sea*, and so many were the waves that had already rolled under them, so many the sudden and threatening crests they had breasted, and behind which appeared once more all the aridity of those plains, consecrated to the sun alone, that it seemed to them that the earth behind them must already have disappeared from sight, abandoning them to their enchanted migration in the midst of the waves. And with exultant cries, they encouraged each other in their flight. And it seemed to Albert that the water was actually *foundering* under them, rushing at an unimaginable speed and would overflow the melancholy shore, while he with his traveling companions pursued a voyage that, in his mind, increasingly took on the character of enchantment. They swam on and on at what seemed to them a constantly accelerated speed. A sharp challenge appeared in their eyes, gaining strength as they pursued this race without a goal. A few minutes more and with the consciousness of the great distance already covered, an icy conviction became fixed in their minds. It seemed to them, to the three of them at the same moment, that now they would *no longer* dare to turn back, would not dare to look toward the shore, and with a glance they exchanged a pledge that bound them body and soul. Each of them seemed to see this mortal challenge in the others' eyes—to feel that the other two were sweeping him along by the whole force of their bodies and their wills—out to sea—farther—toward unknown spaces—toward a gulf from which return would be impossible—and neither of them had any doubt as to the insidious character of this abrupt accord of their wills and of their destinies. *It was no longer possible to retreat.* They swam to rhythmic gasps escaping from their three chests, and with the thrilling chill of death the keen air penetrated their tired lungs. They looked lingeringly at one another. They could not detach their eyes from one anothers', while lucidly their minds calculated the untraceable distance already covered. And in a voluptuous transport, each recognized on the other faces the indubitable signs, the reflection of his own conviction, stronger with every second— now it was certain, they *would no longer have strength enough to return.* And with a holy ardor they plunged forward through the waves, and in the joy of their peremptory discovery, at the price of their common death, every instant more inevitable, each yard gained redoubled their inconceivable felicity. And, beyond hate and beyond love, they felt themselves melting, all three of them, while they glided now with furious energy into the abyss—in one single vaster body, in the light of a superhuman hope that filled their eyes, drowned in blood and brine, with the reassuring peace of tears. Their hearts leaped in their breasts, and the very limit of their strength seemed now at hand—they knew that not one of them would break the silence, would ask to turn back— their eyes shone with savage joy. Beyond life and beyond death they now looked at one another for the first time with sealed lips, and through transparent eyes plumbed the darkness of their hearts with devastating bliss—and their souls touched in an electric caress. And it seemed to them that death would reach them, not when the swelling chasms beneath them should claim their prey, but when the lenses of their staring eyes—fiercer than the mirrors of Archimedes—should consume them in the convergence of an all-devouring communion.

Suddenly Heide's head disappeared under the water and all movement in her seemed to cease. Then Herminien, with a sudden shudder, *awoke* and out of his breast rose an astonishing cry. They plunged into the watery dusk. White shapes floated before their eyes as one or another of their limbs appeared, slowly moving through the opaque greenness in which they seemed profoundly ensnared. Suddenly in this submarine quest their eyes met, and seemed to touch, and they closed them with the sensation of an intolerable danger, as though confronted by the eyes of the abyss itself, magnetic and hideous, engendering an icy dizziness. In this frenzied search, during which it seemed to them that their hands brandished invisible knives, the form of a breast, as hard as stone, suddenly floated into Herminien's palm, then an arm which he seized with desperate violence, and when he opened his eyes above the surface of the water out of the choking terror that had surrounded him, he found the three of them reunited. The sun blinded them like a flow of molten metal. Far away a yellowish line, thin and almost unreal, marked the beginning of that element which they had thought to have renounced forever. A spell was broken.[11]

---

11. Julien Gracq, *The Castle of Argol*, trans. Louise Varese (New Directions, 1951).

CREATION

Working backward from the son to the father, from plant to seed, from earth to solar system and beyond that, to galaxies, going from effects to causes, the mind is faced with the problem of creation. Here, our train of thought gets lost in the most deceitful of mirror tricks. Being tiny and ephemeral fragments of the evolving world, how can we make sense of it as a formed object outside of ourselves? How can we apply our usual thought patterns, which are products of time and space, to what lies beyond time and space? And still, we continue to be haunted by the desire to know how the universe began, to understand how we arrived on earth. Up against such an impossibility, the mind reaches desperately toward the unknown. This exploration leads to the frontiers of the marvelous. To tell the truth, legendary explanations are less concerned with establishing an actual cosmology than with describing how we become aware of the various parts of reality.

To avoid the vulgar dilemmas that lead to the explanation you might give a child, that "someone has to exist to create all this," the reader must put her usual preoccupations aside. Disengaging herself from the mundane worries that map her mental horizon, let her retire to some inaccessible hermitage, taking with her only the basic principles of mathematics. Let her meditate for a long time on the simple numeration she has used since childhood, without the slightest understanding of how it contains within it a summary of all problems. She will begin from zero, the pivot, the separation point between the negative and positive number sequences. She will then go on to unity, one. The distance crossed is inconceivable since she has arrived at total existence from nonexistence, and also at the end of counting, because, having reached unity, the thing is complete. But here, switching levels of reasoning, she will add units to each other, as if she wanted to number all the beings and things in the universe. This infinity can be located in both the positive sequence of realities and in the negative sequence of virtual images. And if, after extending the exploration to its limits, she wishes to close the circle, she can multiply infinity by zero, and the result will again be one, unity. As elementary as it is grand, this assertion demonstrates how unity is the product of nonexistence times the total of all possible existences. The reader then recalls that this theorem in which the marvelous finds its most concise form is the basis for integral calculus. All modern engineering depends upon it. Thus the most abstract metaphysical assertion is, at the same time, the most useful intellectual acquisition.

Despite the vertigo that threatens, let the mind retain its lucidity. The first principles of numeration thus established, next comes the drama of even and uneven, which, in the number sequence, comes to symbolize the joint action of male and female forever uniting and separating for continuous procreation. Next, the imagination will begin to flesh out pure mathematical abstractions with more general representations already linked to tangible elements in the world. Over the framework of numbers will appear the play of shadow and light, that being the first condition of consciousness, then the action of hot and cold, of dry and humid. Arriving at this point in her reflection, the reader can open the sacred books of Brahmanism. At the beginning of the code of Manou[1] she will find the following account:

---

1. Manou, like Menes and Minos, is the name of one of the legendary kings who guided humanity during the most ancient times and who received divine messages. Predating the Vedas, which it cites, the book of Manou seems to come from the eighth century B.C. It reflects the ancient spirit of Brahmanism such as it was before religious schools multiplied and before the Buddhist reformation. The text reproduced here corresponds to the beginning of the first of twelve books that make up the opus.

The Creation
(BOOK OF MANOU)

Everything was immersed in darkness. Nothing could be perceived. Nothing was, nor could be, disclosed or revealed by reason. Everything seemed given over to sleep.

When the time of dissolution came to an end, the Lord, who alone existed, and who had no capacity for the sense perception, made perceptible the world, with its five elements and its other principles, so that it shone in the purest light. The world appeared, the darkness dissipated, and nature developed.

- That which the spirit alone can perceive, which escapes the sense organs, which is eternal, the soul of all beings, which is incomprehensible, opened out in all its splendor.
- Having resolved to issue forth the various creatures from its own substance, it first produced the waters, in which it dropped a seed.
- This seed became an eye, as brilliant as gold, as radiant as the star with a thousand rays, and in which the Supreme Being gave birth to himself in the form of Brahma, grandfather of all beings.
- The waters were called *nârâ* (born of man) because, in fact, they are the daughters of the first man, or the Supreme Spirit; and as these same waters were the place where he first moved, he is called "the one who moved on the waters" (Nârâyana).
- It is from this imperceptible, eternal cause, which actually exists but which does not exist for the senses, which is being and nonbeing, that this divine male, known throughout the world by the name of Brahma, was produced.
- After remaining for one divine year in this egg, the Lord, by his mere thought alone, made the egg split itself in two.
- From these two parts, the creative energy of Brahma made the sky and earth; in between, he placed the atmosphere, the eight celestial regions, and the permanent reservoir of waters.
- This energy drew from the Supreme Soul the feeling of "manas" (which exists by its own nature and not for the senses) and the conscience (which gives internal advice and governs us).
- But before feeling and conscience, it engendered the great intellectual principle, the intelligence, and all that assumes the three qualities, and the five organs of the intelligence meant to perceive exterior objects, and the five organs of action, and the rudiments of the five elements.

- Having joined the imperceptible molecules of these six greatly energized principles (the five elements and the conscience) to the molecules of these same principles transformed into the elements and the senses, he then formed all beings.
- It is because the six molecules emanating from the substance of the Supreme Being are joined together to take the form of the elements and sense organs that the sages are called the visible form of this God Sarira (that which receives the six molecules).
- The elements enter into visible form with the functions that belong to them, just as the intelligence is joined to the organs, and the imperishable cause to the apparent forms.
- This universe is made up of the most subtle parts of these seven principles manifested in a visible form and endowed with great creative energy. It is the changing of the unchanging. Each of these elements acquires the quality of that which precedes it according to the order of succession, in such a way that the further it gets from the primitive source, the more qualities it has.
- At the beginning, he (the Supreme Being) assigned to each creature a different name, different functions, and its own duties.
- He made a multitude of active gods endowed with souls, and many spirits, and the eternal sacrifice.
- He created time and its divisions, constellations, planets, rivers, seas, mountains, plains, and uneven terrain.
- Austere devotion, speech, sensual delight, desire, anger, because he wished to give existence to all beings.

And these words from the Vedas echo throughout Tibetan hermitages. Through yoga, the ascetic has abolished the body's opacity. Its every movement is revealed to the consciousness. The yogi perceives the permanent essence of elements as they go through their transformations. He connects these to the abstractions of the intelligence, resulting in the sublime universal symphony. At these extreme degrees of concentration, an arid chill envelopes thought, the cold, rarefied air circulating around mountain peaks, the cold of interstellar space. The mind expands to the world's scale. It reconstructs the universe according to its own structure. Barriers collapse. Opposites merge. The day is no longer separate from the night, the night of crystal and water where dream still constitutes awakening. Man superimposes poetic images of past experience over the mystery of creation. Having grown to the cosmos's height, he can cast the origin of the world as a representation of his own birth without diminishing it. The sea will open with the woman, and like her. Thus Luonnotar will appear:

Creation in the *Kalevala*

Air's young daughter was a virgin, fairest daughter of creation.
Long did she abide a virgin, all the long days of her girlhood
In the Air's own spacious mansions, in those far-extending regions.
Wearily the time passed ever, and her life became a burden,
Dwelling evermore so lonely, always living as a maiden,
In the Air's own spacious mansions, in those far-extending deserts.
After this the maid descending, sank upon the tossing billows,
On the open ocean's surface, on the wide expanse of water.
Then a storm arose in fury, from the East a mighty tempest,

And the sea was wildly foaming, and the waves dashed ever higher.
Thus the tempest rocked the virgin, and the billows drove the maiden,
O'er the ocean's azure surface, on the crest of foaming billows,
Till the wind that blew around her, and the sea woke life within her.
Then she bore her heavy burden, and the pain it brought upon her,
Seven long centuries together, nine times longer than a lifetime.
Yet no child was fashioned from her, and no offspring was perfected.
Thus she swam, the Water-Mother, east she swam, and westward
*   swam she,*
Swam to north-west and to south-west, and around in all directions,
In the sharpness of her torment, in her body's fearful anguish;
Yet no child was fashioned from her, and no offspring was perfected.
Then she fell to weeping gently, and in words like these expressed her:
"O how wretched is my fortune, wandering thus, a child unhappy!
I have wandered far already, and I dwell beneath the heaven,
By the tempest tossed for ever, while the billows drive me onward,
O'er this wide expanse of water, on the far-extending billows.

"Better were it had I tarried, virgin in aerial regions,
Then I should not drift for ever, as the Mother of the Waters.
Here my life is cold and dreary, every moment now is painful,
Ever tossing on the billows, ever floating on the water.

"Ukko, thou of Gods the highest, ruler of the whole of heaven,
Hasten here for thou art needed; hasten here at my entreaty.
Free the damsel from her burden, and release her from her tortures.

Quickly haste, and yet more quickly, where I long for thee so sorely."
Short the time that passed thereafter, scarce a moment had passed over,
Ere a beauteous teal came flying lightly hovering o'er the water,
Seeking for a spot to rest in, searching for a home to dwell in.
Eastward flew she, westward flew she, flew to north-west and to
southward,
But the place she sought she found not, not a spot however barren,
Where her nest she could establish, or a resting-place she could light
on.
Then she hovered, slowly moving, and she pondered and reflected,
"If my nest in wind I 'stablish or should rest it on the billows,
Then the winds will overturn it, or the waves will drift it from me."
Then the Mother of the Waters, Water-Mother, maid aerial,
From the waves her knees uplifted, raised her shoulders from the
billows,
That the teal her nest might 'stablish, and might find a peaceful
dwelling.
Then the teal, the bird so beauteous, hovered slow and gazed around
her,
And she saw the knee uplifted from the blue waves of the ocean,
And she thought she saw a hillock, freshly green with springing
verdure.
There she flew and hovered slowly, gently on the knee alighting,
And her nest she there established, and she laid her eggs all golden,
Six gold eggs she laid within it, and a seventh she laid of iron.
O'er her eggs the teal sat brooding, and the knee grew warm beneath
her;
And she sat one day, a second, brooded also on the third day;
Then the Mother of the Waters, Water-Mother, maid aerial,
Felt it hot and felt it hotter and she felt her skin was heated,
Till she thought her knee was burning, and that all her veins were
melting.
Then she jerked her knee with quickness, and her limbs convulsive
shaking,
Rolled the eggs into the water, down amid the waves of the ocean,
And to splinters they were broken, and to fragments they were
shattered.
In the ooze they were not wasted, nor the fragments in the water,
But a wondrous change came o'er them, and the fragments all grew
lovely.

*From the cracked egg's lower fragment, now the solid earth was
    fashioned,*
From the cracked egg's upper fragment, rose the lofty arch of heaven,
From the yolk, the upper portion, rose the moon that shines so brightly;
Whatso in the egg was mottled, now became the stars in heaven,
Whatso in the egg was brackish, in the air as cloudlets floated.
Now the time passed quickly over, and the years rolled quickly onward,
In the new sun's shining lustre, in the new moon's softer beaming.
Still the Water-Mother floated, Water-Mother, maid aerial,
Ever on the peaceful waters, on the billows' foamy surface,
With the moving waves before her, and the heaven serene behind her.
*When the ninth year had passed over, and the summer tenth was
    passing,*
From the sea her head she lifted, and her forehead she uplifted,
And she then began Creation, and she brought the world to order,
On the open ocean's surface, on the far-extending waters.
*Wheresoe'er her hand she pointed, there she formed the jutting
    headlands;*
Wheresoe'er her feet she rested, there she formed the caves for fishes;
*Then she dived beneath the water, there she formed the depths of the
    ocean;*
When toward the land she turned her, there the level shores extended,
Where her feet to land extended, spots were formed for salmon-netting;
*Where her head the land touched lightly, there the curving bays
    extended.*
Further from the land she floated, and abode in open water,
And created rocks in ocean, and the reefs that eyes behold not,
Where the ships are often shattered, and the sailors' lives are ended.
Now the isles were formed already, in the sea the rocks were planted;
Pillars of the sky established, lands and continents created;
*Rocks engraved as though with figures, and the hills were cleft with
    fissures.*
Still unborn was Väinämöinen; still unborn the bard immortal.
Väinämöinen, old and steadfast, rested in his mother's body
For the space of thirty summers, and the sum of thirty winters,
Ever on the placid waters, and upon the foaming billows.
So he pondered and reflected how he could continue living
In a resting-place so gloomy, in a dwelling far too narrow,
*Where he could not see the moonlight, neither could behold the
    sunlight.*

*Then he spake the words which follow, and expressed his thoughts in
this wise:*
*"Aid me moon and sun release me, and the Great Bear lend his
counsel,*
*Through the portal that I know not, through the unaccustomed
passage.*
From the little nest that holds me, from a dwelling-place so narrow,
To the land conduct the roamer, to the open air conduct me,
To behold the moon in heaven, and the splendor of the sunlight;
See the Great Bear's stars above me, and the shining stars in heaven."
When the moon no freedom gave him, neither did the sun release him,
Then he wearied of existence, and his life became a burden.
Thereupon he moved the portal, with his finger, fourth in number,
Opened quick the bony gateway, with the toes upon his left foot,
With his nails beyond the threshold, with his knees beyond the gateway.
Headlong in the water falling, with his hands the waves repelling,
Thus the man remained in ocean, and the hero on the billows.
In the sea five years he sojourned, waited five years, waited six years,
Seven years also, even eight years, on the surface of the ocean,
By a nameless promontory, near a barren, treeless country.
On the land his knees he planted, and upon his arms he rested,
*Rose that he might view the moonbeams, and enjoy the pleasant
sunlight,*
See the Great Bear's stars above him, and the shining stars in heaven.
Thus was ancient Väinämöinen, he, the ever famous minstrel,
Born of the divine Creatrix, born of Ilmater, his mother.[2]

And so, was the man who appeared really Väinämöinen, the bard,
who regards creation with such passion that he sings of its beauty? I'm
not convinced of this by the evidence given in the *Kalevala*. Was he the
contemplative disciple of Brahma? That doesn't seem any more likely.
Everything leads me to believe that he was "the conqueror." That singular power that would allow him, after timeless labor, to assert his
supremacy over all species and things was already evident in him. The

---

2. The *Kalevala*, the great popular Finnish epic, was written down in 1835 by
Elias Lönnrot with the help of songs he collected from peasants. Thus, it is a
transcription of folklore. Most of the accounts it contains go back to the thir-
teenth century. *Kalevala*, vol. 1, trans. W. F. Kirby (London: J. M. Dent, 1907).

mystery of the world must have already made him uneasy, because from the beginning, he resisted being an obscure part of creation, wanting instead to be its creator, like the gods, wanting to know the secret of nature in order to master it.

The real tradition of humanity is not one of acceptance but of revolt. It sets humans in opposition to God, it pitches them against the sky, from which they must steal fire to serve their own purposes. The path goes from Prometheus to the hermetics, from them to modern physicists. The latter use the most precise methods and possess the most powerful instruments. But they are nonetheless the legitimate heirs to the tradition of the marvelous.

For humans, true conquest doesn't consist of establishing an ephemeral power over one's peers, but of mastering the elements. "Visit the earth's interior to take its secrets by surprise." That is one of the basic precepts of the ancient masters. Let us go with them to discover the Stone, which is at once the symbol of the Savior, the hidden level of the world, and the necessary material for the Philosopher's Stone. What does that mean to the hermetics? The Philosopher's Stone is something nature employs before our unseeing eyes daily as it draws various metals and species out of chaos. Each of the metals corresponds to an evolutionary period, terminating in the most perfect among them: gold, unalterable and precious. Each of the species moves a step closer to human, the perfect animal. Each individual constitutes a transitory form meant to resemble the prototypical human who, in turn, resembles God, possessing his purity, power, and eternal nature. Thus the endless chain of universal transmutation unwinds. But whoever possesses the Stone and its secret can make these slow operations come about as he pleases. He can make metals come into being before their time, and cure diseases, which are only weaknesses and imperfections. This total science is what Brother Basile Valentin of the Saint Benoît order discusses in the ancient philosophers' *Twelve Keys of the Clavicle of the Precious Stone*.[3]

---

3. This is one of the most important writings in hermetic literature. It treats the origin of the world in the sense of how it was produced. Basile Valentin: Basile means king; Valentin stands for the power and strength of universal medicine. Valentin is the name of an important second-century gnostic, among others. A Valentinian sect developed in Egypt and acquired some prominence. Brother of the order of Saint Benoît or of the order of Beni: many meanings can be drawn from such a title. Thus the very person of Basile Valentin is shrouded in mystery. The same is true for the principle signatories of alchemical or initiatory books. The apparent author or authors are no doubt ficti-

The Manufacturing of the Stone
Basile Valentin

Take a quantity of the best and finest gold, and separate it into its component parts by those media that nature vouchsafes to those who are lovers of art, as an anatomist dissects the human body. Thus change your gold back into what it was before it became gold; and thou shalt find the seed, the beginning, the middle, and the end—that from which *our gold* and its female principal are derived, viz., the pure and subtle spirit, the spotless soul, and the astral salt and balsam. When these three are united, we may call them the mercurial liquid: a water that was examined by Mercury, found by him to be pure and spotless, and therefore espoused by him as his wife. Of the two was born an incombustible oil; for Mercury became so proud that he hardly knew himself. He put forth eagle feathers, and devoured the slippery tail of the dragon, and challenged Mars to battle.

Then Mars summoned his horsemen, and bade them enclose Mercury in prison under the ward of Vulcan, until he should be liberated by one of the female sex.

When this became known, the other planets assembled and held a deliberation on the question, what would be the best and wisest course to adopt. When they were met together, Saturn first came forward, and delivered himself as follows:

"I, Saturn, the greatest of the planets in the firmament, declare here before you all, that I am the meanest and most unprofitable of all that are here present, that my body is weak, corruptible, and of a swarthy hue, but that, nevertheless, it is I that try you all. For having nothing that is fixed about me, I carry away with me all that is of a kindred nature. My wretchedness is entirely caused by that fickle and inconstant Mercury, by his careless and neglectful conduct. Therefore, I pray you, let us be avenged on him, shut him up in prison, and keep him there till he dies and is decomposed, nay, until not a drop of his blood is to be seen."

Then Jupiter stepped forward, bent his knees, inclined his sceptre, and with great authority bade them carry out the demand of Saturn. He added that he would punish everyone who did not aid the execution of this sentence.

---

tious, a means of concealing collective works. As with folklore, we are in the presence of a timeless tradition. [*Les Douze Clefs* was published by Editions de Minuit in 1956.]

Then Mars presented himself, with sword drawn—a sword that shone with many colors, and gave out a beautiful and unwonted splendor. This sword he gave to the warder Vulcan, and bade him slay Mercury, and burn him together with his bones, to ashes. This Vulcan consented to do.

While he was executing his office, there appeared a beautiful lady in a long silver robe, intertissued with many waters, who was immediately recognized as the Moon, the wife of the Sun. She fell on her knees, and with outspread hands, and flowing tears, besought them to liberate her husband—the Sun—from the prison in which, through the crafty wiles of Mercury, he was being detained by the Planets. But Vulcan refused to listen to her request; nor was he softened by the moving prayers of Lady Venus, who appeared in a crimson robe, intertissued with threads of green, and charmed all by the beauty of her countenance and the fragrance of the flowers which she bore in her hand. She interceded with Vulcan, the judge, in the Chaldee tongue, and reminded him that a woman was to effect the deliverance of the prisoner. But even to her pleading he turned a deaf ear.

While they were still speaking the heaven was opened, and there came forth a mighty animal, with many thousands of young ones, which drove the warder before it, and opening its mouth wide, swallowed Venus, its fair helper, at the same time exclaiming with a loud voice: "I am born of woman, woman has propagated my seed, and therewith filled the earth. Her soul is devoted to mine, and therefore I must be nourished with her blood." When the animal had said these words with a loud voice, it hastened into a certain chamber, and shut the door behind it; whither its voracious brood followed, drinking of the aforesaid incombustible oil, which they digested with the greatest ease, and thereby became even more numerous than they had been before. This they continued to do until they filled the whole world.

Then the learned men of the country were gathered together, and strove to discover the true interpretation of all they had seen. But they were unable to agree until there came forward a man of venerable age, with snowy locks and silvery beard, and arrayed in a flowing purple robe. On his head he wore a crown set with brilliant carbuncles, his loins were girded with the girdle of life, his feet were bare, and his words penetrated to the depth of the human soul. He mounted the tribune, and bade the assembly listen to him in silence, since he was sent from above to explain to them the significance of what they had seen.

When perfect silence prevailed, he delivered himself as follows:

"Awake, O man, and behold the light, lest the darkness deceive thee! The gods revealed to me this matter in a profound sleep. Happy is the man who knows the great works of the divine power. Blessed is he whose eyes are opened to behold light where before they saw darkness.

"Two stars are given by the gods to man to lead him to great wisdom. Gaze steadily upon them, follow their lights, and you will find in them the secret of knowledge.

"The bird phoenix, from the south, plucks out the heart of the mighty beast from the east. Give the animal from the east wings, that it may be on an equality with the bird from the south. For the animal from the east must be deprived of its lion's skin, and lose its wings. Then it must plunge in the salt water of the vast ocean, and emerge thence in renovated beauty. Plunge thy volatile spirits in a deep spring whose waters never fail, that they may become like their mother who is hidden therein, and born of three.

"Hungary is my native land, the sky and stars are my habitation, the earth is my spouse. Though I must die and be buried, yet Vulcan causes me to be born anew. Therefore Hungary is my native land, and my mother encloses the whole world."

To make these operations easier for the reader to understand, it seems necessary to cite here the definition of primary matter that Basile Valentin gives in the second part of his treatise.

I am the envenomed dragon that is present everywhere, and at cheap cost; that upon which I rest and which rests upon me is to be found within me. May you diligently seek out my destructive and constituent water and fire; from my body you will extract the red and green lion if you know exactly the five meanings of my fire. A venom emerges from my nostrils; with your craft separate the subtle from the coarse. I enlarge the strength of men and likewise that of women as well as that of the heavens and the earth; I am the egg of nature known to the wise alone, who engender from me the little world. Philosophers named me Mercury; my husband is the philosphers' gold; I am the old dragon, present throughout the world. I am father and I am mother, young and old, strong and weak, quick and dead, visible and invisible, hard and soft. I descend into the earth and rise into the heavens. I am very large and also very small. The natural order is often changed within me in regard to color, number, weight, and measurement, containing natural light, both clear and obscure. I am the very noble earth with which you can transform the metals into gold.

Whatever interest we have in the discovery of cosmic secrets, the mineral universe, and knowledge of the elements undergoing transformation, the origin of life remains at the center of our unease. In trying to understand the appearance of life in the inert world, we return, despite ourselves, to the mystery of our own births. The curiosity that haunts each child becomes generalized. Children have a sense that something fundamental is being hidden from them. They only acquire adult names and powers after learning the mysteries of generation, after having undergone initiation.

The human community has been preoccupied with the same things for centuries. It wants to discover human origin to ensure the species' definitive mastery. Every culture is anxious to know where it comes from in order to find justification for itself, both in its own eyes and in the eyes of others.

We imagine inert material evolving into living substance, vegetable into animal, the most elementary animal into human, going from the simple (?) to the complex. That is the progression we've grown accustomed to because of our civilized intelligence. Yet this kind of reasoning is a relatively recent development. Primitive peoples and children think differently. For them, humanity is the origin of all things.

The Condah Lake tribes give this account of the creation of fire and rain:

Australian Tale

A man threw a javelin into the air, toward the clouds. And to this javelin a rope was tied. He climbed the length of this rope and brought back to the earth fire which he had taken from the sun.

A long time after that, people made their way to the other world by the same means. They all went there, except one man. And it is from this one man who stayed on earth that all other men have descended. The name of this man was Eun-newt; now it is the bat.

It's the crow who sent the first rain.[4]

------

4. These texts are taken from Arnold Van Gennep's remarkable work *Myths*

And here, from the Narrinyeri tribe, the nature of the sun:

The sun is a woman who, when she goes to bed, passes by the country where the dead live. As she approaches them, men gather; then they divide into two groups, leaving a passageway between them.

They invite the sun to stay with them. But she can only accept their offer for a short time because she must be ready to start out again early the next morning.

For the services she renders to a few of these dead, she receives from them the skin of a red kangaroo. So it is that she appears adorned in a red garment in the morning.[5]

The Arunta tribe has this explanation for the arrival of the moon in the sky:

In the time of the Alcheringa, an opossum-man carried the moon in his shield when he went out hunting opossums, his food. All day he hid in the hollow of a rock. One night, a seed-man happened to pass by this spot, and he saw something shining on the ground. It was the moon which the opossum-man had left in his shield when he went off to climb a tree after an opossum.

Very quickly, the seed-man picked up the shield and the moon and ran away. The opossum-man climbed down from the tree and chased the thief, but without success.

Having lost all hope of catching him, he became angry and bellowed out: "Don't let this thief keep the moon, but make it climb to the sky to shine each night."

Then the moon left the shield and climbed to the sky, and there it has stayed ever since.[6]

---

and Legends of Australia. Interest in Australian folklore comes from the fact that primitive peoples there do not conceive of human birth as linked to sex. For them, sexuality is one thing, creation another. Such a concept closely resembles a child's. Australian tales can be superimposed upon the responses obtained by Piaget and his collaborators in questioning school children six to eight years old.

5. Ibid.

6. Ibid.

On the other hand, providing humanity with a marvelous origin, assuring humans some kinship to animals, trees, earth, and stars has been a constant concern. One religion after another feels this obligation. Tribes must be given a mysterious ancestry, humans assigned a creator.

With regard to this "Father," invocations and ceremonies express mixed feelings. He is alternately praised and cursed.

Celebrating rituals, we share his creative power and give him thanks. At the same time, we implore him not to destroy what he has created, or even better, to improve it according to our wishes. Below the Supreme God whose powers are far-reaching and vague, who remains largely unknown, is the tribal ancestor, the creator and redeemer of the community. The ties to this specific ancestor are more direct, the responsibilities more stringent, because we expect his power over us to be greater. Each human group was originally included in the founding legend. Each member of the group plays a distinct part in the ancient unity. Establishing a totemic cult is so basic that there must be a particular version of creation to support it. One of the most curious belongs to a Fan tribe:

Creation of Man
(AFRICAN TALE)

Before there were any things yet, the creator Mébère made man out of clay. He took clay and made it into man. Thus this man had his beginning, and he began as a lizard. This lizard, Mébère put in a pool of sea water. Five days, and so it was: five days passed with him in the pool of water; and he had put him in there. Seven days; he was inside there seven days. The eighth day, Mébère looked at him. And then, the lizard went out. And here he is, outside. But it is a man. And he says to the creator: "Thank you."[7]

The most widely held version is that man was modeled like a statue from earth and that divine powers then brought him to life by using the breath or magic. The image of a divine potter is found throughout the Mediterranean. Not only is the conjecture simple, but it coincides with our taste for simulation. We make beautiful statues resembling

---

7. From Blaise Cendrars's *Anthologie nègre*.

living beings, which are often more beautiful than the real thing. To obtain new beings corresponding to our desires, all we would have to do is bring them to life. But how can we learn this skill, which is God's alone? Either we must discover and steal the secret, or secure it by divine grace. In very ancient times, some mythical heroes or demiurges seem to have possessed this power. At least, that is what Ovid says in his *Metamorphoses*. This episode occurs after the terrible deluge of Deucalion which destroyed all living things.

Origin of Humanity
Ovid

The world had been restored but it was a desert; solitude and vast silence reigned everywhere. At this sight tears sprung to the eyes of Deucalion and he said to Pyrrha: "We two are the only human inhabitants of all the lands seen by the sun during its rise and fall. The sea has taken the rest. Yet still I feel no certainty for our own fate; the clouds still strike terror to my heart. O my sister, O my wife, what would become of us without the other; the human race survives but in us. Thus is the will of the gods."

With these words they decided to direct their prayers to heaven and seek help from the sacred oracle. To the waters of the Cephisius they went accordingly, which, though not yet clear, were again flowing in their normal channels. There they turned their steps toward the holy shrine of the goddess. At its steps they prostrated themselves face against the ground and implored the support of Themis. Moved, the goddess uttered this oracle:

"Depart from this temple with your heads veiled, loosen the girdles of your garments and throw behind you the bones of your great mother."

Having heard these words they remained for a long while frozen in fright; Pyrrha was the first to break the silence by declaring her refusal to obey the goddess. She had fear of insulting the ghost of her mother by disturbing her bones. But after a time the son of Prometheus soothed the fears of Epimetheus's daughter with these words of comfort: "Unless my wisdom deceives me, oracles are pure and never counsel criminal acts. Our great mother, in my opinion, is the earth; and stones are the bones that we have been instructed to throw behind us." Titan's daughter was struck by this interpretation, but she still hesitated to place her trust in the counsels of heaven. But there could be no harm done in putting the matter to the test.

They left the temple, veiled their heads, loosened the belts gird-ing their tunics, and threw the stones behind them as they had been instructed. Who would believe what followed if antiquity did not bear witness to it? These stones began to lose their hardness and gradually took on a tractable quality that lent itself well to taking on new forms. They then lengthened in size and their tenderer nature depicted some features of the human form though still not clearly, like marble under the first blows of the sculptor's chisel. The parts of the stones where a liquid sap blended with the earthy substances were changed into flesh, the solid part that nothing could soften transformed into bone. What had been veins in the rock kept the same form and name. In a brief period of time, by the will of the gods, the stones thrown by the hus-band became men, those thrown by the wife became women. Thus we are a hardy race made for toil; all that we are gives evidence of our origin.

The earth spontaneously created the other animals when it was warmed by the rays of the sun, and the silt lying in the dampened soil was fermented through its nourishing heat.[8]

Did Ovid contribute much to the account he gives? One doesn't get that impression. In his very long poem, he is concerned with bringing together diverse ancient traditions and using this occasion to vaunt the strength of the Romans, to pay homage to the official cults and the emperor. Imposing such an agenda on poetry stifles true feeling and cuts off access to the truly marvelous. All the classics share these limita-tions. Nevertheless, through Ovid's text, the popular legend comes to light and that is what matters to us.

The African tales on the one hand, the Mediterranean tradition on the other, depict very easy creation processes. God, or the demiurges, encounter no obstacles. This is not how it was conceived by pre-Columbian America or what we find in the Popol-Vuh, the sacred book of the Quichés. Here, creating humans seems to have been far from simple. At any moment, the gods may come together to discuss things and are obliged to start their work over again. Here is what happened to the one who is called, ...*the Creator, the Modeler, He who Engenders, He who Begats, and whose names are Possum Blowgun Shooter, Coyote Blowgun Shooter, Great Spiny White Huntsman, the Domineering One, the Plumed Ser-*

8. Ovid, *Metamorphoses*, chapter 1.

pent, Heart of the Lake, Heart of the Sea, Master of the Blue-green Plate, Master of the Azure Bowl.

Here then is the first word, the first eloquence; there was not yet a person, an animal, bird, fish, shrimp, wood, stone, hollow, canyon, field, or forest. Only the sky alone existed. The face of the earth had not yet become. There were only the tranquil sea and all the space of the sky. Nothing had yet formed itself; there was yet nothing that attached itself to something else, nothing that shivered and swayed, nothing that stood erect. There was only the tranquil waters, only the calm sea alone within its borders. There was naught but motionlessness and silence in the darkness, in the night. Alone also were the Creator, the Modeler, the Domineering One, the Plumed Serpent. They that engender and begat were over the water like a waxing light. They were enclosed in green and azure; this is why their name is Gucumatz (Plumed Serpent):

Such is the name of God and that is how it is spoken....

They spoke, they consulted, they meditated, they came to an understanding with one another, they joined their words and their thought. So day dawned as they were consulting and at the moment of that dawn humanity took shape.

Let us make those who will be our providers and nurturers. But how should we proceed so that we are invoked and remembered on the face of the earth? We have already made one attempt at our first work and creature, but they did not give us praise and respect. That is why we are trying to create obedient and respectful people who will be our providers and nurturers. So they say, the creation and formation of humanity will take place, the flesh will be fashioned from potter's clay. They saw that it was not good, for the body was without cohesion, without consistency, without movement, without strength, inept, and watery. Neither would its head turn. Its face was lopsided and twisted, its sight was cloudy, and it couldn't look around. It talked but had no intelligence and was rapidly dissolving into the water before it had even stood up. So the Creator and Modeler talked it over again; the more it is worked upon, the more it is incapable of walking and multiplying, so it requires the making of an intelligent being, they said. So they then again dismantled and destroyed their work and creation and asked themselves, "What will we make?" While they planned together again they said, "We will tell Xpiyacoc, Xmuncane, Possum Blowgun Shooter, Coyote Blowgun Shooter to try again to pull out its fate and its formation...."

Thus it was found to be necessary to make mannequins carved in wood who could speak and reason as they wished, on the surface of the earth. In the same instant that the wood mannequin was fashioned, humanity came into being. They produced, they reasoned, they came into being, and they multiplied; they gave birth to daughter and son wooden mannequins; but there was nothing in their hearts nor in their minds, no memory of their creator. They led a useless existence and lived like beasts. They no longer remembered the Heart of the Sky. They were but a trial and a tentative sketch of humankind; they were speaking at first but their faces dried out. They had no blood, no fat, no sweat, no substance. Their hands and feet were dry. These were the first humans who existed in great number upon the earth.

Then came the end of these mannequins who one and all were put to death; thus the waters were swollen by the will of the Heart of the Sky and he devised a great flood.

A thick resin rained down from the sky. There came the bird Xecoatcovach who gouged out their eyes; there came Camalotz who cut off their heads; there came Cotzbalam who devoured the flesh from their bones; and there came Tecumbalam who tore them open, broke their bones and tendons, then smashed them into powder and dispersed it as their punishment.

The face of the earth grew dark and a black rain began; then came all the animals, large and small; the humans were mistreated by things of wood and stone, by all that had served them up to now: their tortilla griddles, their plates, their cooking pots, their dogs, their turkeys. All abused them, their dogs and turkeys saying, "You have treated us badly, you bit into us. Now it is your turn to be tormented."

Their corn mills said: "Our faces were tormented on your account; now that you have ceased to be people we will grind your flesh into flour." Then their dogs spoke in their turn: "Why wouldn't you give us anything to eat? You chased us outside, you pursued us, we couldn't talk, but now we will destroy you. You will feel the teeth we have in our mouths."

Then the humans were seen to start running. Filled with despair, they wanted to climb onto their houses, but their houses collapsed; they tried to climb up the trees but the trees shook them off; they tried to enter caverns but the caves shut in their faces. Thus was the destruction of the human creatures accomplished. And it is said that their posterity can be seen in the small monkeys who live in the forests today; they survived as a living proof of this because formerly wood alone was used for their flesh.

This is the reason that monkeys resemble people....[9]

What a marvelous text, which leads the mind to the limits of the unknowable! It evokes successive periods of prehistory: the stone age when, hidden in caves, men were one with the earth, the age of clans living in the forests. Almost incidentally it poses the problem of the relationship between monkey and man as well as any Darwinian naturalist could. Many times, standing before the cages in zoological gardens and considering how the monkeys' faces resemble those of old people, examining their looks and finding nothing of the child there, I've believed, like this Quichian storyteller, in the presence of a deteriorated human race, deprived of speech by the curse of who knows what angry spirit.

Besides these echoes from the distant past, the account evokes the mind's eternal question: what is the relationship between the form and the life? Better than all the developments in Neoplatonic philosophy, the names given to the Mexican god present the problem in its most general form. This god, called "the creator and the former," makes models and brings them to life. The Mexican text doesn't reveal how these two phases of creation are linked. On the contrary, it makes us take part in the god's hesitations.

This initial secret of life, central to all mysteries, is what Western hermetics claim to have discovered. They teach it in veiled terms. Among the books of their high science, one of the most marvelous is entitled *The Chemical Wedding of Christian Rosenkreutz.* The author, whose name is purely symbolic, standing for Christ of the Rose-cross, describes the singular journey of an initiate. Summoned by mysterious warnings, the latter surmounts a great many obstacles, which put his courage, insight, and wisdom to the test. He is able to penetrate the castle to assist at the royal weddings. On the sixth day of this journey, guided all the time by a benevolent virgin, the adept finds himself with other companions, predestined like him, in a room of the tower. Having carried out several procedures there, they are granted access to the upper story. And this is what follows:

---

9. Popol-Vuh, *Livre sacré des Quichés.*

The Chemical Wedding of Christian Rosenkreutz
C. Rosenkreutz

Now we having got up there, and the hole having been shut again, I saw the globe hanging by a strong chain in the middle of the room. In this room was nothing but windows, and between two windows there was a door, which was covered with nothing other than a great polished looking-glass. And these windows and these looking-glasses were optically opposed to one another, so that although the sun (which was now shining exceedingly brightly) beat only upon one door, yet (after the windows towards the sun were opened, and the doors before the looking-glasses drawn aside) in all quarters of the room there were nothing but suns, which by artificial refractions beat upon the whole golden globe standing in the midst; and because (besides all this brightness) it was polished, it gave such a lustre, that none of us could open our eyes, but were forced to look out of the windows till the globe was well heated, and brought to the desired effect. Here I may well avow that in these mirrors I have seen the most wonderful spectacle that ever Nature brought to light, for there were suns in all places, and the globe in the middle shined still brighter, so that we could no more endure it than the sun itself, except for one twinkling of an eye.

At length the Virgin commanded the looking-glasses to be shut up again, and the windows to be made fast, and so to let the globe cool again a little; and this was done about seven o'clock. This we thought good, since we might now have a little leisure to refresh ourselves with breakfast. This treatment was again right philosophical, and we had no need to be afraid of intemperance, yet we had no want. And the hope of the future joy (with which the Virgin continually comforted us) made us so jocund that we took no notice of any pains or inconvenience. And this I can truly say too concerning my companions of high quality, that their minds never ran after their kitchen or table, but their pleasure was only to attend upon this adventurous physick, and hence to contemplate the Creator's wisdom and omnipotency.

After we had taken our meal, we again settled down to work, for the globe, which with toil and labour we were to lift off the chain and set upon the floor, was sufficiently cooled. Now the dispute was how to get the globe in half, for we were commanded to divide it in the middle. The conclusion was that a sharp pointed diamond would best do it. Now when we had thus opened the globe, there was nothing more of redness to be seen, but a lovely great snow-white egg. It made us rejoice most greatly that this had been brought to pass so well. For the Virgin was in perpetual care lest the shell might still be too tender. We stood round about this egg as jocund as if we ourselves had laid it. But the Virgin made it be carried forth, and departed herself, too, from us again, and (as always) locked the door. But what she did outside with the egg, or whether it were in some way privately handled, I do not know, neither do I believe it. Yet we were again to wait together for a quarter of an hour, till the third hole was opened, and we by means of our instruments came to the fourth stone or floor.

In this room we found a great copper vessel filled with yellow sand, which was warmed by a gentle fire. Afterwards the egg was raked up in it, that it might therein come to perfect maturity. This vessel was exactly square; upon one side stood these two verses, written in great letters.

O. BLI. O. BIT. MI. LI.

On the second side were these three words:

SANITAS. NIX. HASTA.
Health, Snow, Lance.

The third had only one word:

F.I.A.T.

But on the behind was an entire inscription running thus:

QUOD.
Ignis : Aer : Aqua : Terra :
SANCTIS REGUM ET REGINARUM NOSTR :
Cineribus.
Eripere non potuerunt
Fidelis Chymicorum Turba
IN HANC URNAM
Contulit.
A.

What
Fire : Air : Water : Earth
Were unable to rob
From the holy ashes
OF OUR KINGS AND QUEENS
Was gathered by the faithful flock
Of Alchemists

In this urn
A.D. 1459.

Now whether the egg were hereby meant, I leave to the learned to dispute; yet I do my part, and omit nothing undeclared. Our egg being now ready was taken out, but it needed no cracking, for the bird that was in it soon freed himself, and showed himself very jocund, yet he looked very bloody and unshapen. We first set him upon the warm sand, so the Virgin commanded that before we gave him anything to eat, we should be sure to make him fast, otherwise he would give us all work enough. This being done too, food was brought him, which surely was nothing else than the blood of the beheaded, diluted again with prepared water; by which the bird grew so fast under our eyes, that we saw well why the Virgin gave us such warning about him. He bit and scratched so devilishly about him, that could he have had his will upon any of us, he would have despatched him. Now he was wholly black, and wild, so other food was brought him, perhaps the blood of another of the Royal Persons; whereupon all his black feathers moulted again, and instead of them there grew out snow-white feathers. He was somewhat tamer too, and more docile. Nevertheless we did not yet trust him. At the third feeding his feathers began to be so curiously coloured that in all my life I never saw such beautiful colours. He was also exceedingly tame, and behaved himself so friendlily with us, that (the Virgin consenting) we released him from his captivity.

Our Virgin began: "Since by your diligence, and our old man's consent, the bird has attained both his life and the highest perfection, this is a good reason that he should also be joyfully consecrated by us."

Herewith she commanded that dinner should be brought, and that we should again refresh ourselves, since the most troublesome part of our work was now over, and it was fitting that we should begin to enjoy our past labours. We began to make ourselves merry together. However, we still had all our mourning clothes on, which seemed somewhat reproachful to our mirth. Now the Virgin was perpetually inquisitive, perhaps to find to which of us her future purpose might prove serviceable. But her discourse was for the most part about Melting; and it pleased her well when one seemed expert in such compendious manuals as do particularly commend an artist. This dinner lasted not more than three quarters of an hour, which we still for the most part spent with our bird, and we had to constantly feed him with his food, but he still remained much the same size. After dinner we were not allowed long to digest our food, before the Virgin, together with the bird, departed from us.

The fifth room was set open to us, where we went as before, and offered our services. In this room a bath was prepared for our bird, which was so coloured with a fine white powder that it had the appearance of milk. Now it was at first cool when the bird was set into it. He was mighty well pleased with it, drinking of it, and pleasantly sporting in it. But after it began to heat because of the lamps that were placed under it, we had enough to do to keep him in the bath. We therefore clapped a cover on the vessel, and allowed him to thrust his head out through a hole, till he had in this way lost all his feathers in the bath, and was as smooth as a new-born child; yet the heat did him no further harm, at which I much marveled, for the feathers were completely consumed in this bath, and the bath was thereby tinged blue. At length we gave the bird air, and he sprang out of the vessel of his own accord, and he was so glitteringly smooth that it was a pleasure to behold. But because he was still somewhat wild, we had to put a collar with a chain about his neck, and so led him up and down the room. Meanwhile a strong fire was made under the vessel, and the bath boiled away till it all came down to a blue stone, which we took out, and having first pounded it, ground it with a stone, and finally with this colour began to paint the bird's skin all over. Now he looked much more strange, for he was all blue, except the head, which remained white.

Herewith our work on this story was performed, and we (after the Virgin with her blue bird was departed from us) were called up through the hole to the sixth story, where we were greatly troubled. For in the middle was placed a little altar, in every way like that in the King's hall above described. Upon this stood the six aforementioned particulars, and he himself (the bird) made the seventh. First of all the little fountain was set before him, out of which he drunk a good draught. Afterwards he pecked the white serpent until she bled a great deal. This blood we had to receive into a golden cup, and pour it down the bird's throat, who was greatly averse to it. Then we dipped the serpent's head in the fountain, upon which she revived again, and crept into her death's-head, so that I saw her no more for a long time after. Meantime the sphere turned constantly, until it made the desired conjunction. Immediately the watch struck one, upon which another conjunction was set going. Then the watch struck two. Finally, while we were observing the third conjunction, and this was indicated by the watch, the poor bird submissively laid down his neck upon the book of his own accord, and willingly allowed his head to be smitten off (by one of us chosen for this by lot). However, he yielded not a drop of blood until his breast was opened, and then the blood spurted out so fresh and clear as if it had been a fountain of rubies. His death went to our hearts, and yet we could well judge that a naked bird would stand us in little stead. So we let it be, and moved the little altar away and assisted the Virgin to burn the body to ashes (together with the little tablet hanging by) with fire kindled by the little taper; and afterwards to cleanse the same several times, and to lay them in a box of cypress wood.

Here I cannot conceal what a trick was played on myself and three others.

After we had thus diligently taken up the ashes, the Virgin began to speak as follows:

"My lords, here we are in the sixth room, and we have only one more before us, in which our trouble will be at an end, and then we shall return home again to our castle, to awaken our most gracious Lords and Ladies. Now I could heartily wish that all of you, as you are here together, had behaved yourselves in such a way that I might have commended to our most renowned King and Queen, and you might have obtained a suitable reward; yet contrary to my desire, I have found amongst you these four lazy and sluggish workers (herewith she pointed at me and three others). Yet, according to my goodwill to each and every one, I am not willing to deliver them up to deserved punishment. However, so that such negligence may not remain wholly unpunished, I am resolved thus concerning them, that they shall only be excluded from the future seventh and most glorious action of all the rest, and so they shall incur no further blame from their Royal Majesties."

In what a state we now were at this speech I leave others to consider. For the Virgin knew so well how to keep her countenance, that the water soon ran over our baskets, and we esteemed ourselves the most unhappy of all men. After this the Virgin caused one of her maids (of whom there were many always at hand) to fetch the musicians, who were to blow us out of doors with cornets, with such scorn and derision that they themselves could hardly blow for laughing. But it afflicted us particularly greatly that the Virgin so vehemently laughed at our weeping, anger and impatience, and that there might well perhaps be some amongst our companions who were glad of this misfortune of ours.

But it proved otherwise, for as soon as we had come out of the door, the musicians told us to be of good cheer and follow them up the winding stairs.

They led us up to the seventh floor under the roof, where we found the old man, whom we had not hitherto seen, standing upon a little round furnace. He received us friendlily, and heartily congratulated us that we had been chosen for this by the Virgin; but after he understood the fright we had received, his belly was ready to burst with laughing that we had taken such good fortune so badly. "Hence," said he, "my dear sons, learn that man never knows how well God intended him."

During this discourse the Virgin also came running in with her little box, and (after she had laughed at us enough) emptied her ashes into another vessel, and filled hers again with other stuff, saying she must now go and cast a mist before the other artists' eyes, and that we in the meantime should obey the old lord in whatsoever he commanded us, and not remit our former diligence. Herewith she departed from us into the seventh room into which she called our companions. Now what she did first with them there, I cannot tell, for not only were they most earnestly forbidden to speak of it, but we also, because of our work, did not dare peep on them through the ceiling.

But this was our work. We had to moisten the ashes with our previously prepared water until they became altogether like a very thin dough, after which we set the matter over the fire, till it was well heated. Then we cast it, hot like this, into two little forms or moulds, and let it cool a little.

Here we had leisure to look a while at our companions through certain crevices made in the floor. They were now very busy at a furnace, and each had to blow up the fire himself with a pipe, and they stood blowing about it like this, as if they were wondrously preferred before us in this. And this blowing lasted until our old man roused us to our work again, so that I cannot say what was done afterwards.

We opened our little forms, and there appeared two beautiful, bright and almost transparent little images, the like of which man's eye never saw, a male and a female, each of them only four inches long, and what surprised us most greatly was that they were not hard, but lithe and fleshy, like other human bodies, yet they had no life; so that I most assuredly believe that the Lady Venus's image was also made after some such manner.

These angelically fair babes we first laid upon two little satin cushions, and looked at them for a good while, till we were almost besotted by such exquisite objects. The old lord warned us to forbear, and continually to instil the blood of the bird (which had been received into a little golden cup) drop after drop into the mouths of the little images, from which they appeared to increase; and whereas they were before

very small, they were now (according to proportion) much more beautiful, so that all painters ought to have been here, and would have been
ashamed of their art in respect of these productions of nature. Now
they began to grow so big that we lifted them from the little cushions,
and had to lay them upon a long table, which was covered with white
velvet. The old man also commanded us to cover them over up to the
breast with a piece of the fine white double taffeta, which, because of
their unspeakable beauty, almost went against us. But to be brief, before we had quite used up the blood in this way, they were already in
their perfect full growth. They had golden-yellow, curly hair, and the
above-mentioned figure of Venus was nothing to them.

But there was not yet any natural warmth or sensibility in them.
They were dead figures, yet of a lively and natural colour; and since
care was to be taken that they did not grow too big, the old man would
not permit anything more to be given to them, but covered their faces
too with the silk, and caused the table to be stuck round about with
torches. Here I must warn the reader not to imagine these lights to
have been put there out of necessity, for the old man's intent hereby
was only that we should not observe when the soul entered into them;
and indeed we should not have noticed it, had I not twice before seen
the flames. However, I permitted the other three to remain with their
own belief, neither did the old man know that I had seen anything
more. Hereupon he asked us to sit down on a bench over against the
table. Presently the Virgin came in too, with the music and all necessities, and carried two curious white garments, the like of which I had
never seen in the castle, nor can I describe them, for I thought that
they were nothing other than crystal; but they were soft, and not transparent; so that I cannot describe them. These she laid down on a table,
and after she had disposed her virgins upon a bench round about, she
and the old man began many slight-of-hand tricks about the table, which
was done only to blind us. This (as I told you) was managed under the
roof, which was wonderfully formed; for on the inside it was arched
into seven hemispheres, of which the middlemost was somewhat the
highest, and had at the top a little round hole, which was nevertheless
shut, and was observed by no-one else.

After many ceremonies six virgins came in, each of whom carried a
large trumpet, around which were rolled a green, glittering and burning material like a wreath. The old man took one of these, and after he
had removed some of the lights at the top of the table, and uncovered
their faces, he placed one of the trumpets upon the mouth of one of

the bodies in such a way that the upper and wider end of it was directed just towards the aforementioned hole. Here my companions always looked at the images, but I had other thoughts, for as soon as the foliage or wreath about the shank of the trumpet was kindled, I saw the hole at the top open, and a bright stream of fire shooting down the tube, and passing into the body; whereupon the hole was covered again, and the trumpet removed. With this device my companions were deluded, so that they imagined that life came into the image by means of the fire of the foliage, for as soon as he received the soul his eyes twinkled, although he hardly stirred. The second time he placed another tube upon its mouth, and kindled it again, and the soul was let down through the tube. This was repeated for each of them three times, after which all the lights were extinguished and carried away. The velvet coverings of the table were cast over them, and immediately a birthing bed was unlocked and made ready, into which, thus wrapped up, they were born. And after the coverings were taken off them, they were neatly laid by each other, and with the curtains drawn before them, they slept a good while.

Now it was also time for the Virgin to see how other artists behaved themselves. They were well pleased because, as the Virgin afterwards informed me, they were to work in gold, which is indeed a piece of this art, but not the most principal, most necessary, and best. They had indeed too a part of these ashes, so that they imagined nothing other than that the whole bird was provided for the sake of gold, and that life must thereby be restored to the deceased.

Meantime we sat very still, waiting for our married couple to awake. About half an hour was spent like this. Then the wanton Cupid presented himself again, and after he had saluted us all, flew to them behind the curtain, tormenting them until they awakened. This was a cause of great amazement to them, for they imagined that they had slept from the very hour in which they were beheaded until now. Cupid, after he had awakened them, and renewed their acquaintance with one another, stepped aside a little, and allowed them both to get themselves together a bit better, meantime playing his tricks with us; and at length he wanted to have the music brought in, to be somewhat merrier.

Not long after, the Virgin herself came in, and after she had most humbly saluted the young King and Queen (who found themselves rather faint) and kissed their hands, she brought them the two aforementioned strange garments, which they put on, and so stepped forth.

Now there were already prepared two very strange chairs, in which they placed themselves. And they were congratulated with most profound reverence by us, for which the King himself most graciously returned his thanks, and again reassured us of all grace.[10]

⤱

Thus, from the gold egg, of which Brahma speaks, is born the phoenix, patron of all transformations, the phoenix which the Finnish *Kalevala* legend has turned into a duck. Through the ashes of the bird, human figurines could be given life. Through the fire of the conquered sky, the soul was returned to the king and queen. Having no doubt lost the marvelous secret, profane science has only succeeded so far in building automatons and making dummies move, not recreating the complexity of life.

The history of these automatons is long, and it is connected to an age-old dream of man, who has always yearned for power.

Heron of Alexandria is the most ancient automaton maker whose name comes down to us. Certainly he could not have been the only Egyptian priest who devoted himself to this kind of work. After that, for a long time, the jointed statues were part of the oriental palace treasure. Europe in this period was content with the rigid stone statues that decorated its cathedrals. During the Renaissance, as society became more refined, a taste for these "marvelous" industries reappeared (clockworks for moving figures, jointed horses, etc.). Leonardo da Vinci loved to devise such curiosities for elaborate festivals in Milan, Florence, and Rome. He took as much pleasure in them as in painting. The eighteenth-century philosophy of mechanical materialism resulted in a new wave of automaton construction. Jacques de Vaucanson made astonishing creations in this era. He built a flute player with movable lips and tongue who could modulate the air and thus play a dozen different tunes. He also created a soldier musician, a hunter who shot with great precision, two woman figures—a watchwoman and a spinner. The most famous of these objects was a duck. The animal flapped its wings, swam, stood up on its legs, drank, ate, and digested.

The movements animating these automatons were produced by levers and gears controlled by springs. Since then, the invention of elec-

---

10. This version was edited, from the Foxcroft English edition of 1690, into modern English by Adam McLean and Deirdre Green.

tricity and advances in technology have considerably increased the possibilities for statue-machines. The most marvelous of them are now assembled at the international exposition in New York. The newspapers supply us with curious information on the subject:[11]

Production of Robots

The jointed man measures four meters in height, he has a six-horse-power heart, his bronze voice carries four kilometers. He will light the exposition lights on opening night. A powerful telescope will be directed toward the canopy of heaven and capture the rays of a star. The concentrated light from this star will fall on one of the giant's eyes made of photoelectric cells. There, the celestial fire will be transformed into a current which will activate the right arm of the automaton. One push on a button within reach of his hand will light up the extravaganza. The star at which the telescope will be aimed is Arcturus, in the constellation, Böotes, the Herdsman, which shines with a reddish glow and is located at a distance of thirty-nine light years from our planet. Thus, the rays that will illuminate the New York Exposition of 1939 date back to the beginning of the century. Besides this giant, the public will be able to admire a whole series of automatons approaching extraordinarily close to being human. They walk, talk, calculate, and answer questions. Moreover, spoken language is not the only way of communicating with these artificial humans. Visitors will have a series of whistles at their disposal, each of which will transmit a specific order to a very obedient servant, "Mr. Televox." Made up of a battery of microphones, the brain of this automaton reacts to sound waves which, transformed into electrical currents, activate relays hidden in his body. One relay corresponds to each level of sound. Whistles ensure that the orders are transmitted. Following instructions, Televox will run, stop, and sit himself down in an easy chair. He will even sing to please his master. If you wish, he will recite the names of United States presidents for you, from Lincoln to Roosevelt, or even reveal to you the ages of Hollywood stars. Telelux, another man-machine, run by light waves, is a powerful calculator. In no time, he will give the square root of any number whatever, even one made up of eight digits. The most extraordinary machine is the soldier-machine, invented by Joey Withmann, an engineer from Chicago. This formidable monster

---

11. *Paris-Midi*, February 28, 1939.

is controlled by hertzian waves produced by a special transmitter. In spite of its four hundred and fifty kilograms, it moves with considerable speed, thanks to an eighteen-horsepower heart. With its elephant-like legs, their balance maintained by a gyroscope, it is astonishingly agile. For hands, its steel arms have two constantly rotating discs armed with terrible clubs which could kill a hippopotamus with one blow. With the help of an ingenious relay system, a hidden receptor in the monster's skull transmits to the giant's arms and legs all orders the master communicates by hertzian waves, no matter what the distance. The soldier-machine is blind. Its master commands it and sees for it. Invulnerable warrior, without fear or pity, this steel combatant would be a most formidable adversary.

To create beings with superior capabilities and subservient to humans, magicians thought that rather than using wood or metal, rather than devising complicated gear systems, it would be easier to use the human body itself. Taking a fresh cadaver, they tried their best to resuscitate it and maintain it indefinitely in a secondary state of hypnosis. The individual thus created, existing outside of life and death, is an obedient slave who does those acts for us that we can't, or don't dare, commit ourselves.

Here is the golem born in the ghettos of central Europe from the science of Jewish cabalists. He spreads terror in the palaces of cruel masters. He avenges persecutions suffered by the oppressed race. He is the response raised by hope and science against military power in the Middle Ages.

Here is the monster created by the baron of Frankenstein. Here, in Haiti, are the zombies, those dead who leave their tombs, are reanimated by magic rites of the voodoo sects, and work on the plantations on behalf of the living. They remain between life and death as long as one wishes, under the condition that they not touch either salt or meat. Seabrook tells of having seen these singular characters.[12]

The Dead Slaves of Haiti
W. B. Seabrook

My first impression of the *zombies*, who continued dumbly at work, was that there was something about them unnatural and strange. They were

---

12. W. B. Seabrook, *The Magic Island* (Harcourt, Brace & Co., 1929), 101.

plodding like brutes, automatons. Without stooping down, I could not fully see their faces, which were bent expressionless over their work. Polynice touched one of them on the shoulder, motioned him to get up. Obediently, like an animal, he slowly stood erect—and what I saw then, coupled with what I had heard previously, or despite it, came as a rather sickening shock. The eyes were the worst. It was not my imagination. They were in truth like the eyes of a dead man, not blind, but staring, unfocused, unseeing. The whole face, for that matter, was bad enough. It was vacant, as if there was nothing behind it. It seemed not only expressionless, but incapable of expression. I had seen so much previously in Haiti that was outside ordinary, normal experience that for the flash of a second I had a sickening, almost panicky lapse in which I thought, or rather felt, "Great God, maybe this stuff is really true."

The existence of zombies has preoccupied me so much that I have tried my best to attain further information on the subject. Some have told me that the dead were actually pulled out of their graves. But another source, who carried the bloody mark of voodoo initiation on him, confided to me that these mysterious beings were live humans under a cruel spell that transformed them into slave laborers, less expensive than animals, and lost in an animal-like mindlessness: the wage earners' state that we know in Europe, perfected to its criminal end.

This plausible explanation, which eliminates the unsavory fantastic element, does not divert us from the marvelous. The marvelous exists in the human will to create a new species obliged to serve them. While waiting for inventions to succeed, and for the lack of obedient demons, all the efforts toward transformation are borne by our own species. Whereas the sound human spirit hopes to go beyond the current limits of our possibilities, to elevate individuals above themselves and make them comparable to gods, whereas the sound human spirit traditionally struggles against being enslaved by the forces of nature, other demonic imaginations are haunted by the desire to turn a portion of humanity into complete automatons, deprived of independence, personal needs, and psychological fears. Science fiction films and novels have suggested the possible development, systematically controlled, of inferior races living in the depths of mines or the darkness of factories. An alternative to the dream of constructing robots fashioned like men and relieving them of all their most difficult tasks is the dream of modeling certain social classes to resemble obedient robots, making them into some kind of submissive gnomes, deprived of all capacity for revolt. And such things are not simply nightmares, products of nocturnal imagination or sadistic fits. They are the reality in the concentration camps where thousands of people number among the living dead. Will for power and hatred for people leads political wheeler-dealers and dictators not to elevate themselves to the heights of heroic "supermen," but, on the contrary, to debase humanity in order to enjoy the momentary sensation of finally being on a higher plane.

Under the earth, in the cracks between rocks, in the depths of the forest, live those singular entities called genies or demons, depending on the prevailing religion. Or so one maintains. These entities, who share our intelligence but, by their extraordinary powers, remain attached to natural energy, are invoked by magicians. Over the course of time, a struggle has developed between them and those who call upon them, even heated combat, in which human science has often failed, though human hope for triumph has never been daunted. When one has really wanted to engender one of these intermediary beings in a lasting way, half-demon, half-man, the preferred method has been to resort to a mandrake root, gathered according to a precise ritual. In "Isabelle d'Egypte," Achim d'Arnim tells how Bella, the daughter of the Bohemian king, went about obtaining it.

Harvesting the Mandrake Root
Achim d'Arnim

After spending a week in fruitless research, she finally discovered, in one of these books, a detailed formula explaining the means of obtaining a mandrake root. Moreover it went further on to say what zeal and spirit of rapine, what infallible ruses this root would employ to procure money and everything else that a heart attached to this vile world could desire.

But what difficulties this possession entailed! And yet this was one of the simplest of magical operations. Who in our day could confront all the trials to which it was necessary to submit in order to own the mandrake? Who could successfully meet the demanding requirements of these ordeals? A young girl who could love with her entire soul without seeking the delights of her sex was necessary, for whom the proximity alone of her beloved was sufficient. This first and indispensable condition was realized for the first time, perhaps, in Bella. As she was regarded by the Gypsies as an essentially superior being, she had always seen herself in the same light; and the fleeting appearance of the prince had so struck her as being as sacred and pure as the holy sacrament of the mass, that no ulterior motive had found the occasion to awaken within her.

Then such a young girl must at the same time gather a courage hardy enough to venture out in the middle of the night at which time it is necessary to bring a black dog beneath a gallows from which an innocent victim must have shed his tears (?) upon the lawn. Once there she must plug her ears with cotton and grope with her hands through the dirt until she finds the root. Then despite the cries of this root which is not a plant but is born, rather, from the innocent tears of the hanged man, she must attach a rope made from her own hair and to which the black dog is tied at the other end. Then she must draw away in such a manner that the dog, wishing to follow her, will tear the root from the ground and be struck down without fail by a convulsion of the earth accompanied by a bolt of lightning. At this decisive moment, if she has not stopped her ears she runs the risk of being instantly driven mad by fright.

Bella was perhaps the lone individual, for centuries, in whom all these conditions were met. Who was more innocent than Michael, her father, who had sacrificed his life for his people and who had lived constantly in want and suffering? What young girl would have found the courage to deliberately plan such a midnight excursion if not Bella? She who, for four years, since the time of her mother's death, had led a secret and nocturnal existence and for whom the course of the moon and stars were too well known and common for her to feel any particular feeling of anxiety or despair at night. What young girl had, as she did, a black dog that she detested so much? Since the day it had bitten her as a puppy she could not bear its presence, though now it obeyed her with exemplary zeal and always watched over her, all with such a singular air that it had seemed to her father Michael that there was something of the devil in this dog. What young girl had such luxurious hair as Bella, long enough to furnish a rope, and what young girl would have sacrificed it with such tranquillity? In ignorance of her charms she mused with pleasure at the thought of no longer having to brush such long tresses. Thus, with the rapid snips of her scissors, her hair, in the locks of which the stars were often reflected as in Berenice's hair,[13] fell to the ground around her like a black veil; this she would make into a chain that would be fatal for her dog Samson.

She soon noticed that the dog had understood all that she said for

---

13. A constellation.

instead of going to bury his small pittance of bread and bones in the garden as was his custom, he, to the contrary, started disinterring all his hidden treasures and eating them with an insatiable appetite. Any other individual would have been moved; Bella wasn't in the least. Moreover the dog didn't appear sad; he watched her with a mocking air; and when Friday arrived, for this operation had to occur on a Friday, he ran all over the house, sniffing in all the corners, and, contrary to his normal behavior made a mess of his kennel. But Bella excused Samson more readily than she did the tiresome manner in which her old maid Braka spent her whole day relating the wretched stories of her first loves, broken up by an interminable series of "I said," "he said," "then, he said," and so forth.

If Bella had listened this could have caused her to lose one of the principal qualities required of those who would seek the mandrake; but she was so preoccupied with counting the passing minutes and hours that when midnight sounded, in a fit of impatience, she brusquely arose and, irritated at the prospect of having to put off her business until the following week, grabbed the old woman and started dancing the gypsy crane dance with her, until Braka, out of breath, fell back into her chair coughing and swearing that she hadn't danced so much since her wedding day. She popped a piece of licorice into her mouth to ease her cough and went on her way while saying she was sorry to have to depart so early.

Until that moment Bella had been very troubled, as well as angry at the thought of another week in which to prepare herself; now it seemed preferable. The dog appeared no less desirous of this delay which had given him more time to stuff his belly. Bella intentionally gave him the most delicious morsels, as she knew he was to be sacrificed for her, and often, despite her aversion to the beast, tears sprang to her eyes when she looked at him. However she consoled herself by recalling what the magic book had said, that the soul of the faithful dog who lost his life on this occasion would go to heaven to rejoin his master; and Bella was certain that Samson would be happier with Duke Michael than with her.

The second Friday finally arrived; the weather was beginning to get cold and the water was already freezing in the bogs and the ponds. The old woman had told Bella that she wouldn't be round to see her for a few days because her head cold was keeping her at home. Everything seemed to be going perfectly: the neighbors were all in town, the night was pitch black, and the wind was sweeping the first snowflakes across the ground. Bella reread the book of spells again, her heart beating violently.

At that moment the dog started to rip apart the doll on which Bella had placed the prince's suit. That decided the fate of the undertaking. He would have to expiate this insult made to her beloved; detaching the rope woven of her hair, that she had until then kept on her head in order not to rouse the old woman's suspicions, she struck the dog. He, wishing to get away, headed toward the door. She opened it and they both found themselves transported into the bizarre and mysterious world of winter. First they followed haphazardly a path they were unfamiliar with, finding their way toward the hill where executions took place. Not a person crossed their path, only several dogs that came out of some gardens barking at the top of their lungs and running toward the black Samson. But at the moment these philistines drew near he stopped them in their tracks with a display of his large white teeth. His response was so effective that all of them, large and small, fled in fright with their tails between their legs back to the safety of the gardens where they hid behind the doors emitting piteous yelps.

At the same time two porcupines, their quills garnished with apples and pears that they had gathered by rolling in the gardens, crossed the road. At the sight of the dog they formed into balls but Samson contented himself with relieving them of their loot and devouring it. During this time Bella calmly rested but something did appear out of the ordinary to her; whether she stopped or whether she continued to advance toward the hill, she sensed someone walking behind her so closely that often the tip of the mysterious individual's foot would brush her heel. She dared not look behind her and kept walking at a faster and faster pace, until a violent blow to the head sent her sprawling on the ground. She was merely slightly stunned. As everything remained silent in the neighboring area, she gathered her courage and stood back up. She looked around and saw no one but she did see that she had collided with a toll house barrier and that the presence that had followed in her footsteps was no more than a hawthorn branch that had become stuck in her dress. She laughed at her fear and resolved to be henceforth more rational. She quickly forgot her resolution when a herd of horses sleeping in a stable arose abruptly at her approach and fled, leaping over bushes and hedges.

Bella had arrived at the top of the hill; she saw the opulent city all agleam with lights. One house shone more than any of the others; she thought that this must be the dwelling of the prince. It was just as described by the old woman, and she knew that today was his birthday. She would have forgotten all at this sight, even the withered corpses of the hanged men swaying over her head and bumping into her shoulders as if demanding something, if the dog, on its own initiative, hadn't started scratching at the foot of the gallows. She sought what he had uncovered and felt between her hands a human figure. A tiny human figure whose two legs were still rooted in the earth. This was it! The benevolent mandrake! The child of the gallows. She had found it with no difficulty and with no great expense of time. She attached one end of the hair-woven rope to the root and started to run despite the cries of the root. But she had forgotten to block her ear. She ran as fast as she could and the dog chasing behind her tore the root from the earth. Immediately a dreadful clap of thunder upended both of them! Luckily she had run quite fast and was already around fifty feet away.

This circumstance was her salvation; however, she remained in a swoon for a long time only rising at that hour when satisfied lovers leave their mistresses and seek rest from their bliss. One of these was singing a song spilling over with joy about his beautiful beloved and about the nasty tongues of gossips that betrayed clandestine love affairs; he was half asleep and didn't see Bella. She painfully arose and the first gleams of daylight allowed her to see Samson stretched out dead at her feet. On recognizing him she recalled all the events of the night before in succession; at the end of the rope that she detached from the dog's body she found a being with human form similar to an animated sketch from which the nobler feelings have not yet been extricated, something akin to a chrysalis. This was the mandrake and, astonishingly, on the one hand, Bella had entirely forgotten the prince, the unique cause that prompted her to seek the mandrake. And on the other she now loved it with a tenderness that she hadn't felt since the night she first laid eyes on the prince.

A mother who believes her child lost in an earthquake doesn't greet its reappearance with more joy and affection than Bella felt when she bore this mannequin to her heart, while brushing away the dirt that still covered this tiny being and ridding it of its bothersome sprouts. It appeared to feel nothing of all of this, its breath emerged raggedly from an imperceptible opening that it had on its head. After Bella had rocked it for some time it rapped her chest impatiently with its arms to indicate that this movement was pleasing to it, and it would not have stopped shaking its arms and legs if she hadn't sent it to sleep by the recommencement of that movement.

Following this she hastened to return home with it. She paid no attention to the barking dogs nor to the merchants scattered along the road who were heading toward the city in order to be the first at the opening of the gates. She saw naught but the little monster that she had scrupulously wrapped in her apron. She finally arrived at her room, lit a lamp and examined the small creature; she was sorry that it had no mouth on which to bestow her kisses, no nose to provide passage for its divine breath, no eyes that would let her see into its soul, and no hair to safeguard the frail seat of its thoughts. But this in no way diminished the force of her love. She took her spell book and sought within it for the method to employ to develop the strengths and complete the formation of this carrot adorned with limbs and endowed with life; she soon found it.

It was first necessary to wash the mandrake, which she did. Then she had to sow millet upon its head and once this millet had sprouted and transformed into hair the other limbs would develop on their own. Only at each of the spots where an eye should develop was it necessary to place a juniper berry, and a wild rosehip at the location of the mouth.

Fortunately she was able to procure all these items. The old woman had recently brought some millet seed which she had made off with. Her father used juniper berries to perfume his room; because she couldn't stand their odor, a handful still remained. There was a wild rosebush in the garden that was still covered with rose hips, the last adornment of the dying year. Everything was ready. The fruit of the wild rose was put in the spot indicated, but she didn't notice that in kissing it she had put it in askew; then she pushed in the two juniper berries. It seemed to her that the little being was looking at her which gave her so much pleasure that she would have added a dozen more if only she had found an appropriate setting for them. But in those spots that she would have intentionally given it eyes, such as the back, she feared for their safety. However she finished by giving him a pair on the nape of his neck which we must concede is not to be disdained for its originality. She felt both joyful and sad at having thus created a being which would cause her such torment as all men give to their creator. On the other hand, looking at her formless little monster pleased her as if she were a young artist who had succeeded above all expectations.

She laid it in a small cradle that she had found in the house and wrapped it well in blankets. This secret, which was the first of her life, she resolved to reveal to no one, not even the old Braka.[14]

---

14. Achim d'Arnim, "Isabelle d'Egypte," in *Contes Bizarre.*

THE DESTRUCTION
OF THE WORLD

When I was a child, the news of natural disasters filled me with visceral pleasure. I learned to show no sign of this, and to listen in silence as the grown-ups lamented. In particular, the flood of 1910 elated me. Towns submerged little by little by the inexorable flood tides, streets transformed into rivers, frantic escapes by the inhabitants, driven like rats: marvelous images only to be succeeded by disenchantment when the waters receded and things returned to their ordinary monotony.

Volcanic eruptions which the magazines presented to us in color on their livid first pages: cities swallowed up in one night, the languid flow of lava; in the distance, tidal waves, and huge, heavy vessels wrecked like our little toy boats, which would be capsized by a single gust of wind.

And again, the great fires, like those of the Var forests, flames racing "at the speed of galloping horses," the countryside lit up at night as though for a strange celebration of some monstrous Saint John, the clocks abandoning their regular announcements of the sad masses in order to sound the alarm.

I seemed to be the only person in the world to take pleasure in such misfortunes, and I believed that I was nurturing some demon within me. So, for this reason, I forced myself to keep silent. The war, during which I lived in a dangerous, heavily bombed area for most of the time, would prove that my state was not exceptional. Most of my comrades shared it, I learned through confidences made easier by the freedom we enjoyed at that time. Like all physically weak beings, the child conceals a good deal of sadism. The most attractive images for him are those of natural or inflicted havoc. He nurses a secret affection for Nero, watching, gay and lyrical, as Rome succumbs to the fires set by his own devices. Perhaps catastrophes are interesting because of their exceptional nature; they are the kind of spectacular curiosities that romantics adore. Perhaps the child takes pleasure in seeing the adult community tremble for a moment, losing all its power and authority. Perhaps the child, still so close to the natural phenomena of his own conception and birth, retains some complicity with the cosmic energies? I believe above all that the sadism of the young is an aspect of fear, that essential motivating principle of emotional life. This feeling is so important that humans seem to have agreed not to mention it. They dare to imagine only one of its forms, the most vulgar and repugnant: that moral inhibition which makes some escape necessary, that morbid depression which paralyzes thought and makes us sweat. However, the internal reality is completely different.

Fear of death, you give life its value. Fear of the future, you make the moment precious, you give meaning to health, to riches. Fear, you allow us to marvel at the fragile smile appearing on a woman's face, you evoke the intense feelings that come over us when we meet another being, who, in the next instant, will be swallowed up into the night. The child's sensual fear becomes his excuse for snuggling up with his mother. And finally there is the fear so carefully maintained by stories, recreated by novels, tragedies, and spectacles. Constant presence of the night, filled with night-black mares, without which there would be no light. Intoxicating dialectic of being and nonbeing which reopens the entire question, which creates anxiety, without which life would cost nothing. Source of all our mind's pleasures. The indissoluble union of fear and hope sadistically makes us think that, perhaps, tomorrow the sun will no longer rise, the equilibrium of the seasons will be destroyed once and for all, the fragile comfort of hard-working societies will be ruined, that nothing will remain of the ordinary circumstances of humanity.

It is necessary to have spent a certain amount of time within the tempest, surrounded by mountains seething in the rains, to have been taken up like a helpless plaything into the frenzied dance of the elements. It is necessary to have known, at night, that gradual cold carried by a horizontal wind when the earth seems frozen for eternity, when life is crystallized, dead. And also those other extremes, of torrid heat, when things seem ready to ignite in a universal conflagration. Exhausted, we suffer, but in the midst of our complaints, there remains a demented taste for pushing the extremes, the paroxysms, further. Disturbing limits beyond which life is compromised, you are surely the frontiers and the sources of the marvelous.

This disposition in the human psyche makes our obsessive fears of great cosmic catastrophes a perpetual condition.

Moreover, observation shows that these are not merely obsessive fears. Such catastrophes have already taken place in the past. Stratification in the earth's crust shows evidence of these upheavals which obliterated giant fauna in the Tertiary period and destroyed luxuriant vegetation, leaving only sparse remnants of it on faraway continents. The unconscious associates these geological transformations with mythic events linked to the origin of societies. Searching for a reason for these cataclysms, the mind views them as a necessary means of erasing the bad, of renovating and improving the world. Don't we ourselves destroy the inadequate early drafts of our work and those objects we've worn out? The legend of the flood, found among all cultures, recalls, no doubt a real event, but above all, it expresses a fundamental tendency of the human sensibility and intelligence.

The individual drama of birth, in which waters play so great a role, is magnified to the scale of all of humanity. Humans must be separated from their divine ancestors (and all parents are just that) by a deluge, by waters that must be overcome. The one who survives is a saint, combining the ancient characteristics of heroes and our present nature. He is Deucalion in Greece, Outa Napichtim in Mesopotamia, Noah in the Bible. His virtues have touched the Lord and he has obtained a promise that the catastrophe will not be repeated. He possesses the secret of the covenant.

Alas! This covenant cannot be eternal. Knowing the cyclical nature of life in the universe, Hindus foresee the possibility of future alterations. For Christians, they will be the result of man's progressive changes.

Among the great many versions of the apocalypse that circulated in Asia and Greece during the first century A.D., that of Saint John has remained with us. It has left an indelible mark, lasting two thousand years, on the popular unconscious. The prophet announces future destruction, and, one day soon to come, the onset of plagues.

The End of the World According to Saint John

After this I looked, and, behold, a door was opened in heaven: and the
first voice which I heard was as if it were a trumpet talking to me;
which said, Come up hither, and I will shew thee things which
must be hereafter.

And immediately I was in the spirit; and, behold, a throne was set in
heaven, and one sat upon the throne.

And he that sat was to look upon like jasper and sardine stone: and
there was a rainbow round about the throne, in sight like unto an
emerald.

And round about the throne were four and twenty seats: and upon the
seats I saw four and twenty elders sitting, clothed in white
raiment; and they had on their heads crowns of gold.

And out of the throne proceeded lightnings and thunderings and
voices: and there were seven lamps of fire burning before the
throne, which are the seven Spirits of God.

And before the throne there was a sea of glass like unto crystal: and in
the midst of the throne, and round about the throne, were four
beasts full of eyes before and behind.

And the first beast was like a lion, and the second beast like a calf,
and the third beast had a face as a man, and the fourth beast was
like a flying eagle.

And the four beasts had each of them six wings about him; and they
were full of eyes within: and they rested not day and night, saying,
Holy, holy, holy, Lord God Almighty, which was, and is, and is to
come...

And I saw in the right hand of him that sat on the throne a book
written within and on the backside, sealed with seven seals.

And I saw a strong angel proclaiming with a loud voice, Who is
worthy to open the book, and to loose the seals thereof?

And no man in heaven, nor in earth, neither under the earth, was
able to open the book, neither to look thereon.

And I wept much, because no man was found worthy to open and to
read the book, neither to look thereon.

And one of the elders saith unto me, Weep not: behold, the Lion of the
tribe of Juda, the Root of David, hath prevailed to open the book,
and to loose the seven seals thereof.

And I beheld, and lo, in the midst of the throne and of the four beasts,
and in the midst of the elders, stood a Lamb as it had been slain,

having seven horns and seven eyes, which are the seven Spirits of God sent forth into all the earth.

And he came and took the book out of the right hand of him that sat upon the throne.

And when he had taken the book, the four beasts and the four and twenty elders fell down before the Lamb, having every one of them harps, and golden vials full of odours, which are the prayers of saints...

And I saw when the Lamb opened one of the seals, and I heard, as it were the noise of thunder, one of the four beasts saying, Come and see.

And I saw, and beheld a white horse: and he that sat on him had a bow; and a crown was given unto him: and he went forth conquering and to conquer.

And when he had opened the second seal, I heard the second beast say, Come and see.

And there went out another horse that was red: and power was given to him that sat thereon to take peace from the earth, and that they should kill one another: and there was given unto him a great sword.

And when he had opened the third seal, I heard the third beast say, Come and see. And I beheld, and lo a black horse; and he that sat on him had a pair of balances in his hand.

And I heard a voice in the midst of the four beasts say, A measure of wheat for a penny, and three measures of barley for a penny; and see thou hurt not the oil and the wine.

And when he had opened the fourth seal, I heard the voice of the fourth beast say, Come and see.

And I looked, and beheld a pale horse: and his name that sat on him was Death, and Hell followed with him. And power was given unto them over the fourth part of the earth, to kill with sword, and with hunger, and with death, and with the beasts of the earth.

And when he had opened the fifth seal, I saw under the altar the souls of them that were slain for the word of God, and for the testimony which they held.

And they cried with a loud voice saying, How long, O Lord, holy and true, dost thou not judge and avenge our blood on them that dwell on the earth?

And white robes were given unto every one of them; and it was said unto them, that they should rest yet for a little season, until their

fellow-servants also and their brethren, that should be killed as
they were, should be fulfilled.

And I beheld when he had opened the sixth seal, and lo, there was a
great earthquake; and the sun became black as sackcloth of hair,
and the moon became as blood;

And the stars of heaven fell unto the earth, even as a fig tree casteth
her untimely figs, when she is shaken of a mighty wind.

And the heaven departed as a scroll when it is rolled together; and
every mountain and island were moved out of their places.

And the kings of the earth, and the great men, and the rich men, and
the chief captains, and the mighty men, and every bondman, and
every free man, hid themselves in the dens and in the rocks of the
mountains;

And said to the mountains and rocks, Fall on us, and hide us from
the face of him that sitteth on the throne, and from the wrath of the
Lamb:

For the great day of his wrath is come; and who shall be able to stand?

And when he had opened the seventh seal, there was a silence in
heaven about the space of half an hour.

And I saw the seven angels which stood before God; and to them were
given seven trumpets.

And another angel came and stood at the altar, having a golden
censer; and there was given unto him much incense, that he
should offer it with the prayers of the saints upon the golden altar
which was before the throne.

And the smoke of the incense, which came with the prayers of the
saints, ascended up before God out of the angel's hand.

And the angel took the censer, and filled it with fire of the altar, and
cast it into the earth: and there were voices, and thunderings, and
lightnings, and an earthquake.

And the seven angels which had the seven trumpets prepared them-
selves to sound.

The first angel sounded, and there followed hail and fire mingled with
blood, and they were cast upon the earth: and the third part of
trees was burnt up, and all green grass was burnt up.

And the second angel sounded, and as it were a great mountain
burning with fire was cast into the sea: and the third part of the
sea became blood;

And the third part of the creatures which were in the sea, and had life,
died; and the third part of the ships were destroyed.

And the third angel sounded, and there fell a great star from heaven, burning as it were a lamp, and it fell upon the third part of the rivers, and upon the fountains of waters;

And the name of the star is called Wormwood: and the third part of the waters became wormwood; and many men died of the waters because they were made bitter.

And the fourth angel sounded, and the third part of the sun was smitten, and the third part of the moon, and the third part of the stars; so as the third part of them was darkened...

And the fifth angel sounded, and I saw a star fall from heaven unto the earth: and to him was given the key to the bottomless pit.

And he opened the bottomless pit; and there arose a smoke out of the pit and there came out of the smoke locusts upon the earth: and unto them was given power, as the scorpions of the earth have power.

And it was commanded them they should not hurt but those men which have not the seal of God in their foreheads.

And to them it was given that they should not kill them, but that they should be tormented five months: and their torment was as the torment of a scorpion, when he striketh a man.

And in those days shall men seek death, and shall not find it; and shall desire to die, and death shall flee from them.

And the shapes of the locusts were like unto horses prepared unto battle; and on their heads were as it were crowns like gold, and their faces were as the faces of men.

And they had hair as the hair of women, and their teeth were as the teeth of lions.

And they had breastplates, as it were breastplates of iron; and the sound of their wings was as the sound of chariots of many horses running to battle.

And they had tails like unto scorpions, and there were stings in their tails: and their power was to hurt men five months.

And they had a King over them, which is the angel of the bottomless pit...

And the sixth angel sounded, and I heard a voice from the four horns of the golden altar which is before God,

Saying to the sixth angel which had the trumpet, Loose the four angels which are bound in the great river Euphrates.

And the four angels were loosed, which were prepared for an hour, and a day, and a month, and a year, for to slay the third part of men.

And the number of the army of the horsemen was two hundred

thousand thousand: and I heard the number of them...
And I saw another mighty angel come down from heaven, clothed with
a cloud: and a rainbow was upon his head, and his face was as it
were the sun, and his feet as pillars of fire:
And he had in his hand a little book open: and he set his right foot
upon the sea, and his left foot on the earth.
And cried with a loud voice, as when a lion roareth: and when he had
cried, seven thunders uttered their voices. And when the seven
thunders had uttered their voices, I was about to write: and I
heard a voice from heaven saying unto me, Seal up those things
which the seven thunders uttered, and write them not.
And the angel which I saw stand upon the sea and upon the earth
lifted up his hand to heaven,
And sware by him that liveth forever and ever, who created heaven,
and the things that therein are, and the earth, and the things that
therein are, and the sea, and the things which are therein, that
there should be time no longer:
But in the days of the voice of the seventh angel, when he shall begin to
sound, the mystery of God should be finished, as he hath declared
to his prophets.
And the voice which I heard from heaven spake unto me again, and
said, Go and take the little book, which is open in the hand of the
angel which standeth upon the sea and upon the earth.
And I went unto the angel, and said unto him, Give me the little book.
And he said unto me, Take it, and eat it up; and it shall make thy
belly bitter, but it shall be in thy mouth sweet as honey.

Protected by the insouciance of their vulgar souls, many regard the prophecy as simple dramatic allegory. Since the year one thousand has passed without any demons being let loose, since they have been able to protect their precious selves through wars and epidemics, they now repress their instinctive fear. And the cataclysmic images disappear into the mists. They are abstractions, no longer attached to daily life. We can rest assured, however, that the poet feels the time has come. Leaning over the abyss of his unconscious, like the man resting his elbows on the windowsill in summer watching for the impending evening storm, he notices threatening signs. In familiar objects, he reads the drama that is in preparation. Are his eyes closed or wide open when this glowing red vision appears to him?

The Collapse of a World Condemned

L.-P. Fargue

... And, indeed, we were among men. Ah! Not much more remained. Laos, the Gironde, Peru, Spanish Morocco had all collapsed. It took ten hours to go from Palais-Bourbon place to Bourg-la-Reine, six days to get to Saint-Pierre-des-Corps. Alps of warm asphalt rose between the great centers of Europe. The first hues of the post-mortem landscape appeared at the crossroads. Complete with a locomotive which creaked and balanced on its summit, the towering railroad tracks, sometimes as high as three hundred meters and reminiscent of the treelike ferns of the world's earliest times, came out of the earth, like suspenders at the dormer window of a roof in the old city's past. Rumbling ballistics rose at the cracked lips of craters. One of the first, I lent an ear.

My grandmother used to say that if man's stomach could talk, it would murmur in a plaintive voice, "Carrots, carrots..." The world, which was collapsing like an enormous soufflé, could no longer speak either, of course, but nevertheless we heard it yelping through all the fissures, "I love you... I love you, I love you..." This was not the pieces of swallowed flesh, nor the vertebrae, nor even the earthly throngs, which the planets in the first row recognized by their overcoats, but the feelings. One died by the heart. Confronted with this slide toward nothingness, one was overcome with anguish as if being forced to abandon the beloved forever. And nothing remained to men of their machines, their telegraphs, their gears, their pressure gauges, their films, their politics. Nothing remained to them of what constituted illusion, of what we had all taken for power, for strength. We had only our love on our backs and before our eyes. And we finally learned that love was all that had given us a little sparkle, a little backbone, a little durability.

A singular temperature was dropping on us from the dull skies, initialed by drifting trees hurrying along toward other laws. A bluish temperature which made some cover themselves with furs or newspapers, others wander naked... The dogs stuck out their tongues, but the fish burst like frozen pouches, stiffening in the river beds which emptied like baths, the water running out through gaps toward the Dark Larynx. The door handles were covered with ice, while the fruits were crawling with wasps and, reduced to pulp, fell onto the scaly, flaking sidewalks. The climates, the winds, and the smells were blended together like the colors on a palette. Asparagus could be seen sprouting in bookstore windows. Lemon trees flowered in a pile of streetcars. Mollusks were found where there had been calves' heads, or emeralds, or umbrellas. Nearly all the building façades were still standing, but they were painted with flames or covered with snails, cinders, human eyes. It seemed that ink had run from the upper floors toward the cellars, that the liquid of the sky had fallen down in a form completely different from rain on the remnants of the world in distress. There were rose-colored pools, the pure rose of a young girl in puberty, green ponds, the handsome green of billiard felt, that slept in the provinces. With the speed of a bus, a river of glue came and went in Paris, carrying along chisels, cigarettes, gaping pianos which revealed gazelle skeletons to onlookers. One knew nothing. One heard nothing. The racket was so powerful and so new that it achieved the mysterious immensity of silence. Sometimes a man approached us and hissed:

"Is that you?"

"Yes, it's me," one would respond.

"My God! Tonight the bus conductors have been changed into Easter eggs. Tomorrow, it will be the chiropodists' turn, next come the mailmen, the opticians, the leather workers, the scholars, the noblemen, the ziblostresses, the cacoterms, the pantaguriches, and the bottonglozers..."

"But there won't be any more next days, any more nights, any more days, any more rhythms..."

"That's true, there won't be any more anything... Good-bye. All the same, come tomorrow, Monsieur, we will try to find our neighborhoods again, we will dine together..."

"You are from Paris, you, too?"

"No, I am from Toul... but I've just seen the streets of Toul, there, behind that enormous horse.... I have seen them, as one sees children in the arms of their mothers in Italian paintings. Good-bye, my handsome blonde.... Luterdu pourquil aholoay!..."

And the man abruptly disappeared. He exploded right under one's nose like a lightbulb, and nothing remained of him but a short and comical bit of smoke like that which, at another time, on the stage at the Amboise or Charleville theater, would have signaled the disappearance of Mephistopheles.[1]

The trains arriving in the stations no longer stopped, but ploughed into the lamp room, burst through the façade, killed the newspaper

---

1. Léon-Paul Fargue, "Danse Mabraque," in *Mesure*, no. 2 (April 15, 1939).

vendor on the square, an old woman out of age, bogged down in quick open-faced sandwiches, grazed boulevard Denain, rue de Strasbourg, rue de Rennes, rue du Havre, Königstrasse, cut down passersby, ran off with twenty terraces, went down on the aperitifs, carried off the meeting places on the steps and the lanterns, as well as the heaviest cars, the margin of booksellers, Crainquebilles without curtains, beauty aid boutiques full of nude feet, the merry chains of women workers overturned as on wooden horses, white eyes, the hand over the heart, a large candelabra of bronze lying crooked, all weeping and stinking of bad breath, and all that, passing under the Arc de Triomphe, raking our leaders over the coals, extinguishing the flame, booting President Ricouenne and the ambassador of Wynandie, barreling into Foch and Pétain, rolling on to meet the sea! Then, the neighborhoods reflected each other moving, slowly, then more quickly, with a gymnastic stride, in a thunderous dust. One began to see the stripes accelerating in the same way in order to whitewash, fluid agent! The earth topples in a tempest of rays! People slide from the houses cracked open, already humming with flames, as the rind of a cut fruit, as a concierge one bothers! They were turned out like a rabbit skin, showing the fresh bone of their intimate frame, their organs just uncovered, red and green luggage, their folding chairs, their fibroids, their books, their knowledge, blooming with dripping branchiae, decked out with streamers of black blood which followed the course of the terrible wind. I only had time to give a kick, to gain a height of a good hundred thousand and to skim over the top of this riffraff! That was when I spied among the Elohim a huge divine head, the head of an old master, emerge from some sort of large clinic. He regarded things with his servoradiant monocle.[2]

⤙

He who remains there, stable, amid the catastrophes, impassive before the gusts and squalls of pain, is the one who has in his possession the joint principles of infinite creation and eternal destruction. Piercing through the opacity of space, Lautréamont sees him. He regards him face-to-face, now that the gold and jewels that Saint John described have disappeared from the throne. What remains is the blood, the sweat, the excrement by which the life of man begins and in which it ends. Above the flames, the torrents, and the violent storms, this cruel God's great nightmare takes shape.

2. Léon-Paul Fargue, *Vulturne* (N.R.F.).

Facing God

Comte de Lautréamont

Thus, one day, fatigued from my pursuit on foot of the steep path of this earthly journey, and wending my way, staggering along like a drunkard through life's dark catacombs, I slowly raised my splenetic eyes, ringed with pale blue circles, toward the concavity of the firmament, and I, who was yet so young, dared to penetrate the mysteries of heaven. I lifted my bewildered eyelids higher, and yet even higher, until I saw a throne fashioned from human excrement and gold, on which was sitting, with an idiot pride and a body shrouded in unwashed hospital sheets, he who calls himself the Creator! He was holding the rotting body of a dead man in his hand, carrying it in turn from his eyes to his nose, then from his nose to his mouth; once at his mouth it can be guessed what he did with it. His feet were immersed in a vast sea of boiling blood, on the surface of which two or three cautious heads would emerge all at once like tapeworms in the contents of a chamber pot, and equally as suddenly submerge again with the speed of an arrow. A well-aimed kick on the bone of the nose was the usual reward for breaking the rules occasioned by the need to breathe in another environment; for, after all, these men were not fish! Though at most amphibious they were swimming underwater in this foul liquid!...until, the Creator, finding his hands empty, would seize another diver by the neck, with the first two claws of his foot, as if with pincers, and lift him from the reddish sludge—exquisite sauce!—into the air. This one would be treated in the same manner as the one before him. First he devoured the head, then the arms and legs, and, lastly, the trunk, until there was nothing left; for he crunched the bones. And so it goes for all the other hours of his eternity. At times he would shout: "I made you, so I can do whatever I like to you. You have done nothing to me, I won't deny it. It is for my own pleasure that I make you suffer." And he would go on with his cruel repast, moving his lower jaw which in turn moved his brain-spattered beard. Oh reader, doesn't this last detail make your own mouth water? Couldn't anyone who so desired eat brains just like this, just as good and absolutely fresh, just caught a quarter of an hour previously in a fish pond? Struck dumb, my limbs paralyzed, I contemplated this sight for some time. Three times I almost keeled over, like a man in the throes of an emotion too intense for him; three times I succeeded in staying on my feet. Not a fiber of my body was still; I shivered like lava inside a volcano....

Oh! when you hear the avalanche of snow falling from the frozen peak; the lioness moaning in the arid desert of the disappearance of her cubs; the condemned man howling in prison on the eve of going to the guillotine; and the ferocious octopus recounting to the waves of the sea its triumphs over swimmers and the shipwrecked, then you must admit; are not these majestic voices more beautiful than the sniggering of men?[3]

Before you become indignant over the somber tones that darken this account, before protesting its partiality, literary excesses, and pessimism, comfortable reader, consider the mutilated children, the tortured flesh, the towns disemboweled in the name of virtue and civilization. Listen to the mounting cries of suffering. Those of the twelfth-century weavers reach our ears still:

The Song of the Shirt
Chrétien de Troyes

We ever weave our silken cloth
But are not better dressed,
We always will be poor and bare
And thirst and hunger know;
Never will we earn enough
To know of better meals.
For bread we only have to eat
The morning little, supper less;
Our handiwork will bring us but
A pittance only to survive,
And with that we can never hope
To have sufficient meat and clothes;
With what we earn for our long week
We do not make enough.
Well, you should all know, all of you,
That none of us can earn enough
To hope to flee our misery,
But those who earn, from our hard work,

3. Comte de Lautréamont [Isidore Ducasse], *Les Chants de Maldoror*, trans. Jon Graham. The translated passage is from song II.

Are those for whom we toil
From dawn of day, till late at night,
To earn our meager spoils.
They threaten us to beat our limbs,
Whenever we repose,
So we dare not repose.[4]

The cries of modern wage earners no longer need to rely on help from poets. They come from the mouths of workers themselves. Rising from the hell of American factories, more dismal than Dante's, come the verses of Jim Waters:[5]

Suddenly, as if for an attack,
The wail of the factory whistle fills the air...
A mad rush for the doors...
    And a thousand workers
    are vomited into the streets:
Men, women, children,
They return home after work.
Their tired bodies stagger along
Heavily and sink
Into the darkness of the night.

From Marie L. de Welch, "The Iron Workers":

They will no longer have flesh or blood.
Iron is in their hard eyes and their brazen hands.
Iron sputters in their tough hearts,
Iron invades their guts.
Their strength, their thoughts, their lives change
    Into iron, strong and cold,
    Neither flesh nor blood.

From enslaved humanity, as from a cavern full of blood and tears, the cries of hatred ring out.

---

4. Chrétien de Troyes, *The Song of the Shirt* (end of the twelfth century), trans. Kirk McElhearn.

5. These three fragments of poems come from *Poems of American Workers*, eds. N. Guterman and P. Morhange (France: Edition Les Revues).

From Martin Russak, "A Day of Rage":

Let lightning strike
The roofs of this city,
Let Garret Rock
Fall on the factories below.
Let the demon of thunder respond
To the factory whistle.
Let the sun forget to pass
Over the city of silk for good.

Let it be obliterated, this world of pain. Let the fires of the earth and the waters of the oceans come together into one ultimate convulsion to put an end to this creation capable only of engendering woe. And all humans can hope for is to be buried, rather than to continue suffering. Humans pray for the saving deluge, the angel of extermination. And if the processes of earth seem too permanently fixed in their equilibrium and will not explode, annihilating humankind, if the universe doesn't agree to disappear, at least the current state of things must be destroyed. If the heavens don't accept the responsibility of purifying the earth by fire and water, if they remain deaf to the petitions for death as they have to the thousand-year-old prayers for peace, humans, united in revolt, must bring on the deluge themselves. To entirely sweep away a past of injustice and oppression, to wash to their very cores the rocks soiled by age-old disgraces. The slave knows that nothing can be salvaged from the master's ancient home. The smallest objects there are cursed, and the slave, in turn, feels debased by coming into contact with them.

The authentic poet, also a slave, unable to bear the universal horror, incapable of compromise, knows how deep the gulf is. He knows the distance that separates the real life within him from the social condition of the already fetid dead assembled together in their gangrenous foolishness. And his poetic message prophesies necessary destruction. But such a great goodness remains in humans that it softens him and makes him fear doing injustice. He is afraid that the power of his rage has altered his judgment. At the moment of exerting violence, he suddenly hesitates and says to himself that perhaps a few just souls are living in the condemned world. This fear already affected Abraham. Fleeing from the corruption of Egypt, he led his meager following through the deserts, through hardships, toward holy adventure. Coming head-on into the iniquity of Sodom and Gomorrah, he was warned of imminent destruction, and he tried to stop the exterminating arm, which had grown impatient with the accumulated crimes. Abraham says to the angel of the Lord: "Would you make the just perish with the guilty? Perhaps there are fifty just souls in the city; would you make them perish also? Would you not pardon this city because of them?" And the angel agreed to put off the execution, but fifty just souls were not found, not forty, not twenty, not ten. A single person left, and the city was destroyed.

Today, the slave, fooled a thousand times by the appearance of virtue, by false promises, having searched in vain for a smile among the faces, knows that nothing can be saved. He realizes that the time has come. And then the floodgates are opened.

But why is it that even before everything is destroyed, doubts concerning the days ahead assail him? Is man so sick that he can never be completely hopeful?

After the Deluge

A. Rimbaud

As soon as the idea of the Deluge subsided,
A hare stopped in the clover and swaying bell-flowers, and through the
*   spider's web said its prayer to the rainbow.*
Oh! the precious stones that concealed themselves—and the flowers
*   that already looked up.*
In the filthy main street stalls were set up and boats were hauled down
*   toward the sea, piled high as in old engravings.*
Beavers built. The "mazagrans"[6] were smoking in seedy cafés.
In the large house whose windows still dripped, children in mourning
*   looked at the marvelous pictures.*
A door slammed; and in the village square the small child spun his
*   arms around, understood by weather vanes and steeple cocks all*
*   over, under the beating rain.*
Madame —— installed a piano in the Alps. Mass and first commun-
*   ions were celebrated at the hundred thousand altars of the cathedral.*
The caravans departed. And the Hotel Splendide was built in the
*   chaos of ice and polar night.*
Since that time the moon has heard jackals yelping in deserts of thyme,

---

6. Glazed earthenware cups for drinking coffee.

*and eclogues in wooden shoes growling in the orchard. Then, in
the budding violet forest, Eucharis told me it was spring.*
*Gush forth, pond—Foam, flow over the bridge and over the woods—
black drapes and organs, lightning and thunder, rise and roll
on—waters and sorrows, climb and bring back the deluges.*
*For since they have been dissipated—oh! the precious stones that are
buried and the opened flowers!—it's a bore! And the Queen, the
Sorceress who lights her coal in the earthen pot will never wish to
tell us what she knows and what we don't know.*[7]

---

7. Arthur Rimbaud, *Les Illuminations,* prose poems.

CROSSING THROUGH
THE ELEMENTS

The Enchanted Island: Crossing Through the Water

Reader, I sense your growing indignation. You don't think it's right that, in the name of the marvelous, you are led to these dark land-scapes where you pass your difficult days. No matter how I warned you at the outset of our journey, you still hoped to escape the daily fear, to remain half asleep for a few hours in an imaginary world rich with roses and precious stones, perfume and furs, a world inhabited by beau-tiful slaves responsive to your every sensual desire. Didn't I tell you that we would not accept the arbitrary separation between reality and dream, and that, under no conditions, would we agree to a voyage with some inaccessible paradise as its goal? Going from the round room of the castle to the human heart, the landscape that our long route passes through certainly isn't beautiful, but it is real. The traveler is subjected to those opposing movements that animate all of nature. Sometimes he hopes to create, engender, build. He wants to establish his perma-nence, ensure his power. Sometimes he cries out for destruction. He can't imagine going on without burning up the whole dead past. These contradictory movements of the mind do not even alternate like the ebb and flow of waves. They are simultaneous and indissoluble.

The way of the marvelous goes from the depths of the abyss to sheer peaks. Along it, the traveler experiences anguish; her step falters. Some-times she must overcome obstacles that hostile elements present to her.

Sometimes she must undergo metamorphosis, abandon the ordinary comforts of the thinking conscience. This dangerous route leads to the conquest of knowledge and love, but are those the true and ultimate ends?

Even though the fact of living assumes the victory of hope over despair in us, despair is not diminished by this. The effort to be, which corresponds to a forward, progressive movement, triggers an opposite interior movement, which takes on all the weight of inertia.

As we advance, a sentimental regression turns us toward the past. This longing for birth, for the prenatal state, translates into the idea that in the beginning, perfection reigned. From this golden age, this original Eden, there remains some memory of an island paradise.

Atlantis
Plato

Before the modification of the earth's surface by the deluge, Plato recounts, as he was told by Socrates, who in turn had learned it from Solon and the priests of Egypt, it was possible to cross the Atlantic Ocean. Beyond the Pillars of Hercules there was an isle that was larger than Libya and Asia put together. It was allotted to Neptune, when, after the creation, the gods drew lots to see what lands would be theirs. Toward the sea, but in the middle of the island, there was a plain, which is said to have been the most beautiful of all plains, and distinguished by the fertility of its soil. Near this plain, and again in the middle of it, at the distance of fifty stadia, there was a very low mountain. This was inhabited by one of those men who in the beginning sprang from the earth, and whose name was Evanor. This man living with a woman called Leucippe had by her Clites, who was his only daughter. But when the virgin arrived at maturity, and her mother and father were dead, Neptune being captivated by her beauty had connection with her, and enclosed the hill on which she dwelt with spiral streams of water; the sea and the land at the same time alternately forming about each other lesser and larger zones so that the hill was inaccessible to men.... Neptune adorned the island [by causing] two fountains of water to spring up from under the earth, one hot and the other cold; and likewise bestowed all various and sufficient aliment from the earth. There he engendered and raised five generations of male infant twins. Thus Atlas and his brothers were born and an entire race of great number charged with royal honors.

The isle provided an abundance of gold, and precious and useful metals. The forests contained an infinite variety of trees. All tame and wild animals lived there, together with a prodigious number of elephants. The finest fruits ripened there. Soon pools and canals were constructed for sea-going vessels, magnificent royal palaces, and temples; among these the most beautiful was built on the site where Neptune and Clites had engendered the race of ten kings. There, each year, the ten provinces would come to lay their offerings. This temple was built of silver with golden ledges, just as the god's statue was also made of gold. It was covered with ivory. A sacred woods surrounded it. At predetermined intervals the kings would come to the sanctuary to administer justice. Together they would sacrifice a bull and proceed to the aspersion of blood. They pledged their oaths then judged in a spirit of fairness, in accordance with the law of God. They were just, wise, and peaceful; they despised riches. Alas, this virtue was corrupted across the ages, and Atlantis, by orders of an angry Zeus, was destroyed.[1]

Although tradition maintains it, the fact of this destruction has always been in doubt. People have often thought that the island still remains, but that it exists beyond the limits of their ordinary navigational skills. In all epochs, sailors have talked about it. Sometimes they describe it as deserted, sometimes as inhabited by gods capable of taking on the widest variety of forms, monsters half-animal and half-human, sirens who disappear as the traveler approaches. Some sailors, who have come in contact with barbarian tribes because of wars or maritime commerce, claim that an enchantingly beautiful woman lives there who never ages and has magical powers. Despite their differences, these versions all testify to the hope that paradise is not lost, that it exists somewhere on the earth, and that to find it, all you need to do is look for it. This idea held no small attraction for those voyagers who attempted the first great explorations. The sixteenth-century writer, Tasso, in *Jerusalem Delivered* described one of these enchanted islands of love, locating it beyond the Pillars of Hercules. He opposed its pernicious charm to the Christian duty of the Holy Land. Three centuries later, Charles Robert Maturin alludes in *Melmoth* to a no less marvelous Indian island. This time, the island is no longer the site of forbidden

---

1. Plato, *Timaeus and Critias.*

desires but of the purity that civilization, in its brutal dealings there, has destroyed.

The Enchanted Island
C. R. Maturin

There is an island in the Indian Sea, not many leagues from the mouth of the Hoogly, which, from the peculiarity of its situation and internal circumstances, long remained unknown to Europeans, and unvisited by the natives of the contiguous islands, except on remarkable occasions. It is surrounded by shallows that render the approach of any vessel of weight impracticable, and fortified by rocks that threatened danger to the slight canoes of the natives, but it was rendered still more formidable by the terrors with which superstition had invested it. There was a tradition that the first temple to the black goddess Seeva had been erected there; and her hideous idol, with its collar of human skulls, forked tongues darting from its twenty serpent mouths, and seated on a matted coil of adders, had there first received the bloody homage of the mutilated limbs and immolated infants of her worshippers.

The temple had been overthrown, and the island half depopulated, by an earthquake, that agitated all the shores of India. It was rebuilt, however, by the zeal of the worshippers, who again began to re-visit the island, when a taufaun of fury unparalleled even in those fierce latitudes, burst over the devoted spot. The pagoda was burnt to ashes by the lightning; the inhabitants, their dwellings, and their plantations, swept away as with the besom of destruction, and not a trace of humanity, cultivation, or life remained on the desolate isle. The devotees consulted their imagination for the cause of these calamities; and, while seated under the shade of their cocoa-trees they told their long strings of colored beads, they ascribed it to the wrath of the goddess Seeva at the increasing popularity of the worship of Juggernaut. They asserted that her image had been seen ascending amid the blaze of lightning that consumed her shrine and blasted her worshippers as they clung to it for protection, and firmly believed she had withdrawn to some happier isle, where she might enjoy her feast of flesh, and draught of blood, unmolested by the worship of a rival deity. So the island remained desolate, and without inhabitant for years.

The crews of European vessels, assured by the natives that there was neither animal, or vegetable, or water, to be found on its surface, forbore a visit; and the Indian of other isles, as he passed it in his canoe, threw a glance of melancholy fear at its desolation, and flung something overboard to propitiate the wrath of Seeva.

The island, thus left to itself, became vigorously luxuriant, as some neglected children improved in health and strength, while pampered darlings died under excessive nurture. Flowers bloomed, and foliage thickened, without a hand to pluck, a step to trace, or a lip to taste them, when some fishermen (who had been driven by a strong current toward the isle, and worked with oar and sail in vain to avoid its dreaded shore), after making a thousand prayers to propitiate Seeva, were compelled to approach within an oar's length of it; and on their return in unexpected safety, reported they had heard sounds so exquisite, that some other goddess, milder than Seeva, must have fixed on that spot for her residence. The younger fishermen added to this account, that they had beheld a female figure of supernatural loveliness, glide and disappear amid the foliage which now luxuriantly overshadowed the rocks; and, in the spirit of Indian devotees, they hesitated not to call this delicious vision an incarnated emanation of Vishnu, in a lovelier form than ever he had appeared before—at least far beyond that which he assumed, when he made one of his avatars in the figure of a tiger.

The inhabitants of the islands, as superstitious as they were imaginative, deified the vision of the isles after their manner. The old devotees, while invoking her, stuck close to the bloody rites of Seeva and Haree, and uttered many a horrid vow over their beads, which they took care to render effectual by striking sharp reeds into their arms, and tingeing every bead with blood as they spoke. The young women rowed their light canoes as near as they dared to the haunted isle, making vows to Camdeo and sending their paper vessels, lit with wax, and filled with flowers, towards its coast, where they hoped their darling deity was about to fix his residence. The young men also, at least those who were in love and fond of music, rowed close to the island to solicit the god Krishnoo to sanctify it by his presence; and not knowing what to offer to the deity, they sung their wild airs standing high on the prow of the canoe, and at last threw a figure of wax, with a kind of lyre in its hand, towards the shore of the desolate isle.

Gradually the isle lost its bad character for terror; and in spite of some old devotees, who held their blood-colored beads, and talked of Seeva and Haree, and even held burning splinters of wood to their scorched hands, and stuck sharp pieces of iron, which they had purchased or stolen from the crews of European vessels, in the most fleshy and sensitive parts of their bodies—and, moreover, talked of suspending themselves from trees with the head downwards, till they were consumed by insects, or calcined by the sun, or rendered delirious by their position—in spite of all this—the girls offering their wreaths to Camdeo, and the youths invoking Krishnoo, till the devotees, in despair, vowed to visit this accursed island which had set everybody mad, and find out how the unknown deity was to be recognized and propitiated: and whether flowers, and fruits, and love-vows, and the beatings of young hearts, were to be substituted for the orthodox and legitimate offerings of nails grown into the hands till they appeared through their backs, and *setons* of ropes inserted into the sides, on which the religionist danced his dance of agony, till the ropes or his patience failed. In a word, they were determined to find out what this deity was, who demanded no suffering from her worshippers—and they fulfilled their resolution in a manner worthy of their purpose.

One hundred and forty beings, crippled by the austerities of their religion, unable to manage sail or oar, embarked in a canoe to reach what they called the accursed isle. The natives, intoxicated with the belief of their sanctity, stripped themselves naked, to push their boat through the surf, and then making their *salaams*, implored them to use oars at least. The devotees, all too intent on their beads, and too well satisfied of their importance in the eyes of their favorite deities, to admit a doubt of their safety, set off in triumph—and the consequence may be easily conjectured. The boat soon filled and sunk, and the crew perished without a single sigh of lamentation....

This circumstance, apparently so untoward, operated favorably on the popularity of the new worship. The old system lost ground every day. Hands, instead of being scorched over the fire, were employed only in gathering flowers. The female votarists at last began to imitate some of "those sounds and sweet airs" that every breeze seemed to waft to their ears, with increasing strength of melody, as they floated in their canoes round this isle of enchantment.[2]

Even though the entire surface of the earth has been explored, one hope survives: to rediscover a place like the ancient home of Shiva, a place once inhabited and then abandoned to natural forces. As I've sailed France's rivers and along her coasts, I've felt the mysterious charm of islands, even those well known to us all. Landing on them, one rushes

---

2. Charles Robert Maturin (1782–1825), *Melmoth.*

forward to conquer them. Delicious exploration, the feeling of power that comes with such a conquest, the old proprietary sense surfacing again. To be the first, as if at the dawn of humanity. And if a few dolmens or a few buildings are hidden under the high grasses, to be the first to return after centuries of neglect. I am not thinking of the large inhabited islands like Sein, Ouessant, or Porquerolles, where community life is organized, no matter how different their atmospheres are from the mainland's. With much greater reason, I eliminate Corsica, Ireland, and Sicily, despite the singular wealth of marvelous legends in such places. I am speaking of that isolated little islet surrounded by a narrow waterway. This tiny separation is enough to cause the traveler real trouble, to make sure that his joy is mixed with a vague sense of fear. The new Robinson, suddenly disengaged from civilization, feels himself free from those ancient obligations society imposes. He rediscovers that fresh new sensibility humans have when they first make contact with the world, before there is a name, price, and useful function attached to everything. The barrier of water is the material form the magic circle takes, within which a person's individual power is increased tenfold. Thanks to his increased freedom, the person makes actual contact with living beings and things. They become part of his desire. He sees to it that they participate in his dream's development. He is tempted to regard them as fugitive images ready to metamorphose at any moment. Quivering with anticipation, the explorer nervously waits to be conducted on the great adventure he hopes is waiting for him among the hidden spirits.

If castles surrounded by deep moats provoke similar reactions in us, it is because they possess the same islandlike qualities and, in the same way, the power of magic circles. As soon as the drawbridge, that fragile link to humanity, goes up, a closed and marvelous universe is created. Crossing water gives the one who succeeds the feeling that he has passed through a trial. It is unquestionably the first and the easiest of all those he will encounter during his perilous journey. Those who wish to enter the magic circle that defines a mystical community must submit to ceremonial purification. For those wishing to change the course of their lives, to abandon the past, a liquid barrier must intervene to give the significance of birth to the new present. Such was the necessity presented to Jérôme Bardini, a dissatisfied petit bourgeois, when he wished to give up his gloomy bureaucratic existence to achieve personal freedom.

Jérôme Bardini's Test of Freedom

J. Giraudoux

Without his hat, he was obliged to respond with smiles or gestures to
the grocers, the notary, the state police who greeted him for the last
time, and he regretted having to take leave in so personal, really too
personal, a way to these phantoms. After six kilometers through the
village and then the countryside, he reached the new curve where the
Seine parallels the curve of the Concord nearly to its source. He un-
dressed in the meadow he'd already picked out, left his clothes on the
bank, as he had indicated he would in the letter to his wife, so she
could choose to pass him off for missing or for dead as she saw fit, and
dove in. He swam with delight. It wouldn't be so bad, this business of
man becoming fish. All that had remained on him of Renée's perfume
had already dissipated in Paris, replaced by the smell from the heart of
the Saint-Germain-la-Feuille plateaus. He amused himself by going
against the current. It was pleasant to enact his first gestures again in a
new element. He amused himself by giving in to it, by diving, and by
playing with death, a way of disappearing worth cultivating, perhaps.
He had to get out of the water to get from his wallet the little water-
proof sack with the two thousand dollars that he'd brought, dollars
saved, one by one, over three years, as if for a holiday gift, the gift of a
second life.

Spread out, his clothes took on his shape from a distance. He was
not too upset by his remains, his false cadaver. He congratulated himself for being done with those two buttons on a chain, a present from
Fontranges, with that same old tie pin from Bellita. The jacket and
trousers, which would no longer have the being they'd been cut for
giving them shape each day, had gone limp for good. There lay the first
despair, the first depravity that his departure would cause. He touched
the fabric, he touched his buttonholes with a little pity, as if he were
touching the skin and mouth of the dead Jérôme. He looked at the
spots that were a bit worn, those that his first life had leaned a bit too
hard against. He smoothed his elbow, so shiny, on which he had often
supported this head that had now escaped.

But one doesn't embrace one's headless cadaver. He dove in again,
the sack between his teeth. He reached the other shore, a castaway who
jumps from his raft to gain the island. In one of those hollow willows
where vacationing Parisians think vagabonds and owls live, he found
the clothes hidden there eight days ago and the little hard leather suit-

case with which Wilson walked around Paris. He dressed. Despite himself, he had taken on the air of an American in crossing the Seine, in believing that it was the ocean.... Really, it is only in America that one can walk around incognito among people, and in art, music—and even, he'd noticed, among trees.... Why weren't there blossoms? Why wasn't it springtime? He had loved Renée's flowers, Fontrange's flowers? He tasted their fruits, fruits still green, fruits already bitter.

Then came the second metamorphosis. The animals arrived, the most gentle animals, the cows, an ass, the female animals that whispered in the nursery, whispered over the new Bardini, an hour old. The cow he caressed, the ass whose muzzle he kissed, had no idea that she was the only creature in the world he loved, the first animal formed for him in this new creation. The ideas that had come to Adam occurred to him: to straddle the cow, chat with the ass. A she-goat came also, all alone, newly created, rearing up and flirting around Bardini like an extra from a variety show let out at just the right moment by the stage manager. One sensed that waiting in the wings, for the serious act, were bulls, donkeys, billy goats. Animals each of whom offered a new occupation, a new life, a particular gift of freedom: cowherd, servant, laborer, dairyman, he could be any of these. Carter, horseman, an escapade of careers that led him to the military, to war, supreme freedom.... Moreover, that's why those who believe themselves to be the most free join the foreign legion.... But already, in that kiss with the ground that takes up three quarters of their day, the beasts grazed, disdainful of Bardini.

He stretched out, cut a baguette, and unconsciously let this flash of childhood go, to be replaced with a flash of freedom. He made a whistle out of bark, thought of carving his initials into it, remembered that he no longer had any, asked himself which ones he would choose in the future, what first name would be his, and that visceral uncertainty that he had felt regarding jobs he suddenly felt again regarding names, regarding countries. No! Certainly not! He was not giving up a happy home, a pretty wife, a wealthy district, to keep the attributes and the defects of the French, to call himself "Durand" or "Berthon," to be a specimen of ancient wisdom, defiance, greed, and all the other characteristics of his original nationality. Finally! He could be from whatever country he pleased, from the countries where one is loyal, confident, young, extravagant, which have Vancouver or Christiania for their capitals, which had always represented travel for him when he thought of travel and—as yet he had never completed the phrase with this second word—travel and freedom. The rest he couldn't care less about, he made up this nation all by himself....

A plane passed overhead. He smiled at this symbol of freedom which went from the Romilly camp to the Langres camp on a cord of invisible iron. He was one of the only men who did not exercise their freedom in iron cages, like aviators, like inventors.... A kingfisher flew past.... He smiled, thinking of its invariable itinerary, of its bird soul reappearing as a watch. He recalled having sung as a school child a hymn to freedom in which freedom was Switzerland. What a joke, the Swiss, whose footsteps habit has engraved into the sandstone of the Alps, whose wooden houses sit on the mountain peaks like arcs where Swiss Noahs would continue to live, free, certainly, from Gessler, but with so little freedom from winter, Protestantism, the altitude!

He stood up, stretching himself again. Was he going to take advantage of the freedom that opened before him or sit here, sick with liberty? The sun, still high in the sky, cast a thinner, less attractive shadow than usual. The sun, which no longer marked the time for him, which spun in neutral for a being without birth and without death. Never had he experienced the approaching dusk in this way, without duties or responsibilities. As long as all that he had dismissed from his life didn't reappear in his sleep, seeking vengeance on exactly that part of his day that, in the past, he had almost been able to keep free, thanks to his dreams! He shuddered at the thought of dreaming about the child, the bills, the opened bottle. Suddenly he saw the night as a mirror of the past... But someone walked up behind him. The first human he had encountered since his disappearance stopped a few meters away and stared at him: a woman.[3]

Poor Bardini, I have known your joy and your troubles. Like you, I have stored up a poor treasure piece by piece over the long months. I've cut back on everyday expenses without letting anyone notice. This prisoner's nest egg, I remember hiding it in a bottle. Imperturbable, I continued to play my social roles, to make the daily efforts my family responsibilities required of me. Like you, I waited patiently for the hour when departure would be possible. I know what it was like for you to arrive on liberty's banks, to abandon your old clothes, the proper uniform of the house of the dead. Perhaps you invested too much hope in

---

3. Jean Giraudoux, *Aventures de Jérôme Bardini* (Emile Paul Edition).

the saving virtues of the crossing itself? I'm afraid that, carried along by the violence of your desire to escape, you may have rushed into this too quickly, bringing with you the ancient fear in your heart and all the weight of your poor conscience.[4] Following these naïve experiences, I have since decided to remain on the river itself, leaving me without that alternative voyage out of life into death. Each time, the bank's landscape has changed, the stakes are different, and more and more serious problems have evoked my anxiety anew. And I see people passing by. There aren't many who try to escape into death's domain; most quit life and hurry to annihilate themselves in a long, easy repose. A few others present themselves before the dismal realm to rescue a lost love, to incite revolt there, or to take the hidden secret by surprise.

Thus, one day along comes Gilgamesh, the king of Uruk in Mesopotamia. The son of the goddess Aruru, Gilgamesh remembered having made the voyage to the country of cedars with his brutal companion, Enkidu. There they had fought the cruel giant, Humbaba. Marveling at these feats, the powerful Ishtar fell in love with him, but the hero rejected her erotic propositions. Furious at being scorned like that, the goddess plotted her vengeance. She killed Enkidu. Gilgamesh then embarked upon his great adventure to rescue his friend. He crossed the sea, and then the black river in order to interrogate Utnapishtim, the only man who had survived the Babylonian flood, and so knew the secret of such things.

The Voyage of Gilgamesh
(MESOPOTAMIAN POEM)

"Now which of the gods will let you enter the assembly so that you find the life you seek? Come! Don't sleep for six days and seven nights!"

Even as he sat down upon his haunches, sleep, like a hurricane, blew over him.

---

4. While you wandered at the whim of a fantasy that made you zigzag across the route of the marvelous without being able to follow it courageously, your abandoned clothes came back to life. The little functionary that you were triumphed over the poetic hope that led you for an instant to the banks of freedom. He renounced his failings and took to the ordinary paths of servitude once and for all. He haunted the embassies, the ministries, making himself an auxiliary of the oppression. The prisoner who had escaped for a moment found his place again and became a prison guard.

Utnapishtim said to her who was his wife: "Look at this mighty hero who desires a life! Sleep, like a hurricane, blew over him!"

His wife said to him who was Utnapishtim the remote: "Touch him so this man will wake with a start! By the road he has come he will return in good health. By the great gate by which he has entered he will return to his land!"

Utnapishtim says to her who is his wife: "Humanity is trouble and trouble it will cause you. Come! Bake him bread and place them by his bed, and the days he sleeps you shall mark upon the wall:

"His first loaf is dried out,

"The second is spread out, the third is moist,

"The fourth, his toast, turned white,

"The fifth became old,

"The sixth is ripe,

"The seventh!..." Suddenly he touched the man who woke with a start!

Gilgamesh said to him who was Utnapishtim the remote: "I found myself unmoving, a sleep has been set upon me! Suddenly you touched me and you awakened me!"

Utnapishtim said to him who was Gilgamesh: "Gilgamesh, count your loaves!...so that it may be known to you!

"Your first loaf is dried out,

"The second is spread out, the third is moist,

"The fourth, your toast, turned white,

"The fifth became old,

"The sixth is ripe,

"The seventh... Suddenly, I have touched you and you reawoke with a start!"

Gilgamesh said to him who was Utnapishtim the remote: "What can I do, Utnapishtim? Where will I go? I whom the... a ravisher has seized, in my bedroom, there Death sits!"

Utnapishtim says to him who is Urshanabi the Boatman: "Urshanabi, you who the...is delighted with you, may the crossing bear you away! To him who comes and goes upon the shore, that shore shall be denied! That man before you, whom you have brought here, he whose body is covered by a filthy garment, and he on whom skins have destroyed the beauty of his flesh, take him, Urshanabi, and lead him to the wash-room, and have him wash his filthy garment in the water until it is clean! Let his skins be thrown aside and let the sea carry them off so that his beautiful body can be looked at with desire! Let the turban be restored to his head and clothe him in a robe, a garment of decency, so that he may enter his city and that he may make his way upon his road. The garment will not age but remain ever new!"

Urshanabi took him and brought him to the washroom and washed his filthy garment until it was clean. He hurled off his skins and the sea carried them away, his beautiful body was looked at with desire. The turban was replaced upon his head and he was reclad in a robe, a garment of decency, so he could enter his city, and continue upon his road. The robe will not age but remain ever new! Gilgamesh and Urshanabi boarded the boat, they set it upon the waves and they sailed away!

Then his wife said to him who was Utnapishtim, the remote: "Gilgamesh came, he exhausted himself, he has suffered, what will you give him to return to his land?"

And he who was Gilgamesh lifted pole, and brought the boat closer to shore. Utnapishtim said to him who was Gilgamesh: "Gilgamesh you came here, you exhausted yourself and you suffered, what can I give you to return to your country? I will reveal, Gilgamesh, a secret word, a word of mystery; I will tell you: this plant like a thorn... its prickle like a bramble will pierce your hand, if your hands touch this plant you will attain everlasting life."

On hearing that, Gilgamesh opened the reservoir... he bound heavy stones to himself... they threw him into the ocean... he took the plant and it pierced his hand, he loosed the heavy stones... next he placed it at his side.

Gilgamesh said to him who was Urshanabi the Boatman: "Urshanabi this is a plant of renown, by virtue of which man obtains his life's breath. I will carry it to Erech of the paddocks and I will have them eat it..., I will share the plant! Its name is 'the old man become young': I will eat it and I will return to what I was as a youth!"

After twenty double hours they made the offering to the dead, after thirty double hours they made the lamentation; then Gilgamesh saw a well of cold water. He descended into it and washed himself with the water. A serpent smelled the aroma of the plant, ...it slithered over and carried it away; on leaving, he uttered something shameful.

Then Gilgamesh sat down and wept, the tears flowed down his cheeks and to Urshanabi the Boatman he said: "For whom, O Urshanabi, did I work my arms into exhaustion? For whom have I consumed my heart's blood? I have not done a good deed for myself; it is the lions of the ground for whom I have done this good deed! Now, at twenty double hours, the plant is tossing on the waves. When I opened the reservoir and bore off its property I saw the miracle that was sent as a sign to me. I will head for land and I will leave the boat on the shore!"

After twenty double hours they made the offering to the dead, after thirty double hours they made their lamentation. They made their way to Erech of the paddocks.

Gilgamesh said to him who was Urshanabi the Boatman: "Climb up, Urshanabi, on to the walls of Erech and walk about! Inspect the embankment and the masonry, if its masonry is not added on, and if the seven sages didn't set its foundation. One sar is city, one sar is gardens, one sar that is what has been reclaimed from the debris of the temple of Ishtar. Three sars and the debris of Erech I will amass."[5]

As to the voyage in which the water took the hero back in, the water has kept that mysterious memory to itself. When you walk alone along the banks of a calm lake already misting over as evening falls, you can sometimes hear distant cries, a few vague murmurs. Taken by surprise, the dreamer suddenly returns to himself. He sees nothing, he reassures himself, believing it to be a bird or a snake. But isn't it rather a water sprite who, after stealing the plant of life during the day, returns at sunset to bury its treasure in the palace of algae?

At Dream Level

B. Péret

I followed the lakeshore admiring the luxurious vegetation of smoke blossoming with agates and women's long tresses, of gilded corals, and of clear eyes with long eyelashes, when detouring around a bush of crystal hawthorn, I saw in a field as transparent as the water of a trout-filled stream a little girl running up to the edge of the lake in search of her fairy.

"Fairy where are you? This is definitely the place you gave me to meet you. I am looking for you everywhere: under the ferns and mushrooms, in the calyx of the snapdragons, and in the empty nests, but I don't see you."

From the other side of the lake a loud, clear laugh sounded in response.

---

5. *Legend of Gilgamesh*, in P. Dhorme's translations of Assyrian and Babylonian religious texts, trans. Jon Graham.

"I am not a fish that you can seek me leaning on the water. Don't you see me seated on my throne of roses. Drink the water of the lake and you will be able to rejoin me, but do it quickly, because the dragon is already opening his large mouth above my head. Come quick and ask in my ear for what you desire while there is still time."

I stole away on tiptoe so as not to disturb the dialogue between the last little girl and the last fairy and, after a long hike through the half-light of the undergrowth, I emerged again on the shores of the black lake. But the landscape was transformed. There were no more sparkling fields and music box bushes; a catastrophe had passed through. Pointed rocks reached toward the sky surrounded by the haze of the dawning evening. On one of them a lion growled threateningly.

I fled pursued by the lion and had just enough time to get away through the narrow opening of a grotto that yawned before me. However it wasn't quite a grotto because it was bathed in the strange light of an aquarium that allowed me to contemplate the frozen lace that adorned it at my leisure. Lost in my contemplation I didn't pay any attention to the ground where I was walking and on several occasions, stumbled against footprints, heel prints actually, as if someone had been walking under the ground upside down....

The nocturnal sky was visible through numerous openings. Even the foot of the moon could be seen that seemed about to set itself upon my head and crush me like a bug.

Instinctively I slipped between the mass of fallen, polished rocks that weighed it down and suddenly found myself face-to-face with an anteater-spider who, busy with its personal grooming and the shining of its hairs, didn't notice the bird of prey about to swoop down on it.[6]

Trial by Fire: The Descent into Hell

As soon as water, the first stage of creation, life's original medium, has been crossed, as soon as it no longer serves as the screen separating us from the mystery and the barrier blocking our efforts, our exploration runs into new obstacles, the result of other elements. The disquieting fire arises. Isn't this what holds the respect of hungry animals in the forest? Source of light and consciousness, isn't it humanity's supreme

---

6. Benjamin Péret, "Entre chien et loup," *Minotaure*, no. 8 (1936).

conquest and greatest fright? Behind the flames, we remember that the gods have spoken in burning bushes; Zeus has given his orders during thunderstorms. Fire has retained this same fascinating power for centuries. Also, whoever can pass through it without succumbing to it will have proven the constancy of his courage, the perfect purity of his being. Whoever will not be destroyed by the flames will no longer have to submit to the cycles of evolution. Who else could better deserve to be called hero? Siegfried, the legendary hope of the Nordic race, appears among the small number of the chosen.

Siegfried's Trial

Siegfried went to tell the two kings who had taken care of him in childhood that the moment had come for him to punish King Lynge and the other sons of Huding who had killed his father Sigemund. Hialprek and Alf entrusted an army to him and vessels to transport them to Lynge's country. A terrible battle ensued. Siegfried with his sword Gram struck both men and horses, his two arms were red with blood up to his shoulders. He split Lynge's helmet, head, and cuirass; he cut Lynge's brother in two. He killed all the sons of Huding and destroyed the largest part of the enemy army. When he returned home laden with loot and glory Regin told him:

"Now that you have avenged your father and the men of your race, you must go attack Fafnir as you have promised."

"I have not forgotten my promise," replied Siegfried; "I will keep it."

Siegfried and Regin climbed to the land called Gnitaheide. They found there the place that Fafnir left when he went to drink. Under the habitual path of the terrible beast Siegfried hollowed out a hole where he hid himself. The dragon left the cavern where he lived, sleeping on his gold. His mouth spit forth a poisonous breath. At the moment he passed over the hole, Siegfried plunged his blade into the dragon's heart. Fafnir floundered about with great movements of his head and tail. When he saw Siegfried emerging from the hole he said to him:

"Comrade! Comrade! What race are you who have reddened his gleaming sword in the heart of Fafnir?"

"I am called Siegfried," replied the hero.

"Why," asked Fafnir, "have you allowed yourself to be seduced into taking my life, young man with the shining eyes and son of a dreadful father?"

"Why?" Siegfried responded. "Because my mood impelled me to do so. When one has been a coward in his youth he mustn't wait for courage to come with age."

"Let me give you some advice," Fafnir continued. "Climb on your horse and go far away from this place. The shrill-sounding gold and the wild rings will occasion your ruin. Regin will betray you just as he betrayed me. Good-bye, vanquished by you, I exhale my last breath."

Regin had drawn away during the combat. When he returned he saw Siegfried who was drying the blood from his sword.

"Hail to you victorious hero," he said, "who has delivered us from Fafnir! Of all the men who tread the earth I declare you the most intrepid."

He then approached the dragon's body, drank blood from the wound, and pulled out the heart.

"Now," he said, "I am going to sleep. During that time, Siegfried, hold Fafnir's heart over the fire and cook it so that I can eat it when I awake."

Siegfried sat before the fire and set the heart in it to roast. After a while he touched it with his fingertip to see if it was cooked enough; he burned himself and quickly brought his finger to his mouth. Hardly had his lips tasted Fafnir's blood than he understood the language of the blue-tits chattering in the foliage.

"Regin is lying over there," said one, "planning a betrayal. He wants to rid himself of the young man sworn to him. This misery smith dreams of avenging his brother."

"May this adolescent shorten that old dotard by a head," said another. "May he send Regin to hell; then he alone will possess the gold on which Fafnir sprawled."

A third spoke, "The child will act wisely if he heeds our friendly advice. He should think of himself and leave Regin as fodder for the ravens."

Siegfried then spoke, "The destinies will not allow Regin to gather glory from putting me to death. The two brothers are going to pass on, one immediately after the other, from life into the hereafter."

And he cut off Regin's head. He ate a part of Fafnir's heart and drank some of his blood.

As his hands were covered in dragon's blood he perceived that they had become as hard as horn. He then took off his garments and bathed his entire body in the blood and his whole skin became as hard as horn as well, except for a spot between his shoulders on which a linden leaf had fallen.

Siegfried stretched out beneath a tree, the sweet notes of a nightingale struck his ears. The bird sang of a young Isenland beauty; he sang of the courage a hero would have to possess to get to her. Siegfried resolved to overcome all obstacles and rescue this king's daughter. The nightingale continued his song, which was soon taken up by all the birds in the forest; a concert of praise arose in honor of Brunhilde, imprisoned within the Castle of Segard that is surrounded by eternal flames. The beautiful damsel had been cast into a deep sleep by evil spells. Only the hero capable of traversing the flames could reawaken her.

Mounted on Grani, the horse of the smith Mymer, Siegfried soon reached the sea. There he found a vessel that bore him safely across the furious waves. The nightingale that had become his guide perched upon the top of the mast. The boat then landed on a desert land covered with rocks of sinister aspect. Grani promptly climbed the dunes; he started to buck and neigh when he felt the heat of the blaze that surrounded the castle with its ferocious flames that gave off a light similar to the most blinding rays of the sun.

The closer the impetuous charger approached the incandescent incendiary, the more the song of the nightingale echoed above Siegfried's head.

He said: "The flame surrounds the Castle of Segard on all sides and has done so for fifty years. Brunhilde is a captive but the hardy knight will breech the enchanted barrier of the fortress. Forward, Siegfried, go forward without fear; it is through your courage that you will win the young and beautiful princess."

The wind was silent around the castle; its lord's banner hung immobile from the highest tower. Sweat rolled in great drops down the face of the young hero, the heat was suffocating. There was nothing else to do: Siegfried aimed his charger into that sea of fire. The flames parted and gave him free passage. Having entered the castle, Siegfried remained stupefied; all around him was a deathly silence, and although it had been day for some time, everyone still slept. On the ramparts the guard slept with horn in hand, the dogs slept in the entrance to the lower courtyard, the pigeons and other birds slept peacefully on the portcullis. And when Siegfried started to walk, his footsteps echoed solitarily through the long corridors of the castle; no one came before him in welcome. In the kitchen the cook's assistant was seated, asleep by her skewer; over there snored a servant with chicken in hand ready to be plucked; the cook herself was resting by the chimney. The further Siegfried advanced the greater grew his astonishment for in every chamber he saw nought but men and women sleeping. Finally he entered into the salle d'honneur of the castle where he was stunned to see in a rich and elegant armchair a knight, in armor from head to toe, plunged into a deep sleep. The helmet that girded his head, his hauberk, his cuirass, and the shield hanging at his side were all of a remarkable workmanship, sparkling of gold and precious stones. Siegfried could not resist the desire to pull off the helmet of this elegant sleeper. He did so, and lo and behold a young girl with vermilion cheeks was there before him! Freed from its yellow breastplate her most beautiful, virginal figure appeared in the manner of a rose in full bloom that gleams in the middle of a green wreath. Immediately drawing his sword Siegfried used its edge to free the limbs of the young girl from her armor from which she emerged like a rose from its enclosing bud.

Siegfried, dazzled, felt a soft breath escape the virginal lips of the sleeper and could not prevent himself from placing a kiss upon them. Immediately the eyes of the sleeping beauty opened and looked upon her deliverer with love, like the evening star that sparkles through a veil of diaphanous clouds.

"You are Siegfried, son of Sigemund?" asked Brunhilde, for it was she that now stood before him.

"Who, if not you, could have had the strength to break these bonds imposed by fate and the courage to confront the scorching barrier of flame?"

Siegfried responded, "I am Siegfried, son of Sigemund, the dragonslayer, and henceforth you will be mine."

The proud princess Brunhilde rose out of her seat like a flower that rises on its stalk at the first rays of the sun.

Siegfried walked through the vast chambers of Segard with her and he found all the servants of the castle busy with their duties. Butlers, stewards, and chamberlains all approached their new lord with respect. The spit was now turning in the fireplace, the servants were all occupied in their respective tasks, the dogs were barking in the courtyard, and the horses were neighing in their stables. The watchman sounded reveille from the top of the tower and pigeons fluttered around the castle. All magic was overcome and banished, except that of love, by which Brunhilde was attached to the hero Siegfried.[7]

---

7. *Legend of the Niebelung,* after A. Ehrhard (Piazza).

The test of fire was very widespread among initiatory sects of India and Africa in the past, and is still sometimes used today. The legend of Siegfried, supported by much documentation, proves that it was equally important to Nordic initiations. In contrast, Christianity seems to have attributed a demonic value to fire. Christian thought is closely tied to air and water. Peopled with angels, air is what the Holy Ghost's dove travels through. Water is baptism. It is the surface the Messiah walks on, the lake along which miracles are performed.

Fire is regarded with a singular ambivalence. Origin of life, it is kept burning in the temple, considered the most perfect means of purification, and used to annihilate the heretic. But at the same time, it is seen as the symbol of passion and desire, and diabolical powers are attributed to it. Rest assured that a barrier of fire doesn't surround the marvelous castle. But it does encircle the domain of the dead. Flames shoot out of the menacing mouths of dragons protecting subterranean caves. The devil, god of depths, rules in a world of flame. It is in the midst of such incandescence that the prince of darkness materializes when he is magically invoked by Ambrosio, Lewis's monk.

Invocation of Satan

M. Lewis

She motioned that Ambrosio should be silent, and began the mysterious rites. She drew a circle round him, another round herself; and then, taking a small phial from the basket, poured a few drops upon the ground before her. She bent over the place, muttered some indistinct sentences, and immediately a pale sulphurous flame arose from the ground. It increased by degrees, and at length spread its waves over the whole surface, the circles alone excepted in which stood Matilda and the monk. It then ascended the huge columns of unhewn stone, glided along the roof, and formed the cavern into an immense chamber totally covered with blue trembling fire. It emitted no heat: on the contrary, the extreme chilliness of the place seemed to augment with every moment. Matilda continued her incantations; at intervals she took various articles from the basket, the nature and name of which were unknown to the friar: but among the few which he distinguished, he particularly observed three human fingers, and an agnus dei which she broke in pieces. She threw them all into the flames which burned before her, and they were instantly consumed.

The monk beheld her with anxious curiosity. Suddenly she uttered a loud and piercing shriek. She appeared to be seized with an access of delirium; she tore her hair, beat her bosom, used the most frantic gestures, and drawing the poniard from her girdle, plunged it into her left arm. The blood gushed out plentifully; and as she stood on the brink of the circle, she took care that it should fall on the outside. The flames retired from the spot on which the blood was pouring. A volume of dark clouds rose slowly from the ensanguined earth, and ascended gradually till it reached the vault of the cavern. At the same time a clap of thunder was heard, the echo pealed fearfully along the subterraneous passages, and the ground shook beneath the feet of the enchantress.

It was now that Ambrosio repented of his rashness. The solemn singularity of the charm had prepared him for something strange and horrible. He waited with fear for the spirit's appearance, whose coming was announced by thunder and earthquakes. He looked wildly around him, expecting that some dreadful apparition would meet his eyes, the sight of which would drive him mad. A cold shivering seized his body, and he sank upon one knee, unable to support himself.

"He comes!" exclaimed Matilda in a joyful accent.[8]

Again, it is a wall of fire, Tasso tells us, that obstructs the courageous warrior when he tries to enter the enchanted forest that lies near the walls of the besieged Jerusalem.

The Enchanted Forest Behind the Wall of Fire
T. Tasso

From Godfrey's camp a grove a little way
Amid the valleys deep grows out of sight
Thick with old trees whose horrid arms display
An ugly shade, like everlasting night;
There when the sun spreads forth his clearest ray,
Dim, thick, uncertain, gloomy seems the light;
As when in evening, day and darkness strive
Which should his foe from our horizon drive.

But when the sun his chair in seas doth steep,
Night, horror, darkness thick the place invade,

---

8. Matthew Lewis, *The Monk* (reprint, Grove Press).

Which veil the mortal eyes with blindness deep
And with sad terror make weak hearts afraid,
Thither no groom drives forth his tender sheep
to browse, or ease their faint in cooling shade,
Nor traveler nor pilgrim there to enter
So awful seems that forest old, dare venture.

United there the ghosts and goblins meet
To frolic with their mates in silent night,
With dragons' wings some cleave the welkin fleet,
Some nimbly run o'er hills and valleys light,
A wicked troop that with allurements sweet
Draws sinful man from what is good and right,
And there with hellish pomp their banquets brought
They solemnize, thus the vain Pagans thought.

(Drawing near these thick and shadow-haunted woods and their
savage and frightful paths both travelers and warriors would
shiver with fear and horror; they gave way to the invisible powers
that struck them. They fled and sought to make excuses for their
weakness and cowardice. But Alcaste the leader of the Swiss
stepped forth with a mocking smile and)

He shook his head, and smiling thus gan say,
"The hardiness have I that wood to fell,
And those proud trees low in the dust to lay
Wherein such grisly fiends and monsters dwell;
No roaring ghost my courage can dismay,
No shriek of birds, beast's roar, or dragon's yell;
But through and through that forest will I wend,
Although to deepest Hell the paths descend."

Thus boasted he, and leave to go desired,
And forward went with joyful cheer and will,
He viewed the wood and those thick shades admired,
He heard the wondrous noise and rumbling shrill;
Yet not one foot the audacious man retired,
He scorned the peril, pressing forward still,
Till on the forest's outmost marge he stepped,
A flaming fire from entrance there him kept.

The fire increased, and built a stately wall
Of burning coals, quick sparks, and embers hot,

And with bright flames the wood environed all,
That there no tree nor twist Alcaste got;
The higher stretched the flames seemed bulwarks tall,
Castles and turrets full of fiery shot,
With slings and engines strong of every sort—
What mortal wight durst scale so strange a fort?

Oh what strange monsters on the battlement
In loathsome forms stood to defend the place?
Their frowning looks upon the knight they bent,
And threatened death with shot, with sword and mace:
At last he fled, and though but slow he went,
As lions do whom jolly hunters chase;
Yet fled the man and with sad fear withdrew,
Though fear till then he never felt nor knew...

Godfredo called him, but he found delays
And causes why he should his cabin keep,
At length perforce he comes, but naught he says,
Or talks like those that babble in their sleep.
His shamefacedness to Godfrey plain betrays
His flight, so do his sighs and sadness deep:
Whereat amazed, "What chance is this?" quoth he.
"These witchcrafts strange or nature's wonders be.

"But if his courage any champion move
To try the hazard of this dreadful spring.
I give him leave the adventures great to prove,
Some news he may report us of this thing."
This said his lords attempt the charmèd grove,
Yet nothing back but fear and flight they bring,
For them inforced with trembling to retire,
The sight, the sound, the monsters and the fire.

This happed when woeful Tancred left his bed
To lay in marble cold his mistress dear,
the lively color from his cheek was fled,
his limbs were weak his helm or targe to bear;
Nathless when need to high attempts him led,
No labor would he shun, no danger fear,
His valor, boldness, heart and courage brave,
To his faint body strength and vigor gave.

To this exploit forth went the venturous knight,
fearless, yet heedful; silent, well-advised,
the terrors of that forest's dreadful sight,
Storms, earthquakes, thunders, cries, he all despised,
he fearèd nothing, yet a motion light,
That quickly vanished, in his heart arised
When lo, between him and the charmèd wood,
A fiery city high as heaven up stood.

The knight stepped back and took a sudden pause,
And to himself, "What helps these arms?" quoth he,
"If in this fire, or monster I headlong cast myself, what boots it me?
For common profit, or my country's cause,
To hazard life before me none should be:
But this exploit of no such weight I hold,
For it to lose a prince or champion bold..."

He bolted through, but neither warmth nor heat
He felt, nor sign of fire or scorching flame;
Yet wist he naught in his dismayed conceit,
If that were fire or no through which he came;
And in their stead the clouds black night did frame
And hideous storms and showers of hail and rain;
Yet storms and tempests vanished straight again.

Amazed but not afraid the champion good
Stood still, but when the tempest past he spied,
He entered boldly that forbidden wood,
And of the forest all the secrets eyed,
In all his walk no sprite or phantasm stood
That stopped his way or passage free denied,
Save that the growing trees so thick were set,
That oft his sight, and passage oft they let.

At length a fair and spacious green he spied,
Like calmest waters, plain like velvet, soft,
Wherein a cypress clad in summer's pride,
Pyramid-wise, lift up his tops aloft;
In whose bark upon the evenest side,
Strange characters he found and viewed them oft,
Like those which priests of Egypt erst instead
Of letters used, which none but they could read.

Mongst them he pickèd out these words at last,
Writ in the Syriac tongue, which well he could,
"Oh hardy knight, who through these woods hast passed:
Where Death his palace and his court doth hold!
Oh trouble not these souls in quiet placed,
Oh be not cruel as thy heart is bold,
Pardon these spirits deprived of heavenly light,
With spirits dead why should men living fight?"

This found he graven on the tender rind,
And while he musèd on this uncouth writ,
Him thought he heard the softly whistling wind
His blasts amid the leaves and branches knit
And frame a sound like speech of human kind,
But full of sorrow grief and woe was it,
Whereby his gentle thoughts all fillèd were
With pity, sadness, grief, compassion, fear.

He drew his sword at last, and gave the tree
A mighty blow, that made a gaping wound,
Out of the rift red streams he trickling see
That all bebled the verdant plain around,
His hair start up, yet once again stroke he,
He nould give over till the end he found
Of this adventure, when with plaint and moan,
As from some hollow grave, he heard one groan.

"Enough, enough!" the voice lamenting said,
"Tancred, thou hast me hurt, thou didst me drive
Out of the body of a noble maid
Who with me lived, whom late I kept on live,
And now within this woeful cypress laid,
My tender rind thy weapon sharp doth rive,
Cruel, is't not enough thy foes to kill,
But in their graves wilt thou torment them still?

"I was Clorinda, now imprisoned here,
Yet not alone within this plant I dwell,
For every pagan lord and Christian peer,
Before the city's wall last day that fell,
In bodies new or graves I wot not clear,
But here they are confined by magic's spell,

So that each tree hath life, and sense each bough,
A murderer if thou cut one twist art thou." [9]

In the darkness of the forest where mysterious signs with solemn warning are written, the passageway descending toward the depths opens.

The earth, on its sun-warmed surface, is an accommodating friend, supporting and nurturing life. But below this very thin layer, all that remains is the unknown realm of mineral death. There the telluric powers are held, keepers of the cosmic equilibrium, inexorable and abstract as eternal laws, rigorous as principles, numerous as infinity. It is toward the center of this great magic circle, made up of the entire earth, that the luminous Ishtar goes, the goddess of life, daughter of the moon and mother of men.

Ishtar's Descent into Hell
(MESOPOTAMIAN POEM)

Toward the earth without return, the ground...
Ishtar, daughter of Sin, resolved to go,
So she resolved, Sin's daughter...
Toward the House of Darkness, the dwelling of Nergal
Toward the house where those who enter do not emerge,
Toward the path where one goes with no hope of returning,
Toward the dwelling where those who enter are cut off from the light,
Where dust is their nourishment and mud their food!
They see not the light, in darkness they dwell;
They are clad as the bird in a vestment of wings;
The door, the keyhole are covered with dust.
When Ishtar arrived at the door to the land of no return,
She addressed the porter with these words:
"Ah yes! porter, open the door!
Open the door so that I may enter!
If you do not open the door and I am unable to enter,
I will break down the door, I will smash the keyhole,
I will demolish the threshold and destroy its panels,

---

9. Torquato Tasso, *Jerusalem Delivered*, trans. Edward Fairfax (New York: Colonial Press, 1901), chap. 13, pp. 264–73.

I will compel the dead to reascend and they will eat the living;
The dead will be more numerous than the living!"
The porter opened his mouth and started to speak,
He spoke to great Ishtar.
"Patience! O Lady, don't knock the door down!
I will go announce your name to my sovereign Ereshkigal!"
On his return the porter spoke to Ereshkigal;
"It is your sister Ishtar...
The hostility of the great houses of joy..."
When Ereshkigal heard that,
As when the tamarisks are cut...
As when the reeds are cut down...and he said;
"For what reason has her heart brought her toward me? For what
    reason has her belly borne her toward me?
That one, I with...
As nourishment I eat mud, as intoxicating beverage I drink...
That I may weep for the men who have left their wives behind
That I may weep for the women who have been torn from their
    husbands' breasts
That I may weep for the fragile child who has been struck down before
    his time.
Go porter and open the door for her
See that she follows the ancient laws."
So went then the porter to open the door to her;
"Enter, my Lady, may Kutha welcome you with joy!
May the palace of the land of no return rejoice at your appearance!"
He led her through the first door which was now wide open.
He took the great crown from her head.
"O porter, why have you taken the great crown from my head?"
"Enter, my Lady, for such are the orders of the sovereign of the earth."
He led her through the second door which was now wide open.
He took off the pendants hanging from her ears.
"O porter, why have you taken my earrings off?"
"Enter, my Lady, for such are the orders of the sovereign of the earth."
He led her through the third door which was now wide open.
He took the necklace from around her throat.
"O porter why have you taken my necklace from around my throat?"
"Enter, my Lady, for such are the orders of the sovereign of the earth."
He led her through the fourth door which was now wide open.
He took her finery from her chest.

"O porter, why have you taken my finery from my chest?"

"Enter, my Lady, for such are the orders of the sovereign of the earth."

He led her through the fifth door which was now wide open.

He took off the belt adorned with birthstones that circled her waist.

"O porter, why have you taken my belt adorned with birthstones from
  around my waist?"

"Enter, my Lady, for such are the orders of the sovereign of the earth."

He led her through the sixth door which was now wide open.

He took off the bracelets that she wore on her wrists and ankles.

"O porter, why have you taken my bracelets off my wrists and ankles?"

"Enter, my Lady, for such are the orders of the sovereign of the earth."

He led her through the seventh door which was now wide open.

He took off the last garment from her body that protected her modesty.

"O porter, why have you taken the garment off my body that protected
  my modesty?"

"Enter, my Lady, for such are the orders of the sovereign of the earth."

When Ishtar had descended into the land of no return

Ereshkigal saw her, and in her presence, was troubled.

Ishtar did not reflect, she swooped down upon her.

Ereshkigal opened her mouth and called

To Namtaru, her messenger, she spoke;

"Go Namtaru, Seal her in my palace,

Loose against her the sixty illnesses, loose them against Ishtar!

Visit the sickness of the eyes on her eyes,

Visit the sickness of the sides on her sides,

Visit the sickness of the feet on her feet,

Visit the sickness of the heart on her heart,

Visit the sickness of the head on her head,

On her entire body..."

Since the time Ishtar had descended into the land of no return,

The bull no longer mounted the cow, the ass no longer approached the
  she-ass,

The maidservant was no longer approached by the man in the street,
  The man slept in his apartment,

The maidservant slept turned away on her side.

[on the other side of the tablet the following is engraved:]

The face of Papsukal, the messenger of the great gods, lowered, his
  countenance grew dark,

He donned vestments of mourning, he donned a filthy garment,

Shamash went to Sin, his father, he began to weep.
In the presence of the king his tears began to fall;
"Ishtar has descended into the earth, she has not reemerged
Since the time Ishtar has descended into the land of no return,
The bull no longer mounts the cow, the ass no longer approaches the
    she-ass,
The maidservant is no longer approached by the man in the street,
The man sleeps in his apartment,
The maidservant sleeps turned away on her side."
Ra formed an image in the depths of his wise heart,
He created Asusunamir, the effeminate;
"Go Asusunamir and set your face at the door to the land of no return!
May the seven doors of the land of no return be opened before you!
So that Ereshkigal may see you and rejoice in your presence!
When her heart is calmed and her soul enlightened,
Implore her in the name of the gods:
'Raise your head and direct your attention to the outer Halziquon
Oh, my sovereign queen, may you procure the outer Halziquon for me
    that I may drink its water!'"
Ereshkigal on hearing this,
Struck her thigh and bit her finger;
"You have expressed a desire to me that should not be thought of.
Let's be off! Asusunamir for I enchant you with a great spell!
May the food of city gutters be your nourishment!
May the city sewers serve as your drink!
May the shadow of walls serve as your dwelling!
May the thresholds be your only habitation!
The intoxicated and those who thirst will slap your cheek."
Ereshkigal opened her mouth and spoke
To Namtaru, her messenger, she addressed these words:
"Go, Namtaru, and knock on the door of the palace of justice,
Make an uproar on its threshold that is framed in precious stones;
Cause the Anunnaki to emerge and seat them on the golden throne;
As for Ishtar, sprinkle her with the waters of life and bring her before
    me."
So went Namtaru and he knocked on the door of the palace of justice;
He made an uproar on its threshold that is framed in precious stones;
He caused the emergence of the Anunnaki and installed them on the
    golden throne.
He sprinkled Ishtar with the waters of life and he brought her forth,

*He brought her through the first door and he returned the garment
  that restored the modesty of her body;*
*He brought her through the second door and he returned the bracelets
  to her wrists and ankles;*
*He brought her through the third door and he returned the belt
  adorned with birthstones around her waist;*
*He brought her through the fourth door and he returned the finery
  that adorned her chest;*
*He brought her through the fifth door and he returned the necklace
  around her throat;*
*He brought her through the sixth door and he returned the pendants to
  her ears;*
*He brought her through the seventh door and he returned the great
  crown to her head.*
"If she grants you not his deliverance, turn your face toward her,
For Tammuz, the lover of her youth,
Pour the pure waters, spread the good oil,
*Clothe him in a ceremonial garment so that he may play his flute of
  lapis-lazuli*
May the courtesans contain her anger!"
Bêlili... the treasure she has amassed.
... of precious stones that cover her breasts;
Bêlili heard the voice of her brother, she let fall the treasure that...
She scattered the precious stones throughout her sanctuary.
"O my only brother, do not seek my ruin!
When Tammuz plays the flute of lapis-lazuli with the ring of jade,
When with him the weepers and the wailers make sport of me
The dead will rise again, they will breathe the incense."[10]

---

10. Assyrian and Babylonian religious texts translated by P. Dhorme. Discovered in the library of King Assurbanipal (668–626 B.C.) in 1854, these texts are transcriptions of even more ancient documents, in all likelihood belonging to a group of popular stories collected by Hammurabi around 2050 B.C.

CROSSING
THROUGH DEATH

The Hero's Struggle Against Death:
Myth of the Resurrection

In recounting the exploits of the goddess Ishtar, in describing the celestial and subterranean hierarchies, in delighting in the stories, at once epic and symbolic, of combat waged by supernatural powers, humans define hope. They affirm the desire to vanquish the evil forces of death. Despite defeats, they remain standing, and what's more, they are on the way to attaining the marvelous.

Soon enough, they learn not to put too much faith in the help of the demiurges. Of the gods, those they know best are those they have had to fight, those whose cults have obstructed their lives and their happiness. They know that they must rely on their own strength and skill, and the brotherhood that unites them with others. This idea of mutual fraternal aid is nowhere more evident than in the pre-Columbian American tradition:

The Heroes in Combat Against the Gods of Death
(QUICHIAN TEXT)

Hun-Hunaphu and Vukub-Hunaphu were brothers; they were leading a happy life when one day the Lords of Death, Hun-Came and Vukub-Came and the others of Xibalba, sealed under the earth, became disturbed by the joyful noises they heard overhead. They decided to send messengers and to employ treachery to confound, humiliate, and annihilate the species of courageous men.

Next the envoys of Hun-Came and Vukub-Came arrived and they were told, "Go, captains, go Ahpop-Achih and bear this message to Hun-Hunaphu and Vukub-Hunaphu. Tell them to come with you, that the Lords of Death have summoned them. Tell them we are truly amazed at their ball playing and that we would be most happy to have them come play ball with us. They should bring everything with them that has made such a racket, their yokes and armguards, their gloves and even their rubber balls."

And their messengers are owls: Shooting Owl, One-legged Owl, Macaw Owl, and Skull Owl, as these messengers of Xibalba are called.

As for Shooting Owl he is as swift as an arrow. One-legged Owl has but one leg naturally, then there is Macaw Owl whose nature is fire everywhere. There is also Skull Owl who has no legs but does have wings. These four messengers had the rank of Ahpop-Achih, the captains of the guard.

Leaving Xibalba they quickly arrived with their message above the ball court where Hun-Hunaphu and Vukub-Hunaphu were playing. The owls delivered the message that had been confided to them by Hun-Came, Vukub-Came, Pus Master, Jaundice Master, Bone Scepter, Skull Scepter, House Corner, Blood Gatherer, Trash Master, Stab Master, Wing, and Packstrap as all the Lords of Xibalba are named.

"Have the Lords of Truth truly asked us to accompany you?" asked the two brothers. "And to bring all our playing equipment? That is well, but wait for a moment, we must say good-bye to our mother."

They set along the path toward home and said to their mother, for their father was already dead, "We're going, dear mother, though we just got here, for the messengers of Xibalba have come for us. But this rubber ball will remain as a pledge for our existence here." They then hung it within a niche in the corner of the house.

"We will play ball again when we return; as for you Hunbatz and Hunchouen, continue making music, singing, carving, painting to warm the house and heart of your grandmother. "

They then set out on their way accompanied by the messengers on the road to the underworld. They made a steep descent and came to the banks of a fast-moving river of turbulent waters passing through thorny trees. They passed through countless thorns but were not wounded. They came to the banks of a river of blood. They crossed without drinking of its water. Then they came to a river of pus which they also crossed. They arrived finally at the crossroads, each a different color; one was red, one was black, another was white, and the last was yellow. As they wondered which to take, the black road spoke to them saying, "I am the one you must take, I am the lord's road."

And there they met their defeat and fell into the snare, for this road led to Xibalba and arriving there they had lost the game. The first ones they saw seated there were wooden mannequins. "Hello to you Hun-Came, hello to you Vukub-Came," they said to the wood carvings. The Lords of Death, further back in the room, burst into laughter because they felt they had triumphed; in their hearts they felt Hun-Hunaphu and Vukub-Hunaphu had already lost. Hun-Came and Vukub-Came then said, "It is good that you have come; tomorrow you can prepare your head gear, your armguards, and gloves for a game."

"Sit here in the seat of honor," they were told, but their seat of honor was nothing but a red-hot rock, and sitting upon it they burned themselves. They moved about on this bench but found no relief and hastily arose, having burned themselves. At this sight the Lords of Xibalba wept with laughter; they doubled over and laughed until their sides ached, so heartily were they amused.

"Just go to your dwelling, someone will bring you a resin stick to burn and cigars to smoke," the brothers were told.

They arrived at the House of Darkness, during which time the Lords of Xibalba conferred. "Let's sacrifice them tomorrow," they said, "as soon as possible, for their game is an affront to us."

Hun-Hunaphu and Vukub-Hunaphu entered the House of Darkness as they had been commanded. There each of them was given a stick of resin and a cigar. They were told their lighted sticks and cigars were not to be used up but brought back intact with them at daybreak. Thus they were defeated for the men burnt the resin sticks for light and smoked the cigars.

The tests and trials of Xibalba were numerous. The first was that of the House of Darkness, a place of total obscurity inside. The second was that of the house called Xuxulim, Rattling House, where an unbearably cold wind howled incessantly. The third one was Jaguar House, with nothing but jaguars roaring ferociously inside, and gnashing their teeth. The fourth test was the House of Bats in which there was nothing but a cloud of shrieking, flitting bats. They are locked inside and cannot escape. And the fifth is named Chayim-Ha, Warrior's House or House of Knives. Here there were naught but fighters, either resting or jousting with each other with their lances. These are the first tests of Xibalba, but Hun-Hunaphu and Vukub-Hunaphu never entered any of them but the first house. When they came out the next morning into the presence of Hun-Came and Vukub-Came, they were asked for the resin sticks and cigars that had been brought to them the night before.

"We finished them your Lordship."

"Oh! very well, then you are finished too, today. On this very day your chest will be carved open and you will be sacrificed."

Thus they were sacrificed and buried at the place called the Ash Pit. The head of Hun-Hunaphu was first cut off and his body buried with that of his younger brother. The lords then ordered that the head be placed in the fork of a tree that stood by the road. As soon as this was done the tree bore fruit, which it had never done previously. This is the calabash tree that is still today called "the head of Hun-Hunaphu." The lords looked upon the fruit of this wondrous tree with astonishment. The head of Hun-Hunaphu could no longer be seen: it looked like all the other calabashes.

The Lords of Xibalba then gave orders that no one was to sit beneath this tree or pick its fruit.

From this time on the head of Hun-Hunaphu was no longer to be seen but a maiden heard this marvelous tale and wanted to see this tree for herself.

She was the daughter of Cuchumaquiq, Blood Gatherer, and her name was Xquiq, Little Blood or Woman's Blood. "Why should I not go see this marvelous tree they talk about," she said to herself, "and taste its sweet fruits?" Leaving by herself she made her way to the tree and gazed up within its branches. "Such unusual fruit," she murmured. "Would I die if I just picked one?"

Then the skull that was in the fork of the tree responded, "Are you sure that's what you really want? The fruit of this tree is skulls. Do you still want one?"

"I do want one," the girl said in reply.

"Very well," said the skull, "then reach out your right hand."

The girl extended her hand and the skull spit its saliva squarely into the palm. She immediately looked into her cupped hand but the saliva was no longer there.

"That saliva and that spittle that I have just given to you is my posterity. This head will cease speaking for it is naught but a skull that no longer has any skin. Just like the head of a great lord it is the flesh that gives it its good looks, and when he is taken by death people are frightened by his bones. It is the same with his sons who are spittle and saliva just as are the sons of craftsmen and orators. The father does not vanish but is transmitted across the generations; his face is neither dimmed nor destroyed whether it be that of a lord, an artisan, or an orator. Thus it goes with the sons and daughters he leaves behind as I have done likewise with you. Now climb back to the world's surface; you will not die. Believe in my words," the skull added, "for this is the way things are by command of Hurakan [Hurricane] and Thunderbolt." The maiden returned home, and along her way she was given many instructions. Immediately she conceived in her belly Hunaphu and Xbalanque by virtue of the saliva alone.

Six months had passed since the maiden's return home and her father began to regard her suspiciously; looking closer he saw that she was with child. He went to the lords for their counsel.

"This daughter of mine is pregnant," he said to Hun-Came and Vukub-Came, "and in dishonor."

"Very well, question her and if she won't open her mouth, sacrifice her."

"Very well, your Lordships," Blood Gatherer responded.

He then demanded of his daughter, "Whose child are you carrying in your belly?"

But she responded, "There can be no child, my lord and father, for I have known the face of no man."

"Very well, you are in truth a whore." Then turning to an owl he said, "Take her away for sacrifice, and return her heart to me in a bowl."

The four of them heard and took the bowl. When they left they carried the maiden on their shoulders and they brought with them a flint knife, the instrument of sacrifice.

"You cannot kill me, oh proxies, for I am not guilty of any crime. What's in my belly engendered itself when I went to admire the head of Hun-Hunaphu at the Ash Pit. So please don't sacrifice me!"

"But what can we use in exchange for your heart? There is nothing we would like better than to spare your life."

"My heart does not belong to them. Nor will your dwelling henceforth be here; and not only will you hold the power to kill men but the real whores will be at your mercy. The time will come when I defeat Hun-Came and Vukub-Came and hereafter only blood will be theirs. Now fill the bowl with the sap from this tree," she added.

The sap ran red into the bowl where it congealed and formed a ball. This was the substitute for her heart. The tree was called the blood tree, the croton tree. "There, you will be blessed and everything upon the face of the earth will be your inheritance," the maiden said to the owls.

"Very good, but now we should part and we will leave to return to the lord with an account of our mission."

The lords were assembled and nervously waiting when their messengers arrived. "Have you finished?" asked Hun-Came.

"Here is the heart in this bowl," replied the owls.

Then he plucked it out delicately with his fingertips, and its glistening bloody surface began to fill with blood. He had it placed within the fire and the Xibalbans began to smell its odor; they rose as one and turned with anticipatory astonishment toward this perfume. During this time the owls rose in great numbers and flew from the abyss to the surface of the earth. Thus were the Lords of Xibalba tricked and defeated by a young maiden.

Now the girl Xquiq drew near to the house of the mother of Hunbatz and Hunchouen. She was pregnant and little time remained before the birth of they who would be named Hunaphu and Xbalanque.

Seeing the old woman, Xquiq said, "Here I am my lady and mother. I am your daughter-in-law and I'm the adoptive daughter of your Ladyship."

"Where have you come from and where are my sons? Are they not dead in Xibalba and are these not their two descendants, Hunbatz and Hunchouen, the signs of their words, that you see? Get out of here!" replied the old woman.

"Believe me, I am truly your daughter-in-law. I am the wife of Hun-Hunaphu and what I carry is his. Hun-Hunaphu and Vukub-Hunaphu are not dead and the punishment that has struck them down has made them only more illustrious and you will see their dear faces on those I'm carrying."

But Hunbatz and Hunchouen, who spent their time playing the flute, singing, painting, and carving, began to get mad at the young girl.

"I don't need you for a daughter-in-law; you are a whore and a liar and it is your bastard you carry. Those children of mine you speak of are dead."

Then the old woman thought and said, "If you are truly my daughter-in-law then go gather food for those who must eat; go and fill this large net with what you harvest."

The young girl made her way to the garden that had been planted by Hunbatz and Hunchouen on the trail that they had cleared. She found there but one lone ear of corn, not two, nor three, but only one. Then her heart felt close to breaking, "How unhappy I am; where am I to find the food to fill this net as I've been ordered?" she said to herself. And she prayed to the guardians of food for their aid. Then she took the silk and the end of the ear of corn and gently tore it open; these kernels reproduced themselves until the net was full.

Then the maiden started homeward, but animals took the net from the girl and bore it for her to a corner of the house, like an ordinary burden.

And then when the grandmother saw the large net so full she ran up screaming, "Where has all of this come from, have you destroyed our fields, have you managed to pick every grain? I am going to go see for myself this instant!"

She went off to look at the garden and when she arrived she saw the lone ear still standing in its place. She returned and said to the maiden, "This is proof that you are really my daughter-in-law. I will keep my eye on you and those sages you carry in your belly!"

The young woman Xquiq gave birth. The newborn babies wouldn't sleep.

"They do nothing but scream, throw them outdoors," said the old woman.

They were placed upon an anthill where they slept soundly. From there they were next placed in brambles. And this was what Hunbatz and Hunchouen wanted; they wanted them to die. Hunbatz and Hunchouen were excellent musicians and singers, and as they grew up in troubled times they had become quite wise; everything they did they did well.

They did not show the wisdom they had gained from their past in regard to their younger brothers because of their jealousy. The ill feelings of their hearts had gotten the upper hand over them and they turned against those who were blameless of any harm. The younger children didn't cease to spend their days in hunting and bringing back birds. Nothing was given to them to eat until the others were finished. But Hunaphu and Xbalanque didn't get angry and were content to suffer for they knew their proper place; thus they brought birds back with them when they returned home each day.

But one day they came home empty-handed and the old woman grew furious with them.

"Someone has to climb a tree to get our birds," she said. "Tell our brothers to help us."

They went together to the tree which was full of birds. Though they were struck they would not fall. Hunbatz and Hunchouen climbed up; the tree grew thicker and they couldn't get down.

They called to their brothers for help. Hunaphu and Xbalanque told them to loosen their loincloths and to put them under their bellies with a long end trailing behind them. "Now it will be easy to climb," they said.

These turned into tails and thus Hunbatz and Hunchouen were turned into monkeys because they had become swollen with pride and mistreated their younger brothers.

Hunaphu and Xbalanque now began to work. They cleared land for a garden and requested that their grandmother bring them a meal at noon, they cleared the land for a time, then wearying of the work went off hunting but asked a mourning-dove to keep watch for the arrival of their grandmother. The next day came and they saw all their work of the day before had been undone; it was the work of the puma, jaguar, deer, rabbit, opossum, coyote, peccary, porcupine, and the birds, both large and small. They cleared anew their land, but this time they kept guard and at midnight they heard the arrival of the puma and the jaguar. They tried to grab them but they were too fast. Next were the deer and the rabbit; all they could seize of them were their tails, which is why tails have been so short in those species since then. Then came the opossum, coyote, peccary, and porcupine whom they couldn't catch either. Last came the rat whom they captured. The rat proposed to them that he give them what had belonged to their fathers, that is the gloves, the armbands, and the rubber ball left hanging under the roof of the house.

"These were not shown to you," he explained, "for your fathers died because of them." After the rat had told them they gave him the food they had promised and then took advantage of their grandmother's absence from the house to obtain the ball. Then they went to the ball court of their fathers which they swept clean. There they played and the Lords of Xibalba heard them; again they sent emissaries to make the young men come down to the underworld within seven days. So with the arrival of the messengers the grandmother's heart was broken; however she told herself she must take the message to Hunaphu and Xbalanque at the ball court where they were playing. She charged the louse Xan with this task; on his way he met the toad who offered to swallow him in order to deliver his message more quickly; then came a serpent who swallowed the toad, who in turn was swallowed by a laughing hawk, a large bird. Seeing his arrival the brothers pulled out their blowguns and fired a shot that caught the bird in the pupil of his eye causing him to fall.

"What are you after here?" they asked the bird.

"I carry a message for you in my belly; heal my eye and I will deliver it to you." They pried off a bit of the elastic ball to heal the eye; the hawk vomited the serpent which vomited the toad which then tried to vomit the louse but couldn't as it was stuck to his teeth. They removed it from the toad's mouth and it gave them the message.

Hunaphu and Xbalanque departed leaving behind two reeds in the house that would wither if they died and flower as long as they remained alive. Like their fathers they crossed the river of the raging waters, the river of blood, the river of pus, and arrived at the crossroads. They sent their friend the louse ahead of them on the black road. Once at Xibalba he bit the first mannequin, which said nothing. Then the second, which also remained silent. Then he bit the third who was Hun-Came, who cursed and revealed his name, as did the other Lords of Xibalba in their turn. Thus Hunaphu and Xbalanque were given the correct knowledge and could greet each of the lords by their proper names. They then declined the seat they were offered to sit on. "This is a stone slab for cooking," they said. Then they were told to go to the House of Darkness where they were given resin sticks and cigars. To make it seem as if they had lit their gifts they placed the red tail feathers of the macaw on their torches and fireflies sat upon the ends of their cigars. The next morning, to the surprise of the lords, they returned these items intact. The lords then wanted to play ball, but after spotting the lords' treachery, the brothers insisted that their ball be used and they were victorious. Irritated by their defeat the lords commanded them to go before the next dawn and return with four vases of flowers that they specified, flowers that existed nowhere but in Hun-Came's garden. They were lodged in the House of Knives from which came a constant grating, but they disarmed the blades with promises of the flesh of all animals. They then ordered the ants to go pick the flowers in Hun-Came's garden which was tightly guarded. The ants came back with the necessary flowers; and the lords, furious at their defeat, went to punish their sentries. On their return they suggested another game of ball to the two brothers. After several tied games the brothers put down their equipment for the day.

That night they were lodged in the House of Cold, the next in the House of Jaguars whom they tamed by giving the animals bones. The House of Flame was their lodging the subsequent night, then the House of Bats. It was there that Hunaphu stuck his head outdoors to see if it was dawn and had it cut from his shoulders. One of the reeds left at their grandmother's house withered and died. "It is all over now," thought Xbalanque and called all the animals together; he chose the turtle to take the place of his brother's head so they could return to the ball court at dawn. Xbalanque had it all thought out: at the right moment he hit the ball out of the court. As the lords chased after it, a rabbit ran out and led them far away. Thanks to this, Xbalanque could exchange the turtle with his brother's head that the lords had hung up in the ball court. Thus they triumphed again over the Xibalbans.

The Lords of Xibalba, furious at their defeat, decided to kill the two brothers. They pulverized their bones and threw the powder into the river. Five days later Hunaphu and Xbalanque returned as men-fish, then two days later as two ragged old men who danced and went from town to town to work miracles. Their magic show consisted of burning people and bringing them back to life. By way of example one of the old men burnt his companion and then brought him back to life. The lords were full of surprise and admiration at these marvels; they gave them a dog to kill and resuscitate, then a house to burn and bring back, then a man. Everything vanished in the flames and was brought back to its normal form. Hun-Came and Vukub-Came wanted to try this experience themselves for their own amusement but once they had been consumed by the fire Hunaphu and Xbalanque refrained from restoring them. Thus perished all the Lords of Xibalba.[1]

In this text, you can recognize the elements of folk stories: successive tests proposed to the hero, mysterious rivers that need to be crossed, crossroads where the traveler hesitates over which way to go, helpful animals, the role of the sacred tree, etc. That all this predates the arrival of Europeans in the Americas shows how entrenched these shared unconscious preoccupations are, and how similar the images used to express these fears. The pre-Columbian text brings to bear its own invaluable aspect, however. Here, men are brothers, united as one and only pitted against each other according to generation. After the van-

---

1. Popol-Vuh, *Livre sacré des Quichés.*

quished parents come the older sons, educated but useless. Then come the younger ones who rediscover their ancestral attributes (the rubber ball) against all odds, and triumph over obstacles. Very characteristic also is the woman's intervention. Since the grandmother represents the traditional guardian of the family, the only young female figure is that of Xquiq. Drawn mysteriously to the sacred tree, the tree of knowledge and generation, she gives her virgin body to the cosmic process of resurrecting the hero. Mother and widow at the same time, never does her confidence or her clear-sightedness fail her. She is the faithful and sure ally. No psychological complexity, no interior debate; the Quichian story follows in a hieratic line. It seems essential to compare it to the story of the two brothers, one of the most ancient Egyptian texts of this kind coming down to us. Here the drama results through the fault of a woman. Far from lending aid, the wife of the older brother Anup divides the two brothers by spreading slanderous lies. Subsequently, when Bata is to be given a wife, he confronts the most perilous trials because of her.

The Story of the Two Brothers
(EGYPTIAN TEXT, END OF THE NINETEENTH DYNASTY)

Once upon a time it is told that there were two brothers born of one mother and one father: Anup was the name of the elder and Bata the name of the younger. Anup had a house and wife, and his younger brother lived with him as if he were his son. It was the younger brother who made the elder's garments and herded the livestock into the fields; it was the younger who planted and harvested the fields for his elder brother; it was he who did all the necessary work on his brother's lands. Certainly this Bata was a strapping lad; his like was not to be found in the entire country: his was the strength of a god.

Most of his days were spent in the following fashion: the younger brother would herd his beasts out to the fields, as was his daily habit, and, then, each evening he would return home laden with all sorts of herbs, milk, wood, and with all manner of good things that the fields provided. He would place them all before his elder brother, who would be seated with his wife; then he drank, ate, and left to spend the night alone in the stable surrounded by his animals. And when the dawn illuminated the earth and a new day had arrived, he would prepare a cooked meal that he would set before his elder brother who in turn would give him bread to take with him to the fields. And thus he would drive his cows to pasture. And while he walked behind his beasts they would tell him: "The grass is good in such and such spot"; and he listened to all they said and he led them to the place with the good grass where they desired to go. And the cows whose care he was responsible for became more beautiful to look upon and their births multiplied.

Now during the season of tilling his elder brother said: "Take a yoke of cows for plowing, for the land has now emerged from the water of the flood and it is ready to be tilled; then you will go to the fields with the seeds for we are going to work vigorously on the morrow." This was what he said and his younger brother performed all the tasks as he had been instructed.

And when the earth was aglow with the coming of a new day they went to the fields with their seeds and began vigorously to work; and their hearts overflowed with joy from the efforts of their work from the time they started.

And after many days spent in such fashion, a day came when they were in the fields and Anup, seeing that they were out of seed, sent forth his younger brother saying: "Go look for some seeds for us in the village." There Bata found his elder brother's wife who was getting her hair done. Seeing her Bata said: "Please get up and get me some seeds so that I may run back to the fields where Anup is waiting for me, and be quick about it." She answered him: "Go to the granary yourself and take what you want, I don't want to ruin my hair."

The young man then entered the stable where he obtained a large jar that he intended to fill with lots of seeds. He filled it with barley and wheat and left with his load. The wife asked him: "What is the weight of that which you carry on your shoulder?" He answered: "Three sacks of wheat, two sacks of barley, making five in all. That is what I am carrying on my shoulder." Thus he spoke but the wife addressed him again, saying: "You are great in strength and every day I look upon evidence of your virility." And she desired to know him as a man. She arose and embraced him, saying: "Come, let us spend an hour together, let us lie together. It will be to your benefit as I will make you some beautiful garments in return." Then the younger brother became like a leopard going into a rage because of her base proposition and she became afraid, greatly afraid. Then he spoke, saying: "What! You are like a mother to me and your husband has been like a father to me; Anup is he that has raised me from a child. What abomination is this that you speak? Don't speak of it ever again! I will not repeat it to anyone and I will ensure that it never leaves my mouth for any reason whatsoever." He picked up his burden and returned to the fields where he found his elder brother, and they energetically reapplied themselves to their task.

That evening Anup returned to the house, leaving his younger brother behind with his beasts, and his shoulders laden with all the things from the fields. Bata drove his animals before him back to the stable in the middle of the village where they would sleep.

Now the wife of Anup was filled with fear because of the proposition she had made to Bata. She therefore sought some seed and suet so that she could pretend that she had been beaten and could tell her husband that it was his younger brother who had beaten her.

And when her husband returned to the house that evening, as was customary, he found his wife lying down and pretending to be sick: she poured no water upon his hands as she was accustomed to; she lit no lamps before him; the house was in darkness and she was lying down, vomiting. Anup asked her: "Who has been speaking badly to you?" She answered: "No one but your younger brother. When he came for your seeds and found me seated alone he said, 'Come, let's spend an hour lying together. Put on your wig.' Thus he spoke to me but I did not listen. Am I not as a mother to you, I said, and is not your brother like a father? Thus I spoke to him and he became scared; he beat me so I would not tell of this. But if you allow him to live I will kill myself. When he returns don't listen to him. The idea of this horrendous deed he wanted to commit continues to cause me great pain."

And Anup became like a leopard; he sharpened his spear and took it to hand. He then hid behind the stable door so that he could kill his younger brother when he returned that evening with his animals. Now, when the sun was setting, the younger brother, laden down with all his harvest from the fields, returned to the village. When the lead cow entered the stable, it turned and spoke to their herdsman saying: "Look out! Your elder brother is waiting here with his spear so that he may kill you. Get away!" Bata understood what his cow was telling him. The next cow entered and said the same thing. He then looked under the stable door where he saw the feet of his brother who was lying in wait with his spear in hand. He deposited his burden onto the ground and he fled as fast as his feet could carry him. His brother started after him in pursuit.

Then Bata invoked Pre-Harakhti saying: "My good master! You are he who judges between the criminal and the righteous." And Pre-Harakhti heard all his prayers and caused the appearance of a great expanse of water filled with crocodiles between him and his elder brother. And the younger brother was on one side while the elder one remained on the other. And Anup struck himself twice with his own hand for his failure to kill his younger brother. This latter however called out to him from the other bank, saying: "Remain here until the return of day. When the solar disk rises I will stand in judgment with you before it and it will deliver the guilty one to justice. For I will never live with you again, ever; I will no longer remain in any place where you may be. I am taking myself to the Valley of the Umbrella Pines."

When light again overspread the earth and another day had come, Pre-Harakhti arose and then each of the brothers could see the other. At this time Bata addressed Anup saying: "What is the meaning of your coming after me to treacherously kill me, without having heard the words of my mouth? I am your younger brother, however, and you have been as a father and your wife as a mother to me. Isn't that so? When you sent me for seeds yesterday your wife said to me: 'Come let us spend an hour lying together.' Very well! She twisted the facts and told you the opposite of what happened." And he proceeded to inform Anup of everything that had occurred with his wife. Then he swore by Pre-Harakhti: "You have come, lance in hand, to kill me, at the instigation of a slut!" He then sought a sharp reed and with it cut off his member; he hurled it into the water where it was swallowed up by the silt. He lost his strength and became wretched. The heart of his elder brother overflowed with grief and he stood there crying loudly without being able to reach the other bank where his younger brother was, because of the crocodiles.

Then his brother called out to him: "So, you thought only on the bad deed! And you didn't reflect on some good deed or any of the many things that I have done for you. Return now to your house and take care of your beasts for I will stay no longer in any place where you may be. I am taking myself to the Valley of the Umbrella Pines. As to what you must do for me in the future it is thus: you must come care for me when you learn something has happened to me—for I am going to tear out my heart and place it at the tip of the umbrella pine's flower. If the pine is cut and my heart falls to the ground, and you come in search of it, even if it takes seven years, do not grow discouraged. And when you have found it and have placed it in a vessel of fresh water, I will revive so that I can have my revenge on whoever did me wrong. Now you will learn that something has happened to me when you pick up a pot of beer in your hand and it overflows. You must not delay when that happens."

He then made his way to the Valley of the Umbrella Pines while his elder brother returned home with his hands to his head and all spattered with dust. Once he got there, he killed his wife, threw her corpse to the dogs, then sat down and continued to mourn for his younger brother.

After many like days had passed his brother made his way to the Valley of the Umbrella Pines in complete solitude; he spent his days there hunting the game of the desert, then he would return in the evening to sleep beneath the pine in whose flower rested his heart.

And after many more days had passed he built with his own hands a castle in the Valley of Umbrella Pines that was filled with all manner of good things. One day when he was out he encountered the Ennead[2] who were traveling and occupying themselves with the affairs of the entire country. Then the gods of the Ennead began talking among themselves and then spoke to Bata: "Hey! Bata, bull[3] of the Ennead, are you here all alone, having fled your village because of the wife of Anup, your elder brother? Well then, he has killed his wife and thus you are avenged on all those who have acted evilly toward you." Their hearts filled with pity for him and Pre-Harakhti said to Khnum: "Make a woman for Bata so he doesn't remain alone." And Khnum made a companion for him; she was more beautiful to behold than any other woman in all the land and she had the seed of every god in her making. The Seven Hathors[4] came and speaking as one they said: "She will die by the sword."

Bata was overcome with desire for her. She remained in his house while he spent the day hunting the game of the desert, bringing it back, and placing it before her. And he told her: "Don't set foot outside for the Sea God would then carry you off; you could not escape from him for you are only a woman after all. My heart is placed at the tip of the flower of the umbrella pine and if another finds it I must do combat with him." And he revealed to her all that concerned his heart.

---

2. The Egyptian trinity, which tripled in each of its persons, forms a theoretical group of nine divine individuals who are called the *Pwat Neteru*, "the Ennead, the novena of the gods," or, to use an even vaguer term, "the cycle of the gods."

3. The label of "bull" applied to a eunuch is, to say the least, bizarre. It should not be forgotten that Bata is Osiris and that his misadventure, while removing his virility on earth, does not prevent him from retaining, as a god, his prolific abilities. In one version of the legend the mutilated Osiris succeeds in impregnating Isis and becomes the father of Horus.

4. The Seven Hathors play the role of fairy godmothers in Egyptian legend.

And after many days had passed, one day Bata went hunting as was his habit. This day the young woman left the house to walk beneath the umbrella pine that was beside it. And then she spotted the Sea God who sent his waves rolling after her. She ran fleeing into the house. But the Sea God called out to the umbrella pine saying: "Seize her for me!" And the umbrella pine caught a tress of her hair which he gave to him. And the Sea God carried it off to Egypt and deposited it in the spot where worked the laundresses of the Pharaoh. And the aroma from the tress of hair passed into the Pharaoh's clothing. Quarrels arose with the Pharaoh's laundresses with people saying: "There is the scent of a hair cream in the Pharaoh's clothing." Then quarrels arose between the Great One and the laundresses of that day and no one knew how to proceed. The chief of the Pharaoh's laundresses came to the laundry and his heart was sorely vexed on account of these daily quarrels. He stopped and stood on the stand in front of the tress of hair that was floating in the water. He had someone go in and bring it out to him; finding the odor most agreeable he bore it to the Pharaoh. The scribes and scholars of the Pharaoh were summoned by the Great One. They told him: "This tress belongs to a daughter of Pre-Harakhti in whose making went the seed of all the gods. It is a gift for you from another land. Send your messengers to all foreign lands in search of her; as for the messenger to the Valley of the Umbrella Pines, send with him a large company of men to bring her back." Then His Majesty said: "This is all very good what you say," and the messengers were sent.

And after a great number of days had passed, those who had been sent to the foreign lands returned to report to the Pharaoh except for those who had gone to the Valley of the Umbrella Pines, for Bata had killed them all, save one he allowed to live to report to His Majesty. Then His Majesty sent his troops in great number and also his chariots to bring her back. With them went a woman whose hands held every manner of beautiful feminine adornment. This woman returned to Egypt with the girl and the entire country was elated by her presence. His Majesty loved her greatly and she was given the title of his favorite.

Then the Pharaoh chatted with her to make her tell him all concerning her husband. "Cut down and destroy the umbrella pine," she said. And soldiers were sent with tools of copper to cut the pine. They found the pine and cut the flower on which Bata's heart rested and he instantly fell dead.

And after the sun rose and another day had dawned after the umbrella pine had been cut down, Anup, Bata's elder brother, entered his house and sat down to wash his hands. He was given a pot of beer and it overflowed. He was given another of wine and it grew cloudy. Then he took his staff and his sandals, as well as his clothes and his weapons, and started to walk to the Valley of the Umbrella Pines. He entered his younger brother's castle and found him lying on his bed, dead. He wept to see his brother lying there as a corpse. And he went to seek the heart of his younger brother under the umbrella pine under which his younger brother had slept in the evening. He spent three years seeking it and did not find it; and when he started a fourth year the yearning to return to Egypt grew in his heart. He told himself: "I will go tomorrow." And thus he spoke in his heart.

And after the sun had risen and a new day had dawned he started seeking beneath the umbrella pine; and he spent the entire day seeking his brother's heart, then spent that evening still completely occupied with seeking it. He then found a seed and returned home with it. It so happened that this was his younger brother's heart. He sought out a bowl of fresh water and placed the heart within it, then seated himself as was his daily custom.

And after night had come and the heart had absorbed the water, Bata shivered in all his limbs and began to look at his brother while his heart was still in the bowl. Then Anup took the bowl of fresh water with the heart still in it and made his brother drink it. When Bata's heart was restored to its rightful place he became his former self. They embraced each other and talked into the night.

Then Bata said to his elder brother: "Look, I will become a great bull, adorned with every beautiful color, but of an unknown nature, and you will seat yourself upon my back as the sun rises. When we arrive at the place where my wife is, I will avenge myself. Then you will lead me to the spot where is the Great One, for you will be given all manner of goods and you will be paid my weight in gold and silver for having brought me to the Pharaoh. For I will become a great marvel and the entire land will be elated because of me. Then you will return to your village."

And when a new day had dawned Bata was transformed into the form that he had described to Anup. His elder brother sat upon his back from the dawn and the bull arrived at the spot where was the Great One. His Majesty was informed of his presence and came to see him. He was the cause of great rejoicing in the heart of the Pharaoh and the Great One commanded a sacrifice in his honor, saying: "This is a great marvel that has occurred!" And the entire land was elated because of this. His brother was paid the weight of the bull in gold and silver and he set up house in his village. He was given numerous servants and goods in great number, and Pharaoh loved him greatly, more than all other men in the entire country.

And after a good many days had passed, the bull entered the kitchen and stood at the spot where the favorite was wont to go and started to chat with her, saying: "Look, I am still alive." She asked: "Who are you?" and he responded: "I am Bata and I know quite well that when you had the pine destroyed for the Pharaoh it was because of me, it was to prevent me from living. Very well, then! I am still alive, I am a bull." Then the favorite grew quite scared on account of what her husband said to her. She left the kitchen and went up to His Majesty with whom she sat and spent a pleasant day. She poured a drink for His Majesty and the Great One was very, very good to her. Then she said to him: "Swear to me by God promising that I will listen to what the favorite has to say so as to give her pleasure." And he listened to all that she said: "Give me the liver of this bull to eat so that he may never do anything." The Great One was very grieved by what she said and the Pharaoh's heart was filled with compassion for the bull.

And after the light of the rising sun had overspread the earth with a new day the Great One proclaimed a great festival of offering as an accompaniment to the sacrifice of the bull. His Majesty's first royal butcher was sent to slit the throat of the bull. And this was done.

And then when the body of the bull was already on the shoulders of those who were to carry him away, the butcher struck his throat again so handily that two drops of blood were projected to either side of the doorposts of His Majesty's gate. From these sprouted two large perseas and each was a splendid example of its kind. His Majesty was told: "Two large perseas have sprouted during the night as a great marvel for His Majesty, near His Majesty's great gate"; and this caused great elation throughout the land and the Great One made a sacrifice to them.

And after a good many days had passed, one day His Majesty appeared in his lapis lazuli box with a garland of all manner of flowers around his neck. He climbed into the cab of his golden chariot and left the palace to see the perseas. His favorite went behind him in the company of his retinue. There His Majesty sat beneath one persea while the favorite sat beneath the other. And Bata addressed these words to his wife: "Hey, traitress, I am Bata and I am still alive, despite you. And I know full well that you had the pine cut for Pharaoh because of me. I transformed myself into a bull and you again had me killed."

And after a good many days had again passed, the favorite arose and poured His Majesty's drink and things were pleasant between them. And she said to His Majesty: "Swear to me by God, promising that I will listen to what the favorite has to say so as to give her pleasure." And he listened to all that she said. Thus she spoke: "Have these two perseas cut down and made into beautiful pieces of furniture." The Great One listened to all she said. And His Majesty immediately sent for skilled workers and the perseas of the Pharaoh were chopped down. The royal wife, the favorite, was watching as this was done; a splinter flew into the air and entered her mouth. She swallowed it and became pregnant in the space of an instant. And the Great One made all that she desired from the wood of the trees.

Again after many days had passed, she gave birth to a boy child. And His Majesty was told that a male infant had been born. He was brought forth and given a wet nurse and servants to look after him; there was great rejoicing throughout the land on his account. The Great One sat and spent a pleasant day; the Great One's heart was in jubilation and His Majesty loved the child greatly from the moment he laid eyes upon him and named him the Royal Son of Kuch. And in the days that followed His Majesty named him the crown prince of the entire country.

And after many years had passed His Majesty was taken to heaven. Then his heir, the Great One, said: "May the great administrators of His Majesty be brought before me so that I may inform them of all the adventures that have befallen me." The wife of the Pharaoh was brought before him and they were judged together and the son was deemed the righteous party. The heir had his elder brother brought before him and named him crown prince of all the land. After spending thirty years on the throne of Egypt he left this life and his elder brother took his place as king on the day of his departure.

This tale has now come happily to its end, in peace under the direction of the scribe Gagabu, belonging to the treasure of the Pharaoh, as well as the scribe Hori and the scribe Meremope. The scribe Ennena, the owner of this book, has made this manuscript. Whoever speaks ill of this book will gain Thoth as his enemy. [5]

---

5. *Romans et contes égyptiens de l'époque pharaonique,* trans. with introduction and commentaries by Gustave Lefebvre (Paris: Librairie d'Amérique et d'Orient [Adrien Maisonneuve, 11, rue Saint-Sulpice, Paris - VI], 1949), trans. Jon Graham.

In the preceding texts, we have witnessed the struggle of life against the elements, and while the elements offer plenty of obstacles to overcome in order to win the great secret, the Egyptian story locates the true test of the hero in death itself. To die and be reborn, that is what is required of him. Otherwise nothing can move forward. Separated from his brother by dangerous, crocodile-filled waters, Bata cannot be reunited with him until after he has sojourned in the Valley of Umbrella Pines and been brought back to life. And even then, because of his wife's infidelity, he must submit to a series of transformations, taking the form of animal, then vegetable, before his legitimate rights triumph and he attains supreme power.

Maspero, who circulated this story in France before Gustave Lefebvre, notes that Bata, or Bytis, is one of the popular names of Osiris. With this god, we encounter one of the most ancient forms of the redemptive resurrection myth.

The Osiris legend opposes the human hope of discovering that truth hidden by the mystery of the elements to the need for individual transformation. The body must be destroyed in order to be reborn in a new form.

The Legend of Osiris

Osiris was the son of the god Geb, the earth, and the goddess Nout, the sky. He succeeded his father on the throne of the two Egypts. That was the time of divine dynasties. Ra, the creator of the world, and his descendants, Chou and Geb, had already ruled over mankind. But, suffering from old age and discouraged by general ingratitude, they withdrew to heaven, leaving the task to a more clever god. Osiris was this instructor, awaited since the world's creation. When he was born, "a voice announced that the master of all things arrived by the light." One Tamyles of Thebes had a personal annunciation. Having gone to look for water in the temple of Amon, "a voice ordered him to proclaim that Osiris the great king, the benefactor of the universe, had just been born." Osiris succeeded where his ancestors had failed, thanks to the magical charm of Isis, his wife. The divine couple overcame all difficulties by the power of their beauty, knowledge, and goodness. They taught savage human beings which plants to eat. Isis cut herbs and ground flour. Osiris pressed grapes and made wine. People no longer ate each other. They discovered metals underground and made weapons for killing beasts, tools for cultivating the fields, and statues for honoring the gods.

They learned to speak and write, the methods of science, the rhythms of music and the arts. They could read the stars in the night sky. Leaving Isis to govern Egypt, Osiris traveled all over the earth to spread the good word. Everywhere the charm of his goodness captivated people. Alas, his brother, the violent Typhon, came into conflict with him. Aided by seventy-two accomplices, Typhon organized a festival during which a trunk the size of Osiris was brought in. Everyone tried, but no one could fill it up except the god. When Osiris was inside, the trunk was closed and Typhon's accomplices carried it into the Nile. Soon learning of his great distress, Isis ran everywhere seeking information. Some little children told her which branch of the Nile the trunk had been pushed into. The trunk went as far as Byblos where a bush hid it from view. By virtue of the divine corpse, this bush grew to the point where it became a tree, and the trunk was entirely incorporated into it. One day, Malcantre, the king of the country, had this tree cut down to make one of the columns of his palace. Forewarned by a heavenly revelation, Isis went to Byblos. After many adventures, she was able to obtain the trunk and return to Egypt with it. Out hunting at night by moonlight, Seth found the trunk, and, recognizing the body of Osiris, cut it into fourteen pieces which he flung about the earth. Isis took up her pitiful quest again. She succeeded in reassembling the pieces of the body, all but the phallus which had been thrown into the river and eaten by a crab. Where each piece was found, Isis erected a sepulcher. After that, Horus, the son of Osiris, with the help of Thoth, and Anubis, and the support of all pious men, embarked upon an endless war to wrest from Seth and his followers his legacy, the entire world.

Up till then, gods hadn't known death. When their decrepitude reached its heights, they had withdrawn. Osiris's assassination made it necessary to find a way to escape death. Isis came up with a solution. She knew how to revive the god by magic funeral rites. For humans, these consisted of reproducing the circumstances of the death and resurrection of the god as faithfully as possible. Over the course of the ceremony, these episodes were acted out. Isis had made a statue of wax and herbs into which she incorporated the pieces of the body as they were found. Osiris's family thus devoted itself to the total reconstruction of the divine being. "You have taken back your head," Isis and Nephyths said to their brother, "you have drawn your flesh tight again, your blood vessels are returned to you." The gods watched over the whole operation. Geb, Osiris's father, presided.

Later, during festivals, the ritual required two statues of the god to be made out of earth mixed with wheat, incense, herbs, and precious stones. A separate image was molded for each part of Osiris that each sanctuary was supposed to contain. And these were brought to Osiris's mummy, just as Isis had done. Then the people prayed for the god's return: "Come back to your house, none of your enemies are here, they've been beaten, you will find only your children, stay away no longer." The second act of the drama involved the resurrection. The grains of wheat began to sprout. In place of Isis's charms, priests practiced magnetism to bring the inert body back to life. The body of the god was enclosed in a wooden cow and reborn through the cow's gestation. The soul did not return in the living form of the god. It fled to the moon where it endured the vicissitudes of that night star. There the struggle continued against Seth, changed into some animal or another: pig, bull, gazelle, goose. These animals made up the required sacrifice to the god. In bringing the head, heart, and thighs of the victims to the mouth of Osiris, Horus said to his father, "I have brought you your adversaries, your soul is within." Then Horus touched all the parts of his father's corpse and imitated each of their movements. Thus the life fluid formerly transmitted from father to son returned to the father. The son took it back again to transmit it to the faithful.

In the third act of this sacred drama, Osiris was given a meticulous cleansing, followed by ablutions, fumigations, incensing, and unctions. Then he was arrayed in bandages, collars, and magical amulets. In this way, he entered immortality, no longer fearing his enemies' powers.

The rituals that brought Osiris back to life assured him a second, eternal youth and an immortality that the earlier gods, subjected to senility and the ravages of old age, hadn't known. Osiris's passion became the redemption of gods and men. It was necessary to repeat the resurrection rites for all the other buried gods. And with the help of these same ceremonies, every man achieved the same end. Sons played the role of Horus, wives, the role of Isis, and friends, the roles of Thoth and Anubis.

What was Osiris? The symbol of the overflowing Nile, the sign of beneficial water which Typhon, the fire, dried up. He was the personification of the moon which produces the dew and humidity, promotes the generation of animals and the growth of plants which Typhon, the sun, burns and withers. As Plutarch said, "Each of these explanations alone is false, and taken all together, they are true."[6]

---

6. After A. Moret, *Roi et Dieux d'Egypte* (A. Colin).

In systematizing folk themes into religious myths, in creating a shared, precise representation of the hero, societies aim at practical ends. Just as children find the ways for preparing themselves for their future lives in games, so adults find ways to imitate the feats of gods and heroes in sacred rituals, and so hope to earn, at a lesser cost, their merits and rewards. Repeating the perilous odyssey symbolically, they break out of the ordinary human state and take on the glory and purity of the divine.

This hope may be less puerile than it seems. Think, for example of theater shows: dramatic or cinematic representations provoke the same emotional reactions as dramas in real life. After a few moments, the spectator is drawn in, feeling anger, fear, anxiety, just as if the events were happening to him.

Let us consider, furthermore, how easy it is for physical attitudes to give rise to psychological states. Those who go down on their knees become humble. Those who take a deep breath and stick out their chests already feel more courageous.... Now, over the course of ceremonial rituals, the adept is both spectator and actor, meaning that the adept truly becomes one with the knowledge of the mystery which, at the same time, he performs.

Insofar as certain beings manage to raise themselves above their ordinary mediocrity, these rites belong to the exploration of the marvelous. Although religious cults generally all have their own liturgical apparatus for inspiring the faithful, initiatory sects, because of the secrecy surrounding them, are often more effective in altering the spiritual state of their adherents. Alas, this remark no longer applies to the Freemasons from whom I have borrowed this authentic account of the ceremony that follows.

After having overcome the tests of water, fire, earth, and air, and after having taken his oath, the apprentice has become a companion. He has, hopefully at least, increased his knowledge and purified his conscience by the time he is accepted as a Master, following this ancient and accepted Scottish ritual.

Reception of a Master Following the Scottish Ritual

The lodge is hung with black drapes and is lit by three mysterious stars. In the center of the room, toward the East, is a coffin on which lies the last received Master, with his feet turned toward the East. He is covered with a black sheet and a bloodstained handkerchief has been tossed over his face. The Masters are seated with heads covered, each has a sword in his hand, the tip of which is pointing toward the ground. At the foot of the stairs, before the altar, the Grand Master is sitting.

The candidate is brought into the Chamber of Reflection. The Grand Master says: "My brothers, our companion N. asks for an increase in salary; he is going to be led to the center of the room. I believe I still have need of your approval." This approval is given. The member elect is seized by two brethren armed with swords who lead him to the door of the Temple. The guards, who have been heard knocking, announce to the Grand Master that those knocking are companions [Freemasons].

The Grand Master replies: "Who is this very transient companion that dares enter into these halls? Does he come in insult of our sorrow?" He orders the guards to find out. The guard: "Who is there?" The warden on the other side of the door answers: "We are bringing a companion that we have caught on the outskirts of the Temple and who appears to be immersed in a profound meditation." The Grand Master: "Perhaps he is one of those guilty of the murder that we are mourning; ask him his name and age. What was he doing in the spot where you caught him?" One of the brethren: "This worker, encouraged by the satisfactory reports of his work that he received from his superiors, has conceived the hope of obtaining compensation for it. I know that he has scaled a staircase divided into two landings, one of three degrees and the other of five."

The member elect is marched inside backward, his back facing east. The Grand Master: "Companion, have you totally reflected on the step you are taking, are your hands clean and your conscience untroubled? My brother, a great calamity has fallen upon us. One of those whom Masonry has conferred its benefits upon has basely betrayed it." The Grand Master questions the member elect further on his past, his studies, and his general moral principles; then he tells him: "Turn around." It is at this time that the member elect can see the Master lying on the coffin. The Grand Master: "Examine him who is the subject of our mourning, companion. The light that gave us clarity has disappeared; one of our brothers has been struck down by ignoble murderers. We have the sad certainty that the workers who committed this crime are among the ranks of our companions. Do you have any knowledge of a plot hatched against our Order?.... If you are innocent of this crime you are going to give us proof in a moment. Approach this corpse. If you are not one of the murderers or their accomplices you should have no fear that our brother will rise up before you demanding vengeance and cursing you."

The member elect steps over the body from right to left and from left to right until he reaches the feet of the person lying down who is now behind him. The brother who had been lying down silently stands up and takes back his place amid the ranks of his companions.

The Grand Master speaks: "We are going to reveal to you the circumstances of an unheard of crime of which you will give us your word of honor never to speak, whatever the outcome may be. He whom we mourn is our Grand Master. He had conceived the pious design of raising a temple that would glorify the great architect of the universe. Hiram, learned in architecture as in the transformation of metals, was chosen for this task. The building was almost finished when the enemies of our Order, jealous of his success, decided to wrest from Hiram his secrets in order to continue and finish themselves the work that was so well begun. They were unaware of how scrupulously the Master guarded the secrets that had been imparted to him. They incited three wretches already initiated into the first levels of the art who were workers inflamed with ambition who regarded themselves as too highly trained to remain in the lower ranks. These corrupt individuals jealously regarded those whom talent and virtue had placed above them and who had gained admission to the central chamber. They resolved to enter this sacred spot, by fair means or foul, and to do so, to wrest the sacred word of the Masters from our father Hiram. Having, in silence and shadow, made the arrangements that should, according to their calcu-lations, crown their detestable undertaking with success, they awaited the moment when, at the fall of day as the workers quit their tasks, the Master would be left alone. The temple had three doors: the one on the East that communicated with the central chamber was reserved for the Master, a second on the South, and the third on the West served as the main entrance; it was through there that Hiram was in the habit of retiring. The three plotters lay separately in ambush at each of the doors. Hiram emerged from the central chamber to inspect the works; he saw one of the conspirators hidden near the door and armed with a heavy ruler. Questioned as to the reasons for his presence there, the companion responded that he needed a promotion. Hiram, with his normal goodwill, replied that he must wait for the end of his studies and the decision of his brothers. The companion insisted and threatened; he wished to wrest the sacred word from the Master; he struck him on the head with a violent blow of his ruler. [At this moment the warden strikes the right shoulder of the member elect with his ruler.] Hiram tried to leave by the Southern door; he was prevented from doing so by the second conspirator; he hastily gained the door on the West but the third wretch struck him in the nape of the neck with his tongs. [The first warden gives a light tap to the nape of the member elect's neck.] Stunned, the Master staggered toward the last exit from the temple but he was stopped and struck on the forehead."

At these words the Grand Master strikes the member elect's forehead with a tap from his hammer; the companion is stretched out upon the coffin behind him with a black cloth covering him. His apron is placed over his face. A branch of acacia is placed at his head, a square and compass are placed at his feet.

The Grand Master: "Thus perished this just man, faithful to the last regarding his duty. Alas! My brothers, since the fatal moment that deprived us of our Master, the world has remained in dense shadows, the works have been suspended; is there nothing we can do to regain the light? He alone held the secret of the work begun. Who would dare today present themselves as his successor? However, we won't lose heart, the light can again reappear. Look, my brothers, from West to East, from North to South, until your eyes find the spot where the infamous murderers have left the body of our Master."

The wardens take seven masters with them and circle the lodge three times, then approach the coffin. The second warden says: "This funerary tree, this acacia, indicates a sepulcher; perhaps it overshadows the tomb of our Master."

The first warden replies: "Yes, it is said that science rests in the shadow of the acacia. This sad and empty spot could certainly be the tomb of our Master."

Three Masters armed with swords remain close to the coffin; the others return to their places and tell the tale of their discovery to the Grand Master. He, in turn, comes and stations himself at the head of the coffin.

The Masters are without weapons and are in an orderly grouping. The Grand Master lifts off the apron that is covering the head of the prone figure; he recognizes the face, then pulls off the sheet, uncovering the entire body, and says: "His noble face respected by death has the expression of a calm conscience and peace of the soul. Let us carry these precious remains within the enclosure of the works in order to provide him a worthy sepulcher."

During this time the lights in the Temple have been relit. The wardens seek to restore life to the deceased with the use of magic words: they are unsuccessful.

The Grand Master says: "That is not how, my brothers, you will keep my promise. Do you not remember that in union there is strength and that without the aid of others we can do nothing?"

Then the Grand Master places himself at the feet of the member elect, takes him by the right hand, and practices the secret touches with him. He also bestows the fraternal kiss upon him, whispers something to him in confidence, and then declares: "May the Great Architect of the Universe be praised, the Master has been rediscovered, he appears as glorious as ever."

Immediately the member elect is stood up; the funerary apparatus is promptly hidden away. The Grand Master invites his brothers to rejoice and says: "Our Master sees anew the day; he is reborn in the person of brother N...."

And then addressing his words to the member elect he adds: "Read the history of the past centuries; everywhere you will see talent misunderstood, science scorned, and virtue persecuted; ignorance, fanaticism, and ambition govern the world. To destroy this empire to let reign the truth that is science itself, to defend it against those enemies determined to proscribe it, such is the task imposed upon the Master. My brother, are you agreed to this; do you wish to join with us by your sworn word?"

On the positive response of the member elect the sworn word is uttered by all. The distinctive emblems of his new rank are put in place. He is now the one who can cry out with his hands lifted above his head: "To me, children of the 'widow'!"

He can answer that the acacia is known to him; he is seven years and older. He is presented to all his colleagues and then installed in the place where he can soon resume his work.

The closing ritual of the ceremony can then be spoken.[7]

The Master has made the symbolic voyage beyond death to be reborn in the purified form of his new rank. He is supposed to begin a new existence. To put the profane to death, to kill off the old self, and be reborn by the power of incantations: since the most ancient times, these conditions are required of anyone wishing to enter an order (whatever

7. Masonic chapbook, trans. Jon Graham.

the religion to which this order is attached). No doubt the reader will have noticed that in the case of the reception just narrated, no actual sacrifice preceded it. The new member relived the episodes of the hero's death symbolically. Substituting himself for the hero, he can be considered the hero's legitimate successor. Over the course of the Christian mass, a more complete sacrifice is performed, insofar as the wine, water, and host represent the blood and body of Christ put to death. For adherents to this religion, there will be only one sacrifice in all time to come, the sacrifice of Jesus, which they repent every day. In making use of such symbolic elements, does the ceremony retain its full magic power? For most of the procedures prescribed by magic formulas and practiced by the various esoteric sects, the officiate avoids such substitutions. He is looking for more direct contact with elemental, living realities. That is why the voodoo cult retains the use of blood for joining the novice both to the community and to the divine power. Seabrook describes the ceremony that gave him access to the voodoo mystery.

Voodoo Initiation Ceremony
W. B. Seabrook

On the afternoon of the Friday set for my blood baptism, more than fifty friends and relatives gathered at the habitation of Maman Célie. There was no reason to suppose that we might be disturbed, but as an extra precaution a gay *danse Congo* was immediately organized to cover the real purpose of our congregation. Maman Célie had told me that I would get no sleep that night; so despite the noise I napped until after sunset, when she awakened me and led me across the compound to the *houmfort*.

Through its outer door, which Emanuel stood guarding like a sentinel and unlocked for us, we entered a dim, windowless, cell-like anteroom in which were tethered the sacrificial beasts, a he-goat, two red cocks and two black, an enormous white turkey, and a pair of doves. Huddled there in the corner also was the girl Catherine, Maman Célie's youngest unmarried daughter; why she was there I did not know, and it is needless to say that I wondered.

From this dim, somewhat sinister antechamber we passed through an open doorway into the long, rectangular mystery room, the temple proper, which was lighted with candles and primitive oil lamps that flickered like torches. Its clay walls were elaborately painted with crude serpent symbols and anthropomorphic figures.

At the near end of the room, close to the doorway through which we had entered, was the wide, low altar, spread over with a white lace tablecloth. In its center was a small wooden serpent, elevated horizontally on a little pole as Moses lifted up the serpent in the wilderness.... Grouped also on the altar were earthen jugs containing wine, water, oil; platters of vegetables and fruits; plates containing common bread, and plates containing elaborate sweet fancy cakes, bought days before, down in the plain.

On the altar also was a cone-like mound of cornmeal surmounted by an egg, and before the altar candles were burning and wicks were floating in coconut shells of oil. At the left were the three *Rada* drums, at the right was a low wooden stool placed for me.

At the other end of the mystery room, so that a ten-foot open space was left before the altar, were seated on the ground eighteen or twenty people, all close relatives or trusted friends, who were to witness the ceremony. When I entered, they were swaying and singing:

Hail to Father Agoué
Who dwells in the sea!
He is the lord of ships.

In a blue gulf
There are three little islands.
The African's boat is storm-tossed,
Father Agoué brings it safely in.
Hail to father Agoué!

Once the singing and pouring of libations was over, the *papaloi* began the real service. He stood with arms raised before the altar and said solemnly, "Dans nom tout Loi et tout Mystère"(In the name of all the Gods and Mysteries).

Maman Célie advanced at a sign from the *papaloi* and was invested by him, with the scarlet robe and headdress of ostrich feathers black and red, as *mamaloi* or priestess. This was accompanied by a shrill chant:

Ayiya Oueddo, my serpent goddess,
When you come it is like the lightning flash!

At the same time now I heard through the chanting a sharp, long-drawn, continuous hissing. It was Maman Célie, hissing like a snake, drawing and expelling the breath through her teeth.

I looked for Maman Célie's familiar sweet, gentle face, but beneath the black and scarlet plumes I saw now only what seemed a rigid mask. I felt that I was looking into the face of a strange, dreadful woman, or into the face of something that I had never seen before. As I watched, the cheeks of this black mask were deeply indrawn so that the face became skull-like, and then alternately puffed out as if the skull had been covered with flesh and come alive.

As the chanting died away, she whirled three times and flung herself prostrate before the altar with her lips pressed against the earth.

Emanuel, without donning sacerdotal garb, but now acting as a sort of altar servant, brought in the two red cocks. Each was handled gently, almost reverently, by the *papaloi*, as he knelt holding it, and with white flour traced on its back a cross. One of the small sweet cakes was crumbled, and each cock must peck at it from the *mamaloi's* hand. This was awaited patiently. At the moment when each bird consented to receive the consecrated food, the priestess seized it and rose wildly dancing, whirling with the cock held by its head and feet in her outstretched hands, its wings violently fluttering. Round and round she whirled while the drums throbbed in a quick, tangled, yet steady rhythm. With a sudden twist the cock's head was torn off and as she whirled the blood flew out as if from a sprinkling-pot. The other birds, the black cocks and the dove, were dealt with similarly. As she danced with the white living doves, it was beautiful, and it seemed to me natural also that they should presently die. Blood of the doves was saved in a china cup.

A thing that had a different, a horror-beauty like a mad Goya etching occurred when the black priestess did her death dance with the huge white turkey. Though far from feeble, possessed of great vitality, she was a slender woman, slightly formed, whose nervous strength lay not in muscular weight. When the turkey's wings spread wide and began to flap frantically above her head as she whirled, it seemed that she would be dragged from her feet, hurled to the ground, or flown away with fabulously in the sky. And as she sought finally to tear off its head, sought to clutch its body between her knees, it attacked her savagely, beating her face and breasts, beating at her so that she was at moments enfolded by the great white wings, so that bird and woman seemed to mingle struggling in a monstrous, mythical embrace. But her fatal hands were still upon its throat, and in that swanlike simulacra of the deed, for the male is always like a little death, it died.

So savage had this scene been that it was almost like an anticlimax when the sacrificial goat was now led through the doorway to the altar.... He was a sturdy brown young goat, with big, blue, terrified, almost human eyes, eyes that seemed not only terrified but aware and wondering. At first he bleated and struggled, for the odor of death was in the air, but finally he stood quiet, though still wide-eyed, while red silken ribbons were twined in his little horns, his little hoofs anointed with wine and sweet-scented oils, and an old woman who had come from far over the mountain for this her one brief part in the long ceremony sat down before him and crooned to him alone a song that might have been a baby's lullaby. [Finally on its forehead the *papaloi*] traced a cross and circle, first with flour and afterward with blood of the doves. Then he presented it a green leafy branch to eat.

And the goat nibbled the green leaves.

In the dim, bare anteroom with its windowless gray walls, the girl Catherine had remained all this time huddled in a corner, as if drugged or half asleep.

Emanuel had to clutch her tightly by the arm to prevent her from stumbling when they brought her to the altar. Maman Célie hugged her and moaned and shed tears as if they were saying good-bye forever. The *papaloi* pulled them apart and Maman Célie, no longer as a mourning mother but as an officiating priestess, with rigid face aided in pouring the oil and wine on the girl's head, feet, and breast.

All this time the girl had been like a fretful, sleepy, annoyed child, but gradually she became docile, somber, staring with quiet eyes, and presently began a weird song of lamentation.

And as that black girl sang the inner meaning of her song came to me; a horned beast would presently be substituted in her stead; but the moment for that mystical substitution had not yet come, and as she sang she was a daughter doomed to die.

The ceremony of substitution, when it came, was pure effective magic of a potency that I have never seen equaled in dervish monastery or anywhere. The goat and the girl, side by side before the altar, had been startled, restive, nervous. The smell of blood was in the air, but there was more than that hovering; it was the eternal, mysterious odor of death itself, which both animals and human beings always sense, but not through the nostrils. Yet now the two who were about to die mysteriously merged; the girl symbolically and the beast with a knife in its throat were docile and entranced, were like automatons. The *papaloi* monotonously chanting, endlessly repeating, "Damballa calls you, Damballa calls you," stood facing the altar with his arms outstretched above their two heads. The girl was now on her hands and knees in the attitude of a quadruped, directly facing the goat, so that their heads and eyes were on a level, less than ten inches apart, and thus they stared fixedly into each other's eyes, while the *papaloi*'s hands weaved slowly, ceaselessly above their foreheads, the forehead of the girl and the forehead of the horned beast, each wound with red ribbons, each already marked with the blood of a white dove. By shifting slightly I could see the big, black, staring eyes of the girl, and I could have almost sworn that the black eyes were gradually, mysteriously becoming those of a dumb beast, while a human soul was beginning to peer out through the blue. But dismiss that, and still I tell you that pure magic was here at work, that something very real and fearful was occurring. For as the priest wove his ceaseless incantations, the girl began a low piteous bleating in which there was nothing, absolutely nothing, human; and soon a thing infinitely more unnatural occurred; the goat was moaning and crying like a human child. Old magic was here at work and it worked appallingly.

Other signs and wonders became manifest. Into this little temple lost among the mountains came in answer to goat-cry girl-cry the Shaggy Immortal One of a thousand names whom the Greeks called Pan. The goat's lingam became erect and rigid; the points of the girl's breasts visibly hardened and were outlined sharply pressing against the coarse, thin, tight-drawn shift that was her only garment. Thus they faced each other motionless as two marble figures on the frieze of some ancient phallic temple. They were like inanimate twin lamps in which a sacred flame burned, steadily yet unconsuming.

While the *papaloi* still wove his spells, the priestess held a twig green with tender leaves between the young girl and the animal. She held it on a level with their mouths, and neither saw it, for they were staring fixedly into each other's eyes as entranced mediums stare into crystal globes, and with their necks thrust forward so that their foreheads almost touched. Neither could therefore see the leafy branch, but as the old *mamaloi*'s hand trembled, the leaves flicked lightly against the hairy muzzle of the goat, against the chin and soft lips of the girl. And after moments of breathless watching, it was the girl's lips that pursed out and began to nibble the leaves.

As she nibbled thus, the *papaloi* said in a hushed but wholly matter-of-fact whisper like a man who had finished a hard, solemn task and was glad to rest, "*Ça y est*" (There it is).

The *papaloi* was now holding a machete, ground sharp and shining. Maman Célie, priestess, kneeling, held a *gamelle*, a wooden bowl. It was oblong. There was just space enough to thrust it narrowly between the mystically identified pair. Its rim touched the goat's hairy chest and the girl's body, both their heads thrust forward above it. Neither seemed conscious of anything that was occurring, nor did the goat flinch when the *papaloi* laid his hand upon its horns. Nor did the goat utter any sound as the knife was drawn quickly, deeply across its throat. But at this instant, as the blood gushed like a fountain into the wooden bowl, the girl, with a shrill, piercing, then strangled bleat of agony, leaped, shuddered, and fell senseless before the altar.

At the moment the knife flashed across the goat's throat, the company had begun to chant, not high or loud but with a sort of deep, hushed fervor, across which the girl's inhuman bleating had shrilled sharp as another invisible blade. Now they continued chanting while the celebrants performed their various offices....[8]

8. W. B. Seabrook, *The Magic Island* (Harcourt, Brace & Co., 1929), 54–66.

THE MARVELOUS VOYAGE

The Hero Hesitates, Incantations, Magical Objects, Searching for the Book

To feel terribly alone in the great humming city on a hot evening in June. To be at that anxious moment when adolescence comes to an end. Yesterday, everything was easy, despite the powerless rage of those early years, despite all the pain and grief that shapes childhood. Everything was easy because it was only a question of life or death, and not of the diabolical chain of usury which that machine—human society—involves. To be at the doorstep of the black house where money must be earned, to feel you've been brought there by the person you expected would make you completely free: your wife. Because she asks for the basic comfort of a roof, and flowers, and finery. Because, weary of so much wandering, her smile becomes tense too quickly.

To be at that hour when, yearning to begin building, a man decides he must put his plan into action, that he must stop dreaming and start living the difficult reality. In this moment of choice, this undefined, troubled moment, without present or past, one struggles to the height of the self, like a traveler, reaching the mountain peak after a long trek, who straightens up to see the horizon in the distance beyond the plains. One perceives men's destinies as clearly as roads seen from the cabin of a plane. In this almost unbearably intense moment, it seems that thought is independent of being. It soars free as a spirit of air or fire, a

stranger to human feelings, endowed with an implacable consciousness. And yet the heart, charged with so many desires it dare not acknowledge, beats too quickly. To accept neither sleep nor compromise,
while the perfume of sweat and sperm rises from the noisy city. To refuse
to go down and join in the laughter or take part in the miserable game
that has no risks other than accidents, no grandeur other than hidden
historical significance. To know how to win whatever there is to win
there, even a little more perhaps, but to already be tired of such vain
rewards, vain because social ends are only attained long after the desire for them has faded away. And not to be able to sleep, not to want to
sleep, to refuse that sensuous plunge into cosmic anonymity, free of
responsibilities. To hope for adventure. And not just to take off for
some buccaneer's island or the depths of a tropical forest as the illustrated magazines we remember from childhood would urge. Not just
to play at freedom, as we used to play Indians among the trees in the
public park while our mothers knitted and our fathers checked off sums
in their offices. To take up the human adventure, of which only a few
speak. And even they speak of it mysteriously, reticently, in veiled terms,
as though it were an only partially transmittable secret.

To feel that the marvelous adventure is essential, and then to examine one's powers. To regard oneself as one more recruit filing before a
draft board, a horse being examined by a breeder on the morning of the
race. And if you aren't strong enough to withstand the risks of the voyage? One evening, at the edge of the water, despondency and the ultimate plunge; the asylum where you're led and shut away (poor Vincent);
the hospital in Marseilles where you cut your thigh. Or prison, where
society, rejected, finally gets revenge for the bars within which it finds
itself confined. To know all that, better than a frightened mother, better
than those old timers, full of advice, for whom cowardice is wisdom.

To question oneself anxiously. What if you are the victim of a "momentary exaltation" as they say, if you are finally only suited for regular
jobs such as store clerk or general, if you don't bear that essential destiny within yourself, the star on the forehead? What will you encounter? The winged horse, the daughter of the king of the spirits? Nature's
conspiring approval or its mortal indifference?

Who will provide the magic formulas, amulets, and talismans? Who
will teach the incantations needed to vanquish hostile powers and overcome their obstacles?

At this decisive hour, the uneasy mind recalls the words of Faust. At
the door of the city, Faust says:

The Hesitations of Faust
Goethe

Slow sinks the orb, the day is now no more;
Yonder he hastens to diffuse new life.
Oh for a pinion from the earth to soar,
And after, ever after him to strive!
Then should I see the world below,
Bathed in the deathless evening beams,
The vales reposing, every height aglow,
The savage mountain, with its cavern'd side,
Bars not my godlike progress. Lo, the ocean,
Its warm bays heaving with a tranquil motion,
To my rapt vision opes its ample tide!
But now at length the god appears to sink;
A new-born impulse wings my flight,
Onward I press, his quenchless light to drink,
The day before me, and behind the night,
The pathless waves beneath, and over me the skies.
Fair dream, it vanish'd with the parting day!
Alas! that when on spirit wings we rise,
No wing material lifts our mortal clay.
But 'tis our inborn impulse, deep and strong,
Upward and onward still to urge our flight,
When far above us pours its thrilling song
The sky-lark, lost in azure light,
When on extended wing amain
O'er pine-crowned height the eagle soars,
And over moor and lake, the crane
Still striveth toward its native shore.

Two souls, alas! are lodg'd within my breast,
Which struggle there for undivided reign:
One to the world, with obstinate desire,
And closely-cleaving organs still adheres;
Above the mist, the other doth aspire,
With sacred vehemence to purer spheres.
Oh, are there spirits in the air,
Who float 'twixt heaven and earth dominion wielding,
Stoop hither from your golden atmosphere,
Lead me to scenes, new life and fuller yielding!
A magic mantle did I but possess,

Abroad to waft me as on viewless wings,
I'd prize it far beyond the costliest dress,
Nor would I change it for the robe of kings.

WAGNER:

Call not the spirits who on mischief wait!
Their troop familiar, streaming through the air,
From every quarter threaten man's estate,
And danger in a thousand forms prepare!
They drive impetuous from the frozen north,
With fangs sharp-piercing, and keen arrowy tongues;
From the ungenial east they issue forth,
And prey, with parching breath, upon your lungs;
If, wafted on the desert's flaming wing,
They from the south heap fire upon the brain,
Refreshment from the west at first they bring,
Anon to drown thyself and field and plain.
In wait for mischief, they are prompt to hear;
With guileful purpose our behests obey;
Like ministers of grace they oft appear,
And lisp like angels, to betray.
But let us hence! Gray eve doth all things blend,
The air grows chill, the mists descend!
'Tis in the evening first our home we prize—
Why stand you thus, and gaze with wondering eyes?
What in the gloom thus moves you?

FAUST:

Yon black hound
See'st thou, through corn and stubble scampering around?

WAGNER:

I've marked him long, naught strange in him I see!

FAUST:

Note him! What takest thou the brute to be?

WAGNER:

But for a poodle, whom his instinct serves
His master's track to find once more.

FAUST:

Dost mark how round us, with wide spiral curves,
He wheels, each circle closer than before?

And, if I err not, he appears to me
A fiery whirlpool in his track to leave.

Wagner:

A dog dost see, no specter have we here;
He growls, doubts, lays him on his belly too,
And wags his tail—as dogs are wont to do.

Faust:

Thou'rt right indeed; no traces now I see
Whatever of a spirit's agency.
'Tis training—nothing more.

(Faust has entered his study followed by the dog.)

Behind me now lie field and plain,
As night her veil doth o'er them draw,
Our better soul resumes her reign
With feelings of foreboding awe.
Lull'd is each stormy deed to rest
And tranquilliz'd each wild desire;
Pure charity doth warm the breast,
And love to God the soul inspire.
Cease, poodle cease! with the tone that arises,
Hallow'd and peaceful, my soul within,
Accords not thy growl, thy bestial din.
We find it not strange, that man despises
What he conceives not;
The good and the fair he misprizes;
What lies beyond him he doth contemn;
Snarleth the poodle at it, like men?

But ah! E'en now I feel, howe'er I yearn for rest,
Contentment welleth up no longer in my breast.
Yet wherefore must the stream, alas, so soon be dry,
That we once more athirst should lie?
This sad experience oft I've approv'd!
The want admitteth of compensation;
We learn to prize what from sense is remov'd
Our spirits yearn for revelation,
Which nowhere burneth with beauty blent,
More pure than in the New Testament.
To the ancient text an impulse strong

Moves me the volume to explore,
And to translate its sacred lore,
Into the tones belovèd of the German tongue.

(He opens a volume and applies himself to it.)

'Tis writ, "In the beginning was the Word!"
I pause, perplex'd! Who now will help afford?
I cannot the mere word so highly prize;
I must translate it otherwise,
If by the spirit guided as I read.
"In the beginning was the Sense!" Take heed,
The import of this primal sentence weigh,
Lest thy too hasty pen be led astray!
Is force creative then of sense the dower?
"In the beginning was the Power!"
Thus should it stand: Yet, while the line I trace,
A something warns me, once more to efface.
The spirit aids! from anxious scruples freed,
I write, "In the beginning was the Deed!"

Am I with thee my room to share,
Poodle, thy barking now forbear,
Forbear thy howling!
Comrade so noisy, ever growling,
I cannot suffer here to dwell.
One or the other, mark me well,
Forthwith must leave the cell.
I'm loath the guest-right to withhold;
The door's ajar, the passage clear;
But what must now mine eyes behold!
Are nature's laws suspended here?
Real is it, or a phantom show?
In length and breadth how doth my poodle grow!
He lifts himself with threa'ning mien,
In likeness of a dog no longer seen!
What specter have I harbor'd thus!
Huge as a hippopotamus,
With fiery eye, terrific tooth!
Ah! now I know thee, sure enough!
For such a base, half-hellish brood,
The key of Solomon is good.

SPIRITS (without):
Captur'd there within is one!
Stay without and follow none!
Like a fox in iron snare,
Hell's old lynx is quaking there,
But take heed!
Hover round, above, below,
To and fro,
Then from durance he is freed!
Can ye aid him, spirits all,
Leave him not in mortal thrall!
Many a time and oft hath he
Served us, when at liberty.

FAUST:
The monster to confront, at first,
The spell of Four must be rehears'd.

Salamander shall kindle
Writhe nymph of the wave,
In air sylph shall dwindle,
And Kobold shall slave.

Who doth ignore
The primal Four,
Nor knows aright,
Their use and might,
O'er spirits will he
Ne'er master be!

Vanish in the fiery glow,
Salamander!
Rushingly together flow,
Undine!
Shimmer in the meteor's gleam,
Sylphide!
Hither bring thine homely aid,
Incubus! Incubus!
Step forth! I do abjure thee thus!

None of the Four lurks in the beast;
He grins at me, untroubled as before;
I have not hurt him in the least.

A spell of fear
Thou now shalt hear.
Art thou, comrade fell,
Fugitive from Hell?
See then this sign,
Before which incline
The murky troops of Hell!
With bristling hair now doth the creature swell.
Canst thou, reprobate,
Read the uncreate,
Unspeakable, diffused
Throughout the heavenly sphere,
Shamefully abused,
Transpierced with nail and spear!
Behind the stove, tam'd by my spells,
Like an elephant he swells;
Wholly now he fills the room,
He into mist will melt away.
Ascend not to the ceiling! Come,
Thyself at the master's feet now lay!
Thou seest that mine is no idle threat,
With holy fire I will scorch thee yet!
Wait not the might
That lies in the triple-glowing light!
Wait not the might
Of all my arts in fullest measure!

MEPHISTOPHELES

(As the mist sinks, comes forward from behind the stove, in the dress of a traveling scholar.)

FAUST:
Thy name?

MEPHISTOPHELES:
Part of that power which still
Produceth good, while ever scheming ill
The spirit I, which evermore denies!
And justly; for what e're to light is brought
Deserve again to be reduced to naught;
Then better 'twere that naught should be.
Thus all the elements which ye

Destruction, Sin, or briefly, Evil, name,
As my peculiar element I claim.

FAUST:

Thou nams't thyself a part, and yet a whole I see.

MEPHISTOPHELES:

The modest truth I speak to thee,
Though folly's microcosm, man, it seems,
Himself to be a perfect whole esteems,
Part of the part am I, which at the first was all.
A part of darkness, which gave birth to light.
Proud light, who now his mother would enthrall,
Contesting space and ancient rank with night.
Yet he succeedeth not, for struggle as he will,
To forms material he adhereth still;
From them he streameth, them he maketh fair,
And still the progress of his beams they check;
And so, I trust, when comes the final wreck,
Light will, ere long, the doom of matter share.

FAUST:

Thy worthy avocation now I guess!
Wholesale annihilation won't prevail,
So thou'rt beginning on a smaller scale.

MEPHISTOPHELES:

And, to say truth, as yet with small success.
Oppos'd to nothingness, the world,
This clumsy mass, subsisteth still;
Nor yet is it to ruin hurl'd,
Despite the effort of my will.
Tempests and earthquakes, fire and flood, I've tried;
Yet land and ocean still unchang'd abide!
And then of humankind and beasts, the accursed brood—
Neither o'er them can I extend my sway.
What countless myriads have I swept away!
Yet ever circulates the fresh new blood.
It is enough to drive me to despair!
As in the earth, in water, and in air,
In moisture and in drought, in heat and cold,
Thousands of germs their energies unfold!

If fire I had not for myself retain'd,
No sphere whatever had for me remain'd.

FAUST:

So thou with thy cold devil's fist, still clinch'd in malice impotent,
Dost the creative power resist, the active the beneficent!
Henceforth some other task essay, of Chaos thou the wondrous son!

(He continues speaking to Mephistopheles who admits to being unable to leave because of the pentagram hung above the door.)

To capture thee was not my will.
Thyself hast freely entered in the snare:
Let him who holds the devil, hold him still!
A second time so soon he will not catch him there.

MEPHISTOPHELES:

If it so please thee, I'm at thy command; only on this condition,
     understand;
That worthily thy leisure to beguile, I here may exercise my arts awhile.
This hour enjoyment more intense shall captivate each ravish'd sense,
Than thou couldst compass in the bound
Of the whole year's unvarying round;
And what the dainty spirits sing,
The lovely images they bring, are no fantastic sorcery.
Rich odors shall regale your smell, on choicest sweets your palate dwell,
Your feelings thrill with ecstasy. No preparation do we need,
Here we together are. Proceed.

SPIRITS:

Hence overshadowing gloom, vanish from sight!
O'er thine azure dome, bend, beauteous light!
Dark clouds that o'er us spread, melt in thin air!
Stars, your soft radiance shed, tender and fair.
Girt with celestial might, winging this airy flight,
Spirits are thronging.
Follow their forms of light infinite longing!
Flutter their vestures bright o'er field and grove!
Where in their leafy bower lovers the livelong hour
Vow deathless love.
Soft bloometh bud and bower! Bloometh the grove!
Grapes from the spreading vine crown the full measure;

Fountains of foaming wine gush from the pressure.
Still where the currents wind, gems brightly gleam.
Leaving the hills behind on rolls the stream;
Now into ample seas, spreadeth the flood;
Laving the sunny leas, mantled with wood.
Rapture the feather'd throng, gayly careering,
Sip as they float along; sunward they're steering;
On toward the isles of light winging their way,
That on the waters bright dancingly play.
Hark to the choral strain, joyfully ringing!
While on the grassy plain dancers are springing;
Climbing the steep hill's side, skimming the glassy tide,
Wonder they there;
Others on pinions wide wing the blue air;
On toward the living stream, toward yonder stars that gleam,
Far, far away;
Seeking their tender beam wing they their way.

MEPHISTOPHELES:
Well done, my dainty spirits! now he slumbers;
Ye have entranc'd him fairly with your numbers;
This minstrelsy of yours I must repay.
Thou art not yet the man to hold the devil fast!—
With fairest shapes your spells around him cast,
And plunge him in a sea of dreams!
But that this charm be rent, the threshold passed,
Tooth of rat the way must clear.
I need not conjure long it seems,
One rustles hitherward, and soon my voice will hear.
The master of the rats and mice,
Of flies and frogs, of bugs and lice,
Commands thy presence; without fear
Come forth and gnaw the threshold here,
Where he with oil has smear'd it. Thou
Coms't hopping forth already! Now to work!
The point that holds me bound is in the outer angle found.
Another bite—so—now 'tis done—
Now, Faustius, till we meet again, dream on.

FAUST (awakening):
Am I once more deluded! must I deem

This troop of thronging spirits all ideal?
The devil's presence, was it nothing real?
The poodle's disappearance but a dream?[1]

Why does that controlling mechanism, sleep, always interfere just as we are about to attain mystery? Before abandoning himself to sleep, Faust had taken the devil into his power. If he had had enough vigilant duplicity to feign sleep, learning the secret incantations would have cost him less. Fortunately, a great many incantations have managed to reach us.

Incantation for
Vanquishing His Enemies

I, the god Quetzalcoatl, the Plumed Serpent,
I, the god called Matl;
I, the one who is war,
I mock everything,
Because I know neither fear nor debt.
Now is the time
For me to mock my sisters
And all those who share my own nature.
And in order for us to mock all of them,
Hurry and be my allies.
Gods, ballplayers and warrior gods,
All you others who, together, wound,
All you others who, together, clash,
Because I see my sisters coming,
My doubles in nature;
We will know to mock them
Because they bring their blood and their color
And the fragility of their flesh and their color
But me, I have neither flesh nor blood
And I carry away the priest
With the heat of the summer on my arms.
I carry away the priest and death and the flint

---

1. Goethe, *Faust*, trans. Anna Swanwick (New York: A. L. Burt, 1909).

Who will drink blood before all others
Because red stains the rock,
And blood of the enemy will make the bludgeon drunk,
Will make the earth drunk,
With me and my arms.
Here come my sisters rushing up,
My sisters, men like me,
One of them carries her bouquet
With the feather of roses which is her breath
She carries her cotton fan
And her distaff
To flout me.
So come, you crush of men,
Come thighs,
Come ballplayer gods and warrior gods,
Who, together, wound,
Who, together, clash.
Come priest of the idols,
Those of the East, those of the West
Wherever you may be,
Come animals and birds;
At the four cardinal points I invoke you
For what is going to happen.
See the rabbit standing up
Its head raised or against the earth!
Weapon, your heat will be
Like the heat of the summer
Because you must stain and bloody yourself.
Aim your arrows and don't miss,
Shatter your arrows in their flight.
And you, stone, flint,
Which must be covered with blood,
Listen to the crush
Of the men who follow me.

꧁

Incantation for Netting Birds

I, an orphaned hunter,
For whom Quetzalcoatl alone is god,

I come, an orphaned hunter,
To take my uncles,
The noblemen of the sky;
But, I say,
They are already there, my uncles;
They come close to the ground.
It's here that I set my net,
Which is the home and the dress of my mother;
It's here that I will set a post,
Planting it in the throat,
In the belly, in the flanks
Of this mother whose jewelry
Is made of precious stones.
It's here that I will wait for my uncles,
The ones who fall down out of the sky.[2]

Incantation for the Maguey Plant

The time has come,
staff which loves water,
to plant and make grow
that honored woman
with eight regular leaves:
For you, Great Prince,
I will place her as you wish
in a fertile place
free of nasty weeds,
that honored woman
with eight regular leaves!
Divine Sun which comes out of the darkness
I ask that she be knocked seven times,
beaten nine times!

---

2. The first and second incantations are taken from Hernando Ruiz de Alarco, *Tratado de supersticiones* (1629), not published in French. I owe their translations [from Spanish to French] to my friend, Alejo Carpentier, to whom I address all my thanks.

I begin again full of confidence
in the law of your four conflagrations!
—Ah, my father
who has four flames,
four conflagrations
and a bright red comet!
Father and mother of the gods
Of the four kindling breaths;
being of infinite steps,
whose mouth is a river of black smoke,
Bring along with you the messengers of the rain,
whose heads are all tousled:
those harbingers who are never satisfied,
never calm,
always burdened by
theirs griefs and their tears!
My father
of the four burning breaths,
I will think of you,
before considering myself,
and my pleasure,
I want to offer you the hot blood,
the fragrant blood
of the captive beast!
I want to offer you
the heart
and the head
of the seven rose stag
living on this earth which belongs to you![3]

The incantations are more effective if they are used in conjunction with images or objects capable of retaining the entreaty's power within their actual matter. Talismans open certain doors into the natural world and protect the explorer of the marvelous. I refer readers who wish to make such instruments of power for themselves to more

---

3. Jocinta de la Serna, *Manuel de Ministros de Indios* (National Museum of Mexico, 1892).

specific treatises.[4] Among those formulas known to us, one of the most ancient comes from the magical papyrus, called "Harris."

Take an amulet that represents "an image, painted on clay, of Amon, with four rams' heads, trampling a crocodile, and eight gods worshiping him at his right and his left." Pronounce over it the following prayer: "Back, crocodile, son of Sît!—don't thrash with your tail!—don't grasp with your arms!—don't open your mouth!—Let the water become a sheet of flame before you!—The spell of the thirty-seven gods is in my look—you are bound to Re's great fang—you are bound to the four bronze pillars of noon—to the front of Re's boat. Back, crocodile, son of Sît!—protect me, Amon, husband of your mother!"[5]

But—and this is very mysterious—those talismans and amulets made by magicians with one specific purpose and according to the strict protocol of formulas are not the only ones found to be effective. Experience proves that any object whatever can be charged with real power, however difficult it is to detect at first glance. I am not thinking only of presents given to us by friends. These things bear within them the power of friendship or love. Having penetrated our dwelling places, they enjoy a curious extraterritoriality. Although they belong to us and are subject to our domestic laws, they continue nonetheless to be linked by invisible threads to those who sent them to us. They are true presences. I am thinking of the more general problem of anonymous objects bought by chance from secondhand shops or happened upon in attics, hidden among the rubble. After months or years asleep in the dust, these objects suddenly come back to life once again. These are the instruments fate prefers when it is trying to change the course of events or our thoughts. Believing we have only satisfied some fleeting whim, we let things that hide spirits and demons into our homes.

I recall an experience of this kind, myself. Once when I was making a trip to Brussels, a friend asked me to pay his father a visit there. As the father and I were talking, I noticed a large bronze-colored plaster statue on an old chest. Through a window bordered with geraniums, the room

---

4. See especially P. Piobb, *Formulaire de Haute Magie.*
5. As provided by Maspero.

looked out on a gothic landscape: alleys lined with old, gabled houses dominated by the dark towers of the cathedral. Such landscapes, so common in Belgium and Germany, envelop the visitor in the unsettling atmosphere of medieval tales. I complimented my host on his lovely home and praised him especially for the choice of this statue. For me, it represented Ezekiel, a figure who had always greatly troubled me. To my amazement, in a spontaneous gesture, this gentleman made me a present of the statue. Such a present is not exactly what a tourist wants. Suddenly I found myself with a fragile, heavy, and extremely cumbersome package. Nevertheless, I brought the statue back to Paris. I set it up in my home. And it became the center of inexplicable phenomena. On many occasions, at night, the traces of a fire would be inscribed around it, almost forming words. Strange noises could be heard (very loud cracks, quick knocks... I wasn't the only one to witness these events). The plaster really seemed to be inhabited. After having been moved several times without inhibiting or putting an end to these phenomena, the object disappeared as strangely as it had appeared. It vanished. I had kept it for about four years, and now that nearly ten years have passed, I realize that its appearance coincided with a singular transformation in my life.

In writing down this account, it occurs to me (something I've never thought of before) that the statue disappeared shortly before the friend who had asked me to pay that visit in Brussels died.

When one has had this kind of experience, the account Jensen gives in *Gradiva* seems less astonishing:

The Appearance of Gradiva
W. Jensen

On a visit to one of the great antique collections of Rome, Norbert Hanold had discovered a bas-relief which was exceptionally attractive to him, so he was much pleased, after his return to Germany, to be able to get a splendid plaster cast of it. This had now been hanging for some years on one of the walls of his workroom, all the other walls of which were lined with bookcases. Here it had the advantage of a position with the right light exposure, on a wall visited, though but briefly, by the evening sun. About one-third life-size, the bas-relief represented a complete female figure in the act of walking; she was still young, but no longer in childhood and, on the other hand, apparently not a woman, but a Roman virgin about in her twentieth year. With her head bent forward a little, she held slightly raised in her left hand, so that her sandaled feet became visible, her garment which fell in voluminous folds from her throat to her ankles. The left foot had advanced, and the right, about to follow, touched the ground only lightly with the tips of the toes, while the sole and heel were raised almost vertically. This movement produced a double impression of exceptional agility and of confident composure, and the flightlike poise, combined with a firm step, lent her the peculiar grace.

Where had she walked thus and whither was she going? Doctor Norbert Hanold, docent of archaeology, really found in the relief nothing noteworthy for his science. It was not a plastic production of great art of antique times, but was essentially a Roman genre production and he could not explain what quality in it had aroused his attention; he knew only that he had been attracted by something and this effect of the first view had remained unchanged since then. In order to bestow a name upon the piece of sculpture, he had called it to himself Gradiva, "the girl splendid in walking."

... Yet it was contrary to the young archaeologist's feeling to put her in the frame of great, noisy, cosmopolitan Rome. To his mind, her calm, quiet manner did not belong in this complex machine where no one heeded another, but she belonged rather in a smaller place where everyone knew her, and, stopping to glance after her, said to a companion, "That is Gradiva"—her real name Norbert could not supply—"the daughter of ——, she walks more beautifully than any other girl in our city."

These reflections occupied Norbert's mind for a long time and when spring arrived he decided to take the night train to the South and go down again to the dead city of Pompeii where the memory of ancient life has, nevertheless, remained so living and where he found a spot so kindred to his soul. As he was walking, the only living person in the hot noonday silence among the remains of the Strada di Mercurio, the sun dissolved the tomblike rigidity of the old stones, a glowing thrill passed through them, the dead awoke, and Pompeii began to live again.

Then suddenly—

With open eyes he gazed along the street, yet it seemed to him as if he were doing it in a dream. A little to the right something suddenly stepped forth from the Casa di Castore e Polluce, and across the lava stepping stones, which led from the house to the other side of the Strada di Mercurio, Gradiva stepped buoyantly.

Quite indubitably it was she; even if the sunbeams did surround her figure as if with a thin veil of gold, he perceived her in profile as plainly and as distinctly as on the bas-relief. As soon as he caught sight of her, Norbert's memory was clearly awakened to the fact that he had seen her here once already in a dream, walking thus, the night that she had lain down as if to sleep over there in the Forum on the steps of the Temple of Apollo. With this memory he became conscious, for the first time, of something else; he had, without himself knowing the motives in his heart, come to Italy on that account and had, without stop, continued from Rome and Naples to Pompeii to see if he could here find trace of her—and that in a literal sense—for, with her unusual gait, she must have left behind in the ashes a footprint different from all the others.

Again it was a noonday dream-picture that passed there before him and yet was also a reality. For that was apparent from an effect that it produced. On the last stepping-stone on the farther side, was stretched out a big lizard, whose body as if woven of gold and malachite, glistened brightly to Norbert's eyes. Before the approaching foot, however, it darted down suddenly and wiggled away over the white, gleaming lava pavement.

Gradiva crossed the stepping-stones with her calm buoyancy, and now, turning her back, walked along on the opposite sidewalk; her destination seemed to be the house of Adonis. Before it she stopped a moment, too, but passed then, as if after further deliberation, down farther through the Strada di Mercurio. On the left, of the more elegant buildings, there now stood only the Casa di Apollo and, to the man who was gazing after her, it seemed again that she had also surely chosen the portico of the Temple of Apollo for her death sleep. Probably she was closely associated with the cult of the sun god and was going there. Norbert Hanold stood still without having moved a limb. He did not know whether he was awake or dreaming, and tried in vain to collect his thoughts. Then, however a strange shudder passed down his spine. He saw and heard nothing, yet he felt from the secret inner vibrations that Pompeii had begun to live about him in the noonday hour of spirits and so Gradiva lived again, too, and had gone into the house that she had occupied before the fateful August day of the year 79.[6]

⥱

In the days that follow, Norbert becomes certain that he was not the victim of a wild delusion. The woman who appeared and made a place

---

6. W. Jensen, *Gradiva*, trans. G. Sadoul and E. Zak, in Freud, *Deliriums and Dreams*.

for herself in the young man's emotions, through the inexplicable intervention of the bas-relief, was a living reality. I will not say how, at the end of the story, Norbert marries her, any more than I will report on the highly intelligent, but, in my opinion, very inadequate explanation Freud gives for these disturbing events.

It is in the guise of an Egyptian statue that Doctor Cindarella's invitation for adventure reaches him.

Doctor Cindarella's Plants
G. Meyrink

Do you see this small black bronze statuette sitting here between the candlesticks? It is at the origin of all the strange events that have occurred to me over these last few years. I have sought in vain to distance myself from it; it obstinately reappears as the landmark from which I must trace my way. Whether it ultimately leads me to the light of wisdom or terminates at a point of ever-increasing terror, I have no way of knowing nor do I desire to know. I wish only to hang on to these few short moments of respite that destiny grants me before subjecting me to the next torments.

Stirring through the desert sand with my cane in Thebes, I disinterred this statuette by chance. When I regarded it attentively a morbid curiosity invaded my thoughts; I had to discover its significance. An old Arab collector told me: "It is an imitation of an Egyptian hieroglyph; the strange position of its arms must be in depiction of some ecstatic gesture of which I am ignorant."

I brought the statuette back to Europe and ever since not an evening has gone by without my being absorbed in interminable meditations on the mysterious meaning of this object. I was invaded by a terrible sensation; I was under the impression that I was applying myself to an odious and unhealthy problem that allowed me entry with a diabolic pleasure that erected no serious barriers to my thought but rather little by little infected it with an incurable illness and tyrannically imposed itself over the evolution of my life. One day in which I busied myself with some futile details, the solution of this enigma came to me with such violence that it made me jump.

These ideas that strike us with lightning like swiftness are like meteors in our inner universe; we are ignorant of where they come from and we observe naught but their flamboyant incandescence and their sudden fall.

A feeling of fear... and after a slight... as if... as if some unknown.... What am I trying to say? Excuse me, at certain times I get strangely forgetful ever since my left leg was paralyzed. Then, the response to all my research was there, clearly written: imitate!

It was as if this simple word had breached a wall and caused to surge within me an immense flood of light. Yes, this was the key to all the enigmas, the solution of all our existences, the invisible guiding thread— a secret, automatic, unconscious imitation with no respite. A potent and mysterious guide, a silent pilot with a masked face, has, since dawn, placed his feet on the boat of life. He comes from the chasms where our soul journeys when deep sleep has closed the gates of day. There is doubtless to be found in the inner reaches of physical being a demon statue that demands we model ourselves in its image. Imitate, this curt order that came from who knows where, I found myself constrained to follow it. I made myself comfortable and raised my hands above my head in order to conform to the posture of the statuette. I then lowered my fingers until my nails just brushed across my head.

I waited and nothing happened; no transformation took place, neither within nor around me. Looking at the statuette even more closely I observed that its eyes were closed as if sleeping. I interrupted this exercise until night; I then stopped the noise of the clock's pendulums and went to bed placing my arms and hands again in imitation of the statuette.

Several minutes passed and I don't believe that I could have fallen asleep. Suddenly it seemed to me that a noise echoed inside of me similar to the sound made by a large stone rolling down a chasm. Life left me in leaps: my consciousness seemed to be dragged along by the fall of this stone that was plunging down an endless stairway; it skipped over the stairs, first two by two, then four by four, finally by even larger bounds. As life was disappearing in this manner the visible phantom of death extended itself over my being. What happened next I will not say, no one would ever say it.

People scoff at the idea that the Egyptians and the Chaldeans possessed a well-guarded secret of, a secret never betrayed by, thousands of initiates, and they think that no sworn oath could have such a singular power. That is what I once thought; now I have gained the understanding that it doesn't concern an event of human experience where phenomena occur in a sequential order. In truth, no oath binds the tongue; the thought of even alluding to such things in this world is enough to freeze the heart. The secret is kept because it conceals itself and for that reason will remain hidden for as long as the world exists.

But these considerations have only a slender rapport with the burning shock to which I was subjected and which I cannot cure. Once the mind has breached, be it only a brief moment, the ordinary barriers of consciousness, the fate of the individual in his very actions takes on another sense.

I am living proof of this.

From that night I left my body (I know no other way to describe it), the course of my life has been transformed. My existence, which was once so easy, unfolds now in the midst of enigmatic and terrifying occurrences and seems to wend its way toward a goal that is as dark as it is unknown.

The horrific images grew more frequent; it seemed its goal now was to engender a kind of new madness within me and to install it with a slow and subtle progression into my life. No one could perceive or even suspect the existence of this madness; only the victim has an awareness of it through the torments that he is subjected to. The days following my first experiment with the hieroglyph I experienced things that at first I took for simple hallucinations. I heard strange noises of a potent and jarring quality that tore through the rhythms of everyday life. I caught glimpses of blinking lights that I had never seen before. Mysterious figures loomed up before me that other people could neither see nor feel. These figures acted in an incomprehensible and quite irrational manner, drowned in a kind of half-light. They would abruptly shift shape; stretching out like dead bodies and slithering like viscous cords along the gutters. Sometimes they squatted in stupid immobility in doorways.

This state of extraordinary lucidity doesn't persist; it waxes and wanes according to the phases of the moon.

My detachment in regard to humanity grew. Ordinary hopes and desires now came to me in a very dulled state; they appeared to come from so far away that I have the conviction that my soul is traveling a dark road, where little by little it draws away from the rest of humanity. In the beginning I allowed myself to be led by the premonitions whispered in my ears. Now I am obliged to follow a path imposed upon me, having no more liberty than the horse harnessed to the shaft of a cart.

And so one night I was once more dragged awake and compelled to walk the silent streets of the Malestrana quarter [a neighborhood in Prague]; I wandered aimlessly, feeling only the bizarre emotion provided by old houses. There is no spot in the world as lugubrious as this quarter. It never knows true daylight nor real night; it is bathed in a diffused and dull light that seeps from the rooftops like a phosphorescent exhalation. You go up a street and see nothing but a deathly darkness. At times a mournful ray of light filtered through the crack of a window pierces the eye as if it were a long and diabolical needle. A house looms up in the fog with its shoulders broken and its façade receding. It regards the night sky with its empty dormers like a wounded beast. Next to it another house rises up whose gleaming windows squint greedily down at the well; they seek to know if the goldsmith's child that drowned there a hundred years ago has been found yet. And when you pursue your path among the uneven paving stones, if you suddenly turn to look back you would swear that you saw in the corner several pale faces spying on you with haggard eyes. These faces rise up no higher than the height of large dogs. Yet nobody is in the street; a macabre silence reigns. The very old doors lock their mute lips.

I made my way up Thun Street where the palace of Countess Morzin is located. There perched in the fog was a narrow, hectic, and in truth, wicked house. I came to a halt and felt the growing sensation within of an inner fever. Under such circumstances I act under the control of an alien will and have no idea what I will be commanded to do in the next second.

I pushed open a door that was slightly ajar, entering the corridor, and descended a stairway leading to a cellar, as if it were my own house. Once below the reins that had been guiding me let go; I found myself in the darkness with the troubling certainty of having committed an incoherent act.

Why had I come down that staircase? Why couldn't my mind put a halt to these absurd impulses? I had to be sick—yes, that was it, I was surely ill. This explanation filled me with joy, I was happy to believe that this was all I was dealing with and that no foreign and unhealthy will was guiding me.

But a minute later it came to me that I had opened the door, entered the house, and descended the stairs without colliding into anything a single time just as someone would walk who knew every step of the way, and my hope instantly evaporated.

Little by little my eyes grew accustomed to the darkness and I could see around me. Sitting on a step of the stairs that had brought me to the cellar was a man whom I hadn't touched in passing. His menacing face faded into the gloom; a black beard covered his naked chest; his arms were naked as well. Only his legs seemed to be enveloped in pants or a sheet. The position of his hands was terrifying; they were strangely twisted to right angles. I stared at the man for a long time fixedly. He was as still as a corpse; his contours appeared to be etched into the depths of the gloom where it seemed they would remain until the disappearance of the house itself.

Horrified, I trembled and slid along hugging the curve of the corridor. I came into contact with the wall and I grabbed then a sort of wood trellis similar to those used in the cultivation of climbing plants. There appeared to be a large number of these growing there because I remained as if stuck in a web of stems and tendrils. However, one thing was incomprehensible; these plants, or what I was calling plants, seemed to be swollen with warm blood and touching them gave one the sensation of touching some sort of animal matter. I felt around once more and recoiled in terror; I had felt a round object the size of a walnut that was cold and that immediately shrank back under my touch. I thought it might be some sort of beetle. At this moment a light flickered somewhere and, for the space of a second, lit up the wall that was in front of me.

My emotion surpassed in fright and dismay everything that I had felt as the most atrocious throughout my entire life. Each fiber of my body screamed in an indescribable terror, a mute cry since my voice was paralyzed. It pierced my being like an icy cold. A stalk bearing tendrils traversed by veins climbed the wall to the ceiling; on another vine berries were blooming. These berries were made of hundreds of staring eyes. The eye that I had touched quivered again, it throbbed, and directed a sinister glance in my direction. I think I fainted; I fell back into the darkness. A whiff of unctuous odors reached me, like those earthy perfumes that are given off by mushrooms and ailänthus; my knees were reeling and I was violently thrashing about.

An object, similar to a ring of flames, projected a weak light. It was the reddened wick of an oil lamp briefly flaring up again. I hastened toward it and with trembling fingers managed to turn the wick up a little more. In this manner I was successful in obtaining a little glowing flame. Abruptly I turned around holding the lamp in front of me as if it could offer me some protection. The place was empty. On the table was a gleaming object; I seized on it as if it were a weapon, though it was just something light and rough. Nothing moved. I sighed, a little relieved. Taking infinite precautions to avoid extinguishing my poor light, I cast its glow upon the surface of the wall. Everywhere the same grillwork was to be found and as I could now see it better I could observe the vessels, the veins in tendril form in which blood circulated and throbbed. In this entanglement countless eyeballs cast a frightful gleam. They folded in an instant becoming terrifying tubercles similar to blackberries; their gaze followed my every movement. These eyes were of every shape and color: one a clear and gleaming iris, some dead blue like those of horses who ceaselessly look up at the sky, others black and shriveled like nightshades. The main stalks emerged from phials filled with blood; there they found the juice on which they nourished themselves. I saw bowls full of ashen, greasy morsels where mushrooms grew covered in a glossy sheen. These mushrooms, made from bloody flesh, palpitated at the slightest touch. All these shreds extirpated from living bodies and arranged according to an incomprehensible art were deprived of soul; they subsisted and developed through a purely vegetal mechanism. They were nonetheless alive, for, at the times I approached these eyes with my light, I could observe the contraction of the pupils quite distinctly. Who could the diabolical gardener be that was capable of maintaining such frightful cultivations?

The memory came back to me of the man seated on the stairs to the cellar. Instinctively I searched for a weapon in my pockets; I came up with the odd-shaped object that I had just stuffed there. It sparkled in a dim and scaly fashion; it was a pine cone made from totally pink human fingernails.

Shaken by a shudder I let it fall and gritted my teeth. Leave, leave, even if the man in the stairway should wake up and assault me. I was already close to him; I prepared myself to knock him down when I saw that he was dead. His body was as yellow as wax. The nails had been torn from his contorted hands. Certain slashes on his chest and temples indicated that he had been dissected. I wished to pass close by him and I believe I brushed him with my hand. At that very instant he appeared to glide over the stairs and approach me; suddenly he was standing, his hands folded like the Egyptian statuette. The same position, he had the same position! I know nothing more except that I broke my lamp. I succeeded in opening the door and the demon Tetanus took my throbbing heart between his twitching fingers.

Then, in a state of semiconsciousness I explained to myself: the man had doubtlessly been suspended by a cord tied around his elbows. Thanks to this mechanism his body, in sliding on the stairs, had been able to achieve this singular position.... And then... then, I felt someone shaking me....

"The Inspector is expecting you."

I entered an ill-lit room; there were pipes hanging on the wall and an official's greatcoat. It was a room of the police station; an agent was holding me up. The chief was seated at his table not looking at me at all. He murmured:

"Have you taken his identity?"

"He had some business cards which we took."

I heard the officer reply. Then:

"What were you looking for in Thun Street in front of that open door?"

Another long silence.

"Hey, are you going to answer?" the officer repeated while jostling me.

I stammered something about a murder committed in a cellar on Thun Street. Then the officer left the room. The Inspector still not looking up at me started off on a long speech of which I only understood a portion:

"Just think, the doctor Cindarella is a great scholar and Egyptologist. He cultivates new carnivorous plants: nepenthes and sundews... something along those lines, I believe, right? I don't know.... You really should stay at home during the night."

A door opened behind me. I turned and saw a large man with a beak like a heron, like the Egyptian Anubis. I had a spell of dizziness as the Anubis paid his compliments to the Inspector. He approached me and as he passed by he whispered into my ear, "Doctor Cindarella, Doctor Cindarella."

At this precise moment an important idea crossed my mind, an idea having reference to things past which I immediately forgot. When I looked at the Anubis again he had become a policeman again. He had the air of a bird as he returned my own business cards engraved in my name: "Doctor Cindarella." Now the superintendent was looking at me and I heard him say:

"But that's you, you really should stay home at night."

The agent conducted me outside; in passing I brushed against the greatcoat hanging on the wall. It slowly fell down, remaining suspended by the sleeves. Its shadow on the white wall raised its arms above its head and I could see how it also was attempting to imitate the pose of the Egyptian statuette.

Such is my latest adventure which happened three weeks ago. Since then I have been paralyzed, with half of my face frozen and dragging my leg behind me. I have sought in vain for that narrow and hectic house with the door ajar. As for the police, they have ignored all the incidents of that night.[7]

This statue to which Doctor Cindarella refers, which may exist beyond the tangible world, which would guide our actions and order our thoughts, is the image of fate as humanity has represented it for thousands of generations. It reminds us of Plato's conception of the world. It's a curious fact that in those moments when we find ourselves engaged in the most intense struggles, when we call upon our greatest courage and energy, we continue to feel the external force of an inescapable destiny we were meant to fulfill. So it is natural for us to want to examine this further, rather than to trust our active will to change events. Even the best of us wear ourselves out helping our most diligent efforts fail, while, without apparent reason, successes are showered upon a fortunate few.

In Search of Destiny
(AN INDIAN TALE)

In the country of Gujarat lived two brothers, one of whom was rich while the other was poor and miserable. One night, becoming desperate, the poor brother took his sickle and made his way toward his brother's barley field. Just as he was about to enter, he was stopped by someone who looked like a guard and who asked him what he was doing.

"I have come to take barley from my brother's field because he doesn't want to give me any for my starving children. But you, who are you?"

"I am your brother's destiny, and I protect his possessions."

"If you are my brother's destiny, where is mine, and why doesn't it help me to keep my wife and children from dying of hunger?"

"Your destiny is asleep beyond the seven seas; go there if you want to find it and wake it up."

The poor man left to search for his destiny. He met a mango tree

---

7. Gustave Meyrink, *Das deutschen Spiessers Wunderhorn*, 1913, trans. Jon Graham.

who complained of its fate, an unhappy king, a fish who led a miserable existence. When they learned that the man was going to the country of destinies, these beings begged him to ask what means they should employ to escape their misery. As he walked along, the traveler came upon a nest of eagles. Many of the small ones were being threatened by a serpent who wanted to eat them. The man intervened and removed the reptile, thus saving the birds' lives. Returning from their rounds, the eagles learned that they owed their children's safety to this virtuous man. To show their gratitude, they escorted him beyond the seven seas.

On the deserted shore, a human form descended, wrapped in a sheet. The man understood that this was his destiny. He uncovered its head and, since the sleeper did not wake up quickly enough, he twisted its big toe, crying:

"Lazy fool, don't you know how much trouble you've caused me by sleeping like this all these years? Get up and try not to go back to sleep after I leave."

His destiny promised not to fall back asleep. It answered all the questions that the traveler had to ask. The traveler could then leave the realm beyond the seven seas with great confidence. As he made his way home, he met the great fish who was always writhing with pain on the sands of the river. He told the fish that its suffering was caused by a large piece of gold in its stomach. The man rid the fish of it, taking along the gold as payment. He found the king again, still in despair over not being able to build a tower. He informed him that it was the heavy sighs of his unmarried daughter which kept shaking the construction. As soon as he learned this, the king hastened to give the man the princess's hand in marriage. Then the tower stood, straight and solid. Finding the mango tree again, still complaining that it produced only bitter mangoes, the man, now a king's son-in-law, explained to the tree that its suffering was caused by a treasure buried under its roots. Digging a hole, he did, in fact, find a large copper vase filled with gold and precious gems. As a reward for bringing it relief, the tree allowed him to take these riches. And thus, it was as a rich and powerful lord that the poor man returned to his town.[8]

What the man went to find beyond the seven seas was not gold. Riches, so very ephemeral, came to him as a bonus during his return

---

8. This story is not published in French.

voyage, as payment for services rendered. Our Hindu storyteller refrains from divulging the actual remarks exchanged with that mysterious figure hidden in sleep. But we can believe that the interview turned on universal destiny. Here is what we can imagine of the moving colloquium:

Memorable Vision
W. Blake

An angel came to me and said: "O pitiable foolish young man! O horrible! O dreadful state! consider the hot burning dungeon thou art preparing for thyself to all eternity, to which thou art going in such career."

I said: "Perhaps you will be willing to shew me my eternal lot, & we will contemplate together upon it, and see whether your lot or mine is most desirable."

So he took me thro' a stable & thro' a church & down into the church vault, at the end of which was a mill: thro' the mill we went, and came to a cave: down the winding cavern we groped our tedious way; till a void boundless as a nether sky appear'd beneath us, & we held by the roots of trees and hung over this immensity; but I said: "if you please, we will commit ourselves to this void, and see whether providence is here also: if you will not, I will." But he answered: "do not presume, O young man, but as we here remain, behold thy lot which will soon appear when the darkness passes away."

So I remain'd with him, sitting in the twisted roof of an oak; he was suspended in a fungus, which hung with the head downward into the deep.

By degrees we beheld the infinite Abyss, fiery as the smoke of a burning city; beneath us, at an immense distance, was the sun, black but shining; round it were fiery tracks on which revolv'd vast spiders, crawling after their prey, which flew, or rather swum, in the infinite deep, in the most terrific shapes of animals sprung from corruption; & the air was full of them, & seem'd composed of them: these are Devils, and are called Powers of the air. I now asked my companion which was my eternal lot? he said: "between the black and white spiders."

But now, from between the black & white spiders, a cloud and fire burst and rolled thro' the deep, black'ning all beneath, so that the nether deep grew black as a sea, & rolled with a terrible noise; beneath us was nothing now to be seen but a black tempest, till looking east between the clouds & the waves, we saw a cataract of blood mixed with fire, and not many stones' throw from us appear'd and sunk again the scaly folds of a monstrous serpent; at last to the east, distant about three degrees, appear'd a fiery crest above the waves; slowly it reared like a ridge of golden rocks, till we discover'd two globes of crimson fire, from which the sea flew away in clouds of smoke; and now we saw it was the head of a Leviathan; his forehead was divided into streaks of green & purple like those on a tyger's forehead; soon we saw his mouth & red gills hang just above the raging foam, tinging the black deep with beams of blood, advancing toward us with all the fury of a spiritual existence.[9]

⤛

The one who descended toward the abyss was trying to apprehend his own destiny and the destiny of the world. Both were inscribed by Thoth himself at the beginning of time in the book, which is kept from the greedy eyes of humanity. There are exceptions: free of all greed, William Blake was allowed to contemplate all reality without having to suffer heavy punishments as payment for his enlightenment.

Alas, desire for domination and thirst for profit are so deeply rooted in the human heart that adventure is too often an excuse for satisfying a bad conscience. Begun under the auspices of curiosity and ambition, it turns to confusion for those engaged in it. Many, and we could name them, have had bitter experiences. Let us confine ourselves to recounting what happened to Satni, son of Usimares.

Egyptian Tale of Satni-Khamoîs

King Usimares had two sons: the elder was Satni-Khamoîs, the younger Anukhharerôu. Satni was well taught: he knew how to read the books of sacred scripts, the books of the Double House of Life, and the works carved on the stelae and the walls of the temples. He knew the virtues of amulets and talismans. He understood how to compose and set down writings of great power; he was a great magician. One day as he was speaking with the king's servants, one of them said:

"If you truly want to read a useful book I will tell you the spot where that book written by the hand of Thoth himself is located which will immediately lift you above the gods. You will find two spells within it. With the first you will charm the heavens and the earth, the world of

---

9. William Blake, "A Memorable Vision," in *The Marriage of Heaven and Hell*, First Prophetic Books.

night, the mountains, the waters; you will know the birds of the sky and
the reptiles however many there may be; you will see the fish because a
power will force them to the water's surface. With the second spell,
even though you may be within the tomb, you will regain the form you
had on earth; you will even see the sun rising in the sky, and its cycle of
the gods, and the moon in the form it possessed when first it appeared."

When Satni demanded this precious tome, the old man said:

"The book is not mine. It is in the tomb of Nenoferkeptah, son of
King Minebptah, which lies in the center of the necropolis. Watch that
you don't take this book from him for he will make you return it, with
a trident and staff in your hands and a torch lit on your head."

Satni went before the king and recounted the priest's words, and
asked permission to go down into Nenoferkeptah's tomb accompanied
by his brother Anukhharerôu. They soon reached the Memphis
necropolis where they spent three days and nights searching among
the tombs, reading the stelae and reciting aloud their inscriptions. On
the third day, when they discovered Nenoferkeptah's resting place, Satni
cast a spell. A hole opened in the earth and Satni descended toward
the place where the book was hidden. It was bright within the tomb
because a light shone forth from the book. Nenoferkeptah was not
alone, his wife Ahuri and his son Mihet were also interred with him.
Once Satni entered the tomb Ahuri arose and spoke to him, asking:

"Who are you?"

He responded:

"I am Satni-Khamoîs, son of King Usimares. I have come for the
book of Thoth that I see between you and Nenoferkeptah. Give it to
me, else I will take it by force."

Ahuri said:

"I beg of you, do not take it but listen rather to the misfortunes that
have befallen us on account of this book.

"My name is Ahuri, daughter of King Minebptah, and he whom you
see there at my side is my brother Nenoferkeptah. We were born of the
same mother and the same father and our parents had no other children but us. When I came of age to marry I loved Nenoferkeptah my
brother and wanted no other husband but him. I confided in my mother
who then said to the king:

"'Our daughter Ahuri loves Nenoferkeptah her brother; let us wed
them together as is the custom.'

"The king wished me to wed the son of an infantry general and
Nenoferkeptah to wed the daughter of another infantry general. But

my mother insisted and the king ended by giving in to my desire, whereupon he said:

"'May Ahuri be brought to the house of Nenoferkeptah this very
night. May all manner of fine gifts be brought with her.'

"Thus was it done and Nenoferkeptah spent a joyful day with me;
he received all the things of the royal household and slept with me that
very night without knowing who I was. When he saw that he had slept
with me what could we do but surrender to the love we bore for one
another? When the time of my menses came, I did not have them. The
king was told and his heart overflowed with joy; he had beautiful gifts
of gold and silver, and cloths of fine linen brought to me. When the
time came for me to give birth I gave birth to this small infant you see
before you. He was given the name of Mihet and it was inscribed on the
registers of the Double House of Life. My brother Nenoferkeptah spent
his days in the necropolis of Memphis, reciting the writings from the
tombs of the pharaohs and the stelae of the scribes from the Double
House of Life.

"During a parade an old man said to him: 'If you desire to read a
useful book I will tell you the spot where that book written by the hand
of Thoth himself is located. In it you will find two spells.'

"Nenoferkeptah asked the priest what he wanted in return for this
information; the priest told him:

"'Give me 100 pieces of silver for my sepulcher and have two coffins
like those of rich priests made for me.'

"Nenoferkeptah did as was asked of him. Then the priest said:

"'The book is in the middle of the Coptos River in an iron coffer.
The iron coffer holds a bronze coffer which holds a coffer made of
wood from the cinnamon tree. This cinnamon tree wood coffer holds
a coffer of ebony and ivory which in turn holds a silver coffer. The
silver coffer holds a gold coffer; the book is inside of that. There are
swarms of serpents, scorpions, and all manner of reptile, around this
coffer, and there is an immortal serpent coiled around this coffer.'

"Nenoferkeptah left the temple in search of me. He related all that
the priest had told him. He told me he was leaving for Coptos immediately. I tried to dissuade him, but in vain. He went before the king and
asked for the use of the royal boat and that it be completely equipped:
'I will take,' he said, 'my sister Ahuri and her small child Mihet. I will
bring back this book and to that end I will not remain here a moment
longer.'

"The boat was given to us completely equipped; we made the

voyage and arrived in Coptos. The priests of Isis came down before us; they went toward Nenoferkeptah and their wives came toward me. Then we went to the Temple of Isis and Harpocrates. Nenoferkeptah had a bull, a goose, and some wine brought in; he offered a burnt offering and a libation.

"We were then brought to a beautiful house where four days were spent in our amusement. On the morning of the fifth day Nenoferkeptah bid the high priest of Isis and the other priests come before him. He manufactured a bark [ship] filled with his workers and their tools; he recited a spell over them, giving them life and giving them breath, then tossed them into the water. He filled the royal boat with sand and took his leave of me. I established myself on the Coptos River to learn what would become of him.

"He said:

"'Workers, work to the place where lies this book.'

"And they toiled night and day. At the end of three days a hole had been made in the river. When they discovered the swarms of snakes, scorpions, and all manner of reptiles around the coffer in which the book was placed, he cast a spell over the reptiles but did not make them vanish. He cast a spell on the eternal serpent, he battled with it and killed it; the serpent came back to life and regained its form. He battled with it a second time and killed it again; the serpent again came back to life. He battled with it a third time and cut it in two, then put sand between the pieces; the serpent did not return to life. Nenoferkeptah went to the location of the iron coffer. He opened it and found a bronze coffer, then a cinnamon wood coffer, then one of ebony and ivory, then one of silver, and then one of gold. Finally he opened it and saw that the book was inside. He took it and read one of the spells he found therein. He enchanted the heavens, the earth, the world of night, the mountains, the waters; he knew all that the birds of the sky said, all that the fish of the waters said, and all said by the four-legged beasts of the mountains. He recited the other spell and he saw the climb of the sun into heaven with its cycle of gods, he saw the moon in its rising and the true form of the stars; he saw the fish of the abyss for a divine power forced them to the water's surface. He cast a spell over the workers giving them life, then cast them into the water. Then he told them:

"'Dig to the place where waits Ahuri.'

"They worked night and day. In three days they arrived back where I was waiting; they found me waiting on the Coptos River. I had neither

drunk nor eaten. I was like one who had gone to the Blessed Realm....
I said to Nenoferkeptah:

"'By the life of the king! give so that I may see this book, which we
have taken so many pains to obtain.'

"He placed the book in my hand. I read the spells and the enchant-
ments worked for me. As I didn't write I spoke to my brother Nenoferkeptah who was an accomplished scribe and a highly educated
scholar. He brought forth a piece of virgin papyrus and wrote all the
words that were in the book upon it. He filled it with beer; then dissolved the entire thing in the water. When he saw that it was totally
dissolved he drank of it and knew all that had been written down.

"We returned to Coptos and we passed an agreeable sojourn before
Isis of Coptos and Harpocrates; then we left and made our way north of
Coptos. During this time Thoth learned what had happened in regard
to his book: he spoke of it to the king and demanded justice.

"'May Nenoferkeptah not arrive safe and sound in Memphis, he
and all who accompany him,' commanded the king.

"At that very moment, Mihet, the young child, emerged from under the canopy of the royal boat and fell into the river. Nenoferkeptah
came out of the cabin, cast a spell on the child, and brought him back
to the surface. He cast another spell on him and made him tell all that
had happened and what Thoth had said before the king. We returned
to Coptos with him where we had him guided to the Blessed Realm. We
gathered people around to celebrate his funeral ceremonies and had
him embalmed as befits one of the great; then we took our departure
anew.

"When we passed over the spot where the little child Mihet had
fallen into the river, I came out from beneath the canopy of the royal
boat and fell into the river in my turn. Nenoferkeptah, forewarned,
emerged. He cast a spell on me and brought me back to the surface.
He had me pulled out of the river and cast another spell on me and
made me recount all that had befallen me and the report that Thoth
had given before the king. He returned to Coptos with me, had me
guided to the Blessed Realm, and gathered people around to perform
my funeral ceremonies. He then had me embalmed and placed in the
tomb where our little child Mihet had been placed already.

"Then he left again; when he drew close to the spot where we had
fallen into the river he conversed with his heart saying:

"'Should I not be going to Coptos to rejoin them? If, to the contrary,
I return to Memphis what will I say when the king asks me about my little

boy Mihet? How will I tell him that I have taken his children with me to the land of Thebes? I have killed them yet I live.' He had a band of fine royal linen brought to him and made with it a magic band. He read the book, placed it on his chest, and tightly tied it there. Then Nenoferkeptah let himself fall into the water. The royal bark continued its voyage. When it arrived in Memphis the king came down to the royal boat; he was wearing a mourning coat as were the garrison of Memphis, the high priest of Ptah, and all the members of the king's entourage. It was seen that Nenoferkeptah occupied the cabin of honor in the royal boat in his capacity as an excellent scribe. He was pulled forth. The king had him introduced to the Blessed Realm within the space of sixteen days, reclad him in cloth within the space of thirty-five days, and shrouded him within the space of seventy days. Then he was placed within his tomb.

"Now I have told you of all the misfortunes that have befallen us because of this book."

But Satni said:

"Ahuri, give me that book or I will take it by force."

Nenoferkeptah rose up from his bier and said:

"Would you not rather gain possession of this book through your abilities as an excellent scribe? If you dare play with me let us play a game of fifty-two."

"I accept," said Satni.

The rapier with its long fringe was brought forth and they began a game of fifty-two. Nenoferkeptah won one game over Satni, recited a spell over him, placed the playing sword over him, and forced him into the ground up to his legs. He won the second and third games and forced Satni into the ground up to his groin. The same occurred on the sixth game and he forced Satni in to his ears. With that Satni violently grabbed Nenoferkeptah with his hand and called to Anukhharerôu, saying:

"Get back to the surface without delay, tell the king what has happened, and bring back the talismans of my father Ptah and my magic books to me."

This Anukhharerôu did. He returned with the talismans of Ptah and the books of incantations; he placed the talismans upon Satni's chest and immediately he rose from the earth. Satni reached out his hand to the book and grabbed it, and when he climbed up from the tomb, the light went with him. Ahuri, weeping, said:

"Hail to thee, darkness, hail to thee, light! The power has left our tomb."

But Nenoferkeptah consoled her.

"Do not torment yourself so; I will make him bring the book back, a forked staff in his hand and a torch lit upon his head."

Satni climbed out of the tomb and closed the door behind him. He went before the king and recounted all that had happened to him in regard to the book. The king responded to Satni:

"Take this book back to Nenoferkeptah's tomb before he makes you bring it back."

Satni heard out the king but didn't cease his unfurling of the magic scroll that he then read before everyone.

Following this, it happened one day that as he was passing over the parvis of Ptah's temple, Satni saw a woman of incomparable beauty. She was adorned in gold and was followed by three very young girls; between them they had fifty-two servants. From the moment he saw her Satni lost all presence of mind. He called to his page and ordered him to go toward this woman and find out her name. He accosted one of her entourage and learned that her name was Thubuï and that she was the daughter of the prophet of Bastet, the lady of Onkhtwai. She was on her way to pray before the great god Ptah.

Satni said to the young envoy:

"Go tell the young lady that Satni-Khamoîs, son of King Usimares, has sent you to say: 'I will give you ten pieces of gold to spend an hour with me; if you refuse I will use force. I will take you to a spot so well hidden that no one in the world could ever find you again.'"

The young man went back to Thubuï's entourage and accosted the young servant again who, on hearing these words, began protesting at their insulting nature. But Thubuï told the young man to speak directly to her. The young man gave Satni's message to her.

"Go tell Satni," she responded, "that I am chaste and not a base person. If he wishes to take his pleasure with me may he come to my house in Bubaste, where all will be ready for him and he may then take his pleasure of me with not a soul in the world the wiser, for I am not a woman of the streets."

The page returned to his master with the words of Thubuï. Satni had a bark brought for him and went to Bubaste. There he found an extremely tall house surrounded by a garden that had a flight of steps before a door on the north side. Satni asked:

"To whom does this house belong?"

He was told:

"That is the house of Thubuï."

Satni entered the enclosure. When he came to face the main part of the house located in the garden Thubuï was alerted to his presence. She came down, took Satni by the hand, and said:

"By my life, your journey to the house of the priest of Bastet, Lady of Onkhtwai, to which you have just arrived, is very pleasing to me. Come up with me."

Satni made his way by the staircase to the upper story of the house with Thubuï. This part of the house was inlaid in multicolored patterns with real lapis lazuli and *maf kaït*. There were several beds made with cloth of royal linen, as well as numerous golden cups on the sideboard. A cup was filled with wine and pressed into Satni's hand. Thubuï said to him:

"Please eat."

The stew was set upon the fire. Perfume was brought as if for a royal festival and Satni amused himself with Thubuï without as yet having seen her body. Then Satni said to Thubuï:

"Let us now do what I have come to do."

She responded:

"This house will be as your house, but I am a chaste not a base person. If you still desire to take your pleasure from me then I will have your sworn and written consent that all your goods and all that you own will be given to me."

He responded:

"May a scribe from the school be sent."

He came and Satni wrote out his consent to this donation of all he owned. An hour passed and someone came and announced to him:

"Your children are below."

He said:

"Have them come up."

Thubuï rose and clad herself in a fine linen robe. Satni could see all her limbs through the fine fabric and his desire grew hotter. Satni said to Thubuï:

"Let us do what I have come to do."

She responded:

"If you desire to take your pleasure of me, you will have your children add their consent to your sworn statement, so that they will not contest with my children on the subject of your property."

Satni had his children brought forth and had them add their signatures to his sworn statement. Satni then demanded to know when they would do that which he had come for. She said:

"If you desire your pleasure of me, you will kill your children so that they will not contest with my children on the subject of your property."

Satni responded:

"May the criminal act that has entered your heart be committed upon them."

She had his children slain before him and he had them thrown out the window to the dogs and cats below. Those ate their flesh and he could hear them doing so while he drank with Thubuï. Satni said:

"Let us now do what I have come to do for I have done all that you asked."

She responded:

"Go into that room."

Satni entered the room; he lay down on a bed of ebony and ivory, so as to receive the satisfaction of his desires and Thubuï lay down on the edge. Satni stretched out his hand to touch her; she opened her mouth to the width of a loud scream.

When he came back to his senses he was in a furnace room with no clothing. An hour passed, Satni saw a man, taller than the length of a spear, trampling numerous enemies underfoot. The man had the air of a king. Satni tried to rise up; he couldn't, for shame, as he had no clothing.

The king said:

"Satni, in what state do you find yourself?"

He answered:

"It is Nenoferkeptah who has made me do this."

The king said:

"Go to Memphis. This is what your children have wanted of you, they remain before the Pharaoh."

But Satni asked:

"What means can I use to get to Memphis, seeing that I have no clothing?"

The king summoned a page who found him a garment. He said:

"Satni, go to Memphis, your children live, they remain before the Pharaoh."

Satni went to Memphis and joyfully embraced his children whom he found there, still alive. The king said:

"Is it not drunkenness that has compelled all that you've done? Satni, I have already raised my hand against you, saying that, at the very least, you would kill if you did not return this book. Now return that book with a forked staff in your hand and a torch lit upon your head."

Satni left the presence of the king, carrying a staff and a trident in his hand and a lit torch upon his head. He descended into Nenoferkeptah's tomb. Ahuri greeted him, saying:

"Satni, it is the great god Ptah that has brought you back here safe and sound."

Ahuri and Nenoferkeptah begged him to bring the bodies of Ahuri and Mihet that were in Coptos to the tomb.

Satni left the tomb. He went back before the king and told him what Nenoferkeptah had asked. The king provided him with the royal boat and its crew. He went to Coptos and sought information from the high priests of Isis. He made a burned offering and a libation at her temple.

He went to the cemetery and spent three days and nights searching among the tombs, reading all the inscriptions that they bore. He could not find the final resting place of Ahuri and her child Mihet. Nenoferkeptah knew he would never find the place; he appeared to Satni in the form of an old man and said:

"The father of the father of my father said to the father of my father, and the father of my father said to my father: 'The places where Ahuri and Mihet lie are at the very edge of the meridional corner of the place called Pehemato.'"

Satni, suspicious, took the words of the old man as of little worth, but indeed, the tombs were found at the spot that was indicated. Satni had these great persons transported to Nenoferkeptah's tomb and immediately had the upper room sealed shut.[10]

The reader, I imagine, is growing impatient to attempt the voyage to the country of the marvelous, to bring back his own account of it. Satni's failure should give him pause. Let him consider that neither the initiations of Satni and Nenoferkeptah, nor their extensive knowledge of magic texts and incantatory formulas, could protect them from the dangers such a perilous undertaking involves.

---

10. *Les contes populaires de l'Egypte ancienne,* trans. to French by Gaston Maspero (Paris: J. Maisonneuve, 1889), trans. Jon Graham.

Predestination

Although each of us can rise above the narrow limits society envelopes us in like a shroud, although everyone can achieve the marvelous within by letting the deep currents of emotion penetrate, by listening to the voice of her own unconscious, although "poetry can and must be made by all," despite how much every one of us shares this same treasure, there are a few rare individuals destined to reach the farthest limits, to surmount the ultimate obstacles. It is the same as with a plant containing thousands of seeds, only a few of which are destined to take root.

I understand how debilitating such a claim is. It doesn't correspond at all to our concept of reality as experimental. But do not be too quick to label it an injustice, because the one granted the privilege of succeeding is subject to a series of trials and tribulations others will never experience. And if such determinism still seems unjust, it is worthwhile to consider that only those predestined for the adventure can really carry it out. The individual, male or female, who bears within that sign of election, possesses an unwavering certainty that forces him or her to persevere, despite discouragement and failure. The predestined hero instantly finds before him those things necessary for his progress. His name is Rimbaud, Lautréamont. In another context, he is the fiancé promised to the king's daughter.

The Predestined Fiancé

(TALE FROM THE ARAN ISLANDS)

There was once a widow living among the woods, and her only son living along with her. He went out every morning through the trees to get sticks, and one day as he was lying on the ground he saw a swarm of flies flying over what the cow leaves behind her. He took up his sickle and hit one blow at them, and hit so hard he left no single one of them living.

That evening he said to his mother that it was time he was going out into the world to seek his fortune, for he was able to destroy a whole swarm of flies at one blow, and he asked her to make him three cakes the way he might take them with him in the morning.

He started the next day a while after dawn, with his three cakes in his wallet, and he ate one of them near ten o'clock.

He got hungry again by midday and ate the second, and when night was coming on him he ate the third.

After that he met a man on the road who asked him where he was going.

"I'm looking for some place where I can work for my living," said the young man.

"Come with me," said the other man, "and sleep tonight in the barn, and I'll give you work to-morrow to see what you're able for."

The next morning the farmer brought him out and showed him his cows and told him to take them out to graze on the hills, and to keep good watch that no one should come near to milk them. The young man drove out the cows into the fields, and when the heat of the day came on he lay down on his back and looked up into the sky. A while after he saw a black spot in the north-west, and it grew larger and nearer till he saw a great giant coming towards him.

He got up on to his feet and he caught the giant round the legs with his two arms, and he drove him down into the hard ground above his ankles, the way he was not able to free himself. Then the giant told him to do him no hurt, and gave him his magic rod, and told him to strike on the rock, and he would find his beautiful black horse, and his sword and his fine suit.

The young man struck the rock and it opened before him, and he found the beautiful black horse, and the giant's sword and the suit lying before him. He took out the sword alone, and he struck one blow with it and struck off the giant's head. Then he put the sword back into the rock, and went out again to his cattle, till it was time to drive them home to the farmer.

When they came to milk the cows they found a power of milk in them, and the farmer asked the young man if he had seen nothing out on the hills, for the other cow-boys had been bringing home the cows with no drop of milk in them. And the young man said he had seen nothing.

The next day he went out again with the cows. He lay down on his back in the heat of the day, and after a while he saw a black spot in the north-west, and it grew larger and nearer, till he saw it was a great giant coming to attack him.

"You killed my brother," said the giant; "come here, till I make a garter of your body."

The young man went to him and caught him by the legs and drove him down into the hard ground up to his ankles.

Then he hit the rod against the rock, and took out the sword and struck off the giant's head.

That evening the farmer found twice as much milk in the cows as the evening before, and he asked the young man if he had seen anything. The young man said he had seen nothing.

The third day the third giant came to him and said, "You have killed my two brothers; come here, till I make a garter of your body."

And he did with this giant as he had done with the other two, and that evening there was so much milk in the cows it was dropping out their udders on the pathway.

The next day the farmer called him and told him he might leave the cows in the stalls that day, for there was a great curiosity to be seen, namely, a beautiful king's daughter that was to be eaten by a great fish, if there was no one in it that could save her. But the young man said such a sight was all one to him, and he went out with the cows on to the hills. When he came to the rock he hit it with his rod and brought out the suit and put it on him, and brought out the sword and strapped it on his side, like an officer, and he got on the black horse and rode faster than the wind till he came to where the beautiful king's daughter was sitting on the shore, waiting for the great fish.

When the great fish came in on the sea, bigger than a whale, with two wings on the back of it, the young man went down into the surf and struck at it with his sword and cut off one of its wings. All the sea turned red with the bleeding out of it, till it swam away and left the young man on the shore.

Then he turned his horse and rode faster than the wind till he came to the rock, and he took the suit off him and put it back in the rock, with the giant's sword and the black horse, and drove the cows down to the farm.

The man came out before him and said he had missed the greatest wonder ever was, and that a noble person was after coming down with a fine suit on him and cutting one of the wings from the great fish.

"And there'll be the same necessity on her for two mornings more," said the farmer, "and you'd do right to come and look on it."

But the young man said he would not come.

The next morning he went out with his cows, and he took the sword and the suit and the black horse out of the rock, and he rode faster than the wind till he came where the king's daughter was sitting on the shore. When the people saw him coming there was great wonder on them to know if it was the same man they had seen the day before. The king's daughter called out to him to come and kneel before her, and when he kneeled down she took her scissors and cut off a lock of hair from the back of his head and hid it in her clothes.

Then the great fish came in from the sea, and he went down into the surf and cut the other wing off from it. All the sea turned red with the bleeding out of it, till it swam away and left them.

That evening the farmer came out before him and told him of the great wonder he had missed, and asked him would he go the next day and look on it. The young man said he would not go.

The third day he came again on the black horse to where the king's daughter was sitting on a golden chair waiting for the great fish. When it came in from the sea the young man went down before it, and every time it opened its mouth to eat him, he struck into its mouth, till his sword went out through its neck, and it rolled back and died.

Then he rode off faster than the wind, and he put the suit and the sword and the black horse back into the rock, and drove home the cows.

The farmer was there before him and he told him that there was to be a great marriage feast held for three days, and on the third day the king's daughter would be married to the man that killed the great fish, if they were able to find him.

A great feast was held, and men of great strength came and said it was themselves were after killing the great fish.

But on the third day the young man put on the suit, and strapped the sword to his side like an officer, and got on the black horse and rode faster than the wind, till he came to the palace.

The king's daughter saw him, and she brought him in and made him kneel down before her. Then she looked at the back of his head and she saw the place where she had cut off the lock with her own hands. She led him to the king, and they were married, and the young man was given all the estate.[1]

Here, the hero's patient courage and modest virtue justify those marvelous gifts good fortune reserves for the chosen ones, at least in the eyes of men resigned to their difficult and unrewarding daily struggle. Justice is served. That is less true in the case of Emhammed, whose adventures we will read about next. His life, which turns out to be a series of miracles, does not initially follow the path of virtue. Although they undermine morality, such examples are not uncommon in the folklore tradition. Since ancient times, the collective unconscious, freely expressed in folktales, seems to struggle against moral systems promoted by religions and imposed by social structures. For the popular imagination, the predestined hero is less a man of virtue and wisdom than a bad subject, a malcontent, a social outcast. It is only luck—a miraculous encounter with a god or a loving woman—that allows him to experience extraordinary success.

Ruby
(ARABIAN TALE)

A sultan had married seven wives. The first six had no children. The youngest gave birth to a son who was named Emhammed. He was taught all the sciences, then horseback riding, fencing, and hunting. Nevertheless he ended up becoming a complete scoundrel. Nobody could escape his nasty tricks. Every day his victims came to his father to air their grievances.

Tired of his admonishments going unheard, the sultan resolved to exile his son.

"If you banish my son," his wife said to him, "banish me with him."

He renounced her, giving her animals, money, and all that she would need. Mother and son disappeared into the desert. Finally they arrived

---

1. John M. Synge, *The Aran Islands.*

at a place where there was nothing to be found but cicadas and thirst.

"My son," said the mother, "I cannot go on. I am dying of thirst."

And she fainted. He spread out a cloth and covered her. Then he mounted his horse and began to search for a watering place. Thus, he arrived at a spring. There he drew water and swore this oath:

"By Ta'si and Na'si, as truly as what is on my forehead, I will not drink of this until my mother has drunk!"

He returned to his mother's side, made her drink, revived her, helped her onto her horse, and they continued on their way. They came to a spot planted with trees; they could see a castle far off in the distance. Here they camped.

In the middle of the night, the prince heard moans. He got up and, guided by the sound, approached on tiptoe. Then he saw a very beautiful young woman hung up by her hair. Her blood fell, drop by drop, on the ground. The earth, all around her, was covered with rubies. He gathered them up, filled his pockets with them, and turned to address the young girl who could not respond to him.

He returned to his mother and said to her:

"Mother, there is such and such a thing...."

"I demand that you return those rubies this minute," she answered. "Put them back just as you found them. The property of others is sacred."

He was going to return them when he noticed a black storm cloud approaching, rumbling with thunder. He hid and watched as the storm cloud half opened. A horrible giant came out of it. He approached the girl and blew on her. When she was standing, feet on the ground, he begged her for her love, but she stubbornly denied him. Then he muttered some magic formulas and the girl returned to the way she had been before, hanging from her hair. The giant withdrew.

The prince was rejoining his mother when an angel suddenly rose up before him and said:

"The way in which you have behaved toward your mother has won you personal favor, and thus, your life and hers continue. The reward for your good act has appeared to you in the form of this evil genie, whom nobody has ever gotten the better of."

And the angel vanished.

"Mother, you should have seen! Here is the thing.... Then I heard this and that.... Now, Mother, by Allah! I do not want to leave until I have cleared up the mystery of this girl."

"By Allah!" his mother said to him, "you are not going to return to that spot. We are going to leave here at once."

They left that place and entered the city of another king. There they rented a storefront in the market district.

In the evening, Emhammed closed the door of his living quarters. He had no lamp, only a single ruby lying at the bottom of his pocket. He pulled it out and immediately everything was lit up. The light of the ruby even spread beyond the house and illuminated the street. Every night in this city there were guards on patrol. Emhammed took a book and began to read out loud, in such a charming voice that the guards, rushing up to see this light, spent the night listening to him reading.

That night, a great number of thefts were committed. The next day, the townspeople who were victims of this larceny complained to the king. The king called for the guards.

"So what were you doing?" he asked them.

"Your Majesty, we ask Allah and you for permission to tell everything."

"You have it."

"Well, while we were making our rounds, we noticed a light which dazzled us. As we approached it, we heard a voice soft and sweet enough to make us cry. We stayed there listening to it, and we forgot our duties."

"Go and bring this reader here to me at once."

They brought Emhammed before the king.

"Who are you?"

"My lord, we are strangers whom the one and only God has led here."

"What is the light which lit the night for you?"

Emhammed took the ruby from his pocket and put it in the king's hand.

Now, the king's daughter was married to the son of his vizier. The king gave the ruby to the latter, for him to give to the princess. Then he dismissed Emhammed.

When the princess received the ruby, she said:

"I want another one."

Someone was sent to tell Emhammed, who went in search of another one. The princess then said to her husband:

"I must have a third."

Emhammed brought a third.

Each time he went to that place, Emhammed saw the frightful scoundrel there, the abductor of brides. He also met the angel again who said to him:

"There it is, the kind virtue of your mother. You are being rewarded for not wanting to drink before she did."

And on each of these voyages, he listened carefully to the incantation that the monster spoke to bring the girl back to life, as well as the incantation by which he magically slit her throat and returned her to the state of a woman with a slit throat, losing blood.

The day came when he said to himself:

"By Ta'si and Na'si, by what ordeals God has inscribed on my forehead, I must clear up the case of this young woman. One of two things will happen: either I will save her and bring her back with me, or this will be the end of my life and hers. I know by heart the magic words by which her torturer slits her throat and by which he brings her back to life. And, if God has allotted me victory over this scoundrel, I will put him to death."

He said his farewells to his mother, and, mounting his charger, he departed. Suddenly he found himself face-to-face with the angel, who said to him:

"Go over to that tree in front of you. There you will find a large stone slab. Dismount and lift up this stone. Then, remounting, you will enter on horseback. There you will find a young child. If he addresses you, speak to him. If he is silent, follow his path. You will meet an old man. If you see that his head is bare, greet him. If his head is covered, be silent and go ahead of him. You will find an old man white as the snow-covered peaks. If he is asleep, wake him and say to him:

"'Give me that which is rightfully mine.'

"If you find him squatting, greet him, bow before him, and squat yourself. He will give you that which is rightfully yours without your asking. When he has given it to you, listen carefully.

"If he says to you: 'Leave by whichever way you wish,' by all means, go. If he says to you, 'Follow your path,' be careful, take care not to commit even the smallest impropriety. You will have to fear for your life and you will leave your mother without support in a strange city."

With that, the angel disappeared.

The prince quickly went over to the tree, found the slab, dismounted, lifted the stone, and entered. He saw all those the angel had told him about. Finally, he found the old man, squatting. He bowed before him, sat down, and greeted him. The first words the old man said to him were:

"Are you the one who quenched your mother's thirst before quenching your own?"

"Yes," he answered.

The old man rose. He entered his chamber and returned with a gleaming sword. If you struck a rock with it, it would break it in two. The prince took it in his hand.

"Go as you have come," the old man said to him.

But soon an old man he had not seen before said to him:

"Close your eyes."

He closed them. He found himself right beside the young woman, beside Ruby.

He crouched down in his hiding place and waited. Soon, the angel came to find him.

"Get up," he said to him, "and prepare to do combat with the monster who has stolen so many beautiful women away from their families."

He began to prepare himself. All of a sudden, a black storm cloud approached, rumbling with thunder. It opened and the evil one dropped out like a rock. At the very moment when the monster was about to recite the magic words, the prince struck him a blow with his sword and split him in two. The young woman let out a shrill cry of joy, and not one more drop of blood fell.

"Where is your country, young maiden?"

"Without a doubt," she answered him, "I am your rightful wife."

He helped her mount behind him on his horse and returned home where he got his wife settled in.

As soon as he set foot in the house, his mother said to him:

"If you had not returned today, the king would have thrown me in prison. He was going to take me hostage to ensure your return."

The next day, the guards came and took him to the palace.

"We want you to bring us a red coral necklace," the king said to him. "If it is not here in three days, we'll cut off your head."

He returned home.

"What's wrong?" the young woman said to him. "You've come back worried. Sit down and rest. What has been commanded is already done."

He performed the Fatha ritual for his marriage with young Ruby, and, married, they entered together into a garden of delights. On the third day he said:

"Ruby, this is the last day to deliver the coral necklace."

She took a sharp knife and made a cut in her finger. Blood ran out of it and clotted into a coral necklace. Emhammed took it to the sultan who was delighted. When he presented it to his daughter, she said:

"I want a cloth to cover the entire city."

In hearing this order, Emhammed had a moment of despair.

"So there it is," he said to himself. "This king has decided to cut my throat." He returned home very somber.

"What's wrong with you?"

"I have never heard of a cloth big enough to cover an entire city."

"Nevertheless, it exists," Ruby answered him. "You must go to the spot where you found me hanging. From there, you will see in the distance a castle before which stands a tall tree, visible from far off. You will walk toward the castle. You will knock on the trunk of the tree and not at the castle door. My mother will come to the door. Greet her and say to her:

"'Your daughter sends you greetings. She asks you to give me the cloth with which she played when she was a little girl.'"

When she heard these words, Ruby's mother let out a cry of joy. All the people in the castle were just as happy as she was to hear that the young woman had been delivered from the frightful miscreant, the abductor of brides. What proved that she was safe and sound was her request for the cloth she had played with in her childhood. The prince was treated as a most honored guest. When he was about to depart, he was given a very small cloth, folded like a handkerchief, and the size of the ones carried in pockets. He said his farewells and left, convinced that this cloth could never cover the surface of a city. He returned to Ruby.

"Look, it's only a pocket handkerchief."

"Don't worry. Carry it to the king and let him order a few of the townspeople to climb their terraces, hold it by the four corners and stretch it out. The city will be covered by it."

Emhammed took it to the king and, indeed, the city was covered by it. The king gave the cloth to his daughter.

"The one who has supplied all these things," she said, "obtain from him a gold box that contains all kinds of musical instruments and that plays all by itself."

The king called Emhammed to him.

"I want such and such a thing."

"Fine."

He went to find Ruby.

"That's easy," she said to him. "No need to have the slightest fear. Go knock on the trunk of the tree. Be careful not to knock on the castle door. My mother will come. Say to her:

"'Your daughter wishes you good day. She asks you for the music box which she played with when she was little.'"

She gave it to him. He took it to the king who gave it to his daughter. The princess was enchanted.

"Still I want the one who has obtained all these things for you to bring the man who measures one span, whose beard measures two spans, and whose sword measures two cubits."

"Fine," said Emhammed.

He returned very worried, but Ruby burst out laughing.

"This man is the king of the genies, my own father," she said to him before he had spoken even a word. "Nothing could be easier. Go knock on the tree. My mother will come. Say to her:

"'Your daughter wishes you good day. She asks you to send her father to visit her. She pines away, longing to see him.'"

Mounting his horse, with provisions for his journey, he went to knock on the tree. The mother appeared.

"This is my mission."

"Fine."

Being a genie herself, she immediately understood everything.

"Take the lead," she said to him. "He will catch up with you."

The prince remounted his horse and returned home at a quick pace. Coming inside, he sat down. There before him he saw a man who measured one span, whose beard measured two spans, and whose sword measured two cubits. He greeted him.

Sword in hand, the king of the genies went straight to the palace where the king held court. Only the viziers were there. The king was in his suite. In a flash, the king of the genies transported himself there. He cut off the king's head. After that, he went back to the viziers and proclaimed that his son-in-law was now sultan of the country. Straight away he returned to his castle.[2]

The woman doesn't need to be the daughter of the king of the genies to perform miracles for those she loves. Made up of confidence and disquiet, patient devotion and ardent desires, her love acts to transform the beloved. It enriches him by a mysterious transfusion of energy. Love's clear eyes distinguish the ways of destiny. To say of a woman that her blood is made of rubies, that her tears turn to pearls, is to use

---

2. Recounted by Abderrahman, a native of Aineddefla and a candy seller in Blida. Account taken from E. Cosquin.

age-old poetic images I object to, not because they exaggerate, but because they are too weak.

Blood and tears, combined with smiles and kisses, sighs and abandon, in truth, make up those balms that instantly heal the most serious wounds and that have the power to destroy the most insurmountable obstacles. Nothing is incredible, nothing is impossible, as soon as woman enters the game. For me, the marvelous is so directly linked to the presence of this mediator who reestablishes communication between man and the cosmos, contact arbitrarily disrupted by the intelligence, that the only adventures I find surprising are those in which female help is absent. However, there are cases in which the power of spirits alone carries the traveler along. These are the strange destinies lived out by certain scholars, and a few magi. But then, what heights must be attained as a result of the pain, the deprivation, the desire to know and to triumph. In this regard, it seems to me that the experiences of the one they call "the country doctor," a rather ambiguous title, should be read as very hermetic symbolism.

The Country Doctor
F. Kafka

I was in difficult straits; I had an urgent journey to start upon; a seriously ill patient was expecting me in a village ten miles away; a violent snowstorm was raging in the distance that separated him from me; I had a light coach with big wheels, just right for our large roads; wrapped in furs, my case of instruments in my pocket, I was waiting in the courtyard ready to depart on the journey; but there was no horse to be had, no horse.... Last night my own had succumbed to the anguish of this icy winter; my maid was now running about the village to try and borrow one, but I knew her efforts would be futile, and I stood there needlessly, growing stiffer and stiffer, under the snow which covered me with a heavier and heavier coat. The maid appeared at the gateway, alone and waving her lantern; of course... who would lend a horse on a day like this for such a journey? I crossed through the courtyard once more; I could see no way out; distracted and tormented, I kicked at the ramshackle door of the pigsty that had been in use for years. It flew open and flapped back and forth several times. I was struck by an odor and a warmth as of a stables. A dim stable lantern was hanging there from a rope. A man crouched in this hovel showed me an open, blue-eyed face.

"Shall I yoke up?" he asked crawling out on all fours.

I didn't know what to say and stooped down to see what else was in the sty. The maid was at my side. "You never know what you will find in your own house," she said, and we both laughed.

"Hey Brother, hey Sister!" the groom cried out, and two horses, extremely handsome with powerful flanks, emerged one after the other—their legs tucked close to their bodies and their shapely heads lowered like a camel's—disengaging themselves from the doorway, which they filled completely, by a simple repetition of the trunk. But immediately on getting outside they stood up, their bodies steaming.

"Help him," I said, and the obedient servant hastened to hand the harness to the valet. But hardly had she come to his side when he grabbed her and pushed his face against hers. She let out a scream and came running back to me; the red marks of two rows of teeth stood out on her cheek. In my fury I yelled at the groom, "Brute, do you want a whipping?" But in the same moment I suddenly recalled that the man was a stranger; that I did not know from where he had come, and that he spontaneously offered to help me when everyone else had turned away. It seemed as if he could read my thoughts because instead of being offended by my threat he simply turned to me, while still busying himself with the horses.

"Climb aboard," he said, then, and in fact, everything was ready. I observed that I had never yet traveled behind such a magnificent team of horses, and climbed in happily.

"I will drive," I told him. "You don't know the way."

"Of course," he said, "I'm not going with you, I am staying with Rose."

"No," she screamed and fled into the house with a foreboding that her fate was inevitable; I heard the rattling of the door chain as she put it up, I heard the click of the tumblers in the lock; I saw that Rose had extinguished the light in the hallway, then all the rooms beyond in an attempt to make herself unfindable.

"You will come with me," I said to the groom, "or I will skip my journey, urgent as it is. I wouldn't dream of paying for it by handing that young girl over to you."

"Get moving," he replied, clapping his hands. The coach was carried off like a log in a torrent; I could just hear the cracking and splitting of the door to my house under the blows of the groom; then my eyes and ears were filled with a steady drone that spread to all my senses. But this was only for a moment as it was as if my patient's house opened onto the gates of mine: I was already there; the horses stood silently, the snow had ceased to fall, and the light of the moon bathed everything around me; the parents of my patient rushed out of the house, followed by his sister; I was practically torn from my vehicle; I could understand not a word of their confused speech; in the sickroom the air was almost unbreathable; the neglected stove was smoking; it was imperative that I open a window; but first I had to look at my patient. Skinny, without any fever, not cold, not warm, with vacant eyes, without a shirt, the lad got up from under his comforter, threw his arms around my neck and whispered in my ear: "Doctor, let me die."

I glanced around me; no one had heard him; his parents were leaning forward in silence waiting for my verdict; his sister had pulled up a chair on which to set my instrument case. I opened it and hunted among my instruments while the boy kept clutching at me with his hands to remind me of his plea. I grabbed a pair of tweezers, examined them in the glow of a candle, and set them down again.

"Yes," I said to myself, in disgust, "in cases like this the gods will aid you; they supply the missing horse and even include a second so that you may go even more quickly, topping that they even send a groom...."

It was only then that I remembered Rose. What could I do? How could I rescue her? How could I snatch her away from under that groom from ten miles away, with horses I could not control? These same horses who had somehow slipped their reins and, how, I don't know, pushed open the windows from the outside, where they now had stuck their heads through the window and regarded the patient, undisturbed by the family's cries of alarm.

"I ought to return immediately," I said to myself, as if the horses were inviting me to resume my journey.

But I allowed the sister, who believed I was dazed by the heat, to remove my fur coat. A glass of rum was brought to me; the old man clapped me on the shoulder, a familiarity that was justified by the offer of his treasure. I shook my head; I was suffocating in the narrow confines of his thought; for that reason alone I refused the drink. The mother stood by her child's bedside and called me to it; I obeyed her request, and while one of the horses let out a buglelike whinny toward the ceiling, I laid my head on the chest of the young boy which shivered under my wet beard. What I presumed was confirmed; the boy was quite sound, a little anemic perhaps, a little overdosed with coffee by the zealous solicitude of his mother, but healthy and best given a good shove out of bed. I am no world reformer and so I let him stay. I had been hired by the district's authorities and fulfilled my duty to the full, to the point where it became almost overmuch. Though badly paid I was still generous and helpful to the poor. I still had Rose to deal with; after which, perhaps the boy was right, and I too could ask to die. What was I doing here in this endless winter! My horse had died and there was no one in the village who would lend me another. I had to obtain my team from the pigsty; if luck had not provided me with horses, I would have had to harness swine. That was the situation. And I turned and nodded to the family. They knew nothing of that, and if they had, wouldn't have believed it. It is easy to write prescriptions, but to come to an understanding with people is difficult work. So then my visit here is over; once again I've been disturbed for no reason, I was used to that, the entire district tortured me with my night bell; but that this time Rose was sacrificed as well, that beautiful girl who had lived for years in my house without my paying much attention to her... that sacrifice was too great and I was forced to come to terms with it using my subtlest powers of thought, in order not to fly at that family, which, with all the best will in the world, could not restore Rose to me. But as I closed my case and made a move to take my coat, when I saw the family grouped together, the father sniffing at the glass of rum he was holding up in his hand, the mother apparently disappointed in me—well what do people expect?—weeping and biting her lips, and the sister brandishing a bloody towel, I found myself ready to concede conditionally that perhaps the boy might be ill. I went over to him; he smiled at me as if I were bringing him the most fortifying of broths.... Ah, now the horses started whinnying together; that noise must have been prescribed by a higher power to aid my examination, and now, I saw quite clearly that, yes, the young boy was ill. On his right side, by the hip, was an open wound as big as a saucer. Rose-colored with a thousand subtle shades, dark in the middle but gradually lightening toward the edges, with delicate postula and irregular clots of blood, as open as a mine shaft. This was what it looked like from a distance. But from close up it appeared even worse. Who could look at it without whistling slightly? Worms, as thick and long as my little finger, rose-colored and spattered with blood themselves, were writhing in the depths of the wound that held them back, pointing their little white heads and many little legs agitatedly toward the light. Poor boy, there was nothing more anyone could do for you; I had discovered your great wound; you were dying from this wound in your side. The family was satisfied; they saw me at work, the sister told the mother, the mother the father, the father told several guests who were entering the room on tiptoe by the moonlight spilling through the open door, who were holding their arms outstretched to keep their balance.

"Will you save me?" whispered the boy between sobs, hypnotized by the life swarming in his wound. Such are the people of my land. They are always demanding the impossible from their doctors. They have lost their ancient beliefs; the priest remains at home and transforms his vestments into rags, one after the other; and the doctor must do everything with his skilled hand of a surgeon. Oh well, if that's what they want; I have not thrust myself on them; if they wish to make use of me for some sacred end, I won't stop them. What do I have better to do, I, an old country doctor, whose servant girl has been ravished? And they came, the family members and the village elders, and stripped off my clothes; a school choir with the teacher at the head of it, set up in front of the house, and sang these words to a completely simple tune:

Take his clothes off, he will cure us
If he doesn't heal us, kill him.
For he's nothing but a doctor, nothing but a doctor.

Then I found myself stripped of my clothes and tranquilly looked back at the people, with my fingers buried in my beard and my head leaning to one side. I was in total control of myself and their superior and remained so, though it availed me nothing for they picked me up by the head and feet and carried me over to the bed. They laid me down in it next to the wall, on the side of the wound. Then they all left, shutting the door and stopping their singing; clouds passed over the moon; the covers enclosed me in their warmth; the horses at the open windows tossed their heads like shadows. "You know," I heard at my ear, "I don't have a great deal of confidence in you. You just got thrown in anywhere, besides you didn't even come in on your own two feet. Instead of helping me you are cramping me on my deathbed. If I did what I felt like doing, I would scratch your eyes out."

"It's true," I said, "it is a shame. But I am a doctor. What should I do? Believe me it is no easier for me, either."

"Should I be satisfied with that excuse? Alas! I have to be. I always have to be satisfied with my lot. I came into the world with a nice wound; that's all I came in with."

"My young friend," I said, "your problem is that you lack perspective. I, who have made the rounds of sickrooms, of all sorts, can tell you that your wound is not so bad. Two blows of an ax in a tight corner.

There are lots of people who offer their sides and can't even hear the ax in the forest, even less the one that is coming near them."

"Is that the truth, or are you fooling me in my delirium?"

"It is the truth; believe it as the word of a doctor under oath. Take it with you into the hereafter."

And he took it and shut up. But now it was time to start thinking of my escape. The horses were still there. I quickly gathered together my clothes, fur coat and case; I didn't want to lose any time getting dressed; if the horses went back as fast as they had come, I would be only springing, as it were, from this bed into my own. One of the horses obediently left the window; I hurled my bundle into the coach; the fur coat went too far and was left hanging on a hook by its sleeve. That was good enough. I leapt onto the horse. With the reins loosely trailing behind, the two horses practically detached from each other, the coach following randomly behind, and my fur coat hanging in the snow at the tail end.

"Get a move on," I said, but we didn't go quickly; we went slowly like old men through this desert of snow. For a long time I could hear behind us the new song of the children, a song of children who are fooling themselves:

Rejoice all ye patients,
The doctor has assisted you in your own bed!

I will never get back home at his rate; my flourishing practice is lost; my successor is robbing me, but in vain, for he cannot replace me; in my house the repulsive groom is running wild; Rose is his victim, I don't even want to think about that. Naked, exposed to the chill of this ill-fated age, with an earthly vehicle and unearthly horses, I am sent roaming, old man that I am. My coat is hanging behind the coach and I cannot reach it and none of the fickle rabble who are my patients will lift a finger. Hoodwinked! Hoodwinked! once is enough; I heeded a false alarm... and it is beyond repair forever.[3]

The horses spoken of here should seem familiar. They are the same ones who pulled Hercules's chariot and led him into marvelous adventures, to the trials imposed upon the hero. In Corinth, the winged horse

---

3. Franz Kafka, *The Country Doctor.*

is called Pegasus. Born from the head of Medusa, he is Bellerophon's charger. He drinks from the Corinthian spring, Pirene, before going to battle the Chimera. Isn't this the same horse that Buddha rode as a rich, young monarch, leaving his father's palace to enter the hermits' forest? And it's this same horse again that Grettir is forbidden from meeting when he wants to escape:

The Return of Grettir
(ICELANDIC LEGEND)

Grettir left Plainsport on a night that he didn't wish to be noticed by the local merchants. He obtained a black cloak that he threw over his clothing and made himself quite unrecognizable. He went up Thing Point as far as the Goat Farm. When he got there day was already breaking. He spotted a bay horse in the paddock, went over to it, bridled and mounted it, then went back down along the White River until he was again below the Farm. He then continued to the Flokival River and took the trail that led over Calf Point. Meanwhile at Goat Farm the laborers had risen and informed Svein that someone had run off with his mare. He rose, burst into laughter and made this verse:

A thief has just fled
on the beautiful Sodukolla,
the first in the heart of this warrior;
after lurking
near my house.
This misdeed should not have occurred
and it appears likely to me
that this man is a violent individual.

Then he jumped on his horse and went in pursuit. Grettir galloped as far as the Farm of the Mound. There he met one by the name of Halli who told him he was catching a boat that cast anchor at Plainsport. Grettir spoke this verse:

O spirited warrior! tell
throughout the far flung regions of the land
that you have seen Sodukolla
near the Mound and that a man
who is always lucky with the dice,
clad in a black cloak,

was seated upon the beast.
Now, Halli, go quickly.

Then they went their separate ways. Halli continued to follow the trail and Svein didn't run across him until he reached Calf Point. They hailed each other hastily. Then Svein said:

Have you seen
a babbler, a sly good-for-nothing? He has carried away
(and that is the truth) the beautiful mare
from the nearest farm.
He shall get the just deserts of a thief
if someone catches hold of him.
As for me, if I catch him
I want to whip his back black and blue.

"You can certainly catch him," said Halli, "I met a man who claimed that he rode Sodukolla and told me to tell of it in every farm in the area; he was tall in height and clad in a black cloak."

"He thinks that he is someone important," said Svein, "but I know quite well who he really is."

And thereupon he started back in pursuit.

Grettir arrived at Deild's Neck. A woman was there outdoors. Grettir went up to speak to her and spoke this verse:

Valkure well born of the gold
say to the guardian of the treasure
this amusing verse:
"Grettir, serpent of the earth
just passed this way.
The gods' cup-bearer gallops
so fast that he will not stop
until the Farm of the Torrent."

The woman memorized the verse. Then he continued on his way. Soon after Svein arrived; she hadn't gone back in yet, and as soon as he got there he spoke this verse:

What warrior just passed this way
mounted on a bay horse
galloping in the tempest?
This downfallen and rash man
who does naught but evil,

has today for a long while
been pursued by me.

She recited what she knew. The verse gave him something to think about and he said:

"It is possible that this man is going to cause trouble for me, but I must find him."

He followed his trail from farm to farm; and found traces of his quarry everywhere. The weather was cold and rainy. It was still daylight when Grettir arrived at the Farm of the Torrent. And when Grim, son of Tgorhall, learned of it he greeted him with great pleasure and gave him an invitation to remain with him, which Grettir accepted. He left Sodukolla loose and told Grim from where he had come. When Svein arrived, he got down off his steed and saw his horse. He then spoke this verse:

Who has fled upon my mare?
What benefit does it give me?
Has a greater thief ever been seen?
What is the cloaked man up to?

Grettir had already removed his soaked garments and heard this quatrain.

On the mare I have fled to Grim's,
Compared to whom you are naught but a rascal.
You will receive no benefits at all;
But we must make our reconciliation.

"Of my own free will, and if it always remain thus," replied Svein, "then the horseback ride will have received ample compensation."[4]

The horse and the ship with full sails are the images most frequently encountered in the folktale tradition. For thousands of years, both of them have been the desired means of liberation. They have become irreplaceable symbols in the collective dream. Many centuries will have to pass, many technological changes will have to take place before the image of the horse ceases to haunt the unconscious. A beast of extraordinary power and superhuman intelligence, that is what Edgar Poe has

---

4. *Saga of Grettir,* trans. Fernand Mossé (Montaigne Editions).

borrowed from an ancient Hungarian legend, and what he presents to us in the fantastic tale:

The Horse of Fire
E. A. Poe

The families of Berliftzing and Metzengerstein had been at variance for centuries. Never before were two houses so illustrious, mutually embittered by hostility so deadly. The origin of this enmity seems to be found in the words of an ancient prophecy—"A lofty name shall have a fearful fall when, as the rider over his horse, the mortality of Metzengerstein shall triumph over the immortality of Berliftzing."

Wilhelm, Count Berliftzing, although loftily descended, was, at the epoch of this narrative, an infirm and doting old man, remarkable for nothing but an inordinate and inveterate personal antipathy to the family of his rival, and so passionate a love of horses, and of hunting, that neither bodily infirmity, great age, nor mental incapacity, prevented his daily participation in the dangers of the chase.

Frederick, Baron Metzengerstein, was, on the other hand, not yet of age. His father, the minister G——, died young. His mother, the Lady Mary, followed him quickly. From some peculiar circumstances attending the administration of his father, the young Baron, at the decease of the former, entered immediately upon his vast possessions. Such estates were seldom held before by a nobleman of Hungary....

Upon the succession of a proprietor so young, with a character so well known, to a fortune so unparalleled, no little speculation was afloat in regard to his probable course of conduct. And, indeed, for the space of three days, the behavior of the heir out-Heroded Herod, and fairly surpassed the expectations of his most enthusiastic admirers. Shameful debaucheries—unheard-of atrocities—gave his trembling vassals quickly to understand that no servile submission on their part—no punctilios of conscience on his own—were thenceforward to prove any security against the remorseless fangs of a petty Caligula. On the night of the fourth day, the stables of the castle Berliftzing were discovered to be on fire; and the unanimous opinion of the neighborhood added the crime of the incendiary to the already hideous list of the Baron's misdemeanors and enormities.

But during the tumult occasioned by this occurrence, the young nobleman himself sat apparently buried in meditation, in a vast and desolate upper apartment of the family palace of Metzengerstein. The rich although faded tapestry hangings which swung gloomily upon the walls, represented the shadowy and majestic forms of a thousand illustrious ancestors. *Here*, rich-ermined priests, and pontifical dignitaries, familiarly seated with the autocrat and the sovereign, put a veto on the wishes of a temporal king, or restrained with the fiat of papal supremacy the rebellious sceptre of the Arch-enemy. *There*, the dark, tall statues of the Princes Metzengerstein—their muscular war-coursers plunging over the carcasses of fallen foes—startled the steadiest nerves with their vigorous expression; and *here*, again, the voluptuous and swan-like figures of the dames of days gone by, floated away in the mazes of an unreal dance to the strains of an imaginary melody.

But as the Baron listened or affected to listen, to the gradually increasing uproar in the stables of Berliftzing—or perhaps pondered upon some more novel, some more decided act of audacity—his eyes were turned unwittingly to the figure of an enormous, and unnaturally colored horse, represented in the tapestry as belonging to a Saracen ancestor of the family of his rival. The horse itself, in the foreground of the design, stood motionless and statue-like—while further back, its discomfited rider perished by the daggers of a Metzengerstein.

On Frederick's lips arose a fiendish expression, as he became aware of the direction which his glance had, without his consciousness, assumed. Yet he did not remove it. On the contrary, he could by no means account for the overwhelming anxiety which appeared falling like a pall upon his senses. It was with difficulty that he reconciled his dreamy and incoherent feelings with the certainty of being awake. The longer he gazed the more absorbing became the spell—the more impossible did it appear that he could ever withdraw his glance from the fascination of that tapestry. But the tumult without, becoming suddenly more violent, with a compulsory exertion he diverted his attention to the glare of ruddy light thrown full by the flaming stables upon the windows of the apartment.

The action, however, was but momentary; his gaze returned mechanically to the wall. To his extreme horror and astonishment, the head of the gigantic steed had, in the meantime, altered its position. The neck of the animal, before arched, as if in compassion, over the prostrate body of its lord, was now extended, at full length, in the direction of the Baron. The eyes, before invisible, now wore an energetic and human expression, while they gleamed with a fiery and unusual red; and the distended lips of the apparently enraged horse left in full view his sepulchral and disgusting teeth.

Stupefied with terror, the young nobleman tottered to the door. As he threw it open, a flash of red light, streaming far into the chamber, flung his shadow with a clear outline against the quivering tapestry; and he shuddered to perceive that shadow—as he staggered awhile upon the threshold—assuming the exact position, and precisely filling up the contour, of the relentless and triumphant murderer of the Saracen Berlifitzing.

To lighten the depression of his spirits, the Baron hurried into the open air. At the principal gate of the palace he encountered three equerries. With much difficulty and at imminent peril of their lives, they were restraining the convulsive plunges of a gigantic and fiery-colored horse.

"Whose horse? Where did you get him?" demanded the youth, in a querulous and husky tone, as he became instantly aware that the mysterious steed in the tapestried chamber was the very counterpart of the furious animal before his eyes.

"He is your own property, sire," replied one of the equerries, "at least he is claimed by no other owner. We caught him flying, all smoking and foaming with rage, from the burning stables of Castle Berlifitzing. Supposing him to have belonged to the old Count's stud of foreign horses, we led him back as an estray. But the grooms there disclaim any title to the creature; which is strange, since he bears evident marks of having made a narrow escape from the flames."

"Extremely singular," said the young Baron, with a musing air, and apparently unconscious of the meaning of his words. "He is, as you say, a remarkable horse—a prodigious horse! although as you very justly observe, of a suspicious and untractable nature; let him be mine, however," he added, after a pause, "perhaps a rider like Frederick of Metzengerstein may tame even the devil from the stables of Berlifitzing."

"You are mistaken, my lord; the horse, as I think we mentioned, is *not* from the stables of the Count. If such had been the case, we know our duty better than to bring him into the presence of a noble of your family."

"True!" observed the Baron, dryly; and at that instant a page of the bed-chamber came from the palace with a heightened color, and a precipitate step. He whispered into his master's ear an account of the sudden disappearance of a small portion of the tapestry, in an apartment which he designated; entering, at the same time, into particulars of a minute and circumstantial character; but from the low tone of his voice in which these latter were communicated, nothing escaped to gratify the excited curiosity of the equerries.

The young Frederick, during the conference, seemed agitated by a variety of emotions. He soon, however, recovered his composure, and an expression of determined malignancy settled upon his countenance, as he gave peremptory orders that the apartment in question should be immediately locked up, and the key placed in his own possession.

"Have you heard of the unhappy death of the old hunter Berlifitzing?" said one of his vassals to the Baron, as, after the departure of the page, the huge steed which that nobleman had adopted as his own, plunged and curveted, with redoubled fury, down the long avenue which extended from the palace to the stables of Metzengerstein.

"No!" said the Baron, turning abruptly toward the speaker, "dead! say you?"

"It is indeed true, my lord; and, to the noble of your name, will be, I imagine, no unwelcome intelligence."

A rapid smile shot over the countenance of the listener. "How died he?"

"In his rash exertions to rescue a favorite portion of the hunting stud, he has himself perished miserably in the flames."

"I–n–d–e–e–d–!" ejaculated the Baron, as if slowly and deliberately impressed with the truth of some exciting idea.

"Indeed," repeated the vassal.

"Shocking!" said the youth calmly, and turned quietly into the palace.

From this date a marked alteration took place in the outward demeanor of the dissolute young Baron Frederick Von Metzengerstein. He was never to be seen beyond the limits of his own domain, and, in his wide and social world, was utterly companionless—unless, indeed, that unnatural, impetuous, and fiery-colored horse, which he henceforward continually bestrode, had any mysterious right to the title of his friend.

Numerous invitations on the part of the neighborhood for a long time, however, periodically came in. "Will the Baron honor our festivals with his presence?" "Will the Baron join us in a hunting of the boar?"—"Metzengerstein does not hunt"; "Metzengerstein will not attend," were the haughty and laconic answers.

These repeated insults were not to be endured by an imperious nobility. Such invitations became less cordial—less frequent—in time they ceased altogether.

Indeed, the Baron's perverse attachment to his lately-acquired charger—an attachment which seemed to draw new strength from every fresh example of the animal's ferocious and demon-like propensities—at length became, in the eyes of all reasonable men, a hideous and unnatural fervor. In the glare of noon—at the dead hour of night—in sickness or in health—in calm or in tempest—the young Metzengerstein seemed riveted to the saddle of that colossal horse, whose intractable audacities so well accorded with his own.

There were circumstances, moreover, which coupled with late events, gave an unearthly and portentous character to the mania of the rider, and to the capabilities of the steed. The space passed over in a single leap had been accurately measured, and was found to exceed, by an astounding difference, the wildest expectations of the most imaginative. The Baron, besides, had no particular *name* for the animal, although all the rest in his collection were distinguished by characteristic appellations. His stable, too, was appointed at a distance from the rest; and with regard to grooming and other necessary offices, none but the owner in person had ventured to officiate, or even to enter the enclosure of that horse's particular stall. It was also to be observed, that although the three grooms, who had caught the steed as he fled from the conflagration at Berliftzing, had succeeded in arresting his course, by means of a chain-bridle and noose—yet not one of the three could with any certainty affirm that he had, during that dangerous struggle, or at any period thereafter, actually placed his hand upon the body of the beast. Instances of peculiar intelligence in the demeanor of a noble and high-spirited horse are not to be supposed capable of exciting unreasonable attention, but there were certain circumstances which intruded themselves by force upon the most skeptical and phlegmatic; and it is said there were times when the animal caused the gaping crowd who stood around to recoil in horror from the deep and impressive meaning of his terrible stamp—times when the young Metzengerstein turned pale and shrunk away from the rapid and searching expression of his human-looking eye.

Among all that retinue of the Baron, however, none were found to doubt the ardor of that extraordinary affection which existed on the part of the young nobleman for the fiery qualities of his horse; at least, none but an insignificant and misshapen little page, whose deformities were in everybody's way, and whose opinions were of the least possible importance. He (if his ideas are worth mentioning at all) had the effrontery to assert that his master never vaulted into the saddle without an unaccountable and almost imperceptible shudder; and that, upon his return from every long-continued and habitual ride, an expression of triumphant malignity distorted every muscle in his countenance.

One tempestuous night Metzengerstein, awaking from a heavy slumber, descended like a maniac from his chamber, and mounting in hot haste, bounded away into the mazes of the forest. An occurrence so common attracted no particular attention, but his return was looked for with intense anxiety on the part of his domestics, when after some hours' absence, the stupendous and magnificent battlements of the Palace Metzengerstein, were discovered crackling and rocking to their very foundation, under the influence of a dense and livid mass of ungovernable fire.

As the flames, when first seen, had already made so terrible a progress that all efforts to save any portion of the building were evidently futile, the astonished neighborhood stood idly around in silent if not pathetic wonder. But a new and fearful object soon riveted the attention of the multitude, and proved how much more intense is the excitement wrought in the feelings of a crowd by the contemplation of human agony, than that brought about by the most appalling spectacles of inanimate matter.

Up the long avenue of aged oaks which led from the forest to the main entrance of the Palace of Metzengerstein, a steed, bearing an unbonneted and disordered rider, was seen leaping with an impetuosity which outstripped the very Demon of the Tempest.

The career of the horseman was indisputably, on his own part, uncontrollable. The agony of his countenance, the convulsive struggle of his frame, gave evidence of superhuman exertion: but no sound, save a solitary shriek, escaped from his lacerated lips, which were bitten through and through in the intensity of terror. One instant, and the clattering of hooves resounded sharply and shrilly above the roaring of the flames and the shrieking of the winds—another, and clearing at a single plunge the gate-way and the moat, the steed bounded far up the tottering staircases of the palace and, with its rider, disappeared amid the whirlwind of chaotic fire.

The fury of the tempest immediately died away, and a dead calm suddenly succeeded. A white flame still enveloped the building like a shroud, and, streaming far away into the quiet atmosphere, shot forth a glare of preternatural light; while a cloud of smoke settled heavily over the battlements in the distinct colossal figure of—*a horse.*[5]

~⊗~

---

5. Edgar Allan Poe, "Metzengerstein," in *New Stories of the Extraordinary.*

In Quest of the Grail

Amidst the great inundations of the sun
That bleach perfumes
Amidst the confines of magical seasons
Amidst the inverted suns
Beautiful as water drops
Desires divide in half
For here they have chosen
Tortures of the most contrary sort
Admirable face completely naked
Ridicule refused as rebellious
Out of its depth
Secret cast
Paths of flesh and a head sky
And you miserable accomplice
With your tears between the leaves
And this great wall that you protect
For nothing
Because you will always believe
That you have created evil through love
This great wall that you protect
Uselessly

Under the eyelids in the tresses
I rock those who think of me
They have changed their minds
Since the vulgar times
They carry their own portion of refusal on their arms
Their caresses have not freed their chests
Their gestures I adjust by saying goodbye
The memory of my words demands silence
As audacity engages the whole of dignity.
Listen to me
I speak for those few men who hold their tongues
The best of men.[1]

Despite my desire to place the marvelous adventure in the realm of the spirits and the elements, to raise it to the level of cosmic drama, I cannot lose sight of the fact that it also begins and ends with man, who serves as both necessary agent and spectator. From the human perspective, the marvelous finds its origin in that eternal conflict pitting our heart's desires against our means for satisfying them.

If we want to characterize the human in relation to other live organisms, without resorting to metaphysical hypotheses, we must point to the immense potential for movement that humans alone possess among all living beings. Our psychological complexity stems from our extraordinary mobility which allows us to explore all corners of the world, a mobility we don't just passively acknowledge, but also hope to expand. So far, we can successfully travel through space, plunge into water, overcome fire (not without fear), descend underground, and penetrate objects after examining their surfaces. This feeling of freedom, power, and domination over things keeps us skeptical about any cosmic determinism controlling humanity. We experience a sense of free will. We believe that we make effective, responsible choices. It's impossible for us to imagine the life of a plant or a mollusk, those immobile organisms whose whole evolution occurs in a single place, and who are obliged to wait for the possibility that something outside themselves will move them, either to their advantage or disadvantage. In this respect, one of the most moving natural dramas is that of plant fertilization, of which Darwin has written so brilliantly. Male and female plants live separately.

---

1. Paul Eluard, *Love and Poetry,* trans. Jon Graham.

Since contact is impossible, a chance wind or an insect's fancy is required for pollen to be conveyed to the pistil, and for operations we usually consider more programmatic to be carried out.

However, under scrutiny, our optimistic illusion of conscious power can't be sustained for long. Quickly we realize the limits of our small universe and our freedom. I am not speaking here of those provincial families of the last century that Balzac describes. I am thinking of myself, and of my friends in Paris, that center of exchange where we easily fall into and out of relationships appropriately described as "extensive." Despite everything, our actual universe is limited to a very small number, parents, some neighbors, a few people we admire or argue with because we happen to cross paths. As soon as the personality is formed, it becomes nearly impossible to change this circle. Furthermore, by a kind of irony of fate, those lucky events that we hope will lead to change or renewal bring old friends lost from view close again, and thus shrink our horizons even further. This little circle in which we live is truly a miniature solar system. Possessing, like the latter, a fixed number of planets with stable orbits, it, too, is occasionally visited by comets. And, just as with the distant constellations, beyond the inner circle, it's a matter of shadowy silhouettes, of walkers, workers, members of the various groups to which we belong. We really know nothing about any of these strangers. We exchange passing remarks. Except for those rare moments of collective passion, no real contact capable of breaking through our solitude takes place. And here is the source of that urgent need for love which grows in us, according to its own obscure rhythm. As complex as fire and the cosmic energies, this subconscious force cries out for pleasure. The instinct, with its many conflicting aims, tears us apart. Simple physical desire urges us to look for immediate sexual gratification, without being particular about the ways or means of achieving it. Society, on its part, shows universal hostility toward passionate love. It excuses the physical need by reducing it to a hygienic necessity. It encourages us to link our social persona to another social persona in order to acquire wealth, employment, prestige. Despite being confused time and again by the contradictory signals we get, we retain a deep sense of certainty. Without having any rational proof of it, we know that somewhere, someone waits for us, in whose presence we will find an answer to our anguish, that there lies our only source of happiness. Our feeble minds keep us from imagining the precise traits we desire; our absolute certainty remains an abstraction. Even those who let themselves be won over by society, family, and money retain their core conviction that to discover the being sworn to their hearts, they only need to look.

Animated by our restlessness, we study the looks of passersby, we question the fleeting apparitions. We reexamine those around us, trying to lift the veil that daily habit has woven over familiar faces.

Enclosed within our own horizons, we dream of the mysterious place where this woman lives. We imagine her in the gentle atmosphere of her thoughts, surrounded by her parents and friends. Moved, we linger over the place where she breathes or where she projects the enchantment of her charm onto small things. From then on, the promised land, the marvelous realm, ceases to exist outside of earthly reality; it is there where she waits. But where is this blessed place, garret or palace, or simple room where life will take on its whole meaning? Is it right here, escaping our notice? Is it far off, waiting beyond precipices we must clear and fires we must go through? This uncertainty is at the heart of all human grief. How easy it would be to undertake the struggle if the nature of these obstacles were revealed to us, if we could know toward which corner of the world we should head with our courage. But the prison wall encircling our solitude, separating us from our hope of love, is like those thick fogs the navigator encounters at a certain point in his journey. They travel with him, letting him cross through them, only to have them immediately reform again. How we wish we could possess the rules to this game called life, but alas, no clues are provided, except that it is necessary to resolve it or to die, that victory must be certain, under the condition that we don't betray our pure hope, don't abandon ourselves to physical impulses and make those compromises our bad conscience would recommend.

The young woman waits in her garden. She goes to the door to watch the road, ready to see the knight of her heart coming toward her, whom she'll immediately recognize as her own. Trembling with emotion, and yet, despite everything, confident, she hopes for fate to be kind, just as the orchid offers itself for the insect's miraculous germination. She prepares herself to receive the guest, cultivating herself like an enchanted garden. And the man pursues the quest for the Grail. He travels perilous distances to find the gold chalice, without which the rite cannot be celebrated. He comes up against invisible obstacles, injures himself in fruitless trials. He knocks on closed doors. Trembling, he extends all his efforts toward the beautiful unknown woman, toward her whose presence alone will finally reveal to him his own purpose, give him true knowledge of the world, and, by the virtue of love, break through his sterile solitude once and for all.

The magic includes the entire process by which beings separated by hostile space or human malevolence are reunited. It allows those who carefully focus their desire to attract the Other, the predestined companion. Thanks to secret rituals, any resistance will be overcome.

During the adventure, the smallest signs along the way, a lost shoe, a lock of hair, the gift of a ring, serve the same purpose as prophecies. They are indications or signals to help us interpret our fate. Below is one of the practices that makes the features of the beloved apparent to us:

For Recognizing the Face of the Predestined Fiancé
V. Vend

This is done in secret, in the country, in the depths of a remote bathing place. Baths have always been a refuge for spirits and ghosts. And the more dilapidated they are, the more they lend themselves to all the mystery the imagination can add to such ruins. Few young women or young widows have the courage to brave this test. According to some good women, to go there is to court horrible danger. One only resolves to attempt it armed with all her courage.

Between the hours of eleven and midnight, the postulant goes secretly to the deserted baths. She must remain there absolutely alone. In the lowest chamber—the bath is usually made up of three parts—she places a table, covers it with a white cloth, and sets it. The setting includes lit candles, a plate of fish, bread, salt, a carafe of water, and glasses. She puts a chair to her right, at the empty place. Then she sits down, taking from her pocket a small pair of scissors she has carefully equipped herself with, and hiding them in the palm of her hand, she cries out:

"My predestined one! Quickly! Come dine with me!"

She waits. In the deep silence, she hears only the rapid beating of her heart, the monotonous *cree-cree* of the cricket or the deafening *tic-tac* of insects gnawing the charred beams. The darkness beyond is filled with terrors. In the chamber, the lit up spot of cloth makes the corners seem darker, while the open door makes a gaping, sinister hole, opening out into the mysterious gloom. Suddenly, a fleeting shadow obscures the tiles. The door creaks on its rusty hinges. The loose floor groans under heavy footsteps, strangely paced.... Nearly suffocating, the young woman stifles her cry. She braces herself against the terror overtaking her. Then the silhouette of a man takes shape before her.... he comes closer: it is a handsome man, a young man. If he is rich, she hears coins jingle in his pocket. If he is a soldier, he wears a uniform. But, oh, he is pale! So pale! His look is fixed and glazed over; he moves as if in a dream. Coming close to her, he stands for a moment, completely still. Then he takes a seat. Gathering all her courage, she passes him the dishes she's prepared, offers him bread, a glass of water. Like an automaton, the silent phantom accepts it all. He even eats. Then, pretending to be looking for something under the table, she opens her scissors and quickly cuts off a small piece of cloth from his clothes. Oh! It is at this moment above all that she risks death. If the phantom sees through her ploy, sees what she has done to him, he will strangle her. But the beautiful girl is as deft as she is courageous. Nimbly, she completes her theft. As soon as it's done, she straightens up.

"Dissolve *sgûine!*" she cries out loud at the same time as she crosses herself. "Dissolve in the name of God the almighty. Go! *'Tchour'* protect me.... In the name of Christ, go away!"

At these words, the banished phantom grows pale, wavers, and disappears. The young woman returns home triumphant, the cherished piece of cloth clasped tightly in her hand.

Within the year, she will marry the one she saw that fateful night. Rummaging through his clothes, she will find a shirt tail with a small piece missing, the piece she has kept all this time. But in God's name, may she never speak of this reckless adventure! Her husband would go mad; he would remember that harrowing comatose state the Devil had plunged him into "in order to remove his soul and make it appear elsewhere." Suddenly, his strong love would turn to hate, and from then on, he would want to kill the one who had brought this extraordinary torture upon him.[2]

In order to avoid putting the awaited one through such awful trials, often we are content to make his or her image appear to us in our sleep. Here is the formula used by the young women of Franche-Comté, a very ancient practice poorly disguised by the Christian form it takes.

---

2. Vera Vend, *Une année de fêtes russes* (1896). Cited by Saint-Yves.

Another Magical Procedure
C. Nodier

The novena begins in the chapel of the Blessed Virgin on the evening of the eighth day before February, during eight o'clock prayers. Each day, morning and evening, one goes to the church. Devotion must not slacken for even a moment. On the first of February, all the chapel masses must be attended from beginning to end, all the prayers must be said. One makes her confession; then she enters her room in a state of grace. She shuts herself away, entering into a strict retreat, and meanwhile she assembles what she needs for a banquet. The table must be laid for two people and include two settings complete down to the last knife, in order to avoid the most horrible of misfortunes. This setting requires a perfectly white tablecloth, as new and as fine as possible. The meal is very simple, two pieces of bread blessed at the last service, and two fingers of pure wine. In the middle of the table is a plate of porcelain or silver holding two carefully blessed sprigs of myrtle, rosemary, or any other green plant except boxwood, placed one beside the other but absolutely not crossed. Then she opens the door again to let the awaited dinner guest enter. She takes her place at the table, and, commending herself to the Virgin, she goes to sleep. Then strange and wonderful visions begin. Those with whom the Lord has some unknown affinity in this world will see appearing before them the man who will love them if he finds them, or who would have loved them, if he had found them. This novena sends the same dream to the young man and sparks in him an intense impatience to be reunited with this other half of himself revealed to him in his dream.[3]

The following account comes from Evry-Petit-Bourg and is noteworthy for its great simplicity:

One goes to bed, arranging her stockings in a cross at the foot of her bed. She slips a mirror under her pillow. While falling asleep, she recites the incantation: "I put my foot on the chair rail. I pray that while I sleep, God, Saint Joseph, and Saint John make me see the man I will marry in my lifetime."[4]

---

3. Charles Nodier, *La Neuvaine de la Chandeleur.*
4. I owe my account of this ritual to Brunius, whom I thank here.

Magic rituals throw those who practice them into a very intense emotional state. Sometimes it happens that these props are unnecessary, that the desire itself has sufficient power to provoke the premonitory dream. The account of one such nocturnal vision was communicated to me by a woman who lives in the realm of the marvelous. It is authentic testimony in which religious fervor is not altered by the deadening forms of religious dogma.

A Woman's Dream

A young woman, naked except for the mantle of her long golden hair, crosses the garden. Light, supple, and tall, she doesn't care about the water, or the grass, or the rose-colored stone walk that her feet barely touch. Her gait is not labored or heavy, but perfectly balanced by the weight of the hope she carries within her, a balance which keeps her vertically suspended between her flights toward the sky and her desire to draw from the earth all the joy she asks of it. Hope and joy, she heads toward the temple.

Since I've had this dream, I keep trying to envision the temple's façade clearly. It remains with me only as an imprecise image, like a mirage. Only the garden appears to me clearly, the pools and lawns divided by borders of white stone, the paths rose-colored marble slabs. No flowers, no vegetation except the grass, and, floating on the water, lily pads.

Aware of nothing but her destination, the young woman passes over the lawn leaving no footprints, over the blue water without making the lily pads tremble. The sun begins to rise. There is no sound, no one moving except this young woman who seems to be capturing the light of dawn in order to take it to the one who is waiting.... She does not look like me; she is more like a romantic symbol of my own mind. I remain at a distance from her, an attentive spectator, and yet, I think, hope, and suffer with her, inside of her. For an instant, two images merge for me, one of a rosebud ready to open, and the one of this young woman, so fresh, so bent on living. Then I see only her, but she retains the forgotten flower's perfume and color....

She enters the temple, a great rectangular hall, large but not deep, no openings except the door which she has left gaping on the morning. Four columns, one of them in ruins, stand at the far left side of four steps, an immense stairway as wide as the temple itself and leading to the spot reserved for the priest, the only source of light in this grave and sad place. He is standing on the last step which, being larger than the rest, forms a platform. I cannot distinguish his features, nor the shape of his body which is hidden under a long, luminous robe. His face is covered, encircled in a halo of mist. For me, he is a transcendent being, a priest perhaps, or a god. I call him "the priest who is God."

The young woman approaches him. Her hands are empty. When she kneels on the first step of rose-colored marble, the marble becomes warm and soft as down where her knees have touched it.... Then, a beam of pale light, as wide as her breast from one shoulder to the other, escapes from her. She contains it in her outstretched arms, her hands joined, her fingers forming a cone, a reversed beam, so that there is a great triangle of light ending at the fervent fingers now extending toward the priest this offering, a blue and white flower: the passionflower.

The priest brings it to his lips, and gently he lifts a blue and red bird down from his left shoulder. He says a few words to it in a very low voice. The bird flies up high into the light, then goes through the wall, taking the flower with it.

From a gold chest, the priest takes a robe spun from light and flax, long, wide, and made to fit him. He puts it on the young woman. At first the robe is much too big, but then it slowly shrinks until each stitch is fitted to her skin, and pulled tighter still, embraces her.... And then, nothing in my memory links one day to the next. Each is superimposed immediately over the last, like stage scenery....

The next day, the young woman returns to the temple. Radiant, she seems to be bringing the sun. Her eyes search for the priest. He is standing there waiting for her, the robe of light and flax over his outstretched arms. The young woman kneels on the steps where a river of milk is flowing.

Dressed in sunlight, around her head a halo of sunlight, a beam of gold light extending from her shoulders and outstretched arms to her cupped hands, she offers to God a shard of sun. The priest takes it, holds it to his breast, and makes it penetrate his heart. Then, gently, he dresses the young woman in the robe spun of light and flax, and as before, the robe embraces her. Then he shows her a path. Confident, she leaves the temple. Rising like the bird in the sunlight, going through the wall, she climbs the sky from cloud to cloud, and arrives in a garden of blossoming olive trees. There, birds in mad flight weave a moving canopy above her, multicolored and melodious, a kaleidoscope of colors and sounds. She lies down underneath it. The robe becomes so soft, so close against her own body that for a moment it seems to be God himself, and she feels her heart growing like some fruit within her breast.

The following day, the woman, heavy with passion, kneels on the marble steps which have now turned red. A river of blood flows there. She searches with her eyes for the robe of her joy, but the priest has taken it back. He has laid it in the gold chest, and gravely, he closes it.

Then, desperate, her hands taut, she rips open her breast. She looks for her heart, but all she finds there is an enormous bean. Then, closing her hands again around the beam of the offering which, on this day, is made up of pain and blood, she offers the bean to the priest. The priest, his hands trembling, tries to seize it. But at this moment, the bean shrinks, turns into a haricot, and then a tear, a tear of blood which falls on his bare foot.

At this moment, the violence of my dream wakes me. Immediately I try to reconstruct it, to find it again; perhaps I am putting myself back to sleep again by recording it in my mind, perhaps I was thinking the last part rather than dreaming it.

Besides, the rhythm changes. Now it is no longer a matter of days but of seasons. Suddenly we are in winter. Outside, there is no longer any sun. The woman closes the door. When she enters, she no longer brings light. Only the priest lights the temple where the stones are now covered with moss again. Water trickles down the walls. It is wet and cold. The steps are no longer marble, but brown stone, like the walls. Nevertheless, the woman comes back. Faithfully, one morning after the next, from the width of her shoulders a ray of hope extends to her cupped, outstretched hands, and she offers to him a small green flame. Each morning he will have to crush it against himself, make it penetrate his flesh, and kiss the fingers that offer it. Each day, however difficult, she returns, drawn by her love. She reads his lips, and so learns to love him better and more deeply, to know the routes of the sky, the language of flowers and birds, the meaning of the stars.

Finally, beautiful days return. One morning, a bird enters the temple on a ray of sunlight. In its beak it carries the passionflower. At this moment, the priest rises, takes the flower from the bird's beak, a shard of sun from his heart, the drop of blood from his foot, a green flame from his mind. From his gold chest, he takes the robe of spun light and flax and he turns toward the woman.

Illuminated by a ray of sunlight which seems to have opened a door to the sky high above the walls, she kneels on the steps where a river of gold now flows. She receives the flower, the gem, the tear of blood, and the green flame. Gently, he takes her by the hand, and leads her toward a new path which they have made during their long winter's labor. They arrive in the olive garden escorted by the birds: the bird of fire, the sky bird, the flower bird, the little fairy bird, the bird of the islands, and the bird-fly paint a beautiful fire in the air over their happiness, wings bursting into brilliant colors. Resting lightly on the earth covered again with flowers, their feet receive the gold dust, the pollen of their love.

They lie down under the olive trees, and there, for the love of this woman, he makes himself into a man. He takes the robe spun of light and flax, and, adorning the one for whom it was destined, he gives it to her. The robe adapts itself exactly to the woman's form, the flowers close over her again, the birds join in a chorus of resonant waves of sound, and, lying under the olive trees, she feels she has become one with this man for eternity.[5]

⤶

The Traits of the Fiancé Appearing in a Dream
(PERSIAN TALE)

It was through a dream that Kitaboum, the oldest of three daughters of the king of Roumou, saw long ago the face of the one who would become her beloved. She had reached a marriageable age, and her father had decided to find her a husband. He called together the great sages and wisest advisors. Surrounded by sixteen slaves, Kitaboum paraded through the ranks, holding in her hand a bouquet of roses which she was to offer to indicate her choice. But she did not recognize among any of these assistants the traits she had seen during the night. The king then ordered all those notable for their wealth to gather, regardless of their rank, but with no more success. Not long before, a young stranger had arrived there, and had been received and given hospitality by the head of the village. The village head advised him to go to the palace to take part in the festivities. As soon as she saw him, Kitaboum recognized him and said:

"There is the one my dream revealed to me."

She placed her jeweled tiara on Gouschtasp's head, for that was the young man's name. He was a prince who had left his father's realm to

---

5. Anonymous.

seek adventure. Bound by his oath, the king of Roumou had to give his daughter to the one she had chosen, but he said to him:

"Go, because you will receive neither treasure, nor throne, nor seal."[6]

How mysterious is the origin of these prophetic dreams. The extraordinary powers of the unconscious in direct contact with cosmic destiny astonish us. Our surprise is often so great that we doubt our lucidity. Sometimes it seems that these messages are transmitted to us by spirits.

Crimson, White, and Black Tale

Once in winter a man went for a walk. He killed a crow. The luster of its plumage, the white of the snow, and the red of its blood produced an assemblage of colors that struck the prince. He thought he would be happy if he could meet someone with such crimson and white hues highlighted by perfectly black hair. A voice said to him:

"Go to the empire of the marvelous. In the middle of a huge forest, you will find a tree laden with apples.... Pick three and do not allow yourself to break into them until you return. They will provide you with the kind of beautiful woman you desire."

"The one that I desire," responded the young man....[7]

The Face of the Woman
P. Eluard

You are the only one, I hear the grass blades of your laughter
O you, it is your head that carries you away
From the dangers of a death that comes from on high
Under the foggy globes of the rain of the valleys

---

6. Persian tale dating from the end of the tenth century B.C., in Firdousis, *Book of Kings*.
7. "Crimson, white, and black," in *Nouveau recueil de contes de fées* (1718), reprinted in the *Cabinet des fées* (1786). Note the theme of blood on snow, which is one of the most fundamental in folklore. This is a key poetic image, an image possessing a dynamic power that is always new.

Under the heavy light, under the earthen sky
You give birth to the fall.
Birds are no longer sufficient shelter
Nor is laziness; nor fatigue
The memory of woods and fragile streams
In the morning of whims
In the morning of visible caresses
In the long morning of the absence of the fall.
The barks of your eyes stray
Into the lace of disappearances
The abyss is unveiled for others to extinguish
The shadows that you have created have no right to the night.[8]

Then again he says:

Her eyes have towers of light
Under the brow of her nakedness.
At the level of transparency
The return of thoughts
Annuls the dulled words.
She effaces all images
She dazzles love and its stubborn shadows
She loves—She loves to forget herself.[9]

Our inner certainty that we will meet the person of our dreams, a certainty as unshakable as it is impossible to explain logically, does not grow from nocturnal premonitions alone. Acting as though it had some careful plan, destiny lines our path with unsettling signs. Certain objects take on meanings beyond their ordinary nature's common sense because of the strange contexts in which they appear. They become so many answers to the questions within our hearts, so many bits of evidence meant to quiet our reasonable doubts. The doors of mystery are provided with signs that we must be able to read.

Because of their symbolic language, flowers and jewels play this role in the disquieting exchange between human desire and cosmic processes.

---

8. Paul Eluard, *Love and poetry*, trans. Jon Graham.
9. Ibid.

The Miraculous Jewel
(INDIAN TALE)

A prince who was traveling with his friend, the son of a minister, got lost in a forest. In order to pass the night safely, they climbed a large tree, tying their horses at its foot. All of a sudden they saw an enormous serpent coming out of a pond. On its hood in the form of a crest, shone a jewel which lit up the night for a great distance all around. The gigantic cobra left its jewel on the ground and began searching for prey. It devoured the two horses, then slithered off. Recalling a practice he'd heard about, the minister's son covered the luminous jewel with horse droppings. Now that it was impossible for the serpent to recover what had been its talisman, it perished. Thanks to the jewel which was now in their possession, the two young men discovered a magnificent palace in the heart of the forest. There they found a beautiful princess whom the serpent had held captive and whom the prince married.[10]

Often the object that serves to bring together the man and woman is a ring of gold, lost and miraculously found again.

The Recovered Ring
(INDIAN TALE)

In a palace in India, a cook, having been to market to buy a fish, was very surprised to find a magnificent ring inside it. He presented it to the king. The king had it announced throughout his kingdom that whoever had lost a nose ring should come before him. A man came and told him that the jewel belonged to his sister. The sister was then called before the king. She told her story:

A Brahmin had a wife whom he advised never to eat when he was not present, or else she would turn into a goat. The Brahmani asked on her part, that her husband never eat without her, because otherwise he would be changed into a tiger. A long time after that, when the wife was dishing out food to her children, she ate a small bit of it without thinking about her husband's absence. That very instant, she was changed into a goat. Distraught, the Brahmin did his best to take care of her, but years passed and he remarried. His new wife proved herself to be very

---

10. Tale of Bengale dal Behari Dai, in *Folk Tales of Bengal* (London, 1883).

hard on the children of the first marriage, and gave them barely anything to eat. The goat heard their complaints and watched them wasting away. She told them to knock on her horns with a stick every time they were hungry, and thus, they would receive sustenance.

That is what the children did, and, instead of becoming weaker as the stepmother wished, they grew stronger and stronger. By and by, the evil woman had a daughter. When she was old enough, her mother sent her out to play with her stepsisters and brothers, and advised her to observe carefully how they got food. The little girl reported back to her. The stepmother pretended to be gravely ill and bribed the doctor to prescribe goat meat as the only remedy that would cure her. The Brahmin decided to kill the goat. When the children learned of his plans, they burst into tears before this animal whom they knew to be their mother. She comforted them and told them to bury her bones in a remote spot. When they became hungry, all they would have to do would be to go to this place and ask for food, which they would be given. Sometime later, while one of the stepdaughters was washing her face, her nose ring came out. It fell into the water and was swallowed by a fish. This was the very fish that the cook had bought for the king.

Taking the discovery of the ring to be a sign of destiny, and charmed by the young woman's beauty, the monarch married her.[11]

However much such facts have been repeated for as long as humans have existed on earth, however much universal folklore has served as true testimony, our incredulous minds remain doubtful. Such reservations are not new. They are evident already in centuries long past, in that homeland of legends, the British Isles:

Tristan's Departure

King Marc of Cornwall had such great affection for his nephew Tristan that he had resolved never to marry so there would be no other heir to his throne. But the lords of the realm did not see things in the same vein and they begged Marc to take a wife and extend his lineage. The king was in the midst of thinking of ways he could evade this request, when two swallows attacking each other with their beaks entered by the

---

11. Indian tale collected in Srinagar in the Kashmir valley, in J. Hinton Knowles, *Folk Tales of Chachemir* (London, 1888).

window. During their quarrel they let drop a long, beautiful strand of hair. The king picked it up and saw that it was from the head of a woman. Showing it to his lords he declared that he would wed the woman who was possessor of this hair, as he thought such a subterfuge would provide him a peaceful haven from his subject's unwelcome demands. He was wrong not to pay heed to destiny's warnings. The lords, and with them Tristan, undertook a search for the unknown woman. One day Tristan was tossed by storm onto the Irish coast and wounded in combat with a dragon. The queen's daughter retrieved him from where he lay fallen and cared for him. When he returned to health he learned that the name of this gentle young maiden was Isolde and he could see that the hair carried by the swallows was one of hers.[12]

Despite King Marc's incredulity, here again the magic object allows destiny to triumph over seemingly insurmountable obstacles. Wasn't it a hair that once brought the daughter of the gods to the Egyptian pharaoh? Wasn't it Cinderella's slipper which, against all odds, joined together in love the son of a king and the miserable victim of a pitiless stepmother? Sometimes it happens that no such signs are visible to us. Then we owe our marvelous encounters to chance. How much could be said about the true nature of such chance, its harsh necessity so clear to our minds. At the very least it must be a singular premonition that directs our nervous steps toward that point on the horizon from which she approaches.

The Encounter
René Char

The village was bivouaced on the flanks of the hillside amidst the mimosa-filled fields. It so happened that at harvest time, far from their meadows, there occurred an extremely aromatic encounter with a girl whose arms had been filled with their fragile branches during the day. Like a lamp whose halo of light was perfume, she continued on her way with her back toward the setting sun.

It would have been sacrilegious to speak even a word to her.

Give right of way to the espadrille that is trampling the grass and

---

12. *The Legend of Tristan and Isolde,* after the German poet Eilhart von Oberge.

perhaps you will have the good fortune to see on her lips the moistness of the night.[13]

⮜⮞

His landing in the Indian Isles was driven, it seems to me, by a wind on a very precise course, as precise as the studied trajectory of a missile. We have learned to appreciate the beauties of this place abandoned by men, given over to a natural freedom, and where only a young and pure beauty survives. Here are the memorable circumstances of this encounter:

The Woman of the Enchanted Isle
C. R. Maturin

On the evening of the day after the Indians had departed, Immalee, for that was the name her votarists had given her, was standing on the shore, when a being approached her unlike any she had ever beheld. The color of his face and hands resembled her own more than those she was accustomed to see, but his garments (which were European), from their square uncouthness, their shapelessness, and their disfiguring projection about the hips (it was the fashion of the year 1680), gave her a mixed sensation of ridicule, disgust, and wonder, which her beautiful features could express only by a smile—that smile, a *native of the face* from which not even surprise could banish it.

The stranger approached and the beautiful vision approached also, but not like a European female with low and graceful bendings, still less like an Indian girl with her low salaams, but like a young fawn, all animation, timidity, confidence, and cowardice, expressed in almost a single action. She sprung from the sands—ran to her favorite tree—returned again with her guard of peacocks, who expanded their superb trains with a kind of instinctive motion, as if they felt the danger that menaced their protectress, and, clapping her hands with exultation, seemed to invite them to share in the delight she felt in gazing at the *new flower that had grown in the sand.*

The stranger advanced, and to Immalee's utter astonishment, addressed her in the language which she herself had retained some words of since her infancy, and had endeavored in vain to make her peacocks,

---

13. René Char. Excerpt from a then unpublished collection *Les Loyaux adversaires,* trans. Jon Graham.

parrots, and loxias, answer her in corresponding sounds. But her language, from want of practice, had become so limited, that she was delighted to hear its most unmeaning sounds uttered by human lips; and when he said, according to the form of the times, "How do you do, fair maid?" she answered, "God made me," from the words of the Christian Catechism that had been breathed into her infant lip.

"God never made a fairer creature," replied the stranger, grasping her hand, and fixing on her eyes that still burn in the sockets of that arch-deceiver.

"Oh yes!" answered Immalee, "he made many things more beautiful. The rose is redder than I am—the palm-tree is taller than I am—and the wave is bluer than I am—but they all change, and I never change. I have grown taller and stronger, though the rose fades every six moons; and the rock splits to let in the bats, when the earth shakes; and the waves fight in their anger till they turn grey, and far different from the beautiful color they have when the moon comes dancing on them, and sending all the young, broken branches of her light to kiss my feet, as I stand on the soft sand. I have tried to gather them every night, but they all broke in my hand the moment I dipped it into the water."

"And have you fared better with the stars?" asked the stranger smiling.

"No," answered the innocent being, "the stars are the flowers of heaven, and the rays of the moon the boughs and branches; but though they are so bright, they only blossom in the night—and I love better the flowers that I can gather and twine in my hair. When I have been all night wooing a star, and it has listened and descended, swinging downwards like a peacock from its nest, it has hid itself often afterwards playfully amid the mangoes and the tamarinds where it fell; and though I have searched for it till the moon looked wan and weary of lighting me, I never could find it. But where do you come from? You are not red and diminutive like those who come over the waters to me from other worlds, in houses that can live on the deep, and walk so swiftly, with their legs plunged in the water. Where do you come from? You are not so bright as the stars that live in the blue sea above me, nor so deformed as those that toss in the darker sea at my feet. Where did you grow and how come you here? There is not a canoe on the sand; and though the shells bear the fish that live in them so lightly over the waters, they never would bear me. When I placed my foot on their scolloped edge of crimson and purple, they sunk into the sand."

"Beautiful creature," said the stranger, "I come from a world where there are thousands like me."

"That is impossible," said Immalee, "for I live here alone, and other worlds must be like this."

"What I tell you is true, however," said the stranger.

Immalee paused for a moment, as if making the first effort of reflection—an exertion painful enough to a being whose existence was composed of felicitous acts and unreflecting instincts—and then exclaimed, "We both must have grown in the world of voices, for I know what you say better than the chirp of the loxia, or the cry of the peacock. That must be a delightful world where they all speak—what would I give that my roses grew in the world of answers."[14]

Thus, the most dangerous tests overcome, the man meets the young woman, free, ready to receive him, adorned in the radiance of her beauty. Won over by her many charms, the lover quickly forgets about his past struggles.

Alas! How rarely are we granted such easy access to the marvelous realm. Often the woman is bound by an ancestral curse brought upon her by barbarous families and cruel societies. At the end of his quest, the conqueror must begin another round of labors in order to make all her hidden beauty, all the life held captive within her, spring forth.

The Young Woman Delivered

L. Gonzenbach

Pauline, the daughter of the queen of Sicily, was the prisoner of her mother and her own faith. When she was seven years old, her parents sent her to school.

Each morning, she met a monk who said he was her uncle and who gave her treats. This monk was Saint Francis. One morning he said to her:

"My dear Pauline, ask your mother if it is better to suffer while you are young or when you are old."

Her mother found the question strange and did not want to answer at first. Then she decided:

"It is better to suffer while you're young and then be happy," she said.

---

14. Charles Robert Maturin, *Melmoth the Wanderer.*

Pauline reported this answer to Saint Francis, who took the little girl in his arms and carried her away to a tower in the deserted countryside with only one window and no doors. There he raised the little princess, teaching her everything women of her rank needed to know. Day by day, Pauline became more beautiful and her hair grew marvelously long. Each time Saint Francis went out of the tower or wanted to come back in, he told his adopted daughter to let her tresses down from the window, and he used them as a ladder. One day a king was passing by and witnessed this scene. He waited for the saint to leave and then took his turn at climbing the ladder of tresses. Seeing that this was not her uncle who had gained entrance to the tower, Pauline was very frightened. The king was able to reassure her and convince her to return with him to her castle and become his wife. Pauline followed the king, and the saint never again returned to the tower.[15]

That obstacle was not very serious. Often things can be much more difficult.

In a room in the castle, a young woman lies sleeping, waiting for the one who must awaken her. Thus Siegfried finds her after he has crossed through the circle of fire and the forest. She sleeps covered with a shell of armor which he must split open with his sword in order to reveal her body, resplendent in its beauty.

This very ancient and ubiquitous theme informs stories like "Sleeping Beauty," and also those in the *Peau d'âne* genre. A great many interpretations have been proposed for them. For some, Beauty symbolizes the earth put to sleep by winter and opening to the rays of the spring sun. For others, she represents the lost wisdom of ancient brotherhoods, the flame hidden under the bushel that a predestined hero will one day manage to uncover.

One can see in them as well a representation of the biological processes that are called into play by amorous encounters: in the woman's body, the egg cells, the vehicles for carrying on the life of the species, waiting hidden, sleeping, for the arrival of their male counterpart. The hero's action calls to mind the drama of defloration.

Examined from the point of view of psychology, the story also touches on the metamorphosis women undergo as soon as they experience love.

15. L. Gozenbach, Sicilian tale.

All these explanations, equally valuable, are by no means mutually exclusive. That's why tales from folklore, far from being allegories or apologues, carry all the weight of true symbols. They simultaneously clarify the mysteries of the heavens, the elements, and those of our bodies and hearts. It is worth repeating that the adventure of love duplicates for humans the adventure of the world. This is made very clear in the following tale from Spain:

The Sleeping Prince
(A SPANISH STORY)

D. S. Hernandez de Soto

Once upon a time in winter, a princess was looking out her window and saw a shepherd cut the throat of a lamb, whose blood stained the snow red. In that same moment, she heard a little shepherd singing a song that compared the lovely effect of the red on the white to the coloring of the "king who will sleep and who will not awaken until the morning of our lord Saint John."

She then learned more about this handsome king in a castle very far away (to get there, it was necessary to wear a pair of iron boots). He slept all year round and only woke on the morning of the feast of Saint John. If, upon awakening, he saw no one, he went to sleep again until the following year. If a princess went to the castle, stood watch at the head of the bed, and stayed there until the light of dawn on Saint John's day, the spell would be broken and the king would marry his liberator.

The princess had a pair of iron boots made for her and set out toward the palace of the sleeping king. First she came to the home of the mother of the Sun, and then to the home of the mother of the Stars, but neither the Sun nor the Stars knew where to find the palace. The Wind knew, and he told his mother. He also told her what had to be done to pass unharmed between the two lions who guarded the palace.

Informed of all this by the kindly old woman, the princess proceeded on her way and after having walked a long time, she saw that the iron shoes were worn out. Then she noticed before her the tall towers of the palace.[16]

___

16. Don Sergio Hernandez de Soto, in *Cuentos Populares* (1886). Reprinted by Paul Sébillot, in *Contes espagnols*, and by Cosquin.

And in an account recorded in Bengal, we learn what she did there:

In one of the chambers she saw a beautiful prince lying on a bed, his body all spiked with needles. Immediately she set to work removing these needles, never taking a break even to drink or eat or sleep. A week had passed, a man came along with a young slave he offered to sell. The princess bought her for the price of her gold bracelets.

"Now," she said to herself, "I will no longer be alone."

Then she went back to her work.

Two weeks passed. She had removed all the needles except those in the prince's eyes. Then she asked the slave to prepare a bath for her, but she advised her not to touch the last needles while she was taking it. The slave promised, but no sooner had the princess gone out than the needles were removed. The king came back to life and asked who had saved him.

"I did," said the slave, who identified the princess, when she returned, as her servant.[17]

The first meeting has taken place. The man and the woman have recognized each other immediately. Passion has struck, similar in its intensity to the electrical current that passes between a charged sky and the accepting earth, or between the two electrodes on Leyde's machine. The first spark having abolished the darkness, luminous sensual intoxication would triumph if the intelligence did not apply its corrosive doubt. The man believes himself the prey to an illusion. He is no longer content with this one miracle alone. He demands that others follow to verify it. And the most astonishing thing is that more miracles do follow. In the first moments of their passionate encounter, these two experience such a state of palpable tension that the least desire they have only needs to express itself to be fulfilled beyond all their expectations by subsequent events. It is as though the barrier that has been destroyed has not yet had time to reform so that contact between the two lovers continues even when they are separated from each other. In those moments it is as if all the barriers that, in ordinary everyday life, divide our interior lives from the natural necessity of things no longer exist. An extraordinary complicity is established between the needs of

---

17. Miss M. Strokes, *Contes du Bengale.*

the heart, the thought processes, and the laws of a universe we had mistakenly believed to be mechanical, anonymous, and indifferent. Having experienced days like that, having felt at such times how close one approaches to the center of the mystery, I want to emphasize the importance of André Breton's testimony:

Meeting the Predestined Woman
A. Breton

October 6. So as not to have too long a stroll, I go out at about four, intending to walk to "La Nouvelle France" where Nadja ought to be at half past five. There's time for a detour along the boulevards. Not far from the Opera, I have to pick up my pen from the shop where it's being repaired. I decide to use the right sidewalk of the Chaussée d'Antin, which isn't the route I would usually take. One of the first people I prepare to meet there is Nadja, looking as she did that first day. She approaches as if she doesn't want to see me. As on the first day, I retrace my steps with her. She isn't able to explain why she is on this street and, to avoid more long questions, she says she is looking for Dutch chocolates. Already without thinking about it, we have turned around, and we go into the first café we come to. It seems to me that Nadja maintains a certain distance, is even suspicious. She turns over my hat, no doubt to read the initials on the lining, although she pretends to do this unconsciously, out of her habit of determining the nationality of certain men without their knowing it. She admits that she meant to miss the meeting we had agreed upon. I noticed when I ran into her that she was holding the copy of *Pas Perdu* that I'd lent to her. It is now lying on the table and, glancing at its edge, I notice that only a few of the pages have been cut. They are those of the article entitled "L'esprit nouveau" in which is related a series of striking encounters that occurred one day, a few minutes apart, involving Louis Aragon, André Derain, and myself. The indecision that each of us showed under the circumstances, the trouble we had a few moments later, when we found ourselves at the same table, trying to characterize what had happened to us, that very strange mystical appeal that made Aragon and myself feel the need to go back to the same spots where we had seen this veritable sphinx disguised as a charming woman going from one sidewalk to the other questioning the passersby, this sphinx who had spared us one after the other and, to find her, had made us *run* the whole length of all the lines which, even as arbitrary as they

were, could reunite these points, the lack of results from this pursuit
that the passing of time had rendered hopeless, it was to that that Nadja
had immediately turned. She is astonished and disappointed by the
fact that this account of the day's brief events seemed to me to be able
to go without commentary. She urges me to explain exactly what I think
it means just as it is, and the degree of objectivity I ascribed to it when
I published it. I must answer that I don't know anything about it, that
on such ground, the right to record seems to me all that is permitted,
that I have been the first victim of this abuse of confidence, if it is an
abuse of confidence, but I can see very well that she won't let me out of
this. I read impatience in her look, then consternation. Perhaps she
imagines that I am lying. We continue to feel uneasy with each other.
When she talks about going home, I offer to take her there. She gives
the driver the address of the Théâtre des Arts which, she tells me, is just
a few steps from the building where she lives. On the way there, she
stares at me for a long time in silence. Then her eyes open and close
very quickly, as when you find yourself in the presence of someone you
haven't seen for a long time, someone you never expected to see again,
as though to indicate that "you can hardly believe your eyes." A certain
struggle also seems to be going on within her, but all of a sudden, she
gives up, closes her eyes completely, offers her lips.... Now she speaks of
my power over her, of my ability to make her think and do as I wish,
perhaps to a greater extent than I think I want. She begs me thus to do
nothing against her. It seems to her that even before knowing me, she
held no secrets from me. A short scene with dialogue that occurs at the
end of "Poisson soluble," and that seems to be all she has read yet of
the *Manifest*, a scene that, furthermore, I have never been able to attribute any precise meaning to, and whose characters are like strangers
to me, their agitation completely enigmatic, as if they had been carried
in and taken away again by a flood of sand, gives her the impression of
actually having participated in it, and even of having played the role,
obscure to say the least, of Hélène. The place, the atmosphere, the
respective attitudes of the actors were, indeed, as I had imagined them.
She wants to show me where this happened; I suggest that we dine
together. There must be a certain confusion in her mind, because she
has us driven not to Ile Saint-Louis, as she thinks, but to Place Dauphine, where, curiously enough, another scene from "Poisson soluble"
takes place: "A kiss is so quickly forgotten." (Place Dauphine is one of
the most truly isolated places I know, one of the worst wastelands in
Paris. Each time I go there, I feel myself abandoning, bit by bit, all my

desire to go elsewhere. I must struggle to disengage myself from a very gentle, too seductive, and, finally, crushing embrace. What's more, for some time, I lived in a hotel near this place, the "City Hotel," where the comings and goings at all hours, for anyone not satisfied with the most simple solutions, are suspect.) The day is ending. In order to be alone, we have the wine seller serve us outside. During our meal, for the first time, Nadja shows some frivolity. A drunk keeps loitering around our table. He shouts out incoherent remarks in protesting tones. Among his words, one or two obscene ones keep cropping up, which he emphasizes. His wife, who watches him from under the trees, confines herself to crying out from time to time, "Let's go, are you coming?" I make several attempts to get rid of him, but to no avail. As dessert arrives, Nadja begins to look around. She is sure that an underground tunnel which begins at the Palais de Justice runs under our feet (she shows me from which corner of the Palais, a little to the right of the white stairway) and then circles the Henri IV hotel. She is troubled by the idea of what has already happened on this square and what is going to happen here. Where only two or three couples are, at this moment, fading into the darkness, she seems to see a crowd. "And the dead, the dead!" The drunk continues to joke darkly. Now Nadja's regard sweeps over all the buildings. "Do you see that window over there? It is black, like all the others. Watch closely. In a minute, it will light up. It will be red." A minute passes. The window lights up. The curtains are, indeed, red. (I am sorry, but if perhaps this goes beyond the limits of credibility, there is nothing I can do about it. Nevertheless, on subjects like this I'm supposed to take sides: I limit myself to acknowledging that this window has gone from black to red, and that is all.) I confess that this place is beginning to frighten me, as it also does Nadja. "How dreadful. Do you see what's happening in the trees? The blue and the wind, the blue wind. Only once before have I seen this blue wind in these same trees. It was from a window in the Henri IV hotel, over there, and my lover, the second one that I told you about, was going to leave. There was also a voice which said: You will die, you will die. I didn't want to die, but I felt such vertigo. I would certainly have fallen if no one had held onto me." I think it is high time for us to go. Along the quays, I feel her trembling all over. It is she who wants to go back toward the Conciergerie. She is very relaxed, very sure of me. Nevertheless, she is searching for something. She absolutely insists that we go into a courtyard, the courtyard of some police station, where she quickly looks around. "It is not there.... But tell me why must you go to prison? What are you going to do? Me, too, I have been in prison. Who was I? It was centuries ago. And you, who were you then?" We are walking along the iron railing again when suddenly Nadja refuses to go any further. There, to the right, is a low window which looks out onto the ditch, which she cannot stop looking at. It is in front of this window which has the look of the condemned, that it is absolutely necessary for us to wait, she knows this. It is from there that anything can come. It is there that everything begins. She grasps onto the railing so that I won't pull her away. She hardly answers my questions anymore. For the sake of peace, I finally just wait until she decides to go on of her own free will. The thought of the underground tunnel has not left her, and no doubt she thinks she is at one of its outlets. She wonders who she could have been in Marie-Antoinette's circle. The steps of those walking past make her shudder for a long time. I am uneasy, and detaching her hands, one at a time, from the rails, I finally compel her to follow me. This takes more than half an hour. After crossing the bridge, we head toward the Louvre. Nadja is still distracted. To bring her around, I recite a Baudelaire poem to her, but the inflecions of my voice frighten her all over again, aggravated by the memory of our recent kiss: "a kiss in which there is a threat." She stops again and leans on the stone banister, her gaze and mine cast down into the river which sparkles with lights at this time of night. "That hand, that hand, on the Seine, why that hand flaming on the water? It's true that fire and water are the same thing. But what is the meaning of that hand? How do you interpret it? Let me have a look at that hand. Why do you want us to go now? What are you afraid of? You think I'm very sick, don't you? I am not sick. But what do you think that means: fire and water, a hand of fire on the water? *(Joking):* Of course, it isn't lucky. Fire and water, they're the same thing. Fire and gold, they're completely different." Toward midnight, we reach the Tuileries where she wants to sit down for a minute. Before us is a fountain whose trajectory she seems to be following. "Those are your thoughts and mine. See where they all start from, how they rise, and how it is even lovelier when they fall back. And then, as soon as they reach the bottom, they are taken up again with the same force, all over again, that's this exhausted spurt, this fall, and how it goes on indefinitely." I exclaim: "But Nadja, how strange! Where did you get exactly the image that appears in nearly the same form in a work that you cannot know and that I've just begun to read?" (And I am obliged to explain to her that this image is the subject of a vignette at the beginning of the *Dialogues between Hylas and Philonous,* by Berkeley, published in 1750, where it is accompanied by the legend: "Urget aquas vis sursum eadem, flectit que dorsum," which takes on important significance at the end of the book in the defense of the idealist attitude.) But she is not listening to me, all her attention focused on the activities of a man who keeps passing back and forth in front of us, and whom she thinks she knows, because this isn't the first time that she has been in this garden at this hour. This man, if it is the same man, asked to marry her. That makes her think of her little girl, a child whose existence she has told me of with so many precautions and whom she adores, above all because she is so unlike other children "with that idea of theirs of always wanting to take out their dolls' eyes to see what's behind them." She knows that she always attracts children. Wherever she goes, they have a tendency to gather around her, to come to smile at her. She is now talking as if to herself and not everything she says seems equally interesting to me anymore. Her head is turned away from me. I'm beginning to get tired. But, although I haven't shown the least sign of impatience: "One more point, that's all. Suddenly I felt that I was going to cause you pain. [Turning back toward me.] It's over." We leave the garden and do not slow down again until we reach a bar on rue Saint-Honoré called "le Dauphin." She notices that we have come from la Place Dauphine to le Dauphin. (In that game that consists of looking for correspondences between such-and-such a person and such-and-such an animal, it is generally agreed that I should be a dolphin.) Nadja can no longer tolerate the sight of a mosaic strip that extends from the counter across the floor, and we must leave the bar after having only just arrived. She has our driver stop in front of the Théâtre des Arts. We agree to meet at the "Nouvelle France" not the next evening, but the one after that.[18]

Among the many incidents occurring this day, I keep coming back to that gesture of Nadja's, looking for the initials in the lining of the hat. She wanted to assure herself of this man's identity, even as, a few minutes later, she confessed that there were no secrets she had kept from him, even before she knew him, while her penetrating eyes left no trace of a shadow in the image of André Breton she created for herself.

From the very first moments, the lovers have told each other everything, everything that is essential. True, direct communication occurs

18. André Breton, *Nadja* (Gallimard).

through the looks exchanged, through the mysterious union of the hands, through the whole of the person becoming, for a moment, translucent. Why then must that need for knowing each other according to society's horrible dictates intervene? Why this desire to introduce oneself, why the absurd questions about one's precise social standing, about the contents of one's past, which, it seems, love must wash entirely away. Isn't this instantly recognized, palpable reality more accurate than any image meticulously constructed out of so many sordid details?

Certainly it's indispensable that the masked dancer whose eyes have worked their charm consent to unveil her face. By the confident willingness of her gesture, the woman as abstract symbol of desire becomes this specific woman, the one whom no one else could ever replace. But does love triumph if the mystery is completely destroyed?

A Wife's Curiosity
(INDIAN TALE)

The daughter of a woodcutter had married a merchant. He took her home with him and entrusted to her the hundred keys to his house, forbidding her to enter one particular room. Intrigued, she decided to open the forbidden door one day and through the window she saw a funeral procession entering the cemetery. She watched the burial. Then, she saw her husband among the gravestones, and watched as he turned into an ogre with three eyes, dug up the cadaver and began to devour it. Upon seeing this, she was overcome by a fever and forced to take to her bed.

As soon as he returned home, the husband, seeing his wife in this condition, went up to the forbidden room and found the window open. To find out if his young wife had disobeyed him, and if he was the cause of her illness, he first took the form of his mother-in-law, and then of other relatives, but all this was in vain. Finally, in the guise of the nurse, he made his wife, now at the end of her strength, tell what she had seen from the room. Then, taking his true form, the three-eyed ogre told her that he was going to roast her on a spit and eat her.

The young wife escaped and the camel driver hid her among the bales of cotton his camels carried. Catching up to them, the ogre pierced each cotton bale with his red-hot spit, but he discovered nothing because his wife had born the wound he'd given her in her foot without a cry. The camel driver took her to the king's palace and there her wound was dressed. The king's son fell in love with her and married her. He kept her hidden in a tower, but the ogre managed to gain entry during the night and tossed the "ashes of the dead" over the prince so that he would not awaken. Then he forced the young wife to descend so he could eat her. Going down the steps where she had spilled chickpeas, she gave him a push. He lost his footing and rolled into a pit she had had prepared in advance. And there a lion and a tiger devoured him.[19]

The inquiry of the woodcutter's wife, of Anne, so nervous, in Bluebeard's castle, are specific examples of a more general curiosity that leads us to seek knowledge even as it keeps us from gaining access to the ultimate reality. On its ordinary level, curiosity destroys its object; analytical indiscretion closes doors. A kind of transmutation must occur to arrive at a level of selfless investigation, capable of prolonging real, direct contact. The interpreters have rightly identified in these folktales a defense meant to keep the layman from penetrating the inner chamber, the holy of holies, where true initiation takes place. The analogy is well founded. What chamber is more sacred than the one in which the magic processes of love occur?

Legend of Psyche
Apuleius

Psyche came upon the palace. From the portico onward everything announced that it was the exquisite and noble dwelling of some god. The walls of its rooms were sheeted with pure gold; the very pavement was composed of precious stones arranged to form various pictures. And while she stood gazing upon these riches she heard a voice that said to her: "Why are you astonished at the sight of these treasures? Everything here belongs to you and you are the mistress of all. Give the command and the bath will be drawn for you and the table set." Soon she was immersed in a bath which restored her aching limbs. A meal of delicious wines and various delicious dishes was awaiting her in a neighboring oval chamber. Then a choir of invisible voices burst into melodious song. Then, as it was the fall of day Psyche stretched out upon the bed to go to sleep, but a slight nervousness possessed her. Anything

---

19. Indian tale cited by E. Cosquin.

could happen to her in a place like this but already the unseen husband was climbing into her bed, taking her into his arms, and making her his wife.

At dawn he left her in haste and almost at that very instant she heard the reassuring voices of her invisible servants arriving to prepare the new bride for the new day. On the following night her new husband, whom she still knew only by touch and hearing, warned her: "My beloved, a cruel fate threatens you; your sisters shan't delay to search for you, but refrain from responding to their lamentations, refrain from following their advice, for that would cause me great unhappiness and the worst of woes would befall you."

However poor, weak Psyche didn't heed this prudent counsel and, envious of her happiness, her sisters gave her to understand that her invisible husband only remained invisible because he was a savage and hideous monster. They gave her this advice: "Get hold of a very sharp carving knife and carefully conceal it under your bed; also prepare a lamp full of oil with a good wick that you can keep lit and ready in some niche. Then when the monster has lain down at your side, and you can tell that he has fallen into a deep sleep, procure your light to assist you and cleanly cut off his head."

After the departure of her sisters Psyche remained alone, her soul as turbulent as a stormy sea; her resolve wavered and she was torn by a thousand conflicting presentiments. She hurried, then stopped, grew angry and tremulous by turn; she simultaneously hated the monster and loved her husband. However she hastened to make all ready for her criminal plan.

Night fell and he came to her and together they tasted all the pleasures of love; he then fell asleep. Psyche quietly stole from the bed and got her lamp and carving knife. But hardly had the light shone forth than the truth was revealed! What did she see before her but the gentlest of all wild creatures, Cupid himself, asleep in a most graceful position. Full of surprise at that unexpected scene of wonder, she dropped her weapon. She silently stared at his golden hair; the thick locks spilled in luxurious abandon over the most charming of necks. She saw a skin so white and so delicate that it seemed the caressing breath of a zephyr played over it. At the foot of the bed the god had laid his bow, quiver, and arrows.

Curious, Psyche examined more closely the weapons of her husband and withdrew an arrow from the quiver. Touching the point to test its sharpness, her hand trembled and she pierced herself slightly;

several drops of blood gushed out and fell upon her snow-white skin. Now pierced by Cupid's arrow she burned with greater passion than before for her husband and flung herself upon his sleeping body, smothering him with ardent kisses, fearful only of waking him too soon. However, while she was clinging to him and tasting of such sweet pleasure, a drop of scalding oil fell from the lamp onto the right shoulder of the sleeper. "Ah! bold and imprudent lamp, base vessel of love, is this how you protect lovers?"

Cupid started up from sleep, and seeing that Psyche had betrayed his trust, flew off without a word. However the girl grabbed hold of his left leg, clung to it, and allowed herself to be carried up into the sky until her strength failed her and she tumbled back to earth again. Her god lover settled on the top of a nearby cypress and reproached her: "Here is the misfortune that I always carefully warned you against, this is the danger I begged you to guard against. And now my weak and simple Psyche your punishment is that I must always flee from you."[20]

The ordeals a man goes through to meet his beloved, to reveal her to herself, have hardly ended before the lovers, concerned with building a solid foundation for their love, have to face a new set of trials. It is no longer a matter of overcoming hostile elements, or surmounting dangers, of piercing through the shadowy wall that separates two beings destined for each other. Now, all the social and familial difficulties arise.

Sometimes a mother, envious of the beauty and charm of her daughter and feeling the bitter weight of her own years, seeks to destroy this newborn happiness.

The Mother's Jealousy

Like that pernicious queen, Snow White's mother, this woman of the Inner Hebrides is jealous of her daughter's beauty. She orders her to be killed, and, to make absolutely sure this is carried out, demands that the heart of the unfortunate one be served to her during a feast. But the daughter runs away, thanks to the help of the servants who feel sorry for her. She rejoins her fiancé and marries him. One day when the mother consults her magic mirror, she learns that she has been fooled, and that her daughter is still alive. She also learns where she

---

20. Apuleius, *The Golden Ass.*

lives. She goes there by boat and debarks before the castle. Pretending to be repentant and overcome with maternal affection, she asks to see the young woman. The latter answers that she may not leave the castle. "Then pass only your little finger through the keyhole that I may kiss it." Alas, the girl consents, and her mother sticks the finger with a pin that kills her.[21]

⤫

Other times it is the father who, because of his opposition, is responsible for the ordeals. He imposes them upon the fiancé.

Conditions Imposed Upon the Suitor

Once there was a poor man who was handsome and intelligent. He could compose songs and sing them in a beautiful voice. Because speech came easily to him and he had a lively heart, all men of distinction, viziers, lawyers, and especially sorcerers, loved him.

He was in love with the king's daughter, and never grew tired of passing before the palace in order to charm her with his songs. He did not dare ask for her hand in marriage for fear of having his head cut off. One night while he wandered around outside the castle singing, the princess heard him and fainted away. The next day, when the king went to see his daughter, he found her passed out. Since he, too, had heard the serenade, he guessed that the singer, whom he knew by reputation, was courting his daughter with an eye toward marrying her. He sent his men to find him and had him thrown into prison where he was kept closely guarded. The next day, the young man had disappeared from the prison and could not be found. That night, the king went to watch over his daughter who was still unconscious, her eyes still closed. The young man passed, singing. The princess rose to her feet, ran to the window to listen, and then fainted away again. The king questioned the guards. Even though the prisoner had escaped, the prison door was still secured with seven iron locks. Through divination, the sorcerer had learned that his protégé was imprisoned and, by magic, he had opened, and then closed the locks again. Afraid to be the laughing stock of other monarchs, the king then vowed never to marry his daughter to this good-for-nothing.

"If I were forced to give him to her, I would first impose conditions

---

21. *Tales of the Inner Hebrides*, County of Inverness.

that no one has ever endured up till now." Nevertheless, the sorcerer advised the young man to go right up to the king and ask for his daughter's hand.

"He will impose extraordinary conditions upon you. Demand that he does this before all the country's viziers and noblemen."

By the power of some signs that the sorcerer drew on the young man's forehead, the young man, hesitant at first, felt emboldened and went to make his bid. At his request, the king called together all the rich merchants, viziers, noblemen, and counselors. Before them all, he said:

"The condition that I attach to my consent is that you procure for me a boat that moves on dry ground without the help of horses or wind."

"I accept," answered the young man. "That is easy to do."

The condition had been suggested to the king by his advisor. The sorcerer sent the young man to deliver a note he'd written to an old woman. This was to be the third woman he would encounter in a desert where he'd found himself transported after closing his eyes that evening. The old woman held a golden wand in her hand. She gave it to the young man, explaining to him that some distance away he would find a large flat rock. He must knock on the rock with the wand. The rock would pivot, setting free an enormous African genie, and nearby, he would see a huge boat. Then the young man must follow the genie's directions to another flat rock. All this he did and a child came out and gave him a second wand much like the first. Then he could embark, and, striking the boat with each of the wands, one on the left and one on the right, he began to move. Following a course over the field, the boat came to a river full of water. A man lay face down and drank straight from the river. The young man watched him and saw that he had drunk so much water that the river was dry.

"Master," he said to him, "that is enough. You have drunk the river dry. Come along, you can work for me."

"You can give me work?" the other one responded. "You can provide for me?"

"I will take care of you. Climb aboard."

He helped him up and struck the boat to make it begin moving again. This person he had encountered belonged to the world of the genies.

Further along, the young man met someone with a pile of bread in front of him as high as a haystack. He came down to greet him.

"Master," he said to him, "is that your dinner or your lunch?"

"It is neither, I'm just a little hungry right now."

"Come aboard. I'll take you along with me and give you work."

"But how can you provide for me? You see how much I need to eat even when I am hardly hungry at all."

"Come aboard. I will see to it that you eat your fill."

The genie climbed aboard. Then the man met someone who ran like the wind even though he wore an enormous iron ball and chain around each ankle. A bit further on, a man was kneeling in an orchard, his ear pressed against the trunk of a tree. He was listening to hear if the fruit would soon be ripe.

"You are the one who hears the dew?" asked the young man.

"Oh yes, I hear the dew from far away." After that, there was another person who was uprooting an enormous tree. He had already pulled up a good part of a forest. To everyone's astonishment, our hero finally arrived with his boat before the king's palace. Since they were genies, the five he had brought with him remained invisible. The young man approached the king and declared that the condition set for his marriage was fulfilled. The king went out, examined the boat, and remained silent. He called his advisor.

"You must demand that this suitor find you a man who can drink all the water in the wells you have in your gardens," he advised.

The order was given to the young man, and the drinker was brought forward, and the wells were emptied to their very bottoms. Next came the eater's turn, who put away ten huge plates of couscous, each topped with mutton, in no time.

"Sire, have you another ten of these?" he asked the king. The advisor was called in again.

"We will go, you and I, and sequester ourselves in the very back of the palace," he said. "There we will talk together in private. He must bring us somebody who, even from a great distance away, will be able to repeat all we have said."

The king had the young man called in.

"If you want to marry my daughter, here is the condition."

"That's easy," answered the young man.

And he went to find the one he had discovered listening to fruit ripening. He posted him a great distance from the palace. The king sat down to talk in private with his counselor.

"Have the horse who is tied at such and such a place set loose," his counselor advised him. "This suitor must bring you a runner who is able to keep up with your horse without falling behind."

Thus they spoke, whispering in each other's ears. Then they went out again.

"What is it we have said?"

"You spoke of such and such a horse."

Now this horse had no equal when it came to racing. It flew with the birds.

On the day of the race, the horse was brought in before all the people, and its rider mounted it. For his part, the young man brought in the man with the iron ball and chains, and also the Listener. The king had ordered that the runner be lined up right beside the rider to give them equal chances. But when the signal was given to start, the runner, having begun a conversation with the young man, said to the rider:

"You go first, take the lead."

It wasn't until the horse had disappeared over the horizon that he began to follow, dragging the iron balls at his feet. In less than no time, he had caught up, and no one could see either the runner or the rider anymore. The king asked the Listener:

"Where are they?"

The Listener put his ear to the ground.

"Sire," he said, "the runner is ahead of the rider, but, strangely enough, they have changed directions. They set out toward the east, but they are returning from the west."

He listened again and added:

"The rider has taken a fall. He is barely holding onto his horse by the reins. But now our hero has put your rider back in the saddle. Now they are approaching."

By straining one's eyes, one could see the runner arriving in the lead. When questioned by the king, he confirmed what the Listener had said.

The counselor suggested a new test. The suitor must bring the king a man capable of lifting a particular marble column and carrying it while running without getting out of breath. This column was so heavy that a hundred people together were hardly able to move it. The tree uprooter was brought in by the young man, who begged the king to summon all the witnesses who had been present at the preceding tests. He had them take their places on the top of the column. Then the tree uprooter lifted the whole thing and began to run. Everyone was amazed. Even the young man wasn't aware that he'd been dealing with genies of this kind. Only the sorcerer knew. Furthermore, he'd been constantly listening in to discover the king's requirements in advance and report them to the young man.

The king told the young man to come back to see him in three days.

When the young man reported this to the sorcerer, the sorcerer warned him that a meeting would take place that very night to decide what would be asked of him next.

That night, after completing his divination, the sorcerer asked the young man:

"Do you want to attend this meeting yourself?"

He wrote some magic words on a piece of paper which he then laid down on the ground.

"Fix your eyes on that paper," he commanded.

The young man then saw before him the assembly and heard the king, who said:

"All the other monarchs are going to laugh at me if I give my daughter to him now."

The vizier answered:

"There is nothing else left to do. Only one solution remains. Lure him away somewhere by treachery. There the headsman will meet him and cut his throat, and we will be free of him."

"No," said the counselor. "Kings must not resort to treachery. When the three days are up, we will ask him to prove that that boat can hold all the inhabitants of our country, young and old, as well as the army. And if he succeeds, well then, we will give him your daughter."

On that note, the meeting adjourned. The sorcerer again sent the young man to the place where he had been given the boat. Always following his protector's instructions, this time he received four horses from a being whose voice alone was enough to make one tremble.

"You will attach one of them to each corner of the boat and you will say to the servants you have with you: 'I set you free.'"

This the young man did. The third day, the king announced his new conditions. The public criers assembled all the country's inhabitants to make them climb onto this ship which moved over firm ground. There was room enough for everyone. The young man picked up his sticks, and the boat drifted along until the passengers had had their fill. Then the king explained to his people the reasons for his daughter's marriage. The marriage took place. The young man had the vizier who had advised treachery decapitated.[22]

---

22. Tale recorded in Blida by M. J. Desparmet in 1914, told to him by Abderrhaman Quaid Ahmed.

Such unreasonable tests seem like poetic inventions to us. However, in principle, they are no different from those conditions imposed by bourgeois families upon any young man asking for a daughter's hand.

I'm reminded that I've known of family meetings that were remarkably similar to that gathering of ministers the king assembled in the Arabian tale.

The "suitor," as he was called, saw himself condemned to wait months, if not years. He had to earn degrees, positions with status; sometimes he had to convert.

The future spouse is not the only one who feels the weight of parental will. As though the weak bonds linking father and daughter weren't in enough trouble already, the father must think up ways to destroy her newborn love. In the name of morality or custom, an inhuman persecution begins:

The Metamorphosis of the Fiancée

The daughter of the king of the genies flees from her father's house with the one she wants to marry, Afronk, the prince. The king of the genies pursues them. To escape her father's wrath, the young woman changes the camel who carries them into a house. She transforms the prince into a gardener and herself into a garden full of watermelons. When the king of the genies rushes up and demands if the gardener has seen the fugitives, Afronk talks to him about selling watermelons. Later, the camel is transformed into a mosque, the young woman becomes a school attached to the mosque, and Afronk is the school master. In response to the genie king's questions, he talks about his students.[23]

Again, it is her metamorphosis that allows another princess to escape persecution.

With her own hands she cut out her two eyes using a knife. One eye became a parrot, the other a kind of starling. Then she cut out her heart. It became a great body of water. Her body was transformed into a splendid palace, much grander than the king's. Her arms and legs

---

23. Kabylian tale, published by M. Mouliéras, in *Légendes et contes de la Grande Kabylie*, trans. M. Basset (Paris, 1893).

were the pillars supporting the veranda roof, and her head the dome of the palace. Led there by chance, the princess's husband entered the palace and, by talking to the two birds, he learned that he was inside the persecuted one. Finding his way by following their directions, he found his wife alive and well in a mysterious corner of the palace.[24]

Sometimes a metamorphosis occurs, but not because the young woman victimized by familial struggles and persecutions intended it. Sometimes, through her hateful duplicity and evil powers, the stepmother succeeds in substituting another woman for the original fiancée between the time of the first meeting and the marriage.

The Substituted Fiancée

A virtuous young woman lived with her stepmother. She had, on one occasion, saved the life of a serpent, a son of the world of darkness, who was being pursued by a dangerous enemy. To thank her, it gave her the precious stone from its crest. Thanks to this jewel, she became a dazzling beauty, crying pearl tears and laughing rubies. She met a rajah who fell in love with her and asked for her hand in marriage. The stepmother had a daughter who was ugly and wicked. She sent her to where the serpent was, hoping the same marvelous gifts would be bestowed upon her, but instead she returned uglier than before. The stepmother went to the wedding with rancor in her heart. She was granted the privilege of dressing the fiancée and perfuming her hair. She stuck a magic needle into her head, thus transforming the young queen into a bird. Then she substituted her daughter for the true fiancée. That night the bird perched in a great tree by the palace doors. She asked a launderer to give her the news, to describe the nuptials of the king.

When the bird was told that the king was asleep, she began to cry pearls. When she learned that he had awakened, she laughed rubies. From her beak fell the flowers with which the sun was strewn. The launderer gathered up the precious stones, and when a beggar came asking for alms, he gave him a handful of pearls. The beggar went before the king. He complained that the king's alms were inferior to those of the launderer. The launderer was called to the king. He recounted how his fortune had come to him, and the daily visits of the bird. The tree was

---

24. Mongolian tale.

smeared with glue, and the bird, when it was caught, was taken to the king, who, caressing it, discovered the needle. He removed it, and his true fiancée appeared before his eyes.[25]

The spitefulness of the old woman, the indifferent complicity of the girl who wins favors unjustly, will not come as a surprise to readers accustomed to such base female intrigues. Who could do more dishonor to the human species than such matrons? Who else could cast doubt, if that were possible, on the existence of a pure and selfless love? In contrast, we are more surprised by the prince's passivity. He seems to show singular goodwill in letting himself be fooled. But let us not condemn him too quickly. Rather, let us question our own hearts instead. Romantic conquests are not always as simple as certain legends would have us believe, legends in which the man and the woman act as if they are the only human beings in the universe, and as if the only obstacles in their way are natural: fire to cross through, distance to overcome, dragons to vanquish. These perils are less formidable than inner blindness. The person who appears to the knight at the end of his quest is not alone. Other, equally smiling, equally passionate, faces cloud his judgment. If it alone could be heard, the heart would give him definite enough reassurance, but the seductive murmur of schemes and social intrigues drowns out its voice. And the man hesitates. He allows himself to be fooled. He behaves like the prince in the Indian tale, whose conduct is more understandable than it seemed on first glance.

Here is another of the mishaps encountered by the inattentive man:

The Substituted Fiancée

A prince sets out in search of Anar Pari (the pomegranate fairy) whom he has heard about and wants to marry. The fairy lives on an island guarded by five hundred dragons. A wizard changes the prince into a parrot so that he can surmount all the obstacles and reach the pomegranate tree that bears three fruits, from which he must pick the one in the middle. After a series of adventures, the prince, still in the form of

---

25. Tale originating in the Western Indian state of Gujerat, in "Folklore in Western India," no. 20, in *India Antiquary* (June 1874). I have made additions to this tale from two other similar Indian stories.

a parrot, plucks and carries away the pomegranate. He has been advised not to break it open until he has returned to his father's palace. Then the most beautiful woman in the world will emerge from it. When he has almost reached the palace, the prince stops and convinces himself that he should break the pomegranate open, because if he waits to do so before the entire court, and no fairy appears, he will be mortified. So he opens the pomegranate and a beautiful young woman appears, as brilliant as the sun. Upon seeing her, the prince faints. The fairy rests his head upon his knees so that he can sleep. While he is sleeping, a young woman of a low caste comes to the fountain to draw water. She questions the fairy. Having been told the whole story, the young woman tries to think of a way to rid herself of the fairy and take her place. She suggests to her that they switch clothes.

"Then we will see how you look."

The fairy dresses. Then the woman says:

"Now let us look into the fountain to see which of us is the most beautiful."

When the fairy leans over the water, the woman pushes her in. Then she wakes up the prince, who, after a bit of hesitation, recognizes her as his fiancée and marries her. However, one day when passing near the fountain, the prince sees an amazingly beautiful lily there. He brings it back to the palace. During the night, the false princess tears the lily into pieces and throws them out the window into the garden. A plot of mint has always grown in this place. The cook picks it to season a dish. When he begins to fry it up, a voice speaks from the skillet: "It's I, the true princess whom you are frying to death, while the evil woman who threw me into the fountain has taken my place." Frightened, the cook throws the mint back into the garden. Soon, a beautiful climbing plant grows toward the prince's chamber. The false princess has it pulled up and destroyed. But one of its fruits rolls under a bush. It is picked up by the gardener's daughter, who takes it home. There, the fruit falls to the ground, breaks apart, and out of it emerges the charming Anar Pari. The usurping wife continues to persecute the fairy who will be sacrificed so that her liver can be applied to the forehead of the false princess in order to cure a feigned incurable headache. Before she is killed, Anar Pari asks her executioners to scatter her parts, and to throw her eyes to the wind. These become beautiful birds which fly away into the forest. After many days have passed, the prince happens to pass through that forest. As he rests under a tree, the two birds, perched in its branches, tell each

other the story of Anar Pari. Astounded, the prince exclaims:
"At last I have found you again! Come and be my princess."[26]

So the man triumphs over his blindness. Beneath the woman's poor appearances, imposed upon her by society and bad spirits, he discovers the treasure she contains within. And then, all the others, the nonbelievers who have understood nothing or have done nothing but mock him, suddenly discover riches they failed to recognize before. They intend to make up for this by gaining possession of the newly unveiled precious object either by seduction or by force. It must be admitted that since its discovery, this object has, indeed, changed. Once she has been imbued with a man's desire, the one passed over, unnoticed, becomes the center of all desire.

The Wife Stolen by the Father

The king had three sons. When they came of marriageable age, they went out into the crowd, as was the local custom, and each threw an apple. The fruits that the two older ones threw reached the young women they were to wed. The youngest one's apple fell into a fountain. In the fountain was a pomegranate. The king's son picked it up and took it home. Then he went out. When he returned, a meal had been prepared for him. The same phenomenon repeated itself that night. He hid, and saw that while he was absent, a beautiful young woman quit her form as a pomegranate and did the housework. She advised him to let her retain her secret. But, under the power of his desire, he tore up her pomegranate robe so that she would become his wife.

Coming to visit one day, his father the king noticed this exquisite young woman. He thought of a way to take her from his son. According to his plan, he ordered his son to bring him a carpet so big that the whole army could sit down underneath it. The despairing prince began to weep. His wife, who was near, said to him:

"Didn't I tell you not to destroy my pomegranate robe? But don't be so upset. Go to the fountain where you found me and cry: 'Your daughter asks you to send her father's smallest carpet.'"

The king presented the prince with two other demands, which,

26. Tale recorded by Mistress Dracott at the foot of the Himalayas, in *Simla Village Tales* (London, 1906).

thanks to his wife, the prince was able to satisfy. Finally the king demanded that his son bring him a man one span tall, with a beard two spans long. The prince went to the fountain and cried out:

"Your daughter asks you to send her father's smallest man."

The man was sent to the palace. He reprimanded the king for making such extravagant demands, and for each one, hit him with his fist. His final blow crushed the monarch's head.[27]

It's a dangerous moment when the wife notices the interest she sparks, and is seized with vertigo. She begins to count among her personal attractions all that her lover's passion has added to her charms. As soon as the man has opened the doors of her prison for her, she graciously receives those silhouettes emerging from her horizon. She counters attempts to seduce her with only the weakest of defenses. It is not until after she has let herself be passively led along, after she has tasted what are often too easy pleasures, that she comes back to reality. She understands that those who were unable to discover her cannot assure her happiness. Her only desire is that her true love return, even while he must submit to yet another round of ordeals to reach her.

The Spouse's Disappearance
(CHINESE TALE)

A young man once rendered the king of the sea dragons a service by removing a fish hook from his mouth. The dragon invited him to choose among three parasols. The young man picked one at random, and he learned from the dragon that, when opened in times of drought, this parasol would make it rain so much that he would be able to water his rice paddies.

One day, while using the parasol, he saw a silvery blue fish fall out of it. He put it into a storage jar of clean water. From this moment on, he found all his household chores done, as if by magic. In order to learn if the fish played some part in this business, the young man hid himself in the loft above the jar, holding in his hand a pestle for crushing rice. What he suspected occurred. Changing herself into a beautiful young woman wearing magnificent clothes (she was one of the

27. Tale of Pari Banou, in Fr. Macler, *Contes et légendes de l'Arménie* (Paris, 1911).

dragon king's daughters), the fish came out of the jar and began to do the housework. Immediately, the young man let the pestle fall, smashing the jar. He seized the young woman who no longer had water at hand, and so could not return to her fish form. And so they were married.

One day while the young man was out in the fields, the king's soldiers passed by, and, seeing the beautiful young woman, they carried her off to the king. The king married her immediately, giving her the rank of number one queen and neglecting all other women to be with her.

Returning home, the young man could not find his wife and became desolate. But then he noticed a trail of cabbage seed beginning at the house and extending across the countryside, and he told himself that this was his wife's way of showing him where she'd been taken. So he set out walking in that direction, and he walked for so long, so long that his worn-out clothes made him look like a beggar. At last he arrived at the capital, and at the king's palace.

Just then, his wife happened to be in the courtyard before the palace, and seeing him, she began to laugh with joy. Seeing this, the king said to the queen:

"For a whole year, despite my tenderness, despite all I've done to prove my love, I have never seen you smile. Then this beggar's getup makes you giddy. From now on, I'll dress like him."

Immediately, he went off to trade his royal garb for the young man's rags, but when he wanted to return to his queen's side, the palace dogs didn't recognize him without his gowns. They threw themselves upon him and tore him to pieces. Then the queen brought her true husband into the palace, where, seeing him dressed in the royal robes, everyone took him for the king. And he reigned wisely and well from that moment on.[28]

If this danger presents itself to the woman in the guise of a friendly seducer, if, for her, it adorns itself in the false splendor of luxury, for the man, it wears the mask of complacence. The man considers resting from his labor, and a mortal inertia takes hold of him, compromising

---

28. Tale recorded by Captain Bonifacy at Tonkin in the province of Tuyen-Quang at *les Tabus de race Man* (in southern China), in *Bulletin de l'Ecole Française d'Extrême-Orient* (1903), vol. 2. Cited by Cosquin.

the results of his long and courageous efforts. Haven't we witnessed the weakness of the prince who lets his true fiancée be replaced with a substitute? Here is a more serious case. In order to be united with the woman of his dreams, the prince of this adventure has not hesitated in the face of a thousand dangers. He has risked his life. But the moment he is about to receive the inestimable reward for his struggles, he lets himself go and sinks into sleep. A very specific biological reality can be seen at work in this story. How many beings, at the height of their desire, see themselves reduced to impotence. But this interpretation may be too narrow. The Kashmirian story that we will read next has more general significance. One of the most disquieting characteristics of human psychology is that desire disappears as soon as it becomes realizable, as soon as the desired object becomes available.

The Hero's Insouciance

A prince arrived in another realm in disguise, accompanied by his friend and advisor, the son of the vizier. With his companion's skillful assistance, he set about abducting the king's daughter, whom he ardently desired and wished to make his wife.

Having arranged a rendezvous with the princess for the prince, the vizier's son waited with him at the appointed spot that night. The first watch passed, then the second. The prince slept. During the third watch, the princess arrived. Seeing that the prince was sound asleep, she noticed a pot of milk that happened to be there. She daubed the milk on the prince's lips. And then, again using the milk, she made three spots on the sleeper's forehead. After that, she withdrew.

The prince awoke and was about to protest to the vizier's son that he had been tricked, and that the princess had not come. But the vizier's son pointed out to him the traces of milk. And when the prince asked him to explain, he said:

"Ah, prince, if she daubed your lips with milk, that is supposed to mean that you are still a milk drinker [like a little baby], and the three marks on your forehead mean: I came during the third watch."

A second rendezvous was arranged, and again the prince fell asleep while waiting. This time the princess put two walnuts in his left hand and one in his right. Then she replaced one of the prince's shoes with one of her own. This time, again, the prince asked the vizier's son for an explanation:

"The switched shoes again prove that she came. Furthermore, she wished to say that you are still one of those who play with walnuts."[29]

This abrupt loss of desire doesn't occur only when a man comes face-to-face with the object of his love who is finally willing to satisfy his passion. It recurs in all those situations when, after a long effort, results are about to be attained. Such weakness causes attempts courageously carried out up to that point to fail. It is what usually lies behind those great unforeseeable and logically incomprehensible defeats. This pattern has been seen, and no doubt with good reason, as a kind of psychosis, a neurotic transformation that mental therapy can treat (psychoanalysis offers to fulfill this function). Another more pessimistic and religious theory claims that it is less a mental problem than an actual, deep curse, dating back to the origin of the human species. This curse forbids the perfect realization of desire, and thus, of complete happiness. In fact, anyone about to reach this goal is seized with a fear that approaches terror.

I remember, not without some emotion, the last conversation I had with my great friend, the archaeologist L.-Ch. Watelin. Since he was ten years old, he dreamed of exploring Easter Island. He had traveled the world, carried out his most passionate excavations in Mesopotamia, but this desire remained the dearest to his heart. He was over fifty when a marvelous convergence of circumstances made the expedition possible. It was 1934. Before leaving Paris, he confided to me that he was apprehensive. "Finally, my life's goal has been achieved!" After some weeks passed, I was not too surprised to learn that he had died in the Patagonian channels shortly before arriving at the island of his dreams.

Something within us, perhaps the ancient weight of our inherited guilt, inclines us to believe that realizing our desires constitutes a kind of offense against the natural order, and such acts must lead to death. This feeling is so strong that even the most ardent lovers can't imagine their love complete without thinking that it must, necessarily, disappear. They fear that after having reached this summit of happiness, life, with its constraints and customs, will violate the intensity of their passion.

For us to fully realize our desires, it seems as though we must give up everything within us and around us that does not converge toward

29. A Kashmirian tale told by the pundit Sahajabhatta in a forest village and recorded by Johannes Hertel, 1908, in *Zeitschrift des Vereins für Volkskunde.*

that end. Any indifference, any difficulty, is unbearable to us. It is an almost religious fervor that compels us to strip them away. "To sacrifice to desire," this popular phrase embodies the ceremonial ritual that serves as preparation for an act that promises to transfigure us. To free passion of its shackles, to make the internal fire burst forth, is to let the slag heap burn, to incinerate our very beings.

Will, an American fabric worker, has a clear perception of this mystery. On this summer evening which is so much like all other miserable, stifling evenings, in this house just like every other one along a street noteworthy only for its repetition of such unfortunate mediocrity, by the sheer force of his flesh, he is going to lift off, he knows, a thousand-year-old ceiling of opacity, of spineless slavery, of desperate obedience. He will not do this like a lawyer, careful afterward to avoid the consequences of his acts, but like a man who stands up and faces the world, ready to die at once, struck down by lightning. And, in fact, he is struck by lightning a few days after the scene reprinted here takes place.

The Drama of the Possession

E. Caldwell

He was looking at her when she found the courage to look up. He was looking at her as if he had never seen her before.

"Stand up Griselda," he said calmly.

She stood up immediately, rising eagerly at his command. She waited for anything he might tell her to do next.

"I've waited a long time for you, Griselda, and now is the time."

Rosamond made no move to speak or to get up. She sat calmly in her chair, her hands folded in her lap, waiting to hear what he would say the next moment.

"Ty Ty was right," Will said.

All of them wondered what Will meant. Ty Ty had said many things, so many things that it was impossible for them to know what Will had in mind.

But Griselda knew. She knew precisely the words he had used and to which Will now referred.

"Before you go any further, Will," Darling Jill said, "you'd better not forget Buck. You know what he said."

"He said he would kill me, didn't he? Well, why doesn't he come over and do it? He had the chance to try this morning. I was over there among those God damn pot holes. Why didn't he do it then?"

"He can still do it. There'll be time enough for it."

"I'm not scared of him. If he ever makes a move at me, I'll twist his neck off and throw it into one of those God damn pot holes, and him into another."

"Will," Rosamond said, "please be careful. Buck can't be stopped once he sets his head on doing something. If you put your hands on Griselda, and Buck ever hears about it, he'll kill you as sure as the world we stand on."

He was no longer interested in hearing them express their fear of what Buck would do.

Griselda stood before him. Her eyes were closed and her lips were partly open, and her breath came rapidly. When he told her to sit down, she would sit down. Until then she would remain standing for the rest of her life.

"Ty Ty was right," Will said, looking at her. "He knew what he was talking about. He told me about you, lots of times, but I didn't have sense enough to take you then. But I'm going to have it now. Nothing in God's world can stop me now. I'm going to have it, Griselda. I'm as strong as God Almighty Himself now, and I'm going to do it."

Darling Jill and Pluto moved nervously in their seats, but Rosamond sat calmly quiet with folded hands in her lap.

"I'm going to look at you like God intended you to be seen. I'm going to rip every piece of those things off of you in a minute. I'm going to rip them off and tear them into pieces so small you'll never be able to put them together again. I'm going to rip the last damn thread. I'm a loom weaver. I've woven cloth all my life, making every kind of fabric in God's world. Now I'm going to tear all that to pieces so small nobody will ever know what they were. They'll look like lint when I get through. Down there in the mill I've woven ginghams and shirting, denim and sheeting, and all the rest; up here in this yellow company house I'm going to tear hell out of the cloth on you. We're going to start spinning and weaving again tomorrow, but tonight I'm going to tear that cloth on you till it looks like lint out of a gin."

He went toward her. The veins on the backs of his hands and around his arms swelled and throbbed, looking as if they would burst. He came closer, stopping at arm's length to look at her.

Griselda stepped backward out of his reach. She was not afraid of Will, because she knew he would not hurt her. But she stepped backward out of his reach, afraid of the look in his eyes. Will's eyes were not

cruel, and they were not murderous—he would not hurt her for anything in this world—they were too tender for that now—and his eyes
were coming closer and closer.

Will caught the collar of her dress, a hand on each side, and flung
his arms wide apart. The thin printed voile disintegrated in his hands
like steam. He had ripped it from her, tearing it insanely in his hands,
quickly, eagerly, minutely. She watched him with throbbing excitement,
following the arcs of his flying fingers and the motions of his arms.
Piece by piece he tore like a madman, hurling the fluffy lint in all directions around the room when he bent forward over the cloth. She
watched him unresistingly when he flung the last of the dress aside and
ripped open the white slip as though it were a paper bag. He was working faster all the time, tearing, ripping, jerking, throwing the shredded
cloth around him and blowing the flying lint from his face. The final
garment was silk. He tore at it frantically, even more savagely than he
had at the beginning. When that was done, she was standing before
him, waiting, trembling, just as he said she would stand. Perspiration
covered his face and chest. His breathing was difficult. He had worked
as he had never done before, and the shredded cloth lay on the floor at
his feet, covering them.

"Now!" he shouted at her. "Now! God damn it, now! I told you to
stand there like God intended for you to be seen! Ty Ty was right! He
said you were the most beautiful woman God ever made, didn't he?
And he said you were so pretty, he said you were so God damn pretty, a
man would have to get down on his hands and knees and lick something when he saw you like you are now. Didn't he? Yes, so help me
God, he did! And after all this time I've got you at last, too. And I'm
going to do what I've been wanting to do ever since the first time I saw
you. You know what it is, don't you, Griselda? You know what I want.
And you're going to give it to me. But I'm not like the rest of them that
wear pants. I'm strong as God Almighty Himself is now. And I'm going
to lick you, Griselda. Ty Ty knew what he was talking about. He said
that was what a man would do to you. He's even got more sense than all
the rest of us put together, even if he does dig in the ground like a God
damn fool."

He paused for breath, going toward her. Griselda backed toward
the door. She was not trying to escape from him now, but she had to go
away from him until he caught her and dragged her to another part of
the house. He ran, throwing his hands on her.

For a long time after they had gone Darling Jill sat squeezing her fingers with savage excitement. She was afraid to look across the room at her sister then. The beating within her breast frightened her, and she was almost choked with nervousness. Never before had she felt so completely aroused.

But when she did not look at her sister, she was afraid of being alone. She turned boldly and looked at Rosamond, and she was surprised to see such composure as Rosamond possessed. She was rocking a little in the chair, folding her hands and unfolding them without haste. There was an expression of sereneness on Rosamond's face that was beautiful to behold.

Beside her, Pluto was bewildered. He had not felt the things she had. She knew no man would. Pluto was speechless with wonder at Will and Griselda, but he was unmoved. Darling Jill had felt the surge of their lives pass through the room while Will stood before them tearing Griselda's clothes to shreds, and Rosamond had. But Pluto was a man, and he would never understand how they felt. Even Will, who brought it, had acted only with the guidance of his want of Griselda.[30]

❦

Does the terror provoked in us by the idea of complete happiness translate into a cosmic law (a law, for example, that keeps stars apart, that prohibits the collision of planets attracted to each other) or is it only the result of traditional family and religious teachings?

In recounting the adventures of Chosha Sultan, the Tartan story that we are about to read emphasizes the role maternal jealousy plays in the origin of misfortune. But the story does more than that. It shows— and this is a capital notion to my way of thinking—how the beloved woman can come to vanquish this so-called human curse through her confidence and encouragement.

The Triumph of Love
(A TARTAN TALE)

A young man named Chosha Sultan lived with his mother. He kept them fed by trapping wild ducks along the shore of a lake. One day Chosha caught a golden duck.

"Do not kill me," said the duck. "I am the princess Kara Kys."

As he was reluctant to believe her, she showed herself to him in her

---

30. Erskine Caldwell, *God's Little Acre* (1933).

true form. She promised him, by oath and also in writing, that she would come back.

Chosha Sultan let her go and fell sick with love. He did not want to tell his mother why he was sick. His mother begged her son's friend to try and learn his secret. The friend returned and said:

"He is in love with a young woman who is going to come here, and we are both going to go wait for her."

The mother cried out:

"If my son leaves me, what will I live on? He is the only child I have."

And she added:

"Before the young woman arrives, pierce my son's shirt with this pin while he sleeps. Then he will not wake up."

And the mother gave the friend a pin.

During the night, the two young men went to the shore of the lake. Chosha Sultan's friend said to him:

"The young woman won't arrive until daybreak. Let us get some sleep."

When Chosha Sultan was asleep, his friend stuck the pin into his shirt. As the sun rose, a boat carrying the princess appeared on the lake. She sent for Chosha Sultan, but he could not be awakened. After the boat sailed off, the friend removed the pin, and Chosha Sultan woke up. He called out, but the men on the boat couldn't hear him. The next day, the princess came with two boats, and the day after that, with three, and each time the pin cast Chosha Sultan into a sleep like death. Finally the princess tried in vain to wake him herself. Irritated, she said:

"I have come for you with three boats. You have hardened my heart. I have changed it into a stone like an egg. This stone I have put inside a duck, the duck in a hare, the hare in a chest, and this chest I have put under a boulder as big as a house. As long as you have not found this stone egg and have not melted it with fire, I will be resolute and not soften. You, my people, never say the name of Chosha Sultan in my presence. Whoever does so, I will cut off his head."

Upon awakening and seeing the three boats sailing off, Chosha Sultan was desperate, and went to tell his mother that he was setting off to find his wife. When he reached the princess's country, a kind old woman gave him lodging and reported to him what the princess had said about the stone egg.

Thanks to the help of various animals (a goat, a dog, an eagle, and a fish) whom he agreed not to kill during the course of his journey,

Chosha Sultan gained possession of the egg. Butting it furiously with his horns, the goat moved aside the enormous boulder. The dog caught the hare which fled when the young man opened the chest. The eagle seized the duck which escaped when the hare's stomach was slit open. Finally Chosha Sultan let the stone egg fall in a river when he was leaning over to drink, but the fish returned it to her benefactor.

Then the old woman put the stone egg in the fire. When it was completely melted, Kara Kys arrived.

"Now," she said to Chosha Sultan, "I love you."

She married the young man and conferred upon him the power of a prince.[31]

It was obviously not princely honors—is it even necessary to mention this?—that Chosha Sultan dreamed about while he slept under his mother's evil spell. The dream pushed aside those false temptations of gold, precious stones, flowers, and lace. Caught between his mother and the object of his desire, he experienced through dream the great hesitation of the cosmic drama. The transcendent reality of physical endeavors overcame his subconscious anxiety.

The Mystery of Desire
A. Jarry

Listen to what I saw suspended on the star Algol, though a sulfur rain was falling, and to how I would have gathered the penna of flying fish if I hadn't lingered to listen to the four symmetrical birds conversing on the suffering of Jesus on the cross.

Under the green hell sky, the colonnades raised their fists whose veins spattered themselves into leafy capitals from the domes of which gleamed shields.

Beneath the rain of sulfur and bitumen, the mocking city opens its parasols, but in the meantime the great tortoises with their elephantiasic feet remain in a daze, stuck over the clouded lake that doesn't mirror their gold breastplates at all.

---

31. Tale recorded by M. W. Rodloff among the Muslim Tartars of the Tobol region, in *Proben der Volkslitteratur der Turkischen Stoëmme Sud Sibérien* (Saint Petersburg, 1872).

And up above, passing back and forth, the bats with burned cardboard wings open and close their fans.

And still the city raises its menacing fists at the heavens from where its enemy threatens to overwhelm it. But God never lets his eyes rest upon his wingspan traversed by all; much further below, his toes have the subterranean veins of gold for rings, which the divine grape picker crushes so their light will flow up like perfume; much further above, his beard sweeps the clouds, and his fingers, when he is reflected in the black firmamental tapestry, pierce it with holes. But from the star Algol—that I leaped to in a single bound to contemplate this receding scene, the image of which was lost like the circles that radiate away from a stone that is hurled through the liquid infinite—I saw his sacred phallus, called lingam by the Hindus, creeping across a crumbling temple. He bent his ivory tower, and his naïve skull, that bears no sagital suture whatsoever, similar to the eye of an albino chameleon.

And the great Phallus, like a water serpent and especially like a galley with three banks of oars, glided over the smooth pool of bitumen. And the crowd, in making way for this monster with their feet that had been until that moment welded like flies to a pot of honey, radiated in the glittering bursts of the thousand feet of the scolopendra.

And the celestial voice fell slowly and gravely like a parachute:

"They all will perish who have not respected my laws; they, the mages, the diviners, and those who consult the spirits of Python will perish, because they have violated the norm; and those who have coupled with beasts, because that is a confusion, and those who wish not at all to reproduce their race such as I created them, because they are abominable in the sight of my rule."

And the rain of sulfur and bitumen fell with the voice from the heights of the clouds, and covered the flat earth mounting little by little like a sea. And the mages, the diviners, and those who consulted the spirits of Python, and all those condemned by God, seemed to descend very slowly into the rising flood or to melt like a taper that is placed like a hot iron. And as the Phallus looked at one of them, this mage, to hear and to delay this untimely demise, stood on his head and spread out the great wings of his robe over his outstretched arm, sheltering the ground beneath him from the rain of fire and revealing to my sight his sex organ, beautiful as an owl hanging by its claws.

And the voice of the hautboy warbled:

"By me and despite me will perish those who don't obey my master and have not maintained my role; those who dream of sexes purer than those brought forth by God from the silt and who invent the A sharps and flats of Eros, taking over from the brutal plainchant."

And shamed for having said too much, for having pitied those who disappeared into the bitumen that was opening its trapdoors, two rose phoenocopter wings sprung suddenly from its sides—at least that is how they appeared in the gleam of the liquid fire—and it climbed straight up, after razing the plunging city, soaring like a flying fish.

A fire-gray cormorant, whose sleek body covered the entire city, emerged into the sky without delay and pursued the Phallus in wrath. Behind him the flame soared ever higher in the air until I could no longer see them.

Then, I suddenly saw like a snowfall, swirling, large feathers falling from the sky and the invisible west that the marine snouts of the tapirs will smell. And I descended to walk along the road on which I knew now lay, in the faraway valley, the large white and black penna that are beautiful as the skeletons of whales.

I advanced toward the golden cross. Caeser, Antichrist will tell you.

II

Vulpian and Aster sat on the high rocks enamored of their judges' robes. O the lubricity of their green eyes and the rime of their chestnut tree glances! In their eyes, Vulpian and Aster possess the fortunate joys of the dead, the violators of nothingness. And the fan of their green eyes palpitates like Lybian palm trees.

VULPIAN:

I tell you it is so, this day is the day of our mortal dishonor. Where are the curtains that we have breathed as smoke from trees?

ASTER:

The four-handed wind has quintupled its sybilline whip. Spill your fingers over my knees like the trunk of a dead elephant. The thunder has spoken, "I will write." And it has placed its three-cornered hat in the storm.

VULPIAN:

The night and its opaque ivory shoulders has closed my eyes without spectacles. Aster, the gorse has ramified its flashes and firecrackers. And the furze has flowered like opening mussels.

ASTER:

The rocks have grown green again and the avaricious cold has borne away the caviar of its eggs under its palms. Why have you spilled the night upon the reflection of your ten ivory phalluses?[32]

This is what leads us farther and farther from the traveled route. We have gotten through the brambles, the walls of fire. The drawbridge is lowered. We have stayed awake, not allowing pain and weariness to force shut our eyes and weaken the vigilant strength of our arms. The temple is situated at the very center of the castle, now grown to the size of a holy city. Which building is it? There is only one temple. Long ago, Solomon lived there. We are now very near the door, on the temple square, and already the songs of the Sulamite rise, praising the mysteries of love.

Song of Songs

The voice of my beloved! behold, he cometh leaping upon the mountains, skipping upon the hills.

My beloved is like a gazelle or a young hart: behold, he standeth behind our wall, he looketh forth at the windows, shewing himself through the lattice.

My beloved spake, and said unto me, Rise up my love, my fair one, and come away.

For, lo, the winter is past, the rain is over and gone;

The flowers appear on the earth; the time of the singing of birds is come, and the voice of the turtle is heard in our land;

The fig tree putteth forth her green figs, and the vines with the tender grape give a good smell. Arise my love, my fair one, and come away.

O my dove, that art in the clefts of the rock, in the secret places of the stairs, let me see thy countenance, let me hear thy voice; for sweet is thy voice, and thy countenance is comely.

Take us the foxes, the little foxes, that spoil the vines: for our vines have tender grapes.

My beloved is mine, and I am his: he feedeth among the lilies.

Until the day break, and the shadows flee away, turn, my beloved, and be thou like a gazelle or a young hart upon the mountains of Bè-ther.

---

32. Alfred Jarry, "Les Prolégomènes de Haldernablou," in *Minutes de sable,* trans. Jon Graham.

By night on my bed I sought him whom my soul loveth: I sought him but I found him not.

I will rise now, and go about the city in the streets, and in the broad ways I will seek him whom my soul loveth: I sought him but I found him not.

The watchmen that go about the city found me: to whom I said, Saw ye him whom my soul loveth?

It was but a little that I passed from them, but I found him whom my soul loveth: I held him and would not let him go, until I had brought him into my mother's house, and into the chamber of her that conceived me.

I charge you, O ye daughters of Jerusalem, by the gazelles, and by the hinds of the field, that ye stir not up, nor awake my love, till he please.

Who is this that cometh out of the wilderness like pillars of smoke, perfumed with myrrh and frankincense, with all powders of the merchants?

Behold his bed, which is Solomon's; threescore valiant men are about it, of the valiant of Israel.

They all hold swords, being expert in war: every man hath his sword upon his thigh because of fear in the night.

King Solomon made himself a chariot of the wood of Lebanon.

He made the pillars thereof of silver, the bottom thereof of gold, the covering of it of purple, the midst thereof being paved with love, for the daughters of Jerusalem.

Go forth, O ye daughters of Zion, and behold King Solomon with the crown, wherewith his mother crowned him in the day of his espousals, and in the day of the gladness of his heart.

Behold, thou art fair, my love; behold, thou art fair; thou hast doves' eyes within thy locks: thy hair is as a flock of goats, that appear from mount Gil-é-ad.

Thy teeth are like a flock of sheep that are even shorn, which come up from the washing; whereof every one bear twins and none is barren among them.

Thy lips are like a thread of scarlet, and thy speech is comely: thy temples are like a piece of pomegranate within thy locks.

Thy neck is like the tower of David builded for an armory, whereon there hang a thousand bucklers, all shields of mighty men.

Thy breasts are like two young gazelles that are twins, which feed among the lilies.

*Until the day break, and the shadows flee away, I will get me to the
mountain of myrrh, and to the hill of frankincense.*

Thou art all fair, my love; there is no spot in thee.

*Come with me from Lebanon, my spouse: look from the top A-má-na,
from the top of She-nir and Hermon, from the lions' dens, from the
mountains of the leopards.*

*Thou hast ravished my heart, my sister, my spouse! How much better is
thy love than wine! and the smell of thine ointments than all
spices!*

*Thy lips, O my spouse, drop as the honeycomb: honey and milk are
under thy tongue; and the smell of thy garments is like the smell of
Lebanon.*

*A garden inclosed is my sister, my spouse; a spring shut up, a foun-
tain sealed.*

*Thy plants are an orchard of pomegranates, with pleasant fruits;
camphire, with spikenard,*

*Spikenard and saffron; calamus and cinnamon, with all trees of
frankincense; myrrh and aloes, with all the chief spices:*

*A fountain of gardens, a well of living waters, and streams from
Lebanon.*

*Awake, O north wind; and come, thou south; blow upon my garden,
that thy spices thereof may flow out. Let my beloved come into his
garden, and eat his pleasant fruits.*

*I am come into my garden, my sister, my spouse: I have gathered my
myrrh with my spice; I have eaten my honeycomb with my milk:
eat, O my friends; drink, yea, drink abundantly, O beloved.*

*I sleep, but my heart waketh: it is the voice of my beloved that
knocketh, saying, Open to me, my sister, my love, my dove, my
undefiled: for my head is filled with dew, and my locks with the
drops of the night.*

*I have put off my coat; how shall I put it on? I have washed my feet;
how shall I defile them?*

*My beloved put in his hand by the hole of the door, and my bowels were
moved for him.*

*I rose up to open to my beloved; and my hands dropped with myrrh,
and my fingers were sweet smelling myrrh, upon the handles of the
lock.*

*I opened to my beloved; but my beloved had withdrawn himself, and
was gone: my soul failed when he spake: I sought him, but I could*

not find him; I called him, but he gave me no answer.

The watchmen that went about the city found me, they smote me, they wounded me; the keepers of the walls took away my veil from me.

I charge you, O daughters of Jerusalem, if ye find my beloved, that ye tell him, that I am sick of love.

What is thy beloved more than another beloved, O thou fairest among women? What is thy beloved more than another beloved, that thou dost so charge us?

My beloved is white and ruddy, the chiefest among ten thousand.

His head is as the most fine gold, his locks are bushy, and black as a raven.

His eyes are the eyes of doves by the rivers of waters, washed with milk, and fitly set.

His cheeks are as a bed of spices, as sweet flowers: his lips are like lilies, dropping sweet smelling myrrh.

His hands are as gold rings set with the beryl: his belly is as bright ivory overlaid with sapphires.

His legs are as pillars of marble, set upon sockets of fine gold: his countenance is as Lebanon, excellent as the cedars.

His mouth is most sweet: yea, he is altogether lovely. This is my beloved, and this is my friend, O daughters of Jerusalem.

Whither is thy beloved gone, O thou fairest among women? Whither is thy beloved turned aside? that we may seek him with thee,

My beloved is gone down into his garden, to the bed of spices, to feed in the gardens, and to gather lilies.

I am my beloved's, and my beloved is mine: he feedeth among the lilies.[33]

She doesn't expect royalty from Solomon, prince and sage, she hopes it only from her love. That is what the intellect, what modern scientific analysis, however important its discoveries, fails to understand, and what the hermetics have taken into account by using the image of the royal marriage (in *The Chemical Wedding*, for example) to depict the terms of the conquest. The poet is not fooled. He knows where the secret that the uninitiated look for in all the wrong places resides.

---

33. Song of Songs, 2:8–6:3.

Royalty
A. Rimbaud

One fine morning, in a land of very gentle people, a proud man and woman cried out in the public square: "My friends, I want her to be queen!" "I want to be queen!" She laughed and trembled. He spoke to his friends of revelation, of a trial ended. They swooned over each other in joy.

Indeed they were sovereigns for an entire morning, when all the houses were draped with crimson tapestries, and for the entire afternoon when they made their way toward the garden of palm trees.[34]

The Nuptial Countenance
René Char

O vault of effusion on the crown of her belly,
murmur of dark dowry!
O the movement run dry of her diction!
Nativity, guide the rebellious that they may discover their foundation,
the almond believable in the new day to come.
Evening has sealed its pirate's wound where dim rockets soar among a
*   sustained fear of dogs.*
In the past are the micas of mourning upon your face.

Unextinguishable pane: my breath was already level with the friend-
*   ship of your wound,*
arming your inconspicuous royalty.
And from the lips of fog descended our pleasure with its dune threshold
*   and its roof of steel.*
Awareness increased the shivering array of your permanence.
Faithful simplicity extended throughout.

Tone of the matinal motto, offseason of the early star,
I race to the term of my arch, interred coliseum.
Kissed long enough the nubile hair of grain:
The carder, the obstinate one, our confines subdue it.

---

34. A. Rimbaud, *Les Illuminations*, trans. Jon Graham.

Cursed long enough the haven of nuptial imitations:
I touch the depths of a compact return.

Streams, neume of the anfractuous dead,
you who follow the arid sky,
mingle your progress with the storms of he who could heal desertion,
hitting against your salubrious studies.
In the center of the roof bread suffocates carrying heart and light:
Take my thought, the flower of my penetrable hand,
without awakening the darkened crop.

I will not see your flanks, those swarms of hunger, wither and fill with
    brambles,
I will not see the mantis replace you in your greenhouse.
I will not see the wandering minstrels come, troubling the reborn day,
I will not see our freedom's lineage be subserviently sufficient unto
    itself.

Chimeras, we have ascended to the plateau.
Flint shivered beneath the vine shoots of space,
the word, weary from staving in, drinks at the angelic wharf,
no savage survival:
The horizon of roads to the afflux of dew,
the intimate unraveling of the irreparable.

This is the dead sand, this is the salvaged body;
Woman breathes, Man stands erect.[35]

After so many accounts of the encounter, after abundant descrip-
tions of the ordeals, an almost perfect silence follows once the supreme
ritual has been carried out. A silence thick with passion, solemn in its
happiness, and shivering with terror.

Then a Great Silence Was Made
J. Mégnen

A hand of light has lifted the floodgate. Slowly the water lifts him to
the heightened state of this woman whose ardor flows to him and will

---

35. René Char, from "The Nuptial Countenance," trans. Jon Graham.

henceforth be his bread. Hull open wide and arms crossed, black sails and mast flapping, in an eruption of iron and foam, the boat takes its passenger.... A great silence is made, a silence in which the joys and dangers, the promises and the beating hearts of the city, the breathing of machines all merge for an instant, suspended. Silence in which the suffocating mist falls on them, and then the air, moving in the opposite direction, seems to rise so high that nothing remains around them but the void, in which their own life, turned intensely in on itself, finds no more external obstacles, no more echoes. The foreboding silence of a heavy storm in which their unimaginable accord gets lost, as well as the vast complicity of this void encompassing all that was not them and fusing forever their recaptured freedom. Then, as if the transfusion of their beings established once and forever the movement, in them, around them, the boat began to move and the man's song could be heard. His voice pierced the fog, and through the gap that it made, the pure air came to them and the sun shone. His voice lifted the stones high that rolled along the way, and their stubborn cascade was brought to an end. His voice lifted high the hot and mortal trees and merged with the song of the rays which came toward them.[36]

Why is it that nothing that can be expressed in words manages to reach the central chamber of the castle, the chamber of love? Perhaps humanity doesn't dare to speak of its joy, as it did, so verbosely, of its difficulties. Perhaps our experience of happiness is too limited to prepare us for this confession. But perhaps also, the silence surrounding the mystery of love is a required necessity. Subject to the processes of the law of strict economy, the world has no doubt invented the Word as a means of acquiring, seducing, conquering, and not of singing. Tools of discovery and power, words are not accustomed to speaking of our joy.

Is there anything else two beings can do, joined for the moment and forever in the communion of love, besides feel the depths of that mystery and remain silent? This is the point, the marvelous limit, where the Word breaks off, defeated, and the pure act triumphs. Beyond this threshold, no word sounds....

But as soon as the rite is interrupted, as soon as the lovers disen-

---

36. Jeanne Mégnen, an unpublished story.

gage themselves, and their communication with the universe grows fainter, then the murmur of humanity picks up again, the sad cries and complaints rise, the conflicts and regrets. Listen to the appeals of those who cry out for love to rejuvenate them, to screen them from loneliness and old age. Who needs such aids but those who, out of weakness, let themselves be defiled by the contagion of society, those who have lost the purity of the emotion they felt, those who have violated the law of passion? Reverting back to nonbelievers, they are excluded from the celebration of the actual sacrifice. The energies of the world no longer penetrate the opacity of the spruce uniforms they once again wear. Let us leave them to the mundane satisfactions of pride, abandon them to this vast hospital that the earth, left in their care, has become.

Let us take one final and fond look at the lovers as they continue, the two of them, along the adventure's way, united now in the strength that they draw from each other. The enemy they have already encountered and defeated so many times now rises up as that unique and ultimate obstacle: death.

Song of the Dove and the Phoenix
Shakespeare

Let the bird of loudest lay,
On the sole Arabian tree,
Herald sad and trumpet be,
To whose sound chaste wings obey.

But thou shrieking harbinger,
Foul precurrer of the fiend,
Augur of the fever's end.
To this troop come thou not near!

From this session interdict
Every fowl of tyrant wing,
Save the eagle, feather'd king:
Keep the obsequy so strict.

Let the priest in surplice white,
That defunctive music can,
Be the death-diving swan,
Lest the requiem lack his right.

And thou treble-dated crow,

That thy sable gender makest
With the breath thou givest and takest,
'Mongst our mourners shalt thou go.

Here the anthem doth commence:
Love and constancy is dead;
Phoenix and turtle fled
In a mutual flame from hence.

So they loved, as love in twain
Had the essence but in one;
Two distincts, division none:
Number there in love was slain.

Hearts remote, yet not asunder;
Distance and no space was seen
'Twixt the turtle and his queen:
But in them it were a wonder.

So between them love did shine,
That the turtle saw his right
Flaming in the phoenix' sight;
Either was the other's mine.

Property was thus appalled,
That the self was not the same;
Single nature's double name
Neither two nor one was called.

Reason, in itself confounded,
Saw division grow together,
To themselves yet either neither,
Simple were so well compounded;

That it cried, How true a twain
Seemeth this concordant one!
Love hath reason, reason none,
If what parts can so remain.

Whereupon it made this threne
To the phoenix and the dove,
Co-supremes and stars of love,
As chorus to their tragic scene.

Threnos
Beauty, truth, and rarity,
Grace in all simplicity,
Here enclosed in cinders lie.

Death is now the phoenix' nest;
And the turtle's loyal breast
To eternity doth rest.

Leaving no posterity:
'Twas not their infirmity,
It was married chastity.

Truth may seem, but cannot be;
Beauty brag, but 'tis not she;
Truth and beauty buried be.

To this urn let those repair
That are either true or fair;
For these dead birds sigh a prayer.[37]

Only a few books in the library have been read. Many more must be opened. The complexity of man and his dream, of things and of so much knowledge has been reduced to a panorama whose brief outline is wholly inadequate. The evening is drawing to a close, the world is dark, the night peopled with storms. The woman is sad, ill at ease. The dead phoenix has been buried. But our hands are still joined. Impalpable signs that penetrate the darkness already let me know that the dawn is not far away. From the marvelous rises the vigorous song of hope. Tears fallen on the funeral urn mix with blood, and reawaken life.

Above the noise of wars and crime, the prophetic voice rises:

The Hope of Man
W. Blake

"I am Orc, wreath'd round the accursed tree:
The times are ended; shadows pass, the morning 'gins to break;
The fiery joy that Urizen perverted to ten commands,

---

37. William Shakespeare.

What night he led the starry hosts thro' the wide wilderness,
The stony law I stamp to dust; and scatter religion abroad
To the four winds as a torn book, & none shall gather the leaves;
But they shall rot on desert sands, & consume in bottomless deeps,
To make the deserts bloom, & the deeps shrink to their fountains,
And to renew the fiery joy, and burst the stony roof;
That pale religious letchery, seeking Virginity,
May find it in a harlot, and in coarse-clad honesty
The undefil'd, tho' ravish'd in her cradle night and morn;
For everything that lives is holy, life delights in life;
Because the soul of sweet delight can never be defil'd.
Fires inwrap the earthly globe, yet man is not consum'd;
Amidst the lustful fires he walks; his feet become like brass,
His knees and thighs like silver, & his breast and head like gold. "[38]

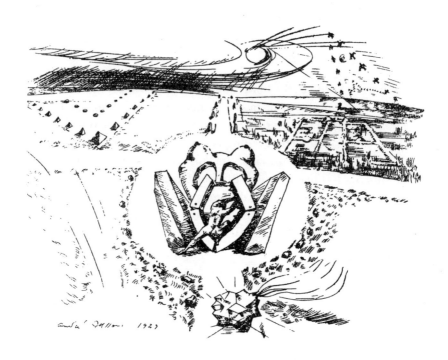

---

38. William Blake, *America* (First Prophetic Books).

INDEX OF BOOK REFERENCES

Incantations

Legends

INDEX